DR. STRANGE BEARD

A WINSTON BROTHERS NOVEL

PENNY REID

WWW.PENNYREID.NINJA

COPYRIGHT

CHAPTER ONE

"The past beats inside me like a second heart."

— JOHN BANVILLE, THE SEA

Roscoe

M OST PEOPLE HAVE approximately eleven or twelve stories, and that's it.

When I was a kid, I used to think older people were just forgetful. A ten-year-old me considered folks over thirty-five "older people." But as I grew older myself, I realized people of all ages were forgetful. Well, a lot more forgetful than me.

I also realized nobody wants to be told that they're repeating themselves, that they're sharing the same tales and anecdotes for the seventh, eighth, or twentieth time. Folks hate that, even more so if you remembered their story better than they did.

Every time I reminded someone that they'd already told me a particular story, on such and such date and time, or I tried to correct their recollection, they'd get irritable and frustrated. Like it was my fault for having a good memory and not theirs for having a poor one.

I learned to keep my trap shut. I let people tell me their eleven or twelve stories over and over, pretending each time like it was the first time I'd heard it. This was a skill I'd perfected, acting interested, surprised, laughing believably at the good parts or looking sad and troubled at the bad ones.

I was a real good actor. I was excellent at being disingenuous, and I rationalized the insincerity of my outward reactions by reminding myself that the deceit was due to necessity, not design. I sincerely didn't want to be obnoxious, or to piss people off.

Which, I suppose, is the main reason why I preferred my own company to anyone else's. Memories of solitude don't clutter the mind. But if I had to be around people, I preferred the company of strangers to longtime acquaintances, and my family's company over everyone else's.

Strangers' stories are always new, so there's that.

I love my family, and their stories almost never got old. Though, every once in a while, if I wasn't in the mood for another telling of a familiar tale, I could get away with complaining about the repetition. They might get testy, but they had to love me, no matter what.

It wasn't until I was seventeen when I realized it was rare for people to tell stories for the benefit of the listener. Usually, but not always, a story is told mostly for the benefit of the teller. The story about "how I got so drunk that one time I climbed the fence of that celebrity's compound and was invited to breakfast," or "how I rescued those folks from a rattlesnake" demonstrates how the teller has lived a life full of adventure, of meaning; that they're comical, self-deprecating, and brave; that they're ultimately a person worth knowing.

It's as though folks need to remind themselves of their own worth, and they do this through telling and retelling their favorite eleven or twelve stories, the anecdotes that fundamentally define who they are.

And therein lies the burden of having an above-average memory, and why I'm rather finicky about making memories.

I don't get to decide which stories to remember. The stories never fade. I remember them all. I have a lot of stories, ones I never tell, even though they might fundamentally define who I am, and many I'd prefer to forget.

But I couldn't.

That's why, sitting in my car, staring out my windshield and through the large wall of windows into the small roadside diner, I was undecided about what to do. I was also assaulted by a gamut of vivid memories. All my memories were vivid, but these were ones I'd prefer to forget. But I couldn't.

Simone Payton wasn't supposed to be at Daisy's Nut House.

Today was a Thursday, the last Thursday of the month. Simone wasn't home on Thursdays, and never during the last week of the month.

For five years now (five years, four months, and twelve days), Simone always arrived on the first Friday of the month, her flight landing at 5:16 PM at the Knoxville airport, which meant it was safe for me to grab dinner at Daisy's until about 6:00 PM. After that, I knew to steer clear of the diner until Simone took her plane back to Washington, DC on Sunday night.

No doughnuts the first weekend of every month was a small price to pay for avoiding making any more memories of Simone Payton.

But here she was. On a Thursday. The *last* Thursday.

Frustrating.

I crossed my arms, I scratched my neck. Somewhere nearby, what sounded like a motorcycle engine roared past, seemed to draw closer, and then abruptly cut off. I hadn't yet cut my car's engine because I hadn't yet decided whether to stay or go. The question was, how badly did I want a doughnut?

Pretty bad.

I'd just spent four hours on the road with several reoccurring thoughts occupying my mind, the most prevalent one being how nice it would be to treat myself to a fine doughnut from the original Daisy's Nut House upon arrival in Green Valley. In fact, I'd been feeling generous. The plan was to pick up three dozen for the next morning's breakfast, share them with the whole house.

And wouldn't they be surprised. Just last month, Cletus—that's my middle brother—had chewed me out for never "thinking beyond my own nose," all because I moved his laundry out of the washer without putting it in the dryer.

First of all, the towels in the dryer weren't completely dry. Instead of moving his wet clothes in, I restarted the dryer for the towels. And second, when the towels were dry, I needed to dry my own clothes if I wanted to get on the road prior to sundown. And third, I *told* him when I left the house that he needed to put his clothes in the dryer.

I did my due diligence, right?

He didn't think so and had called me seventeen times since, once for every article of clothing he'd had in the washer, to leave a voice-mail detailing how repugnant each item now smelled. I could even hear him sniff.

Long story short, Cletus overreacted, as he was prone to do.

Rolling my eyes at the memory, I brought my attention back to the beautiful girl pouring coffee for two locals—Garrison Tyler and Jeff Templer—sitting at the counter. She flashed a smile, the sight making me grit my teeth at the reflexive twinge in my chest.

Tearing my eyes away, I admitted to myself that Simone wasn't a girl anymore. I reckoned she hadn't been a girl in quite a while, but I'd missed all that.

I never did this. I never sought her out, and I certainly never watched her like a creeper, sitting in my dark car in one of the Nut House's shadowed spots just after sunset. I avoided her, like my brother Cletus avoided stupid people. I'd missed everything after we'd turned sixteen ten years ago, and I had no plans on catching up now.

Maybe . . .

Maybe I could act like I was in a hurry. Maybe I could pretend I was on an important phone call, which would make meaningful interaction or even chitchat impossible. Maybe I could order, run out as though I needed to check something, and come back when I saw she had the doughnuts ready.

Or maybe you should man up and just get it over with.

. . . Nah.

Cutting the engine, I formed a defensive strategy: I'd go in, pretend I was on the phone, order utilizing as few words as possible, walk to the back of the diner—to be polite, so as not to be one of those obnoxious public-phone-talkers standing in the middle of the restaurant—until my order was up. Then I'd place a twenty on the counter and leave, all the while still on the phone.

Perfect.

I set my hand on the door handle, stalling. I opened the door, reconsidering, ultimately breathing out as I stood from the car. I stalled again, reconsidered again, and shut the door behind me while reaching into my back pocket.

Pulling out my phone, I stared at the screen.

Actually . . . better idea, I'd call my sister Ashley. I'd make her stay on the phone with me until I had our doughnuts in hand and was on my way back out. Yes. My sister would understand. She wouldn't tease even if I explained the reason why I called. She was the best.

Yep. Good plan. Good, good plan.

Swiping my thumb over the screen, I clicked on my phone contacts, navigated to recently dialed, and was just about to tap on my sister's name when I heard the sound of approaching footsteps, crunching closer on the gravel lot.

Absentmindedly, I glanced over my shoulder. I did a double take, my mind went blank, the hand holding my phone dropped to my side, and I backed up a step.

It was my father.

More accurately, it was my biological father. He was twenty or so feet away. Cold, grayish light of a late winter evening peeked through the tall oaks of the surrounding forest and offered little illumination. I could see him just fine.

I didn't know this man well, but I'd know this man anywhere. Even if his face hadn't been visible, I knew his walk, the way he moved, with a swagger so like my oldest brother Jethro's.

Presently, I marveled at how ageless—how exactly like my

memory—he seemed to be. His hair was still salt and pepper, but mostly pepper. His form was still tall and lean and strong, looking like a man twenty years his younger. His face was nearly free of wrinkles, except the deep grooves of laugh lines around his vivid blue eyes and mouth.

But what struck me dumb was how much I looked like him. My father was smiling my smile. At me. I was momentarily beset by an unnerving sense that I was watching myself.

I stiffened, my sluggish brain realizing that he meant to intercept me, meet me where I stood gaping at my car door. He was going to talk to me.

Which had me wondering, *Why?*

I hadn't seen my father since the day of my momma's funeral, my last glimpse had been him carted away in the back of a police car after trying to kidnap my sister and brother Billy.

Before that, he'd shown up to our family's house at twilight, the day after my momma died, making threats and demands.

The last time before that, he'd picked me up from school unexpectedly—he never picked me up from school—and I'd been happy to see him. He'd asked me all about myself, about school, about girls, about my momma and how she was doing.

It had felt like the best day of my life until he'd dropped me off in the middle of Hawk's Field, grinning his grin, telling me to find my way home. If I could. I needed to prove to him that I was a man worthy of carrying his blood.

I'd been twelve.

But here he was now, his boots crunching the gravel, his stride smooth and unhurried, looking at me like he knew who I was better than I knew myself.

Why is he smiling?

I could only wait dumbly, confounded by his approach. But I did manage to snap my mouth shut, my brother Cletus's voice in my head saying, *"Close your mouth, no one wants to see your papillae."*

Darrell Winston slowed his steps, coming to a complete stop

approximately five feet away. His eyes moved over me with a peculiar gleam.

"Son," he said warmly, his voice startling me. It was deep like my brother Billy's, but roughened, presumably due to years of cigarettes and breathing motorcycle fumes. "What a nice surprise."

"Is it?" I asked and wondered at the same time. My own voice hoarse with astonishment, I fumbled in my confusion.

He was the last—and I do mean the absolute last—person I'd expected to see. Ever. Not just now, but ever.

"Of course it's nice to see you." Darrell's grin spread a little more, his eyes glittered with what looked like amusement. "How have you been?" he asked in a tone laced with a sincerity and interest that had me blinking.

Standing straight, I lifted my chin and crossed my arms. It was instinctive, a defensive posture, as though I could protect myself against his show of sincerity.

The sincerity wasn't real. Like I said, I didn't know my father well, but I knew when someone was faking sincerity.

"What do you want?" I asked, annoyance eclipsing my surprise, and made no effort to return his show of politeness or interest.

Darrell's eyes moved over me, still looking amused. "You going inside?" He gestured to the diner. "Let me buy you dinner."

My nose wrinkled, all on its own, the beginning of a sneer. "No."

"No?" He chuckled, like he was dealing with an adorable toddler, one he had a long-standing affection for. "Come on now, Roscoe. I haven't seen you in, what is it now, three years?"

"Six years and four months." *And twenty-two days.*

Now he was full on grinning, looking pleased as punch by my accidental correction of his poor recollection, and definitely reading too much into it. I remembered the date and time of each and every one of my last encounters, with each and every person I met. He wasn't special in this regard.

My father spoke through his laughter. "Yeah, I can see you haven't been missing your old man at all."

Frustrated, I ground my jaw and looked away, determined to set

7

my gaze anywhere but on this man who—if the bits and pieces of stories I'd managed to overhear throughout the years were true—had wrecked my family in all ways that matter.

And that's when I spotted Simone Payton.

She was no longer in the diner, passing out smiles and pouring coffee. She was walking over, her eyes on me, her foot just about to leave the sidewalk and step on the gravel of the lot. I froze for a split second, rocked back on my feet, and promptly returned my attention to my father.

Something about my unintended expression change must've caught his notice, because he was now looking over his shoulder. A second later, he was standing taller, watching her approach. A few seconds after that, his gaze swung back to mine, assessing, a small smirk tugging at his mouth.

"Well, look who it is," he said, steady and quiet, like this— Simone's sudden appearance and my reaction to it—also amused him.

I need to leave.

I wouldn't leave.

There was no way I was going to leave. Not with Darrell here, not with Simone all alone. Well, technically, she wasn't all alone. Garrison and Jeff were still in the diner, but she may as well have been alone.

I tried to tell myself I'd behave in a similar fashion with any person, but this was a bald-faced lie. I wouldn't suffer through my father's company for many, and Simone was probably near the top of that list. Even if she'd been surrounded by the entire police force, there was no way I was going to leave Simone Payton with my father.

Hell. No.

Anchoring my legs, determination—to keep her safe—calcified my chest and breath and bones.

Darrell's smirk widened and he openly scrutinized my face. "Looks like your girl is all grown up."

There was no mistaking his tone, and a thirst for violence such as

I've never experienced exploded outward from my gut, a shock wave coursing through my veins.

I opened my mouth to respond, maybe to threaten him.

Before I could, Simone called out, "Roscoe? Roscoe Winston? I thought that was you."

I didn't look at her, my attention focused solely on the menace in front of me, my eyes narrowing into slits when my father answered for me, "Yes, darlin'. Here stands Roscoe Orwell Winston."

Darrell turned to her again. I glared at his profile as his mouth curved into a full smile.

"And is that . . . is that Mr. Winston?" she asked, sounding pleased by the possibility, and this brought me up short.

I could not believe my ears. First of all, Simone hated my father. At least, she'd always said so when we were kids. Second, the way she was talking was . . . weird. Like, she was putting on an accent, wearing it. I doubted my father could tell, but I certainly did.

I had a southern accent, so did Simone's momma, Daisy, and her grandfather, the judge. But Simone didn't have an accent—not ever —nor had her daddy, her sister, nor her brother. They'd always sounded like Yankees.

Darrell tipped his head in her direction, unfazed by the oddness of her enunciation. "Hello, Miss Simone."

That's what he'd called her when we were kids, when he'd drop in unexpectedly and she'd been over at my house. He always said it with an air of amusement and mock respect. It hadn't charmed her then.

But now, she laughed lightly, the sound causing my frown to deepen.

"Well, Mr. Winston, look at you. Long time no see," she said, drawing even with my father.

My notice flicked over Simone without really seeing her, more concerned with watching the scene unfold than the details. She held out her hand for a shake. He reached for it. Instead of shaking it, he held her fingers between his palms, like her hand was a precious thing.

"I was just saying to my son"—his voice adopted a gentle, intimate quality, one that had me balling my hands into fists—"I can't believe how much you've grown. How old are you now?"

"Same age as Roscoe." Her answer carried a smile.

Simone pulled out of his grip and turned to me. She moved close, closer, acting reluctant to approach.

But I hadn't looked at her.

I kept my eyes fixed on my father, not missing the way his gaze lowered to her legs. It rose leisurely, conducting a deliberate, admiring perusal of her backside. I fought the urge to blacken both of his eyes as she stepped forward into my space.

I understood why patricide was illegal. That said, given who my father was and how he was presently ogling Simone, I also understood why it happened. These were my thoughts when she slipped her arms around my torso, catching me off guard.

On autopilot, I wrapped my arms around her while I held my anger closer, telling myself that my father's presence—and my enduring hatred for him—would be enough to keep this quick embrace from becoming a plague, like so many other moments involving this woman.

I knew noticing her couldn't be helped. I'd lived my adult life greedy for her even as I'd avoided all mentions and news of her person. There was nothing I could do about committing at least parts of this quick moment to memory, despite my best intentions.

Except, it didn't end up being a quick hug.

Simone inhaled a sharp breath as our bodies met, and that caused my focus to waver. She then held me for several beats, her arms growing tight, disrupting my thoughts from the violent intent coursing through me.

I blinked. My attention shifted.

She smells like midnight jasmine.

Now, there's no such thing as midnight jasmine, but there is such a thing as the fragrance of jasmine in the middle of the night, and that's what she smelled like.

Closing my eyes until they were scrunched tight, I did my best to grasp at the anger.

I would not remember what it felt like to have her in my arms. I would not remember how she pressed close, how she fit, how she was both soft and firm. I would not remember how warm she was or how her cheek and lips felt next to the skin of my neck.

I will not.

Dammit.

I was so screwed.

CHAPTER TWO

✖ ✖ ✖

"Between memory and reality there are awkward discrepancies..."

— EILEEN CHANG

Simone

HOLY COW.
Holy. Cow.

In fact, holy mother of all bovines, I was hugging Roscoe Winston. After ten years of virtually no contact, how nuts was that?

Even nuttier, his jerk father was there, apparently watching us hug.

Darrell Winston, the guy nobody could find, the guy who randomly skipped out on his parole for kidnapping his adult children just three months prior to completion of his sentence just, you know, hanging out in the parking lot of my mother's doughnut shop, shooting the shit with his youngest son like half of the FBI field office wasn't desperately trying to track him down.

I couldn't believe my luck and I couldn't wait to call it in.

Really, I couldn't wait.

I would definitely be calling it in.

Definitely.

I snuggled closer to Roscoe.

Right after this hug is over.

#Priorities.

I hadn't meant to hug him. Hugging hadn't been on my radar when I'd spotted Roscoe talking to an older man outside the window of the diner. I wasn't usually much of a hugger. I was more of a high-fiver, or a fist-bumper, or a single-head-nod-and-tight-smile-giver.

My attention had been focused almost entirely on the older man when I left the diner, a hunch pulling me outside. Not Roscoe.

Okay, maybe a little bit Roscoe.

It had been one heck of an unlikely hunch, and I'd been right. The older man was Mr. Winston, second in command of the Iron Wraiths motorcycle club, the only known confidant of our number one suspect, and a super-duper outlaw. If I could call this rare sighting into the office quickly—and we were able to apprehend Winston quietly—I'd be Agent Nelson's favorite person for at least six months.

Except now, I was randomly hugging Roscoe, my ex-best friend from childhood. So I couldn't call in Mr. Winston's sudden appearance, and I had no idea how I'd arrived at this moment, in Roscoe's strong arms, pressed against Roscoe's strong chest, smelling him.

Hold up, why was I smelling him?

He smells good. Just go with it.

This Roscoe smelled different—a lot better than that other Roscoe, who developed the faint musk a la teenage boy around twelve. You know what I mean, corn chips and the pungent, tangy aroma of sock sweat.

My older brother had introduced our family to the smell when I was ten and I'd been a little afraid of becoming a teenager because of it. Y'all can chill though, because not all teenagers reek of swamp foot. Only boys.

I snuggled closer, irritated with myself because I didn't want to let go.

Helpless to this sudden inexplicable hugging urge, I endeavored to retrace my steps, figure out how this had happened.

I'd shaken hands with his slimy biker father, I'd looked at Roscoe, and then . . .

And then I'd experienced *feelings.*

Oh for fuck's sake.

I'm not opposed to feelings, in general. I'm sure feelings are great for other people, and I'm happy for those other people and their feelings. I hope they lived a nice life together.

Don't get me wrong, I have feelings. I just choose not to be preoccupied by, ensnared by, or guided by them. That's not what feelings are for. If I wanted to be guided, I would open Google Maps or consult a Sherpa.

Therefore, I was most definitely opposed to ungainly, sudden feelings that distracted me from my job. Yet, here I was, experiencing ungainly, sudden feelings. And hugging.

Nostalgia. That's what this is.

How many times had we hugged growing up? So many I'd lost count. Not that it occurred to me to count. If I'd known then that our hugging days would come to an end so unexpectedly, I might've counted. But I didn't know, so I hadn't counted the hugs.

Instead, I'd counted on him, always being there, always having my back.

Yeeeeeah, no. That had been a mistake.

But time, as they say, heals all wounds that aren't affected by sepsis or gangrene. I'd stopped thinking and wondering about Roscoe Winston a long, long time ago.

Plus, in his defense, we'd been kids. Just sixteen. Roscoe hadn't poisoned the well when he ditched me for the cool crowd. He hadn't spread rumors or lies. We were friends on a Friday, and by Monday he'd disappeared.

He'd lost interest. We'd grown apart. Whatever. It happens. *Over it.*

Speaking of being over stuff, Roscoe was all over me. His arms were heavy around my back and torso, the good kind of heavy.

Substantial, strong. His hold tightened and I snuggled even closer, pressing my nose against his neck, emotion-inertia taking the wheel.

But I couldn't get over how strange and normal this felt. It was like going back in time, but not. He was familiar and comforting, and oddly . . .

Exciting? New? Tantalizing?

No. Not Tantalizing. Tantalizing is an unnerving word. No one should use the word *tantalizing*. It was almost as bad as *titillating*.

Abruptly, I sensed a shift in him, a restlessness. He tensed, and I realized we'd been hugging for a long time. Too long. Roscoe's hands slid from my back to my shoulders, and I released him—a rush of rare embarrassment and confusion heating my neck and cheeks— just as he set me gently away.

He didn't let me go far, tucking me under his arm in a movement that felt protective, both of us facing his father.

On reflex, I looked up, completely perplexed by my impulsive actions, discombobulated to the max, and watched this new Roscoe as he glared at his father.

"You should leave," he said. Coldly.

Whoa.

Oh yeah, this Roscoe was much, *much* different. I couldn't imagine old Roscoe speaking to his father this way. My mind sped to keep up and I pushed aside my embarrassment for the moment, attempting to reconcile past Roscoe with this present version.

Mr. Winston didn't flinch, nor did he look surprised. Instead, he stared at his son calmly, a faint smile on his lips.

"I have a better idea." The older man scratched his jaw, his gaze coming to me. "We'll go inside and catch up. How's that momma of yours, Miss Simone?"

"My mom?" I pressed my fingers against my chest. "Oh, she's—"

"Darrell." Roscoe's voice dropped lower, and with it the temperature outside seemed to plummet. "I don't know what you're playing at here, but I'm not interested."

"Darrell?" his father asked, lips twisting to the side as he examined his youngest son. "Since when do you call your daddy by his Christian name?"

"There's nothing Christian about you."

Whoa!

Buuuurn.

Winston straightened at his son's flat tone, or maybe it was the eyeball daggers Roscoe was pointing in the old man's direction.

Whatever it was, Mr. Winston seemed to decide something, nodding, his tone hard and bitter as he said, "I see your brother Billy poisoned you against me, like he did your sister, like he did with Jethro."

Roscoe scoffed, and seemed as though he wanted to respond, but Winston cut him off. "Or was it Cletus?" he asked with an acrimonious snort. "That boy never did have the sense of a blank sheet of paper, the half-wit."

I nearly choked, because *that* statement was patently false. Cletus Winston was almost as brilliant as me.

"You don't know what the hell you're talking about." Roscoe shifted forward, like he planned to get in his father's face. I used my arm around his waist to keep him next to me. This new Roscoe might've been tougher than the boy I'd known, but—unless he was now a martial arts expert—I was pretty sure his father could still beat the crap out of him.

I'd read enough about Darrell Winston to know the man was a dirty fighter, always had been, and had no compunctions about beating his kids and wife. If Darrell beat on Roscoe, then I'd have to beat on Mr. Winston, and. . . well *you know.*

Awkward.

Thank goodness, Roscoe allowed me to keep him in place, but he did taunt, "You don't know us. And we don't want to know you."

I glanced between the two men. Instinct and misplaced loyalty wanted me to cheer for my ex-BFF, but duty and logic knew that was a bad idea. I needed to do the opposite. I needed Mr. Winston to *stay.* Mr. Darrell Winston was wanted, and not just for skipping out on his parole.

Clearing my throat, I squeezed Roscoe's torso, and doing my best to sound completely free of ulterior motives, I asked, "Maybe y'all could come in and have some pie?"

"We?" Darrell paid no mind to my suggestion. Or maybe he heard me, but wasn't interested in pie so much as poking at his son with a verbal stick, his eyes flashing dangerously. "You speak for everyone now?"

"Yeah." Roscoe didn't hesitate. "I do."

This wasn't going well.

I blamed the weird hug.

I opened my mouth to try again but didn't get a chance. Roscoe, his arm now along my back, his hand hot and firm at my waist, propelled us forward. He steered us toward the diner, leaving his father standing in the lot.

Glancing over my shoulder, I watched Darrell Winston, hoping for my sake—and sorta not hoping for Roscoe's—that he would follow. The biker stared at the gravel near his boots, still as a statue, yet seemed to grow smaller the further we walked away, and not just because of the distance.

His eyes lifted and settled on Roscoe's back. The older man's shoulders slumped, his chest rose and fell quickly, and his features were . . .

He looked upset.

Not angry.

Upset.

Huh. Interesting.

Unable to walk normally and peer behind me any longer, I faced forward, a hand dipping into my back pocket for my phone. Roscoe let me go as we approached the diner door, holding it open while he glared in the direction of his father.

I walked in first, hurriedly unlocking my phone, navigating to my messages, and sending a text to Agent Nelson with just three words: *Darrell Winston @Daisy's.*

She was at the safe house where Lundqvist and I were set to

convene at midnight. This meant—assuming Winston didn't leave immediately—she had a fifty-fifty chance of apprehending him.

Man, why didn't I text her before going outside? That was sloppy, unlike me.

I heard Roscoe's footsteps close behind at first. They shuffled to a stop just as I walked past the counter.

Finishing my text, I tucked my phone in my pocket and twisted to see if he was still following. He wasn't. He'd turned his back on the diner and was facing the wall of windows by the door. His arms were crossed and he was watching his father who was—thank goodness—still there.

Keeping one eye on Roscoe's stoic back and one eye on Darrell loitering in the lot, I quickly checked in with the two customers at the counter. Once I was certain they were happy, I peeked at my phone while meandering closer to Roscoe.

Nelson: *On our way.*

Payton: *Hurry. He's in the east lot.*

My heart did a little skip, excitement and pre-adrenaline putting a spring in my step, one I worked to squash as I approached my ex-friend. Putting my phone away, I stopped at his shoulder and glanced at him.

Scratch that, I glanced *up* at him, because this new Roscoe was tall. Really, really tall.

I blinked at his profile, my heart doing a different little skip—like a thud, an *inconvenient* hard beat—at this fully formed realization of his tallness.

Okay. Don't hate on me, but tall men are my thing. Every girl has a thing, whether it be abs or beards or hands or jaws or eyes or muscular thighs or soft middles or red hair or hairy chests. You can't help your thing, it just is.

Love it. Own it. Thing it.

That said, I didn't have time for indulging, loving, or owning my thing right now—and especially not with Roscoe Winston of all people—so I pushed the realization away. Instead, I concentrated on the way new Roscoe's jaw ticked, visible beneath his close-cut beard.

He was upset. But unlike his father, he was angry-upset.

"Hey," I said, hesitated, and placed a hand on his arm. I figured a hand-on-arm touch paled in comparison to the weirdly long hug I'd given—and he'd accepted wordlessly—just moments ago.

Roscoe didn't look at me.

I took a half step closer. "Are you okay?"

He nodded in a way that looked absentminded, still not looking at me, jaw continuing to flex and release. He was grinding his teeth. He used to grind his teeth when he was angry with me, when he sulked and refused to speak, shrugging in response to every question I asked.

It used to drive me up the wall. I would sing catchy show tunes or jingles—the kind that got stuck in your head—until he laughed or relented and told me why he was angry.

An unbidden smile tugged at one side of my mouth. I'd forgotten about that. Or rather, I hadn't forgotten. I just hadn't thought about it —or him—for a really, really long time.

I can't believe he's here.

There was that dratted nostalgia again.

The sound of a loud engine starting yanked my attention to the parking lot and my heart plummeted. Darrell Winston was leaving.

Shit.

Shit shit shit shit shitter shiticker shite shoot shat shit.

Shit.

For just a split second, I entertained the thought of running out to the lot and arresting him myself. If it had been just the two customers in the diner, I might have. But with Roscoe there, I couldn't.

Huffing my frustration, I tracked the target as he pulled up his kickstand and sped out of the lot on his bike, heading north.

Once more retrieving my phone, I turned slightly away from Roscoe and typed out a quick message to Nelson, updating the perp's status, his direction, what he was wearing, the make and model of his bike, and anything else I could quickly type that might be of value.

If only I'd . . .

But there was nothing I could've done. I was undercover. Unlike most undercover agents, I had a real-life reason to be on my assigned stakeout, and a believable backstory because it was mostly true. I was playing a version of myself. One who'd just quit her job at the Justice Department, after graduating with her master of forensic science in forensic chemistry from The George Washington University two years ago, and was currently trying to figure out what to do with her life.

So, a flaky, fictional version of myself. Only my parents knew I was actually working for the bureau, and I definitely couldn't tell them why.

I knew I couldn't be the one to arrest him, but I was still frustrated. If I hadn't been in such a hurry to rush outside, if I'd texted Nelson prior to leaving the diner, if I hadn't hugged Roscoe, if those inconvenient feelings hadn't flared, then maybe I would've been able to lure Mr. Winston into the diner. I would've kept him well supplied in food and drinks and whatever it took to keep bad biker dudes in one place.

Finished with my message, I glanced up at Roscoe again, surreptitiously putting my phone away. He continued staring out the window, but his gaze was unfocused, and he'd stopped flexing his jaw. Instead, he was biting his bottom lip thoughtfully, releasing it, pulling it through his teeth, and biting it again.

I took advantage of his inattention to openly study this new, tall Roscoe. I had so many questions.

He was so different, and at the same time so familiar. In addition to his height, he'd gained width, all muscle by the looks of his shoulders, the bulk of his chest, and the trimness of his waist.

Huh. Maybe he is a martial arts expert.

It was like someone had taken my friend and put his essence in the body of this . . . this . . . *man.*

The way he'd spoken to his father had also been a surprise, and the way he'd looked at him, like he might call upon the wrath of God from the Old Testament—not Jesus, Jesus was too warm and fuzzy, except that one time in the temple—I'm talking about starving people for thirty or forty years just for putting a pretty cow in their town square.

New Roscoe was fierce.

Fierce wasn't my thing. I preferred my guys quiet, thoughtful, and reflective, slow to anger and quick to theorizing. There wasn't much that got my engine running like a good theory, *amiright ladies?*

Tall and bookish; thick glasses not thick necks; that was my bag.

But ferocity suited this Roscoe. Ferocity looked good on him. Fierce was definitely his color.

Also, there was no denying the truth, this Roscoe was hot.

Not that it mattered, but hot is neither my thing nor not my thing. Hot guys are fine, not hot guys are also fine. In my experience, whether a guy was outwardly hot didn't make much of a difference in the long run. All men are fugly as soon as they demonstrate an inability to carry on a conversation about issues that matter. Or if they don't empty the dishwasher. Or if they poop with the bathroom door open.

No one wants to see that. Even I—ye old goddess of crime fighting—have accepted that some mysteries in life are better left unsolved, such as the facial expressions associated with a boyfriend's constipation.

Hard. Pass.

Wait. Where was I?

Ah, yes. Tall, fierce, hot. New Roscoe.

I looked him over, nodding once to myself and thinking, *Good for him.*

Yes. Good for him. Good for Roscoe growing up, and living his life, and finding his own way, and becoming this tall, fierce, hot man.

Good for him.

Looking away from his square jaw and handsome face, I rubbed my sternum. An inexplicable ache and a creeping sense of melancholy settled in my chest.

More nostalgia.

I ignored it. When that didn't work, I forcibly pushed it away because capturing Darrell Winston should be on the forefront of my mind. If he slipped away from Nelson and Lundqvist, I would have to be prepared next time, and there would be a next time. Remembering how Winston had stared after his youngest son made me certain of that. I had a hunch Winston would be sticking around.

Sucking in a quiet, bracing breath, I turned back to this guy I used to know, pleased when I felt nothing but dispassionate interest in the man, and how I might use him to help me capture his father.

"Hey," I said, putting on a smile and stepping closer. "I can make a pot of coffee, if you want to—"

I didn't get any farther than that, because Roscoe flinched. He darted a quick look in my direction—a haunted, discomfited look that didn't quite meet my eyes—and promptly walked around me.

"Uh, Roscoe?" I called after him, too surprised to do anything else other than watch him leave, which he did.

That's right. He left. He walked out and across the lot, opened his car door, slid inside, started his engine, and left, heading due south.

He disappeared.

Huh.

I crossed my arms, unable to stop the bitter thought, *Just like old times.*

CHAPTER THREE

"Humans, not places, make memories."

— AMA ATA AIDOO

Simone

E AST TENNESSEE HAD a population of approximately 800,000. Twenty-four dead bodies weren't going to escape the notice of law enforcement. However, they seemed to escape the notice of the locals. Or maybe they just didn't care.

"Tell me you got him."

I didn't say hi, I didn't ask about their day, I didn't comment on the pile of dishes stacked in the sink—but I did notice them—I got right to the point. Twenty-four unsolved murders, all dates of death clustered around the end of June/beginning of July for the last two years. It may have been late-March, but it felt like the clock was ticking.

Nelson and Lundqvist exchanged a quick look, with Lundqvist exhaling a frustrated breath and Nelson shaking her head. "No sign of him."

Damn.

That explained why they hadn't returned my last text asking for a status update. There was nothing to report.

Even though I'd been assigned full time to the case squad somewhat recently, I was already ready to be done. Based on what I'd learned about these case agents in the short time we'd known each other, I suspected they were both anxious to get this thing resolved as well.

I studied them, the disgruntled narrowing of their eyes, the unhappy curve of their lips, confirming that they were just as frustrated as I was.

Hisako Nelson had been working undercover as a stripper at the G-Spot for nineteen months, since the first string of murders two years ago this coming June. The strip club was frequented by all the motorcycle clubs in the area. She'd been assigned just after the eighth body had been found. Hisako had seniority on the case, which meant she gave me and Lundqvist our day-to-day direction.

Oscar Lundqvist had been brought in when the number of dead bikers officially reached eighteen last July. That was nine months ago. The body count had risen to twenty-four, but they'd all been murdered in June, according to the coroner in Knoxville.

Lundqvist was currently working his way into the Black Demons motorcycle club, playing the part of a potential new recruit. The Demons had been one of the clubs hit hardest by the string of murders with seven members dead.

Of course, there was Isaac Sylvester, and I knew for a fact he was more than ready to find the killer.

Neither Nelson nor Lundqvist knew Isaac's identity, though they knew he existed. More precisely, they knew the bureau had someone inside the Iron Wraiths, but they didn't know who. I suspected Isaac would be the reason we ultimately broke the case. That was, if he survived long enough.

Like me, Isaac Sylvester had grown up in Green Valley. Unlike me, he'd joined the army just after high school, disappeared for several years and returned a changed person. Everyone in town thought he'd turned to the dark side, including my parents.

He hadn't turned to the dark side. He'd been an undercover ATF agent. But when people started dying, Isaac had been loaned out to the bureau, and now here we were.

"Did you bring any doughnuts?" Lundqvist asked, his eyes widening with a hint of hope.

I thought about saying, *"You don't deserve doughnuts, Lundqvist."*

Instead, I nodded, throwing my thumb over my shoulder. "They're in the car."

He didn't need to be told twice, excusing himself with a lopsided smile and darting out of the room.

Nelson and I exchanged a look. Her dark brown eyes beneath perfectly manicured eyebrows felt judgmental as they moved over me, but I knew it was nothing personal. Nelson had an air about her, like she'd been royalty in another life. Or maybe this life. Whatever, it was just her way.

Also, her posture was magnificent. When I was around her, I stopped slouching. I'd never experienced better posture by association, but there you go. True story.

Nelson gestured to one of the four chairs set around the small kitchen table. "Take a seat and tell me what happened."

I sat in the chair she offered, finding myself mimicking her posture, my shoulders didn't touch the back of the chair. "It was completely random. He seemed to be on his own, no meetup, no posse."

Her gaze narrowed, causing the epicanthal fold of her eyes to be more pronounced. "You're telling me Winston just showed up? Out of the blue on your first day full time?"

"That's what I'm telling you. I was serving coffee, glanced out at the lot, and spotted a car I recognized. Then I saw two figures standing and talking by the car. I recognized the younger one as Roscoe Winston."

Her thick black lashes swept down and then up, her gaze turning fuzzy for a second. "The youngest. The vet."

"The veterinarian, that's right."

Her stare refocused on me. "You knew him. The two of you went to school together, right?"

I nodded, giving her nothing more.

Despite my best efforts, the irritating nostalgia from earlier hadn't dissipated. Instead, the long-forgotten memories were floating to the surface of my mind. Bits and pieces of conversations from my childhood and adolescence, life moments I'd wallpapered over or packed up and put in mental storage, darted in and out of my vision like gnats.

On the drive over, I remembered how Roscoe and I had played Monopoly, one game spanning eight years, from the age of eight to sixteen. It had been his idea. He'd watched his sister Ashley and her childhood pal Jackson James run a game for nearly as long, and he liked how they'd added their own spin to it, printed their own money, and made clay models for skyscrapers.

We'd added our own spin on it, too. But instead of skyscrapers, we'd added a seedy, criminal element, with smugglers and thieves. The houses became safe houses, the hotels became business fronts for money laundering, and if you could steal from the bank without the other person noticing, you could.

Going to jail was never a respite from landing on each other's property. If one of us ended up behind bars, we had to stop the game, and the jailbird was forced to do push-ups in the prison yard—the middle of his room—once a day, make the other person lunch and fork over his or her real-life allowance for a week.

It had been so, so much fun.

Sometimes we engaged in heated debates and fought. Sometimes we played FBI (he was always the bad guy). Sometimes we baked in my mother's kitchen. Sometimes we purposefully got lost in the woods, but never seemed to have a problem finding the way home at suppertime. Sometimes we simply sat and read together. Or read to each other.

I frowned at the amalgamation of memories, now jumbled and knotted together like one of those long, bright orange extension cords, wrapped badly and shoved in a corner of a garage. It was an apt analogy, my brain as a garage seemed about right. But a super awesome, clean, tidy garage, with a place for everything and everything in its place.

Pay no attention to those haphazardly discarded extension cords in the corner.

"You recognized Roscoe Winston's car?" Nelson asked, bringing me back to the present.

I nodded again, taking a deep breath. "Yes. His brothers—the twins, Beau and Duane—gave it to him for his sixteenth birthday. It's a 1955 Chevrolet 3100."

"Crap. Where do they fall in the family tree again?" Nelson turned toward the laptop she'd left open on the table. "There's so many of these Winston brothers and they all look the same."

"Do you think so?" I didn't think so.

Roscoe looked like a combination of Jethro, who was the oldest, and Billy, the second brother. He had Jethro's lean frame and mannerisms, and Billy's electric blue eyes and well-groomed dark hair and beard.

But Roscoe didn't look anything like Cletus, number three in the family. He had messy light brown hair, curly and chaotic, with streaks of blond. His eyes were greenish, like Jethro's. He was also shorter, stockier, and his beard was longer.

Whereas the twins, Beau and Duane, only looked like each other, with bright red hair and cornflower blue eyes.

"Ah, yes. I remember seeing a picture of that car." Nelson nodded at something she saw on her laptop screen. "The Winston twins run the auto shop and they all seem to drive classic cars." She sounded like she was speaking mostly to herself, clicking around and waiting for the screen to load again.

It was an ancient laptop in terms of latest technological advances, but we were lucky to have it. It was our link in the field to all the various law enforcement databases—and there were many, many databases—scattered across the government web.

"No. Cletus, he's the third brother, and Beauford, one of the twins, run the auto shop. The other twin, Duane, lives with his wife, Jessica James-Winston, in Italy."

"Cletus is married to the baker?"

"Yes. Cletus and Jennifer Winston are married, and she's a baker," I confirmed.

"No kids . . ." Nelson's eyes narrowed as she read. "And Jennifer Winston was arrested for—"

"That was years ago." I waved away Jennifer Winston's arrest record. It wasn't pertinent to the present case.

"Cletus is the third, and Ashley is the fourth." Nelson continued reading. "And Ashley is married to Andrew Runous, one daughter." Nelson paused, her eyebrows jumping. "Ah, yes. Senator Runous's son, the senior senator from Texas."

"Correct."

"That's quite a family connection." Nelson grabbed a pen and wrote something in her notebook, continuing. "Beauford is with the famous one. Stacy something."

I wavered, feeling protective of both Beau and his partner *Shelly*, not Stacy. "Shelly Sullivan. She's a famous artist."

I really liked Shelly. She and Beau had come into the diner every Saturday I was in town for the last five years and they were freaking adorable. There was something about the way she meticulously cut her banana that I found soothing. The way he looked at her and the way she looked at him, talk about ungainly feelings.

They almost made me want a life partner. Someone who knew, accepted, and cherished me on a fundamental level.

Almost, but not quite.

Ultimately, I knew my cloth wasn't cut that way. I liked my own space, only cleaning up after myself, working as much as I wanted and going to sleep when—or if—I wanted. So as much as I liked the idea of a partner who looked at me the way Beau Winston looked at Shelly Sullivan when she cut her bananas into perfect, one-fourth inch cylinders, I wanted to sleep in the middle of the bed, consult no one on my decisions, and shower at my leisure even more.

"No, wait, I'm thinking of Jethro Winston." Nelson snapped her fingers, pointing at something she read on the screen. "Jethro Winston is married to Sienna Diaz, the filmmaker. They have three kids." Then to me she asked, "Their address is listed as Green Valley. Do they live here? I haven't seen them."

I shook my head and shrugged. "I honestly don't know. I've seen Jethro maybe three times in the last five years, always with one or more of his kids and always a quick stop in to pick up doughnuts. Maybe their permanent address is here, but my guess is he and the kids go where she goes."

"He used to be a park ranger though, right?" Nelson scrolled through a page, her eyes scanning the contents.

"Jethro was a park ranger. Runous and Jethro used to work together at the Park before Jethro married Sienna."

"And they had kids. And now Jethro is a full-time dad." A glimmer of respect shone in Nelson's eyes, there and gone in an instant. Her attention flickered to me. "William Winston, state congressman, is the one engaged to your sister."

I carefully schooled my expression. "Correct."

Nelson examined me before saying, "Everyone is related to everyone in this town."

"Not everyone."

"Oh really? Duane—the other twin—is married to Jessica James-Winston. She is Sheriff James's adopted daughter, and Jackson James's —sheriff's deputy—adopted sister." Nelson spoke slowly, clearly trying to connect mental dots and understand the web of relationships.

I nodded, not adding that Jessica James-Winston wasn't just the sheriff's adopted daughter, but also his niece on his wife's side, the biological daughter of Janet James's sister, but the biological father was unknown. That level of detail would just confuse Nelson. Heck, it would confuse me if I didn't already know all these people. Plus, again, it wasn't pertinent to the present situation.

"That means," she went on, "the Winston family is related to the local sheriff, a movie star, a senator, your family—"

"Billy and Dani aren't married."

"—who owns the mill, and your grandfather is a judge, and your mother owns those restaurants, and your dad owns a bank—"

Oh brother.

"He doesn't own the bank. He's a vice president."

"Whatever." She looked away from the computer screen, releasing a tired sounding sigh. "Let's get back on track. Tell me what happened tonight."

"I didn't recognize the target right away, only identifying him from the window as an older man fitting the description." *But I had a hunch.* "As soon as I was outside and I approached, I made positive identification."

"That's when you messaged us?"

"No." *Much to my regret.*

I continued with my report, leaving out the awkward hug, but filling her in on the argument between father and son, how Roscoe had stormed off, how the target had watched him go, and how I'd made contact as soon as it was feasible. Nelson listened thoughtfully, as did Lundqvist when he finally returned with the two boxes of Nut House doughnuts I'd brought.

My narrative at an end, I leaned back in my chair and crossed my arms. Sitting perfectly straight was a pain in the neck, I didn't know how Nelson managed it all the time.

Nelson and I stared at each other as Lundqvist started on his second doughnut.

I sensed her thought processes were roughly similar to mine—another hunch—because her eyes were moving over me with speculation, her lips compressing. I was learning her mannerisms, and this expression seemed to indicate she was about to ask me to do something I might not like.

Actually, she never asked. Over the last week and a half, she just told me how it would be.

"Intel from the Black Demons and my information gathered at

the G-Spot points to Razor Dennings as the murderer. Winston is second in command and the closest known associate to Dennings—aside from Dennings's woman, Christine St. Claire. Roscoe is of interest to Winston. You'll get close to him," she said, right on schedule.

I knew precisely who she meant by *him*.

That pang of nostalgia was back, almost as overwhelming as it had been in the parking lot of my mother's diner, but I was careful to make no outward sign of it.

"I will if I can." It was a pragmatic response to a pragmatic suggestion.

"Why couldn't you?" Her gaze moved over me again, as though assessing my physical suitability for the task. Then, as though deciding I wasn't an ogre, she asked, "Is he a racist?"

"No," I answered quickly. "Not at all. The Winstons were raised by their mother, Bethany. Bethany was a . . ." *a good soul.* "She wasn't racist, not even a little."

"Everyone is a little racist," Nelson responded flatly, giving me a pointed look.

Lundqvist spoke around a bite of doughnut. "Hey!"

We both ignored him.

"You know what I mean," I said, echoing the flat inflection of her words.

She shrugged, like she was shrugging off my statement. "Then what's the problem? According to your statement last year"—she gestured to the laptop screen—"you two were friends in childhood."

"Correct," I said, even though *inseparable* was the word I would have used.

Her gaze sharpened, and she asked again, "What's the problem?"

"There is no problem." I was proud of myself for how unperturbed I sounded.

"You want to switch assignments?" she asked conversationally. "I'll get close to the kid, you take my job at the G-Spot?"

Now, I was proud of myself for not grimacing, but I was also irritated with myself for the odd spike of antagonism pinging my chest and ringing in my ears.

My first thought was unlike me, and annoying. It was about Nelson getting close to Roscoe. Nelson with the long legs, and perfect body, and high cheekbones, and gorgeous tawny brown skin, and alluring smattering of freckles, and the long, shiny, perfectly behaved obsidian hair?

Oh. Hell. No.

See? Annoying. What was wrong with me?

I still blame the weird nostalgia inspired hug.

My first thought should have been about my fitness—or lack thereof—for her role.

I'd joined the bureau immediately after graduating with my masters. But I'd never wanted to be a case agent working in the field, and I'd definitely never wanted to be an undercover agent. I'd wanted to be a subject matter expert, working within a division, ideally in Washington, DC.

Guess what? Mission accomplished. I'd joined the research and development lab and I loved my work. I couldn't wait to get back.

There was no way, *no way,* I would be able to take on Nelson's role in this case. My cloth wasn't cut that way, and she knew it.

Which is why she didn't wait for an answer to her prior question before asking, "What is it? Do you need more training?"

I inhaled quietly, gathering composure with the breath, and reminding myself that I respected this human. I respected the hell out of Special Agent Hisako Nelson. Apparently, one of her favorite things to do was to remind me that I was the youngest and most inexperienced person on the squad. Her reminders never bothered me much because they were true.

I was the youngest and most inexperienced. Truth.

But she didn't give me enough credit.

I knew these people. I'd grown up here. I understood the relationships. If she wanted to get technical about it, I'd also been involved in one capacity or another with investigations into MC activity in East Tennessee for much longer than she had.

Five years ago, neither the bureau nor the ATF had any local contacts that could consistently rendezvous with Sylvester without breaking his cover. They'd gone through twelve field agents in one year, a new liaison each month, and—from what I'd been told—he'd grown frustrated with the lack of a consistent contact and had given the ATF my name.

Why he'd thought of me, I could only guess. Isaac Sylvester was several years older and had been homeschooled by his parents even though his father had been the local high school principal at the time.

I'd been a senior in college when the ATF reached out, interning at the Virginia Department of Forensic Science. After numerous interviews and meetings with several of my professors at George Washington, they'd explained the situation.

All I had to do was visit my parents once a month, volunteer to work in my mom's flagship diner location in my hometown, serve Sylvester coffee Sunday morning, collect his tip, and fly back home to Washington, DC Sunday night.

The tip money went to the ATF, I assumed it contained some sort of message, and I went back to college, or graduate school, or work —whichever was correct at the time. It was only supposed to be for two years. Two years became four and a half, and Sylvester had been on the precipice of extraction when the bodies began piling up.

I'd continued being his point of contact as per normal, but two months ago I'd been pulled out of my lab at the Counterterrorism and Forensic Science Research Unit, gone through a crash course repeat of my training for undercover work, and assigned to the case full time. Isaac Sylvester wanted me in town so he could pass on information whenever he needed. I hoped this meant we were close to finding the killer.

Or, I guess maybe killers.

"No. I don't need more training," I responded evenly, holding her dark eyes. "I know what I'm supposed to do."

Nelson regarded me, her gaze flickering down and then up, and lifted her chin. "You'll get close to him."

"I will."

"Whatever it takes."

"Yes."

She nodded, seemingly appeased, and glanced over at Lundqvist. He'd watched our exchange passively and was now working on his third doughnut.

"I know you're not going to keep all those to yourself." Nelson reached for the box and tugged it away from him. "Give them here."

"Your mother is a genius, Payton," Lundqvist said around a mouthful of chocolate coffee cake doughnut.

"I know." I tried to muster a smile, but couldn't. I didn't like making promises I wasn't sure I could keep, and getting close to Roscoe . . .

How am I going to do this? He won't even look at me.

Lundqvist pointed to me with the hand holding the remainder of his third helping. "How come you're not eight hundred pounds? I'd be eight hundred pounds."

"Because I don't have an endocrine disorder or other medical condition that causes weight gain, nor do I lack self-control."

"See," he gave me his lopsided grin, showing his gold tooth, his longish blond hair falling forward on his forehead. "That's the difference. I have no self-control."

Nelson snorted, rolling her eyes, and picked up the cherry-topped Boston cream pie doughnut from what remained of the original dozen.

We both knew Lundqvist's statement wasn't true. He was a weird guy, but this white dude seemed to have self-control in spades. I'd read his file, so I knew.

His parents were immigrants from Switzerland and had both died when he was young. He'd been placed in foster care, graduated from Annapolis, was a decorated navy officer, and received a law degree from Yale before joining the bureau ten years ago. Since joining, he'd worked mostly undercover assignments.

Why he wanted to act like a fool, I had no idea. Maybe he had difficulty breaking character? Or maybe he thought he was breaking the tension between Nelson and me. Or maybe he was just weird.

My attention flickered to Hisako as she took a bite of her doughnut. She then set it down on a napkin. I watched her as she paused mid-chew, closing her eyes, breathing in through her nose, and showing less inhibition in that moment than I'd ever seen from her before. The woman looked close to orgasm.

"My God," she said, gripping the table with both hands. "I think I'm going to cry."

Now I did smile, but I quickly hid it before she opened her eyes.

"If I meet your mother, I'm going to ask her to marry me." Lundqvist devoured the rest of the coffee cake doughnut and licked the tips of his fingers, his eyes on me. "It's a cliché, but it's true: the way to a man's heart is through his stomach. If you want to get close to the youngest Winston brother, maybe just bring him a dozen of these."

* * *

I APPROACHED THE front door as quietly as possible, careful to avoid the squeaky boards on the steps and porch. Just as quietly, I pushed my key into the lock, twisted it slowly, and slipped inside the house. I breathed out silently as soon as I'd closed and locked the door behind me.

But the foyer was dark, and that gave me pause. The foyer was never dark—ever, and definitely not at night—unless there was a reason for it.

My mother was awesome. I loved her dearly and respected her even more. She and my dad had been tough on us as kids, the good kind of tough, the kind of tough that came with high expectations. Her favorite thing to say to us had always been, "Why are you so anxious to build yourself a ceiling? Why don't you build a rocket instead?"

She was amazing.

But—and you knew there was going to be a "but"—she was prone to dramas in order to get her point across. I'm not talking about loud dramas, with screaming and hollering. Oh no. These were much worse (and therefore better).

I'd never been on the receiving end of the dark-foyer-drama, which consisted of flipping on the light to the unnerving and immobile image of my mother suddenly there, in her bathrobe and glasses, a look of intense disapproval on her face.

She used to do this often to my sister Daniella, when Dani would try to sneak back into the house after a late night and a broken curfew. I'd avoided this fate by being an avid spectator of Dani's adolescence. Since I was nine years younger than my sister, I watched, learned, and adjusted my behavior accordingly. As such, when I hit the curfew years, I always arrived home a half hour early.

Maybe it wasn't fair, but I couldn't help reflecting on my older sister's life and experiences as a cautionary tale.

Case in point, Dani had fallen head over heels in love with a guy when she was in high school—like, *crazy* in love, disrespecting our parents in love, acting like a moody fool 24-7 in love. She ran away from home when I was eight and broken my parents' hearts.

Basically, she'd let her feelings be her guide when she should have consulted Google Maps or a Sherpa.

When she returned after three months, all was forgiven. She'd been in her senior year, had been a straight-A student her entire high school career, and had already been accepted to Howard. Her teachers were sympathetic, just as forgiving as my parents, and allowed her to make up her course work so she could graduate with everyone else.

Dani went off to college and that was that, like it had never happened. Except, it had happened.

I'd been there, witnessing my parents' heartache, their worry, their sleepless nights. They'd held me tighter, reluctant to drop me off at school, or play at anyone's house. This didn't change when Dani returned. Their trust—in my sister, in their children, in life— had been shattered. None of us were the same after.

But I've gotten way off track. Back to the dark-foyer-drama.

According to Dani, our mother would get more and more creative each time. One time, the last time as far as I knew, Dani flipped on the light, ready to face my mother. But she wasn't there.

Dani turned to the entryway closet—which had a full-length mirror attached to the outside of the door—opened the door, put her bag away, closed the door and nearly had a heart attack. In the few short seconds it had taken Dani to put her bag away, my mother had soundlessly apparated to stand directly behind my sister.

It was one of my favorite stories, how Dani had screamed at the image of our mother standing behind her in the mirror. It woke up the entire house, but we had all laughed and laughed at the expense of my sister. If you knew my sister, this story was even funnier. No one laughed at Daniella Payton.

Except her family.

Hilarious.

Which was why I paused just inside the suspiciously dark foyer, holding my breath and listening to the house.

My mother was there. I couldn't see her, but my hunch-senses were tingling. Bracing myself, I flipped on the foyer light. The entryway was empty. I waited, scanning the area. After a full minute, I walked quickly to the living room and flipped on that light as well, careful to keep looking behind me.

She was nowhere to be seen.

A shiver raced up my spine.

Dammit.

Attempting to keep my attention pointed in every direction, I walked backward into the entryway, pressing my back against the wall next to the closet door, and slipped off my shoes.

I didn't think she would jump out. That wasn't her way. She would just abruptly appear, lips pressed together in a stern line, eyebrows slightly raised, which was way worse (and therefore better).

I reached for the knob of the closet, my attention swiveling around the tidy space behind me as I opened the door, my heart pounding in my chest in anticipation of her inevitable appearance, and hurriedly faced the closet to—

"Simone."

I screamed, jumping back, dropping my bag, and gripping my chest, because there was my mother.

Inside the closet!

Fuuuuuck . . . and drat.

I should have seen that coming.

"Oh, did I scare you?" she asked, sounding unperturbed, but her face communicated a different story.

She was pissed.

"Mom." I laughed lightly, closing my eyes and telling my body to calm down. The aftereffects of having the shit scared out of me left my hands shaking and my heart on high alert.

She was quiet, so I opened my eyes, meeting her Spartan stare.

"Was that scary?" Holding my gaze, my mother stepped out of the closet, wearing her bathrobe and glasses and a silk scarf on her head.

"Here we go," I whispered under my breath, still grinning. I couldn't believe how good she got me. Man, I was *impressed.*

"So I guess maybe you can understand—just a little—how I felt, waiting for you to come home."

I released an elongated breath, my gaze growing hooded as I glared at her in return. "I'm working here. I can't always call and tell you where I am."

"You can text if it's going to be after midnight."

"Not always."

She examined me in that piercing way of hers, a way that sometimes had me convinced my mother could read minds. "But you could have tonight."

I didn't respond, because she was correct about tonight—see? Mind reader—but that wasn't the point.

Dragging my feet as I closed the distance between us, I pulled her into a hug. "Can we please just let this drop? I'm exhausted."

"So am I." She wrapped her arms around me and squeezed me tight. "But I can't sleep when I don't know where my babies are."

"Do you know where Dani is right now? Or Poe?" Poe was my

brother Adolpho's nickname; as a two-year-old I couldn't say Adolpho, but I could say Poe.

She leaned away, giving me a flat look. "Don't be smart with me. Neither Dani nor Poe are living in my house right now, and neither of them are determined to take crazy risks—"

"I work in a lab!" I growled, walking away.

"Then why are you here?" she called after me, following me into the kitchen. "There are no labs in Green Valley."

"That you know of," I corrected gently, trying to infuse my tone with humor. She did not smile.

I opened the fridge and—*Oh, leftovers!*—pulled out the leftovers dish, carefully lifting the aluminum foil so as not to tear it. There wasn't much that irritated my mother more than perfectly good aluminum foil being ripped.

Cashew chicken and egg rolls.

Man, I loved being home.

"You make me crazy." My mother mimed a strangling movement with her fingers, a rare display of frustration, and it made me smile.

I set the leftovers dish on the counter, giving my mother a kiss on her cheek as I stepped around her, heading for the sauce packet drawer. "I'm honestly not trying to drive you crazy."

"Between you and your aunt Dolly, I'm going to sell the business and move to Tahiti."

My grin was immediate. Mom had been making this threat for years.

"That sounds nice." I dug around the packets, searching for duck sauce.

I had no idea why, but miniatures of foodstuffs made me happy. I especially enjoyed those fish-shaped mini pods of soy sauce with the red cap, tiny bottles of Tabasco, and miniature jars of seedless blackberry jam.

Blackberry jam was my favorite.

"Simone," she said, and something about her tone, a particular rawness, had me looking up. Her eyes were a little glassy, like she was fighting tears. "*Please* be careful."

I went to her and hugged her again, and again she held me tightly, more tightly than normal.

"It's fine," I tried to soothe, rubbing my hand down and then up her back.

"It's not fine." She leaned away, but held my upper arms and captured my gaze with hers. "When you said you were joining the FBI, your father and I didn't say a word. You said you weren't going to be an agent in the field, you said you were going to stay put in DC, work in an office or a lab, do research, stop terrorists using science, give support to folks in the field."

"Yes." I nodded patiently, because this was not the first time we'd had this conversation in the last ten days. "And that's still the plan. They needed me here for a temporary assignment. I am only here for a short time."

Her eyes moved between mine, like she was reaching inside my head, seeking to read my thoughts. "But you don't know how long."

"No. I don't."

"So how can you say it's temporary?"

I sighed, but she wasn't finished.

"You are too bright—too brilliant—to put yourself in danger like this."

"I'm not in danger." I was in a little bit of danger. A very little bit. A wee, itsy-bitsy, teeny-tiny bit of danger. But she didn't need to know that.

"Ha!" The sound was strangled, full of fear, and she pulled me against her again.

I understood my mother's terror. Her half brother, who'd been fifteen years older than her, had died in Vietnam, and she had two uncles that had died in World War II.

"This country doesn't deserve you." She placed a kiss on my neck and I sighed again, because those were the same words she'd said to my brother when he'd seriously considered joining the navy.

These also happened to be the same words my sister Dani had said to me when I told her I was joining the bureau.

So I repeated the response I'd given to my sister. "Be the change you want to see in the world."

My mother laughed, it sounded desperate but also amused, and maybe a little proud.

Whereas my sister had simply glared, unimpressed. Her perspective was more, *You don't need to live in the world to change it. Become powerful enough, and you can bend the world to your will.*

Ah, dearest Dani. Warm and fuzzy, she was not.

We stood silently for a while, hugging in the kitchen, the clock on the wall ticking softly the only sound in the room, other than our soft breathing. My stomach growled, and my mom laughed again.

Sniffing and stepping away, she held my cheeks in her hands and captured my eyes once more. "I'm proud of you, I hope you know that."

"I do."

"Just . . . don't take any unnecessary risks," she said firmly.

"I won't."

"And text me if you're going to be later than midnight."

My protest died on my lips when I perceived the slight flicker of fear behind her eyes. So I nodded.

"Good." She let me go and straightened the front of her bathrobe. "I'm going to bed. I don't need to tell you to clean up after yourself."

She didn't need to tell me. Working for the bureau carried some risk, but not cleaning up after myself in my mother's kitchen was taking my life in my hands.

"I will."

She yawned and turned for the hall leading to her room. I watched her go. Taking a deep breath, I turned for—

"Simone."

I jumped, gasped, clutching my chest, because there was my father, standing directly—like six inches—behind me, his arms crossed, bathrobe and glasses on, stern expression on his face.

"Dad!" I hit his shoulder.

"Oh"—he lifted an eyebrow—"did I scare you?"

My mother's laughter carried all the way to the kitchen.

CHAPTER FOUR

❋ ❋ ❋

"What matters in life is not what happens to you but what you remember and how you remember it."

— GABRIEL GARCÍA MÁRQUEZ

Roscoe

THE HOUSE WAS quiet when I made my way downstairs Friday morning. That was to be expected since I reckoned I was alone.

Jethro, Sienna, and my nephews were still in Boston where she was filming her latest movie. Billy—who, when in Green Valley, lived in the main house when Jethro's family was gone, and in the carriage house when the family was in town—had probably already left for work. My brother Billy split his time between the state capital when government was in session and our hometown, where he still managed the day-to-day operations of Payton Mills.

Cletus and Jenn had their own place, but if anyone was around this morning—likely skulking—it would be Cletus. He liked to drop in at odd times, fiddle around, do his laundry. He said the old house missed him when he was gone. My brother Cletus often had odd ideas, so this notion wasn't out of his range of normal.

Ashley, Drew, and their daughter lived up on Bandit Lake in a house deeded to his family. Beau and his lady friend Shelly also lived on Bandit Lake, in the old Weller house, which was more like a mansion than a house. Beau said he'd won it from Hank Weller in a staring contest. This wasn't outside the realm of possibility. Hank Weller was eccentric on a good day, nuts on a normal day, and downright insane on a bad one.

Duane and his wife Jess were settled in Italy for the time being as they awaited the arrival of their first child. We were all planning a visit come summer, and I could not wait. I'd only been to Italy once, when I'd taken a semester off college and traveled part of the world with Drew. The entire country ranked high on my list of most beautiful places in the world.

Convinced of my solitude, I hummed lightly to myself as I descended the stairs. Since I hadn't picked up the doughnuts, there was no reason to call anyone over for breakfast, and maybe that was for the best. After last night's events, which I hadn't allowed myself to dwell on in any meaningful way, a little solitude before meeting Drew for a day's work vaccinating bear cubs sounded like a good idea.

I didn't mind the quiet. The old house provided more than enough smells, sights, and sounds that I could easily fill the space with my family if I chose to, vivid memories of louder, happy times.

I was recalling one of these times, specifically Cletus trying to teach a fourteen-year-old me how to pack sausage and Beau mucking everything up to Cletus's chagrin, when I walked into the kitchen and stopped short. The house was quiet, but my earlier assumption that I was alone had been a faulty one.

Cletus sat at the kitchen table, as did Beau, Shelly, Billy, Drew, and—amazingly—Jethro. They all glanced up as I entered, peeking over their newspapers, magazines, and other sundry reading material, with Jethro lifting an index finger to his lips.

"The baby is asleep," he whispered, as though that would explain what in the heck everyone was doing in the house on a Friday morning at 8:00 AM, making no noise whatsoever.

I looked around the table at my family, my gaze settling on Drew. "Is Ashley here?"

He nodded and pointed at the ceiling.

"Where's Bethany?" I asked, thoroughly confused. Bethany was their daughter, who was two and a half, and the great love of my life.

He pointed at the ceiling again, whispering, "With Ashley."

I thought about that, scratching my head. "Are they—"

"Shhh." This curt chastisement came from Cletus. He was frowning, a deep V between his eyebrows, and peering at me. "Your curiosity is not an emergency."

I glared at my brother, but said nothing else, moving to the cupboard where the coffee cups were kept. I retrieved a cup, closed the cupboard door, and came face-to-face with Cletus. He'd moved across the kitchen without making a sound, or at least no sound that I could hear. I hated it when he did that.

"Cletus," I whispered. "Don't do that."

"Do what?" he asked, his eyes never leaving my face as he reached for the coffee carafe, filled his cup, and set it back on the warmer.

"Sneak up on people," I said, though I would've thought it was self-evident.

"I didn't sneak up on you. You need your hearing checked. If you wake up that baby, you're responsible for getting him back to sleep."

"I won't wake up the baby." I rolled my eyes at his histrionics. "Besides, Drew and I should be leaving soon. I'm working with the sweep team on vaccinations today."

"You're not going anywhere if you wake the baby," he warned.

I reached in front of him for the coffee carafe. "I'm not going to wake the baby."

"Would you two quiet down," Billy rough whispered from his seat at the head of the table, glaring at us over his newspaper. "You're going to wake the baby."

Cletus turned a flat-lipped, somber expression toward me, his eyes hooded as though to say, *See what you did?*

I ignored this look, concentrating instead on pouring my coffee as quietly as possible, because I didn't want to wake the baby.

Before Jethro and Sienna had their first child, I didn't understand parents and their obsession with naptime and bedtime. My ignorance on this matter had swiftly been rectified. Benjamin, their oldest son, never slept. So when he did sleep, Jethro and Sienna would become rabid about the need for absolute silence, with Jethro convinced Ben could detect minor seismic shifts of the earth and infrared radiation —because why else would a baby wake up just a half hour after falling asleep?

As it turned out, Ben had adenoid problems. Once those suckers were removed, he'd started sleeping through the night just fine. But by then, Andy had arrived and the whole hypervigilant process started all over again.

Cletus meandered back to the table and I followed, sipping my coffee and wondering what the chances were that I could talk Beau into making breakfast. He made a mean omelet, always getting the egg cooked through without browning the outside and the cheese perfectly melted.

Maybe if I prep the ingredients, he'll cook it for me.

Then, the doorbell rang.

Everyone tensed.

Panicked, wide-eyed stares were swapped until Beau whisper-hissed, "Someone go get the door before they ring again."

Na-ah.

Not me. If the baby woke up, Cletus would say I'd walked or turned the doorknob too loudly. As I glanced around at my brothers, I saw everyone was having similar thoughts.

Shelly, the only one who didn't look near a fit, folded her paper, setting it neatly on the table, and stood calmly from her seat.

She announced quietly, "I will get the door," and left, the rest of us on high alert, straining our ears and staring at the baby monitor.

But before we heard the door open, it happened. A wailing cry pierced through the speaker of the portable monitor, and Jethro sighed mightily.

"Sorry, Jet," Billy said, using his normal voice. "We tried to buy you some time."

"It's fine." Jethro shoulders slumped as he stood. "It was going to happen sooner or later. Besides, I got to read half an article. That's a miracle."

Drew stood, too. "I might as well go check on Ashley and Beth."

"Now that the baby bomb has exploded, will someone tell me what's going on?" I stood in the middle of the kitchen, looking at each of my siblings.

"Everyone is home for the long weekend. Mystery solved." Cletus took his seat again and picked up his paper, adding under his breath, "If you would check your email, you'd know."

"Why can't y'all use a group text message like normal people?"

"Because we're not normal and because some of us don't like group text messages," Jethro responded as he left the room.

I heard his voice a moment later—further away—say, "Oh, hey. Hello. How're you?" A pause, then, "Yeah, that's the youngest."

"None of us like group text messages." Billy folded his paper and glanced at his phone.

"I like group text messages," I mumbled, taking the seat Jethro had vacated and peeked at the magazine he'd been reading, *Family Knitting.* On the cover was a picture of a man, woman, and baby. They all wore matching sweaters, and I smirked. I wouldn't put it past Jethro to knit his entire family matching sweaters.

"She brought doughnuts," Shelly's voice announced from the other room, sounding like she was just outside the kitchen. The words *she* and *doughnuts* snagged my attention and I glanced up from the magazine to the kitchen entrance.

"That was nice of you," Drew said, sounding farther away.

"It's no problem. I'll make sure they save some for you guys," a friendly voice responded.

And I froze. Because that friendly voice definitely belonged to Simone Payton.

What . . .

What the hell was she doing here?

I stood, backing away from the table and turning toward the back door.

"You already done with your coffee?" Cletus asked, and I looked at him. His eyes were moving over me like he suspected I was untrustworthy. "'Cause if you're done, you need to wash your cup before you leave. We're not here to do your dishes."

Sending a quick glare to my brother, I grabbed my cup, dumped it out in the sink, and moved to the back door.

"I said *wash* it. Don't just leave it dirty in the sink, that's no help."

Exhaling through clenched teeth, I stomped back to the sink and flipped on the faucet, reached for the soap, and washed my freaking coffee cup. All my siblings treated me like I was still a kid sometimes, but Cletus was the only one who did it *all* the time.

"Here is everyone," Shelly said from someplace behind me, making me tense, because now Simone was in the kitchen and I'd lost my chance to escape. Heat crawled up my neck, but I didn't turn around. I'd successfully avoided looking directly at her last night and I wasn't keen on avoiding eye contact again this morning.

"Simone."

"Well look who it is."

"'Morning."

Chairs scraped against the wood floor. I imagined Beau, Cletus, and Billy were now standing from the kitchen table and closing in on the woman. Noise followed, a general chatter as I dried my coffee cup and put it back in the cupboard, all the while pushing back against the scene playing in my head.

"Simone."

"Yes?" She had her eyes closed, her dark lashes feathered against her cheeks, her head lolled to one side, long braids spilling over her shoulder.

She was so pretty.

I wondered if she'd remember this tomorrow. I knew I would.

I shut my eyes tight and brought forth the memory of kayaking in Doubtful Sound with Drew. I'd been nineteen. Dolphins appeared and swam next to us, white haze rising from the water, a tumbling waterfall in the distance, looming mountains. My kayak was orange. The dolphins looked lavender up close. The water moved like quick-silver. I could feel the mist in my face.

When unhappy or painful memories were forefront in my mind, I'd learned I could usually push them aside by focusing on the task at hand, reciting the dictionary, or superimposing other recollections. Basically, I distracted myself.

Every memory was always there—every single one, like books on a shelf—but I usually had some control over which took precedence at any given time as long as I remained calm. But if I wasn't calm, if I had to battle both emotions in the moment and the emotions from multiple memories of different times, keeping my mind ordered and focused was near impossible. I'd have to retreat, confront the recollections while alone, talk myself down.

I wasn't so good at this when I was a kid or a teenager, which meant folks often thought I was off sulking, or brooding, or too sullen to respond to a question. In reality, I was trying to reorder my brain, calm down, so I could engage in the present.

Thankfully, I was much better and faster at this now. I was also better at avoiding situations that might spark a cascade of unhappy memories.

Take now, for instance.

Currently, as the conversation behind me flowed, hope arose anew that I'd be able to slip out the back door undetected and completely avoid interacting with Simone or making any new memories of her. I could then text Drew from the backyard and tell him I'd meet him at the north Cades Cove station rather than riding over together.

I'd opened the back door, stepped outside, and was just closing it behind me when I felt resistance and was forced to look up.

And there she was. Round amber eyes with starbursts of gold, big happy smile bordered by full luscious lips, her gorgeous face was framed by a halo of brown curls, which I knew would have highlights of auburn and copper in the sun. Basically, the woman was loveliness incarnate.

Motherfucker.

That's right, go clutch your damn pearls and take a powder. That word was the worst, most heinous curse as far as I was concerned, and this moment required it.

"Hey Roscoe," she said, her voice like silk, coming out of the door and shutting it swiftly behind her. "I was hoping you were here."

Heartbreak, that hopeless, empty, all-encompassing sensation, dimming and numbing everything but the focus of your desire and the pain of the unobtainable, hit me in the chest and stomach. A one-two sucker punch, I almost grunted at the impact.

Motherfucking motherfucker.

Simone's smile waned as her gaze moved over my face and took on a slightly forced quality when I said nothing.

I couldn't speak.

"I'll never love anyone that way." Simone frowned at me, then at the hand at my side. *"Especially not you."*

I winced, ready to relive any memory—any memory at all—except for that one.

My memories were an emotional time machine, which meant I was as raw and speechless now as I'd been then. Nothing I could do about that.

But what I could do was tear my eyes away and clear my throat; I could take a few steps back to lean against the rail of the porch; I could cross my arms and distract myself by thinking about whether the porch needed a new coat of paint. So I did.

She said nothing, just hovered by the back door watching me. After a time, during which I struggled to breathe normally, focus on the cracks in the paint by the porch beam, and school my expression, I sensed Simone move closer.

"I wanted to check on you," she said with her lovely voice. "After last night, with your dad, I was—uh—worried."

"I'm fine." I peered over my shoulder, squinting at the mountain behind our house and the withered wildflower field leading to its base.

A memory floated to the surface, seeing the field like this, cold and frozen, and I grabbed hold of it. My momma had given Simone and I food to leave at the edge of our property, which ended at the border to the Great Smoky Mountains National Park.

"For the fairies," she said.

"Do fairies eat fried chicken?" I asked dubiously, my mouth watering as I catalogued the contents of the plate. Fried chicken, lima beans in butter, bacon collard greens, mashed potatoes with gravy.

"I have questions. Has your father been bothering you?"

I shook my head.

"Of course. Everyone eats fried chicken," my momma said, wiping her hands on a dark blue and white gingham apron, covering the food with tin foil. "Simone, you carry the food, and Roscoe will carry the milk and chocolate cake. Leave it under the box and remember to put the sandbag back on top. That fried chicken is for fairies, not raccoons. And I'll bring the blanket."

"When was the first time he made contact with you?"

Something about the tone of her voice grabbed my attention, like the question was an official one, and I chanced a quick glance at her.

"Why're you so interested in Darrell Winston?" I found myself asking.

She was close enough that I could see her freckles had faded. They were still there, faint against the brown topaz of her complexion.

Also, she was breathtaking.

Now that I'd allowed myself to look again, I couldn't stop.

Her face appeared longer, her cheekbones more defined, as were the lines of her graceful jaw and the point of her chin. She looked a bit like that poster Simone's sister Daniella always had hanging up in her room, where the model was smiling and wearing big, gold hoop earrings, curls framing her face in a way that reminded me of a lion's mane.

Gorgeous.

She was taller than I remembered, and definitely had more curves than I remembered, too. When we were fifteen, Simone had told me she always wanted to look like a boy. I'd asked her what the heck she was talking about, because I didn't think she looked anything like a boy.

She glanced down at herself, at her small frame beneath the white T-shirt and green cargo pants she wore. I knew she was wearing kid-size ten, because she kept complaining about it. The pants had a hole at the knee.

"Flat chest, for one. If I had big boobs, they would affect my aerodynamics."

I rolled my eyes, careful not to let her see. Yeah, she wasn't buxom by any stretch of the imagination, but I'd loved everything about the way she looked. She was prettier than any other girl I knew, and I wasn't the only one who thought so. I wanted to tell her that, but if I did she'd torture me by singing "It's a Small World After All" for who knows how long. So I kept my mouth shut.

Girls were confusing.

Presently, gritting my teeth and frustrated with myself for noticing current Simone's new shape, I decided I could definitely get away with describing her as buxom. I'd noticed last night when we'd hugged, but I'd immediately pushed the awareness away. Not so easy now that she filled my vision.

Time had been especially kind to Simone Payton.

Knowing I'd pay for this indulgence later, I grew restless at her silence and turned from her.

Descending the steps quickly, I walked around the back of the house, calling over my shoulder, "See you later."

I would not see her later.

Billy and Simone's sister Daniella were engaged, and so I'd probably see Simone at the wedding—if they even had a family wedding—but I doubted there'd be many events between our two families celebrating the joy of the union.

Don't get me wrong, I loved Daisy and Trevor Payton. Trevor Payton had been more of a father to me than my own. But I wasn't the only one who thought the impending marriage between Daniella Payton and my brother was based on what could be gained by an alliance rather than deep affection.

Daisy seemed resigned to it.

The one time I'd run into Trevor while grocery shopping, we'd gone out for coffee to catch up and, while at the diner, he'd sighed like he was exhaling a world of worries.

"I love my daughter, and I have an affection for your brother, I do. But I don't think they love each other." Trevor sounded sad and his gaze lost focus as it moved to a spot over my shoulder. "I told your brother as much when he came by to ask our permission."

I snorted my disbelief. "I can't believe Daniella was okay with that."

"She wasn't. When she found out, she was fit to be tied." Trevor gave me a faint grin and chuckled a little. "But you know how your brother is. And Daisy appreciated the gesture, as did I."

What he meant was, Billy was old-fashioned. This was likely because we'd been raised by our momma and our Grandma Oliver. Well, I wasn't raised by Grandma, as I was young when she died, but the rest of my siblings were. And Grandma Oliver had been a stickler for etiquette and good manners.

We were in the cereal aisle and I'd just put granola in my shopping cart. I'd have to sneak it into the house and hide it. All of my siblings were granola fanatics.

"Has Daniella mentioned when the wedding will be?" I asked, hoping Trevor had more information than Billy had shared with us. At least Billy had told the Paytons in person. We'd found out about the engagement by reading about it in the paper.

Trevor shrugged in a way that seemed frustrated and helpless, not a look I was used to seeing on Trevor Payton. "She says they haven't decided."

"Wait, Roscoe. Wait." I felt Simone's hand close over my arm, the warmth of it cutting through to my consciousness and banishing my recollections.

I stopped.

She came around in front of me, her hand still on my forearm, and searched my gaze. "What are you doing later? As in, later today?"

"Why?" I asked quietly, taking another look at her, and why not? The damage had already been done. This Simone, as she was now, would forever be branded in my mind.

She shifted on her feet, her hand falling away as her eyes held mine. A small, tentative smile curved her lips, drawing my attention to her mouth.

"It's been a while. And, you know, I'll technically be your sister soon."

My . . . sister?

My heart gave a sluggish, aching lurch as my chest filled with fire.

Oh. Hell. No.

"And I thought maybe—"

I walked around her again, my lungs so tight, every breath painful as I marched away.

"Roscoe Orwell Winston," she called to my departing back, frustration seeping into her voice. "You are a rude ass." But she didn't follow this time.

I cleared my mind, marched to my car, slipped inside, and drove away. I would text Drew when I made it to Cades Cove. He would understand.

But try as I might, I couldn't stop conjuring this new image of Simone, or the exasperation lacing the cadence of her lovely voice.

She thought I was an ass? Good.

I'd much rather her think of me as an ass than as a brother.

CHAPTER FIVE

"It is easy to love people in memory; the hard thing is to love them when they are there in front of you."

— JOHN UPDIKE, MY FATHER'S TEARS AND
OTHER STORIES

Simone

MOODINESS WAS MY sister's modus operandi. Moodiness and grudges. No one held a grudge like my sister Daniella.

Well, no one except maybe Cletus Winston.

But that was a different story.

My brother's temperament was on the opposite end of the spectrum; Poe had often been described as robotic, too literal and logical for his own good. He didn't have a spiteful bone in his body, having too much curiosity for spite.

If someone treated him poorly, he was likely to spend all afternoon questioning that person until he reached the root of their motivations. Above all else, he sought to understand.

I considered myself a mixture of both my siblings, with a dash of Simply-Simone-Spice thrown in. Which meant I was rarely moody.

Unfortunately, today was one of those rare days.

After Roscoe had left me yesterday, standing on the side of his family's house as he drove away, I'd shaken off his rudeness and spent the rest of the day troubleshooting how best to crack the man's seemingly impenetrable shell of dumbassery.

I also tried to reconcile this new Roscoe—tall, fierce, hot, dumbass—with the sensitive, sweet boy I'd known growing up, and with the boy who'd ditched me for greener pastures when we were teenagers. I endeavored to channel my inner Poe: what could possibly be the root of Roscoe's rudeness?

Root of Roscoe's rudeness . . . *say that three times real fast.*

"Root of Roscoe's rudeness. Root of Roscoe's rudeness. Root of Roscoe's rudeness," I muttered under my breath, listening to how the words morphed and changed until they sounded funny.

The Saturday morning and afternoon rush had finally died down and my shift was almost over. Thank goodness. My feet hurt and my brain hurt and I hadn't been able to shake off my foul mood all day. I attributed this mood to Roscoe being a dumbass by a factor of three.

Firstly, Roscoe shouldn't be able to affect my mood. I didn't know him anymore. I'd gotten over the dissolution of that friendship years ago. I'd even burned items that reminded me of him, tossing pictures and mementoes into a campfire in our backyard. He'd been exorcised from my life. Done.

Secondly, Roscoe did affect my mood. The fact that Roscoe affected my mood was extremely irritating, especially since I didn't understand how it was possible.

Thirdly, the fact that I'd allowed feelings to creep into this assignment irritated me further. I needed to get close enough to Roscoe so that I could ascertain what he knew about his father's whereabouts and report back to Nelson. Feelings about Roscoe and his rudeness should have been the last thing on my mind.

The bell chimed over the diner door, announcing the entrance of customers, and I scowled at the page of the book I hadn't been reading. Sighing as I closed the cover, I walked out of the kitchen, glancing at the entrance to inspect the new arrivals.

I blinked my surprise, straightening, my movements faltering in my astonishment.

The new arrival was Isaac Sylvester, and he was alone, and it was a Saturday afternoon. I'd never seen him on any day other than Sunday, and always in the mornings, and always in a crowd. But right now, aside from Rebecca stocking supplies in the back room, we were alone.

His eyes moved over me, his expression stoic, his muscular form clad entirely in leather—jacket, gloves, pants, boots—and he walked like a soldier. How he conducted himself had been the first thing I'd noticed about him during our initial contact. He had an economy of movement, never turning his head if he could shift his eyes instead, never fiddling or fidgeting, holding still for long moments, like he was more statue than person.

Isaac claimed a stool at the counter and flipped over the coffee cup, tapping it with his index finger, his hard stare holding mine.

"Coffee. Please."

So many questions . . .

I reached for the coffee, lamenting the fact that it was now three hours old and likely stale, but brought it to his cup in any case. Pouring, I let my notice flicker over him. He looked pale.

It was winter, so it's not like I expected him to be sunbathing, but his white skin looked paler than usual, a touch of grayish green in place of his usual healthy hue.

"How are you?"

My eyes jumped to his and I did my best to mask my confusion. This was the first time he'd spoken to me aside from, *Coffee. Please,* and, *Keep the change.*

"Fine," I lied, glancing behind him to the parking lot—because I was paranoid—and met his eyes again. "And how are you?"

He swallowed a sip of coffee, licking his lips as he placed the cup back on the counter. "Winston is at the Dragon. Arrived Friday morning. He and Razor are holed up, no one has seen either since yesterday."

As he spoke, I reached under the counter and grabbed the salt, busying myself by unnecessarily filling saltshakers that were already mostly full. I nodded subtly to indicate I'd heard him, but said nothing, because there was nothing that needed to be said.

Razor Dennings, president of the Iron Wraiths, hadn't left the Dragon Biker Bar—as far as we knew—for three years.

Also, there was no way we could extract Winston from the Iron Wraiths' compound. Make no mistake, the Dragon Biker Bar was a compound, a maze on the inside, with false doors, walls, and tunnels leading to a range of hidden exits. Even if Isaac told us exactly where Winston's quarters were and drew us a detailed map, it wouldn't matter. The target would be long gone by the time the extraction team made it to the room.

"Something else," he lowered his voice, his eyes forward. "I've been given orders to pick up Roscoe Winston."

An unanticipated squeeze around my heart and jolt of feelings had me spilling salt on the counter.

Are you fucking kidding me right now?

Stupid feelings.

I breathed out, frustrated with my display of clumsiness.

"I have questions," I said, cleaning up the mess with a napkin. "First of all, why Roscoe?"

"Winston wants him."

"Are they going to hurt him?" I cursed inwardly at the slight catch to my voice and told myself lies like, *I'd be concerned for anyone.*

I would be concerned for anyone, so that part wasn't a lie. The lie was that I wouldn't be this hands-shaking, heart-racing concerned for just anyone.

Stupid dumbass Roscoe, giving me feelings and unsteady hands.

"I don't know." Isaac rubbed his eyes with the base of his palms. "Winston seems to think he'll come willingly, but I'm supposed to use force if he doesn't."

Shit.

"When?" I tossed the salt and the napkin in the trash. "How long does he have?"

Maybe I could warn Roscoe.

Or maybe I could just show up wherever he was, that would certainly drive him out of town.

The only conclusions I'd been able to draw with any degree of certainty about Roscoe Winston were: he couldn't stand the sight of me, didn't like me, and was therefore avoiding me.

Why he felt this way—other than him being a dumbass—I had no idea.

The disappearing act had been distressing when I'd been sixteen. Not only did he stop coming by the diner, stop returning my calls, and never seemed to be at home when I bicycled over, he'd also changed his schedule at school and joined the football team.

This had been quietly devastating to me at the time because he switched out of our shared shop class, developing a mysterious and sudden interest in the trumpet, and therefore band class in third period.

I don't have anything against the trumpet or band. But shop class had only been fun because of him. He let me do all the cutting and nailing. He did the measuring and gluing. Our bird houses had been a triumph of modern architecture and design. Life had been good.

Until it wasn't.

Keeping it real, his absence in shop class wasn't the issue, but rather an allegory for everything. I was good at solving puzzles, he was good at remembering facts. I didn't know how to be "Simone" without "and Roscoe."

For weeks I'd wondered what went wrong. I'd searched for clues, I'd questioned anyone who might've had relevant insight into the behavior patterns of teenage boys. Why had my best friend ditched me for band, football, and the girls' volleyball team?

Oh, yeah. The girls' volleyball team. He dated them. *All* of them. One right after the other, like he'd needed to fill out a punch card with their names on it in order to get a free smoothie or five dollars off his dry cleaning.

Whatever.

After a few months, I let it drop, his abandonment forever left unsolved. And that was okay. This was a character trait where I resembled my sister rather than my brother. I may have been obsessed with solving mysteries, just not about myself or about other people's feelings regarding me.

You don't like me? That's cool. You do you.

Which was why I'd let Roscoe go ten years ago. Yes, I'd thrashed against it for a time. But in the end, I wasn't one to force my company on folks who didn't want it.

Their loss, because I was awesome.

I'm so awesome, I'm magic.

Jazz hands.

MAGIC!

Irritatingly, I didn't have the luxury this time of letting it go. It wasn't about me or us. I needed Roscoe to talk to me. More than that, I needed him to trust me.

"Winston gave me two weeks to bring in Roscoe." Isaac stared at his coffee, his expression blank, but his eyes looked tired.

Two weeks.

One important detail could be extrapolated from this information: Winston planned to stay put for at least two weeks.

"One more thing."

I felt Isaac's stare on me, so I lifted my head and looked out the window to the parking lot behind him. Finding it empty, I gave Isaac my eyes.

"Razor is going to the Kentucky Derby."

My lips parted in surprise and I felt my eyebrows pull together before I could halt the expression of confusion.

"Pardon?"

Isaac's jaw ticked, but a weak smile tugged at one corner of his mouth. "Kentucky Derby."

"Why?"

He didn't answer, just looked at me. That, I had to assume, meant my guess was as good as his.

Isaac stood. Reaching into his pocket, he pulled out a dollar and fifty-one cents, and placed the bill and coins on the counter.

"Exact change?" That couldn't be right. Isaac always left a twenty and the twenty was what I handed over to the ATF or the bureau.

My head was swimming. Razor was leaving the Dragon for a trip to the Kentucky Derby. Winston was in town for the next month. Roscoe was a dumbass, about to be kidnapped—or, dumbass-napped —and Isaac Sylvester had given me exact change.

"The coffee was stale," he said, standing and turning for the door. "No tip today."

* * *

I DECIDED TO put a tracker on Roscoe's car.

Wait.

Hear me out.

This was a good idea, I swear.

There existed a possibility that Isaac wasn't the only Iron Wraiths lieutenant tasked with bringing Roscoe in. If one of those other guys caught up with the youngest Winston first, I didn't like the real possibility that Roscoe would be seriously hurt.

After leaving the diner, I texted my mother to let her know I'd be home after midnight. I didn't know for a fact that I'd be home after midnight, but better to be safe than scared half to death upon entering my house after midnight.

I then drove to the safe house and left a report in the case file, alerting Nelson and Lundqvist separately via text that there was new intel from *The Cat*.

The Cat was Sylvester's code name, for . . . obvious reasons to anyone who was a *Looney Tunes* fan.

Grabbing a GPS vehicle tracking device from the supply locker in the bedroom, I set out in search of Roscoe. Or more precisely, his car.

I checked his house first. Nothing.

Then the Winston Brothers Auto Shop. Still nothing.

Then his brother Beau's and his sister Ashley's houses around Bandit Lake. Nothing and nothing.

I'd noticed the police vehicle on my way into the private road that snaked around Bandit Lake, but I hadn't thought much of it. However, when I pulled to a stop at the end of the loop, and saw that same cop car behind mine, a jolt of terror hit me like a lightning bolt.

Calm down, I told myself, *calm down, this is Green Valley, calm down.*

I huffed a laugh at my silliness.

A second later, the lights flashed and I jumped in my seat again, my heart hammering in my chest. Peering into my rearview mirror, I tried to figure out who the heck was pulling me over.

I knew most of the sheriff deputies in this area. Sheriff James's wife—Janet James—was a dear friend of my mother's. When I was home in Green Valley, I didn't tense when I spotted a police officer, I didn't check the volume of my voice or my car's radio, I didn't conduct a self-assessment, to make sure my expression was appropriately respectful, not like I did in other small towns.

If I was pulled over in Green Valley, it was because I was speeding around the switchbacks or I had a taillight out or my tag had expired.

So this, being pulled over for no apparent reason, was an odd experience for me in my hometown.

Maybe I have a taillight out? I didn't think so, but maybe I did.

I steered my vehicle into Ashley Winston's driveway. I'd spotted her car parked out front and logic told me her driveway felt safer than pulling onto the twisty side road where one car might pass by every half hour.

Just in case.

I cut the engine, rolled down my window, and kept both hands on the wheel, hoping this was just Jackson James—the sheriff's son—wanting to say hi.

It wasn't.

My mouth went dry and the terror returned. An officer I didn't recognize strolled up to my window, but this wasn't why my mouth went dry. His hand was on his weapon. It was still holstered, but his hand was on it. He bent slightly to peer inside my car, unsmiling.

"What do you think you're doing here?" He sounded angry, aggressive.

Maybe it was my imagination, but I didn't think so. And, I swear in that moment, all I could think about was Sandra Bland.

I swallowed around the tightness in my throat—part frustration, part fear, part incredulity—and told myself to refer back to my training at the bureau. I was a professional. This was no big deal. This man was a fellow law enforcement officer. I'd met and worked with hundreds of police officers, all great guys and gals, all on the same team.

I plastered a small smile on my face. "I'm looking for a friend."

He huffed a disbelieving sounding laugh and his gaze darted over my Audi. "Yeah right. Is this your vehicle?"

"Yes, sir," I said, careful to keep my tone respectful.

"Driver's license, insurance, and registration. This better be your car."

Heat climbed up my neck and I took a deep breath. I began drafting a speech in my head for when this was over, how I would—calmly, politely—explain to him that he was behaving inappropriately. I told myself again that this was no big deal. I told myself that I was overreacting.

None of that helped. Call it a hunch, but there was just something about this guy that didn't seem right. Nevertheless, I reached for my glove box.

"Whoa! Slowly," he warned, taking a step back and shifting his weight to his left foot, unclipping the latch holding his gun.

Oh my God.

The polite proposed speech and everything else fled my brain as survival instinct kicked in.

Calm down. You're a freaking FBI agent. Nothing is going to happen. Calm. Down.

I had my gun on me, I knew how to use it, but that wouldn't make a difference if this guy shot first and asked questions later. No amount of training could stop a bullet. In that moment, I thought about both Chris Kyle and Sandra Bland.

Just tell him you're FBI.

I rejected the idea as soon as it formed. I couldn't. My life wasn't the only one at stake here. Blowing my cover might mean Isaac, Nelson, and Lundqvist were exposed, too. I wouldn't do that to them. Plus, there were the folks who'd been murdered and those who might be in danger if the killer struck again in June, according to his/her pattern.

This case was bigger than me and my fear, or my safety.

So I moved slowly, hating the way my hands were shaking and how angry and scared I was, how I couldn't think and was unable to stop the chanting thought, *I belong in a lab. I belong in a lab. I belong in a lab.*

This was the reason I didn't take road trips. I cringed at the thought of Green Valley becoming a sundown town, rejected it on a visceral level. I loved this place, I loved these people, I didn't want it to change.

Just as I fished out my registration, I heard someone holler, "Hey, what's going on out here?"

Holding out the registration, my attention shifted to the woman standing in the doorway behind the officer and the little girl on her hip.

I breathed out, relief rushing to the surface of my skin. It was Ashley Runous and her daughter.

The officer glanced at me, then at Ashley. "Sorry, ma'am. I'm just responding to a disturbance."

My mouth fell open and I nearly choked on the short, hysteria-laden laugh that tumbled from my lips.

Disturbance my ass.

Ashley charged forward, her expression somewhere between confused and mad as hell. "Is that Officer Strickland? What the hell do you think you're doing? Get your hand off your weapon, you damn fool."

"Uh . . ." His eyes swung back to mine, not dropping his hand from his weapon, but he did clip it back in place.

By now, Ashley was next to the car and stood between my open window and the officer. "First of all, we have cameras on the house, so don't you get any ideas. Plus, Bitty Johnson is watching us out her window." She turned her head and jutted her chin toward the house across the street, quickly rushing to add, "Secondly, Drew is on his way home, and will be here any minute. Thirdly, that"—she pointed at me—"is Simone Payton. *Payton.*"

I couldn't see the officer, but I could sense in the silence that he was putting two and two, and two and two together, and that equaled not being able to get away with his present behavior. Also, he must've known who my family was because he couldn't seem to find anything to say.

Ashley made a short, satisfied sound. "Yeah. Right. I see now that you understand your er-*ror.*" Her tone was hard and angry, and she'd overpronounced the word *error*, making it two syllables.

She made like she was going to turn to talk to me, but then seemed to think better of it. "You see this man, Bethany? This man is a racist."

I started in my seat, a new wave of fear crested at Ashley's over-reaction.

Was it an overreaction, though?

I honestly didn't know. Racist wasn't a word to be thrown around lightly, and she seemed to know this man well enough to feel comfortable calling him such in front of her daughter.

She continued, "He pulled over your Uncle Juan for no reason. He pulled over this wonderful woman just because of her skin color. Don't be like this man, Bethany. See people, see their differences, rejoice in those differences, but don't judge folks for something as stupid as the ability to absorb vitamin D. Racists are ignorant assholes."

He seemed to puff out his chest. "Now-now-now, see here—"

"You're really going to try to defend yourself? *Really?* You just got off suspension for what you did to Sienna's brother when he had the audacity to visit his family. You just had your hand on your gun. So may I suggest you think long and hard about what you're going to do next." She didn't raise her voice, but I could tell she was furious.

I saw over Ashley's shoulder that he'd snapped his mouth shut. Now he was turning red. Officer Strickland's gaze moved to me and his face turned redder. I held my breath.

"I'll be going," he said, promptly turning and walking to his car.

I watched him go in my rearview mirror. I watched him slide into his car, start the engine, and leave.

Breathing out, I felt myself deflate.

Thank God.

I looked at Ashley.

"I'm sorry," she said, a pained expression on her face, like she was apologizing for his behavior.

I wasn't able to speak. I needed a minute. I was going through too many emotions: relief, anger, gratitude, frustration at needing to be grateful in the first place, guilt for being frustrated for being grateful, more relief.

See? *This.*

This right here was why I eschewed feelings. Feelings were the worst.

Just say thank you.

I closed my eyes, concentrating on my breathing while my mind slowed.

I should say thank you. I was hugely grateful. But . . .

It stuck in my throat. This was my sister's part of my personality shining through, this stubbornness, this sense of righteous injustice.

I really liked Ashley Winston. She'd always been kind to me when I was a kid and when she came into the diner. But the fact was that she—a white woman—had been able to holler at Deputy Strickland and get away with it, while I—a black woman—couldn't reach too fast for my glove box. That wasn't Ashley's fault, it just was.

I felt grateful. So grateful.

I also felt wretched and powerless.

I *hated* feeling powerless.

She huffed. "You're not the first person he's harassed. He pulled over Sienna's brother Juan when he visited. Called him horrible names and demanded his passport. He arrested him on some BS charge, got suspended for three months over it. They should have fired him. I'm sorry if I crossed the line, but that man is just nasty."

I nodded, putting away my registration, coming down from the adrenaline high.

She wavered, looking embarrassed, eventually blurting, "Will you come inside?"

"No, thank you." I glanced behind her at nothing in particular, a creeping numbness weighing heavy in my stomach. I figured, while I had her here, I might as well ask the pertinent question. "Do you know where Roscoe is?"

"Actually—" she breathed a short laugh "—I do. He and Drew just finished up at the Park. Drew should be home soon. We have a sitter for tonight and we're meeting everyone—including Roscoe—at Genie's for drinks and dancing." Her stare darted over me. "Do you want to come with? Shelly and Beau will be there." She added this last bit like it was an incentive.

Usually, she'd be right. The thought of getting to know Shelly Sullivan outside of our monthly chats at the diner was a big pull.

But I had a job to do.

I started my car. "I'll think about it." "Uh, do me a favor?"

"Anything."

"Don't tell my parents about this? Or my cousins. Or Sheriff James." The last thing I needed was my Aunt Dolly making a fuss about a DWB (driving while black) episode. I needed to keep the lowest of profiles while undercover, and *that* would certainly draw all the wrong kind of attention.

She looked confused. "Uh—"

"And Genie's. Thank you for the invite."

"Okay." She nibbled on her lip, her eyes anxious. "I hope you come."

I considered her, my attention moving to her daughter who was looking at me squarely, in that quiet forthright way that kids have, before they learn about guilt and shame and prejudice.

And I decided something.

"Can I give you some advice, Ashley?"

"Advice?" She shifted, redistributing her weight to the hip where her daughter perched. "Yeah. Sure."

"The next time you see someone behaving like Officer Strickland . . ." I held her gaze with mine and gave her a small, genuine smile. "Absolutely intervene. You did the right thing coming out here, thank you so much for that."

She studied me, a question between her knotted brows. "But?"

"Not really a *but*. More like, consider. Instead of rescuing the person being harassed, and if you judge that the person isn't in imminent danger, may I suggest you amplify that person's voice instead?"

Ashley tilted her head to the side, her gaze cloudy with confusion. "How do you mean?"

"Next time, ask me if I'm okay and if I've been treated fairly. Give me a chance to defend myself, to use my own voice."

Her blue eyes moved between mine, so like Roscoe's, and a wobbly half-smile tugged at her lips; her cheeks flushed. "Yes. Okay. I'm sorry."

"Oh no! Don't apologize, please don't!" *Crap.*

I reached out with my hand, palm up. She held it. We smiled at each other.

"Don't apologize," I repeated. "And please, please, please don't feel bad. God, never feel bad about being an excellent person. Just, if you think of it, let capable people speak for themselves. Let us use our voices. People like Officer—" I thought better of what I was going to say, and restarted, "Wouldn't it be great if folks everywhere were used to listening—really listening—to people who didn't look like them? Instead of discounting a voice because it doesn't come from a mouth and face that resembles theirs, what if they got used to valuing those voices? The only way people learn and change—I believe—is by practicing. So that means we need to give them more opportunities to practice listening. We need more voices like mine speaking to folks like Officer Strickland."

She nodded, her smile steadier, and sniffed. "That makes sense. I'll try. But you know how we Winstons are, always poking our beaks into other folks' business, always squawking, flapping our feathers, out to rescue someone."

"I don't typically need to be rescued, so thanks for rescuing me today," I said, laughing at her description of her family and letting our hands swing gently. "But I'll never turn down an ally."

CHAPTER SIX

"One of the keys to happiness is a bad memory."

— RITA MAE BROWN

Roscoe

ASHLEY TOLD US the story over drinks at Genie's.
I'm not going to lie, my first instinct was to go out, find Officer Strickland, and—

"Now there's a man who deserves leprosy," Cletus announced, stroking his beard thoughtfully.

Jennifer, sitting next to him, nodded.

"But I'm confused." Beau scratched his jaw. "Simone was upset with you for sticking up for her? You'd think she'd be grateful."

Ashley shook her head vehemently. "No. That's not at all what happened. The sense I got was that Simone was relieved I was there, and grateful, and she's just so lovely—but can I just say here, how awful is it that she was put in a situation *at all* where she had to be grateful for someone stepping in and defending her for doing absolutely nothing but driving her car, so frustrating—"

"Think of it this way," Shelly cut in, likely because Ashley was getting herself all worked up again, and turned to Beau. "If someone was yelling at you and threatening you for no reason, and Jackson James came over to diffuse the situation, would you want a chance to use your own voice? Or would you be fine with Jackson James always speaking for you?"

"Okay, yeah. I see your point." Beau nodded thoughtfully.

"And," Cletus added, "in addition to providing my services for ally amplification, I know where the armadillos are."

Drew chuckled, exchanging a glance with Beau, who was also chuckling. I didn't know why they were laughing, it wasn't funny.

"Why are you laughing?" I demanded, working hard to keep my voice steady. "You wouldn't think it was funny if it happened to Shelly," then to Drew I said, "or to Ash."

Drew's expression softened. "No, no, Roscoe. We're laughing at the idea of giving Strickland leprosy, not at what happened to Simone."

Beau chimed in, "I assure you, this could have happened to anyone and I'd be equally delighted at the prospect of Cletus's plan."

"Cletus has had this idea in his back pocket for years, just waiting for the right asshole to use it on." This came from Jenn and, I swear, even in my current state, I think I gasped. I'd never, not in my whole life, heard Jennifer cuss. Not once.

I wasn't the only one shocked. Ashley, Beau, and Drew were all staring at her, equally flummoxed.

But Cletus didn't seem surprised.

Neither did Shelly.

"Let me know if you need help catching armadillos." Shelly set her beer down, turning to Cletus. "I can build a trap."

"I'll help too," I said.

But the idea of revenge didn't help the sick feeling in my stomach or the rage pounding through my veins.

I wish I'd been there. I would have . . .

I probably would have gotten myself arrested. Or shot. Or both.

"We're not giving anyone leprosy," Ashley cut in, giving each of us in turn a look that communicated she meant business. "We're filing a report with Sheriff James. That man needs to be fired. We'll do this the right way."

Cletus continued to stroke his beard thoughtfully. "And if that doesn't work, we're all agreed." He hit the table with his closed fist, as though it were a gavel. "Leprosy it is."

Ashley made a sound, but I said before my sister could object, "Do you think she'll file a report?"

I wondered how Simone was doing. I wondered if she was regretting moving back to town. I wondered a lot of things.

Drew told me on Friday, while we were making our rounds at the Park, that Simone had moved back in with her parents. That she'd quit her job in the government because—and this was according to Trevor Payton—she needed some time to figure out what she wanted to do.

I called bullshit.

Simone had always known what she wanted to do. She wanted to solve crimes, catch bad guys, and keep good folks safe. End of story.

"We have those cameras at the house"—Drew glanced at Ashley—"and you said Bitty watched the whole thing. So maybe Simone doesn't have to file a report."

Ashley's brows pulled together and her eyes lost focus, as though she were remembering something. "Like she said, it's not up to us. It's up to her." My sister turned to look at her husband. "We leave it up to her, she decides. We'll let her know we're here to help, but that we'll follow her lead."

"Speaking of leading"—Cletus checked his watch—"does anyone know where Jethro is?"

"What does Jethro have to do with leading?" Beau took a swig of his beer, giving Cletus a face.

"Nothing. Our plan is decided, no need to rehash the details. I just wanted to change the subject." Cletus looked to Ash. "Did Jet message you?"

"He did." Her mouth formed a sympathetic smile and her

eyebrows looked regretful. "He decided to stay in and catch up on sleep."

"I thought Jackson was babysitting for him. So he could have a night out." Jenn sat up straighter.

"Jackson is babysitting. Even so, Jethro wanted to stay in and get some sleep." Now Ash looked like she was holding in laughter.

I was only half listening to the conversation, the remainder of my attention still absorbed by Ashley's tale and my clumsy behavior with Simone on Thursday and Friday.

My memories were an emotional time machine, which is one of the main reasons I'd been avoiding Simone. The other big reason was because I didn't want to make any new memories with her. But I reflected that didn't mean all the experiences I'd had between a particular moment and now ceased to exist. I could learn from interactions between a particular moment and the present, learn to see it differently, but this took a great deal of effort and determination.

As an example, my memory of being abandoned at Hawk's Field by my father was painful every time I thought about it, just as painful and frightening as it had been when it happened. I'd avoided the place like my brother Billy avoided the Iron Wraiths, at all costs.

But over the last few months in particular, I'd worked to compartmentalize that memory, so it didn't have such a hold on me, so it didn't matter as much. I retrieved it on purpose. I camped at Hawk's Field on the weekends, making new memories there, ones where I was in control.

But people weren't fields. If I decided to stop avoiding Simone now, I couldn't control the memories made moving forward.

I picked up my beer, took a drink, considered the two short interactions I'd had with Simone this last week, what I understood now about being an idiot teenager, what little I knew about heartbreak—drawing mostly from what I'd observed in my family over the years and their struggles—and layered it all together.

A conversation I'd had with Beau while he was drunk, sitting on the back steps of our house five years, six months, and twenty days ago struck out at me.

"How do you know?"

"What?" Beau looked like he was having trouble keeping both his eyes open at the same time.

"How do you know whether a woman has substance? Whether her feelings for you go as deep as your feelings for her?" I'd often wondered this, not allowing myself to get close enough to anyone to find out for sure.

I'd wanted to, over the years. I'd go on a date, maybe two. Then the woman would do something, say something that rubbed me the wrong way. It didn't have to be a big something, anything at all might stick in my craw—not liking my alma mater, gossiping about their friends, a word said in anger—and I couldn't forget. And I didn't feel enough for the woman yet to merit staying, so I'd move on.

He didn't answer right away, and I thought maybe he wasn't going to, but then he said as he breathed out, like the words cost him, "She makes you a priority."

Becoming a priority to Simone Payton wasn't going to happen, not the way I wanted. But maybe there was a way I could interact with her and remain in control of the memories made.

I wasn't paying attention to anything but my own contemplations, so when someone bumped my shoulder as they passed our booth, I knocked over my beer. Everyone leaned away from the table and Beau quickly caught the puddle with the few napkins we had, keeping it from the edges.

"Shoot." I stood, checking the front of my clothes and lamenting the loss of my beer.

"Calm down. Your haute couture is safe, Roscoe," Cletus drawled. "Go get a towel from Patty for us plebeians."

I ignored Cletus's surliness, because he was always surly with me, and glanced around the table. "Anyone need anything while I'm up?"

"I'll take another margarita." Ashley gave me a big smile, and I made a note to bring my sister some flowers the next time I drove back from Nashville.

I wonder if they're ready for that puppy.

When Bethany was born, I'd told Drew and Ash that I had dibs on buying my girl her first puppy. I wondered if they'd forgotten.

Navigating through the crowd, I decided to order myself a water instead of replacing my spilled beer. It had been a long day and I didn't feel much like drinking.

Careful to keep my eyes forward, I tried not to make eye contact with folks as I passed by, instead waiting on people to stop me, if they so choose. This practice had become a force of habit after I'd made the mistake a few times of recognizing people who didn't recognize me.

That's another funny thing about having a better than average memory, I usually remember people after meeting them just once. Nothing disconcerts folks like being remembered, the assumption being that they must've made a big impression, or I particularly valued making their acquaintance. This is seldom the case.

I'll remember my waiter or waitress, regardless of whether I received noteworthy service, just because I saw his or her face.

Therefore, I don't look at people's faces unless needs be.

Traversing the crowd successfully, I stepped up to the bar and searched for Genie, hoping to catch her eye. Seeing it was me, she came over after a short delay and I placed our order.

"I'll bring it over when it's done, hun." She lifted her chin toward the booth where my family sat.

"One more thing," I began regretfully. "I spilled my beer."

"You need a towel," she guessed, her grin understanding, looking at me like I was her favorite. "Don't worry about it, baby. I'll bring one over when I bring Ashley her margarita. You want your water now?"

"Yes, please."

She made a clicking sound with her tongue, filling up a water glass. "You Winston boys are so polite. I wish they were all like you." She passed me the glass.

"Thank you, Genie."

"You're welcome, baby," she said, giving me a wink and turning away to reach for the tequila.

I took a sip of my water. Pulling the straw out, I bit one end flat and picked up my glass. But as I turned, I came face-to-face with Charlotte Mitchell.

"Roscoe Winston."

I straightened, giving her a smile, because I was happy to see her. "Charlotte Mitchell."

Charlotte had played trumpet with me in high school; she'd been first chair, I'd been second. We'd sometimes meet up after I was done with football and she was finished with band practice, just to hang out, or maybe practice together.

In the spring, when she had volleyball and I had track, she'd often bring along all her teammates and we'd go hiking or to the library, where my momma worked. I'd ended up taking the entire volleyball team to prom our junior year.

There'd been nothing between Charlotte and me then, just kids doing kid things. I'd told her all about what happened with Simone, and she'd told me all about her breakups. She'd been a friend to me, a good friend, when I'd needed one.

"Aren't you going to buy me a drink?"

I chuckled, because, for the last six months, we always started this way.

I knew what to say next. "I would, but my brother confiscated my wallet."

"Why'd he do that?"

"Because he knew if I saw you, I'd want to buy all your drinks."

Charlotte laughed, her gaze moving over me like she approved of my answer. She should, it was the same one I gave every time we happened to run into each other at Genie's.

It was good to see her smile. A few months ago, I doubted it was possible. But seeing her come through this dark time was a good reminder that the present—the moment we're living right this minute —isn't the rest of our lives. Sometimes it can feel that way, when things get overwhelming, but it's simply not the case.

My momma would say, *"Like thunderstorms and time, this too shall pass."*

Charlotte had dropped out of college when she got pregnant with her first and married the father. They had another kid almost immediately and moved to Vegas. Unfortunately, her husband wasn't the good sort and had left her and their kids eight months ago for another woman. Charlotte had moved back in with her folks.

I felt for her. She was a good person. She deserved to be happy. As I studied her now, I was pleased to see she seemed to be doing better, if looks were anything to go by.

"Well then." Charlotte set her purse on the bar. "Allow me to buy you a drink."

This was new. "Nah. That's all right. I think I should stick to water."

"Already?" She glanced between me and my cup. "The night is young, Roscoe. Live a little."

"I'm living." I let a slow smile spread over my features and unleashed an eye-twinkle. "I'm talking to you, aren't I?"

Charlotte tried to look unimpressed, but I knew that look. She loved flirting with me just as much as I did with her. I enjoyed making her happy.

"Go on"—Charlotte gestured to the row of liquor over the bar —"order anything you like."

"What do I need alcohol for?" I bent forward and whispered in her ear, "You're already intoxicating enough."

"Oh my goodness"—Charlotte threw her head back and laughed —"that's a terrible line."

As I leaned away, I chewed on my straw and watched her, laughed with her, taking in her reaction. She attempted to roll her eyes and fight a smile at the same time. Then she flipped her hair, her cheeks flushing with pleasure, her eyes lowering as she took a steadying breath.

Flirting was easy, fun.

I loved it.

Making women smile—especially women like Charlotte— watching them light up, it was like a drug for me.

Maybe they sensed I had no expectations, there was no pressure, that all I wanted was to brighten their day. Or maybe I'd had so much practice, I knew exactly the right things to say. Either way, it was easy.

Pressing her lips together, but still smiling, her eyes flicked over me, a question in her assessing gaze, "Why do you always tease me?"

"Am I teasing?"

"You say such pretty things." She tucked her brown hair behind her ear, leaning an elbow on the bar and bringing our faces close together. I noticed she was wearing the same earrings she wore to our church's high school graduation party. "You talk a great game, Roscoe. *The best* game. But . . ."

"But what?"

"You never actually do anything." She looked confused, as though she'd clicked the pieces together and arrived at this conclusion at just this very moment.

Inwardly, I sighed. Because as much as I liked making her smile, nothing was going to happen between us. We were never going to seal the deal, not because there was anything wrong with Charlotte and not because I wasn't attracted to her. She was smart and funny and damn sexy, but I didn't seal deals.

If things didn't work out, she'd forget being with me. Regrets, if there were any, would fade. It might be a rosy memory for her, or it might simply disappear under a pile of other encounters.

I didn't have that luxury.

So I tried to play off her question, looking up and to the side, knowing she'd think it was adorable. "Maybe I just like seeing you smile."

She laughed again, but as she straightened away from the bar, I detected sadness there, too. "You're cute."

I was about to launch into another flirt attack, hoping to chase away her sudden blues, when movement at the end of the bar caught my attention. My words stalled, my thoughts hijacked.

It was Simone.

*She swayed a little, laughing, and shaking her head. "Why'd you
let me drink so much?"*

*"Let you?" I laughed, too. "Nobody lets Simone Payton do
anything."*

"Damn straight." She slurred the word straight *and abruptly sat
on the grass in an ungraceful heap.*

*I vacillated a second, sat next to her, and wanted to put my arm
around her shoulders, to support her, hold her close, but I didn't
know how she'd react to that.*

How did I not notice her come in?

Three stools from where I stood, she was shaking her head
subtly. A wry smile on her lips, her eyes were on the drink in front of
her. I had no doubt she'd overheard the conversation I'd just had
with Charlotte, or at least some of it.

Interestingly, my first thought wasn't the cutting memory of her
rejection like usual, but rather the spike of alarm I'd experienced
when Ashley had told us what happened this afternoon.

Charlotte stirred and glanced over her shoulder. She then turned
back to me, giving me a knowing smile.

Leaning close and holding my gaze, she mouthed, "Still
Simone?"

I took a deep breath, my own smile regretful, and a look of
understanding passed between us.

It had always been Simone. I'd gone to Charlotte's wedding with
no date. Whenever it came up, I'd admitted I had no girlfriend. She'd
tried to set me up, I'd always declined. Junior year, senior year, all
through college and vet school.

Always Simone.

Charlotte nodded, like she'd just decided something. She lifted to
her tiptoes and pressed a kiss against my cheek.

"Go get her," she whispered.

Charlotte then picked up her purse, stepped around me, and
walked past, presumably to the dance floor or one of the high top
tables clustered around it.

Gathering a deep breath, I looked at Simone.

She sat in profile on a stool, her elbows on the bar top while she stirred her drink with two miniature straws. It might've been soda water or it might have been something mixed with soda water. Either way, her glass had a lime in it.

More and more, I'd wanted to touch her. And she'd been letting me. We'd always hugged, but now holding hands wasn't unusual, and —I reminded myself—she'd been the one to pat my backside first.

"Simone."

"Yes?" *She had her eyes closed, her dark lashes against her cheeks, her head lolled to one side, long braids spilling over her shoulder.*

She was so pretty.

I wondered if she'd remember this tomorrow. I knew I would.

I blinked away the memory, pushing it to the side by recalling where I'd left off in the dictionary. *Besot.* To make dull or stupid; especially to muddle with drunkenness.

Hmm.

The word was timely.

I didn't want her to always be "still Simone." I didn't want this woman, who I'd been avoiding for a decade and who was never going to return my affections, to matter so much.

Taking three steps forward, because that's all it took to reach her, I claimed the seat next to hers and breathed through the ache in my chest. Not going to lie, it hurt, and I was nervous, and I wasn't sure what I was going to say.

I settled on, "Hey."

Simone lifted her chin, her eyes sliding to mine. She then made a show of looking in the other direction, on her other side, as though searching for someone.

Turning back to me, she gestured to herself and wore a mask of exaggerated astonishment. "Oh. Are you talking to me?"

I rolled my lips between my teeth.

"Hi," she said, "I'm Simone." She held out her hand, "And who are you?"

I lifted an eyebrow to disguise the way my heart galloped.

"What would you say if I told you I love you?" I was so nervous. Even drunk as I was, I was nervous. But the liquor helped.

A laugh, a wide grin, exquisite amber irises moving over my face. "I love you, too. Of course I do."

"I mean"—I reached out, my fingers closing gently over her wrist and a thrill shot through me to see my hand on her skin—"what if I told you I'm in love with you?" My voice cracked a little on the last three words.

Her smile fell as understanding sharpened behind her eyes, disappointment, dismay.

She covered my hand with hers, prying away my fingers.

I slipped my hand into hers, watching our palms meet, and I swallowed a rush of nerves. She felt the same, and it devastated me. Unthinkingly, I twisted my wrist so that the back of her hand was visible to my eyes, and I spotted the scar—now faint—she'd gotten when she'd insisted on learning how to throw knives. I brushed my thumb over it, my heart in my throat.

"This looks different," I said and thought.

She made no move to pull her hand away, instead twisting in her seat until her knees knocked mine. "Scars fade over time."

Maybe for some people.

I exhaled a laugh, shaking my head and letting her hand go.

"Roscoe . . ." She'd never said my name like that before, like it was a word to put distance between us. She blinked like she was trying to bring me into focus. "No. No, no, no."

I studied her, holding my breath, feeling like my life and heart were balanced on the edge of a knife.

"Why no?" I whispered.

Her head swayed a little, and she blinked, and I saw she was real drunk. I cursed. Guilt had me gritting my teeth and shaking my head at myself. I was drunk, too. But I wasn't as drunk as she was.

"We'll talk about this later."

"Still no."

"Roscoe."

I swallowed reflexively, gathered a bracing breath, and lifted my eyes to hers. Once more I was tangled up in her, by how beautiful she was. Her eyes were gentle now, patient, like she sensed I needed a minute to reacquaint myself, or steady myself.

"You know, I have a lot of questions . . ." she started, pulling me out of my thoughts, tilting her head to the side as her attention moved over me. "Starting with, why were you so rude yesterday?"

I considered her, thinking back to yesterday, and nodded. "I was. I'm sorry."

Her eyes narrowed. "Anything else you're sorry for?"

I rolled my lips between my teeth again, but this time—despite the enduring ache in my chest—it was to stop a smile.

"Hmm." I stroked my chin, trying to mimic the way my brother Cletus might do it, forcing levity I hoped I'd soon feel. "Let's see."

"Do you need some paper? Or a pen?" Simone made like she was going to reach for her bag. "Maybe you want to make a list. I don't know if I have enough paper for *everything*, but maybe for the first hundred or so things."

Now I did smile, and I caught my bottom lip with my teeth to keep it from growing too wide. A moment later I frowned, remembering the worst part.

I swallowed a lump in my throat, her words like a punch in the stomach. "Let's get you home. I'll call Billy. He'll drive us." I stood, offering her my hand.

"No. Never." She didn't seem to be speaking to me, but rather to a conversation going on in her head.

"Come on." I shook my hand, gesturing for her to take it. "Tomorrow, when you're sober, we'll talk." And I'd make a romantic declaration, not take the chickenshit, coward way out and try to pry answers from her while we were drunk.

"The answer will still be no," she said, loudly.

I winced, my hand dropping.

"I'll never love anyone that way." Simone frowned at me, then at the hand at my side. "Especially not you."

Simone examined me, her teasing smile becoming something else. She looked like she wanted to say something, or ask something, but I wanted—needed—to distract myself from the hurtful recollections.

So I asked, "What happened today?"

Her grin immediately dissolved, as did her good humor.

She glanced to her right, studying the glass of clear liquid on the bar. "It's nothing I wish to discuss."

"Are you going to file a report?"

Her eyes came back to mine, and it was easy to see she was confused. "What business is that of yours?" She sounded honestly curious and—since I'd known her so well once upon a time—I also detected a faint hint of bitterness.

"You shouldn't have to put up with that kind of behavior."

Her eyes narrowed, like she was inspecting me. "Who did Ashley tell? Just you?"

"Just our family."

"She's not going to tell my parents? Or my grandpa? Or my Aunt Dolly? Or Deputy Boone? Or Sheriff James? Or Jackson?"

Her questions surprised me. "You mean you're not going to tell them?"

"No. I'm not," she said firmly. "As far as I'm concerned, it's no big deal."

"Are you kidding? That man, he—" I didn't know what to call it, no word seemed adequate, so I settled on, "You shouldn't have to put up with being harassed."

The side of her mouth lifted. She was looking at me like I was cute. I was used to this, folks—women especially—looking at me like I was cute. Hell, Charlotte had just called me cute. It never bothered me.

But from Simone, it pissed me off.

"Let's talk about something else," she said. Perhaps she sensed my mood shift.

She picked up her drink, took a gulp, and set it back down, keeping her eyes on me the whole time.

Seeing she really didn't wish to discuss Officer Strickland, and knowing I had no right to push the issue, I nodded, speaking through clenched teeth, "Fine. What are you—"

"Billy and Daniella are getting married," she blurted, her eyes dropping to where our knees were touching, one of mine between hers, one of hers between mine. Her voice lowered, "We might be seeing more of each other, after the wedding."

Staring at her, trying to figure out where she was going with this, I hoped to God she wasn't going to call me her brother again. If she called me her brother again, I was liable to do something crazy, like kiss her to prove a point.

My eyes moved to her mouth and a different memory, a much better one, one I hadn't allowed myself to think about for years, surfaced.

"It's time for another pact." Simone handed me my fishing pole, *she'd just put a worm on the end. I was grateful because I hated hooking the worm. I'd always felt badly for them.*

Poor worms.

But I did like to fish.

"Okay." I tossed my line into the lake, placing my elbows on my knees. "Shoot."

"If neither of us have been kissed by the end of this year, we have to kiss each other."

I found myself grinning, my attention still on her mouth.

Her lips were soft, I knew that much. When she kissed she did so with her whole body, wanting to be close, wrapped together, like she needed to hold on. If I licked my bottom lip—I drew it between my teeth, swept my tongue over it—I could almost taste hers.

I sensed Simone tense and my stare darted to hers.

She was blushing, and she was gaping. Her eyes were wide, like I'd done something surprising, shocking even. Her attention flicked to a spot over my head and she blinked.

Giving her a questioning glance, I turned, checking to see who might be eavesdropping—in a town like Green Valley, you could usually bet on someone "accidentally" overhearing—and found Ashley and Cletus at the bar right behind me.

I straightened, and they jumped, looking everywhere but at me in a way that made me suspicious and them appear incredibly guilty.

"Do you mind?" I asked, incredulous.

Ashley gave me an apologetic smile. "Sorry, real quick—"

"For the record, I mind," Cletus sniffed, looking down his nose.

My sister ignored our brother. "We just wanted to stop over and invite y'all back to the table, after you're finished with . . ." Her blue eyes moved between us, her smile growing by the second. "Well, when you're finished. No rush."

Looping her arm through his, she pulled Cletus back in the direction of the booth. I tracked them as they went. That's when I noticed my entire family looking at us, at Simone and me. They waved cheerfully at both of us. Jennifer had her hands folded beneath her chin, her eyes dreamy; and Beau gave me a thumbs-up with a small nod.

I covered my face and rubbed my forehead.

Good Lord.

It was my fault, approaching Simone at Genie's. Granted, I didn't plan on engaging her in discussion or remembering the first time we'd kissed, but I certainly didn't want an audience.

Simone's laughter had me peeking between my fingers. Her eyes were still on the booth where everyone was sitting, and she was making faces, crossing her eyes and sticking her tongue out. Beau was making faces back. They used to do this often, across my momma's dinner table, when we were kids.

But we weren't kids now.

A spike of impatience had me grinding my teeth. I was trying here, I really was. I was struggling against a current I'd swam with for ten years, pushing her from my mind so I wouldn't have to deal with any of this.

Here, now, just moments ago, I'd been making progress. I was beginning to think that if I wanted a future with anyone, I needed to put Simone in my past once and for all. Which meant I needed to stop avoiding her, giving her memory so much power. In much the same way I'd confronted being abandoned in Hawk's Field, I needed to confront having my heart broken by Simone.

Standing, I pulled out a twenty, left it on the bar next to her drink, and reached for her hand. "All right, let's go."

Simone did a double take, looking between me and the money. "It's just tonic water."

"Then Genie will appreciate the tip."

I pulled Simone past the bar, out the door, and into the parking lot, part of me surprised she allowed it, another part of me determined to figure this out.

The sooner I could speak to her without feeling that ache, the hollow, constant heartbreak, the sooner I could compartmentalize memories of her in the past and those made in the future, the sooner I'd finally be able to move on and place the specter of her where she belonged.

CHAPTER SEVEN

❀ ❀ ❀

"Ghosts don't haunt people--their memories do."

— ALEXANDRA BRACKEN, NEVER FADE

Simone

O KAY.
So.

I've never been a fan of Neanderthal or gladiator displays. They're weird, a la pep rallies in high school, where you sit daydreaming about your science fair experiment while the cheer-leaders act manic. Meanwhile, you're just happy you got out of English because the quiz was supposed to be on *Romeo and Juliet*, and you hate those melodramatic a-holes and you're glad they died because they were self-involved poor listeners. But, you're also irri-tated and sad that they died for some reason and you can't figure out why.

The comparison here—between pep rallies and Nean-derthal/gladiator displays—is the amount of frenzied emotion involved. I do not have that much energy to spare. I hoard my energy for things that matter to me. Therefore, I can't bring myself to get excited about something so transitory and, usually, pointless.

Nope.

Plus, most people—men or women or other—can't get away with barking orders or making demands. They just can't.

Like . . . *Calm down, Kenneth. I read the memo. Why are you shouting?*

You know what I mean? It's not that I experience a visceral reaction against taking loud orders. There's no part of me that hates it.

Like . . . *Dude, why? Why are you so hyped up? Relax.*

However, I will admit that sometimes, in rare instances—unlike pep rallies, which never make sense—being a bossypants is done so skillfully, it's a thing of beauty. I find myself *wanting* to be bossed and amped.

Like . . . *Dude, yes! Let's get serious about this thing.*

Roscoe was doing a beautiful job of being bossy at present. Taking me by the hand, pulling me off my stool, leading me out of the bar, through the door, across the parking lot to his truck. He was taking charge of the situation, and I approved.

But I also must point out that in order to arrive at this admirable crest of bossitude, he'd laid the groundwork while we were sitting inside. This wasn't a sudden or random take-charge moment.

Exhibit A: The quiet, soulful way he'd studied the scar on the back of my hand. Goodness. I'd remembered Roscoe being sensitive, not soulful. When had that happened?

Exhibit B: How he'd immediately apologized for his behavior on Friday instead of arguing with me. Everyone makes mistakes, but so few take responsibility for their mistakes. Big yes to people who don't dodge or try to explain away their bad behavior. It's *alluring*. Almost as alluring as theories. But I digress.

Exhibit C: The way our lower halves tangled, his knees bumping lightly against mine, our legs fitting together like two puzzle pieces. And how strong his thighs were. The boy had nice thighs, nicely shaped, good femur length. A++

Exhibit D: How he looked at my mouth while biting and sucking on his bottom lip. That whole business had scattered my wits.

Heinrich Rohrer, take the wheel.

And, while you're driving Heinrich, please tell me what that whole lip-sucking-eye-smolder thing was about.

Studying Roscoe's back as he pulled me along, my first guess was that Roscoe had been flirting with me. I mostly dismissed this guess right away. I'd witnessed Roscoe with Charlotte just moments prior, and his reluctant interactions with me were night and day different to how he gleefully got his flirt on with Charlotte Mitchell.

No. He hadn't been flirting with me.

But still, something was going on, something my Simone-senses hadn't picked up prior to tonight, likely because he'd avoided me like I avoided Shakespearean tragedies. The man hadn't looked me in the eye for a decade.

Stopping at the passenger side of his truck, he opened the door and I looked at him, catching his eye. He stilled, his gaze adopting an arrested quality, like he was a little lost, or I'd caught him off guard.

Huh.

Dropping my eyes to the asphalt of the parking lot, I slipped into the front seat, marinating in this fascinating development as a whisper of a hunch formed in my mind.

Does . . . does Roscoe have a crush on me?

Like my first guess, I tried to immediately dismiss this notion, but it lingered. So I argued with myself, no one has a crush for ten years. No one. That would be weird and troubling. That's stalker, needs-to-get-professional-help, please-don't-lock-me-in-your-base-ment-with-your-taxidermy-collection level kind of stuff.

Right?

And how would that work? How could the crush possibly endure? We hadn't seen each other, or spoken, or interacted in forever. Not that I had a ton of experience with crushes, but wouldn't he seek me out if he was crushing? I'd done exactly that in college and grad school, putting myself in the path of the crushee, hoping to get noticed. That's what normal people do.

Right?

Roscoe walked around the bed of the truck and entered through the driver's side. Once his door was closed, he leaned his elbow on the windowsill and studied his side mirror.

"Sorry about that," he said, not looking at me.

I shivered, because I was cold. "About what?"

"Cletus and Ash, interrupting."

"They were fine." I smiled at his family's blatant eavesdropping.

The Winstons were fun and hilarious. More precisely, all the Winston siblings Cletus and younger. I didn't know Jethro Winston well growing up; he was so much older and he'd been a pain in the butt when we were kids, running around with the Iron Wraiths and giving his mother heartburn.

And Billy . . . there was nothing fun or funny about Billy, but I understood why. I felt a small pang of sadness for my sister, who was vivacious and spirited. I worried for her, marrying the second eldest Winston, knowing the burdens he'd shouldered.

We sat in silence for several seconds, maybe a full minute. Roscoe kept his eyes forward and I glanced at him in intervals. He seemed to be struggling with how to begin, or deciding what he wanted to say. He looked nervous.

And I was cold, so I shivered again, folding my arms over my stomach and holding my arms. I wore a light sweater, but my coat was hanging up inside the bar.

My small movement seemed to catch Roscoe's notice and his brows drew together, studying how I was sitting.

"You're cold," he said, and released a frustrated sounding breath. He turned in his seat and reached behind it.

Pulling out a neatly folded, soft fleece blanket, he handed it to me.

I took it and hurriedly covered myself, my teeth chattering. "Thank you."

He eyed me. Then he faced forward, clearing his throat.

Rubbing my hands together beneath the blanket, I studied the pattern of the red, black, and turquoise design. "Where'd you get this blanket?"

"Near the Grand Canyon, from a Navaho shop on the side of the road."

I nodded, looking at it more closely. "It's a nice blanket." I rubbed the material between my fingers and realized it wasn't fleece. It was wool. "It's so warm."

"I use it when I camp," he said, still looking out the windshield. His voice sounded gruff.

"Do you camp often?"

He shrugged. "Once a week, whenever I'm home."

I paused, absorbing this information. He camped once a week, when he was home. Which meant he came home once a week. How had I not known this? How had we not seen each other over the past five-freaking-years?

He's been avoiding you.

My heart balled up, then expanded, making me think of a once smooth piece of paper that had been crushed, and then straightened. I blinked at the lights from the bar, and at nothing in particular, irritated that any part of me—and in particular my heart—was reacting to this man at all.

This is so messed up.

Thank goodness I'd placed a tracker on his car. Apparently, Roscoe Winston was as adept as Carmen Sandiego at avoiding.

Suddenly, I wanted to get this over with. I wanted to get out of the car and drive away and avoid him, too. I wouldn't be able to do that, however. I needed to gain his trust, and you can't gain the trust of someone you're avoiding.

So I cleared my throat and breathed in through my nose to cool my brain, which felt hot and aggrieved. "As I was saying, Dani and Billy are getting married. Fact. We might be seeing each other more because of it. Also fact. So I think, whatever it is that made you ditch me in high school . . ." I glanced at him, feeling grimly satisfied that he was now super still, like maybe not even breathing. "Whatever that thing was—and for the record, I have *no idea* what that thing was, or is—and, whatever it is, I guess you could continue keeping it to yourself, or tell me, or not. Whatever, that's cool."

Dammit. I was rambling. I needed to wrap it up, because my voice was no longer steady. *How can I possibly be feeling so much about this?*

I cleared my throat again. "I think we just need to forget about it and try to get along. For Dani and Billy's sake."

His head gave a small series of nods. "That's fair," he agreed quietly, but he still wasn't looking at me.

I had the sudden urge to do something shocking, like grab his face and kiss him, or flash him, or scream at him. It was confusing. I swallowed that urge.

But I was still raw with frustration.

"Roscoe."

"Yes?"

"Look at me."

His eyes cut to mine, and the swirling mess of feelings there hit me right in the chest. I couldn't untangle them before he looked away, returning his gaze to some spot beyond the windshield, the muscle at his jaw jumping. My earlier hunch that he had a crush on me, or strong unresolved feelings of some sort, solidified.

Exasperatingly, the crumpled sheet of paper that was my heart softened. I hated that it softened. I was glad that I didn't let feelings be my guide because my feelings were clearly dumb as rocks.

"Okay," I started again, determined to get this over and done with so I could leave. "What I think we should do is—"

Kiss!

"Is—uh—"

What the heck? Where had that thought come from?

Not understanding myself, or the jump in my pulse, I doubled down on my attempt to focus, and started again, "If we happen to be at the same place at the same time, we should stop and talk to each other. That's what I'm suggesting. Over the coming weeks and months, leading up to the wedding, whenever that is, if we happen to be in the same place at the same time, we should be friendly and exchange words," I finished on a rush, now much too hot beneath the blanket.

Holy crackers, what was wrong with me?

"If we run into each other, I can do that," he said evenly, giving me the impression that Roscoe Winston would do everything in his power to avoid me. Again.

Well, the joke was on him.

That tracker would tell me precisely where his vehicle was at all times. Luckily, a ruling by the Ninth Circuit Court of Appeals allows for law enforcement to secretly place tracking devices on cars without getting a warrant, even if the car is parked in a private driveway. Roscoe's truck had been parked at Genie's when I'd placed the tracker.

He could put that in his pipe and smoke it . . . should he take up pipe smoking.

"I guess I'll be going now," I said, shoving the blanket off and opening the door, half expecting steam to rise from my skin and somewhat surprised when it didn't.

As I stood, I took the time to refold his blanket and place it in the front seat. In the time it took me to do so, he'd come around to my side and shut my door when I was finished.

"Are you going back inside?" he asked easily enough, looking at me now.

I studied him and his carefully stoic features. Actually, they weren't stoic. They were lacking in all expression.

"I need to get my jacket, but I think I'll head home."

He nodded, stuffing his hands in his pockets.

Inexplicably flustered, I turned and walked to the bar. He came around and opened the door to Genie's for me before I had a chance to reach for it. I didn't think much of it, all the Winston boys were like this, they were stubborn in their chivalry. My brother and my dad were the same way.

It was a southern thing.

Anyway.

Finding and grabbing my coat, I walked back through the door—which Roscoe still held open—and gave him a small nod.

"Goodbye, Simone," he said, like it was truly goodbye, the last time we would meet, his gaze soft as it traveled over my features.

I pulled on my coat and glared at him. "I'll see you later," I responded, like it was a threat.

Because it was.

* * *

I DIDN'T "ACCIDENTALLY" run into Roscoe the next day, although I could have.

When I watched his car depart Green Valley on Sunday via the GPS, I felt relief. I needed time to stew and simmer in my hunch.

My relief was short-lived, because Nelson wanted a progress report mid-week and wasn't pleased that I'd obtained no new intel about Darrell from Roscoe.

"He's in Nashville during the workweek, according to his brother Beau," I explained, having learned as much from Beau and Shelly when they'd come in to the diner on Monday evening for pancakes. "Roscoe drives home—to Green Valley—every Thursday. I'll find out more this weekend."

Nelson made a face. "He's a grown man who drives home, four hours, every weekend? He's your age, right?"

"Yes. But his family is really tight-knit."

"No. That's not being tight-knit with your family. That's being twenty-six and unable to cut the apron strings."

Instinctively, I bristled at that, but said nothing because Nelson was mostly right. There was something off about Roscoe. The way he'd flirted with Charlotte but shot her down, that was strange.

Right?

Right.

"What's the plan? How are you going to get him to speak to you?" Nelson stood from the kitchen table where she'd been taking notes and moved to the safe house's fridge. Opening it, she pulled out a vitamin water.

"I think . . ." I recalled the way Roscoe had looked at me in the bar and in his truck. Maybe more important was the way he wouldn't look at me. "I think he has a crush on me."

Actually, I was 97 percent certain he had a crush on me.

I'd been putting the pieces together for the last few days. The hunch had ceased being a hunch. It had developed into a full-fledged hypothesis and was on its way to becoming a theory.

Contributing evidence: When we were young, just after my sixteenth birthday, we'd kissed each other a few times on a few different occasions, mostly because neither of us had kissed anyone. It had been fun, at least I'd been having fun. But he'd put a stop to it, making some excuse about the sacredness of kissing and an impassioned speech about wanting to save himself for someone who loved him, or something like that.

As I've mentioned, Roscoe was sensitive. A romantic, through and through.

So I'd taken him at his word and we'd stopped.

But shortly after that, he'd ghosted me.

I'm not saying correlation equals causation, I'm just saying the evidence was piling up in support of my hypothesis.

"He has a crush on you?" Nelson said the word *crush* with derision. "What is he? Ten?"

An image of Roscoe, as he was now, came to mind.

No. Definitely not ten. Nope.

"We were friends growing up. He abruptly stopped talking to me when we were sixteen." I stood as she sat down, crossing to the fridge for my own drink. "It hadn't occurred to me at the time, but looking back, I think he stopped talking to me because he wanted more from the friendship."

"And you didn't?"

I thought about her question as I reclaimed my seat.

My pragmatic, too-literal heart hadn't considered the possibility when I was sixteen. It wasn't that I had a low self-image, not at all. This is usually everyone's first assumption when I discuss my teenage self, or my *now* self, and my priorities, goals, and interests. My self-image is based almost entirely on my brain and my brain's interests, which seems to be a difficult concept for most people to grasp.

I've never been into romance and such, finding puzzles, mysteries, and science more alluring and interesting than almost anything else. The marriage of chemistry and physics was the only kind of marriage that had been of interest to me.

"No. I didn't," I finally answered. "If he'd asked me to be more than friends, I would have turned him down. Maybe he knew that or figured it out somehow."

"And he still has a thing for you now? Which is why you're having trouble getting intel out of him."

"I'm not having trouble." I was having trouble.

"You could use his crush, his feelings, to your advantage." Nelson typed as she spoke. "Go on a few dates, get the info that way."

My entire person rejected her suggestion on a cellular level. I didn't owe Roscoe anything other than the same basic level of respect I had for all humans, which meant he didn't deserve to be led on, manipulated, or lied to.

I needed information from him, but I wouldn't stomp on his heart to get it.

"Speaking of Roscoe"—I opened my vitamin water and fiddled with the cap—"Are we going to allow Isaac to pick him up?"

Nelson ceased typing and looked me squarely in the eye. "We are."

I huffed, disgruntled—which I'd expected—but also acutely alarmed, which I hadn't expected. "Really?"

"If Winston wanted to hurt him, he would have done so last Thursday, when he had him alone."

"I was there."

"Winston isn't the kind of guy to let a waitress stop him. He would have found a way to deal with you both, if he'd wished to."

She wasn't telling me anything I didn't already know. "Assessment is that Winston wants to talk to Roscoe, not injure him."

I studied my bottle cap and thought back to the look Darrell had given Roscoe last Thursday as we'd walked away. It wasn't the look of a man who wanted to harm anyone; it was the look of a man who wanted a relationship with his son.

"So the Wraiths take Roscoe . . ." I would be shadowing Roscoe constantly whenever he was in town. Where he went, so I would go. If the Wraiths took him, I wouldn't be far behind. "And we don't even give him a heads-up."

"That's right." Nelson took a swig from her drink, nodding. "And when they let your boyfriend go, you'll find out what Winston wanted."

Boyfriend.

I snort-laughed lightly, shaking my head, while Nelson's mouth curved into a rare smile.

During the ensuing moments of quiet, the word settled around me and I found my throat grow tight. Curtis Hickson had been my sister's boyfriend. They were always in fights, always making up and breaking up, wreaking havoc on each other until they'd run away together, and then they wreaked havoc on us all.

So, no.

Roscoe wasn't my boyfriend.

I'd never had a boyfriend. Nor did I want one.

CHAPTER EIGHT

"I can only note that the past is beautiful because one never realises an emotion at the time. It expands later, and thus we don't have complete emotions about the present, only about the past."

— VIRGINIA WOOLF

Simone

TRACKING ROSCOE HAD become just as much of my routine as checking for friend and celebrity updates on social media. Of note, some of my favorite celebrities to follow were Neil deGrasse Tyson (informative), Issa Rae (hilarious), and Merriam-Webster (informative and surprisingly hilarious).

NERDS UNTIE! ... er, unite. Not untie.

You know what I mean.

Anyway, I'd discovered quite a lot about this new Mr. Roscoe Orwell Winston, Local Man of Mystery, since placing the tracker on his car.

He woke up early. I knew this because he arrived to work early, a veterinary clinic in Nashville. It had a specialty consult for large animals in addition to a prosaic pets practice.

Also, in case I haven't mentioned it prior to now, Roscoe was a veterinarian. This was information I'd read in his file several months ago, and information I already knew just from overhearing folks in the diner gossip over the past few years. But it was also information my dad made a point to share with me when Roscoe had been accepted into the veterinary program, and when Roscoe started the program, and when Roscoe graduated from the program.

I think my father took Roscoe's sudden disappearance from my life—or, more precisely, *our lives*—harder than I had. Furthermore, I sometimes got the impression he still wasn't over it.

But anyway, back to tracking Roscoe.

He must've packed a lunch to work every day or walked to get it, because he didn't leave work until after 5:00 PM. He would then drive to an animal shelter, a different one each night, where his car remained until 9:00 PM or so. After which, he'd go back to his apartment.

Curiouser and curiouser, I searched for him online, scoured social media, which was something I'd sworn to myself years ago I would never do. But since it was for work, I rationalized the intel gathering was necessary for the case.

I didn't find much. Roscoe didn't have a Twitter or Facebook account. So, on a hunch, I looked up the Facebook page for the vet clinic where he worked. Lo and behold, there he was on the banner, surrounded by adorable puppies.

As I'd scrolled through, I couldn't help but smirk. The photos of Roscoe had more hearts and thumbs-up than any of the other content. And, let me tell you, the comments were a journey. Several had me laughing uncontrollably, especially the one shot of Roscoe holding a kitten. Who knew there were so many suggestive puns about felines? Now I did. The replies were a masters course in cat-vagina
euphemisms.

Presently, I was sitting in the safe house on Thursday night, watching his car travel closer to Green Valley. Roscoe had left work promptly at 5:00 PM and it was now 8:30 PM. Interestingly, he hadn't taken I-40 for most of the trip, preferring smaller state roads, like the Oak Ridge Highway.

I'd been told it was a scenic drive on the Oak Ridge Highway between Oliver Springs and Knoxville. I'd also been told there were historic Cherokee caverns just before Karns which were decorated with lights and displays around Christmastime.

Beyond Knoxville, I'd never driven on the Oak Ridge Highway, though I'd always wanted to see the caverns. When my family drove any significant distance—like to Nashville—we stuck to the large freeways, and ventured out only during daylight hours, never at night.

Roscoe was approaching Solway now, and I watched as he took the exit for the Pellissippi Parkway. This route made sense if he didn't want to drive through Knoxville. Assuming he didn't make any detours, he'd be in Green Valley in about an hour.

Biting my thumbnail, I fretted. In case it wasn't apparent by now, I wasn't much of a fretter. When I fretted, it was usually about TV shows and fictional characters.

The plan for this coming weekend was to magically pop up wherever Roscoe happened to be and remind him of his promise to talk and interact with me if we ran into each other. This plan also had the happy byproduct of ensuring the Wraiths didn't get a chance to pick him up. If they took Roscoe, they were going to have to take me, too.

It's not that I didn't trust Nelson's assessment of the situation. More so, it's simply that, for some people, I would never be able to sit on my hands and do nothing if I knew there was even a slight possibility that they were in danger.

Obviously, my family was included in this group; so were Neil deGrasse Tyson, Issa Rae, and whoever was in charge of the Merriam-Webster Twitter account; three of my good friends from college and the little old lady in my building back in DC—who made me enchiladas on Tuesdays—were lumped into this crowd; and to a mixture of surprise and *well-of-course-he-is*, so was Roscoe Winston.

I was beginning to suspect—a hypothesis, not yet a theory—that my affection for Roscoe hadn't ended when he'd cut off communication, but rather had lain dormant within me, biding its time, just waiting for him to make contact again.

How infernally frustrating.

I didn't particularly have any interest in exploring this hypothesis. I found the idea of having a case of uncontrollable affection for someone who'd ghosted me after sixteen years of best-friendship abhorrent.

So what if he'd had a crush?

Get over it, man.

Best friends don't ghost best friends.

And what did this lingering affection say about me? Shouldn't I feel dispassionate at best about this person?

Besides, it really didn't matter if my latent-Roscoe-fondness hypothesis were true, because I was leaving Green Valley ASAP. My life was in DC, my friends, my Tuesday enchiladas, my job which was my purpose and passion. Not to mention my favorite brownie pan—the kind where each square has edges—tucked away in my kitchen cabinet. This mysterious residual affection would just have to remain unresolved and dormant forever.

Forever and ever.

The end.

That's all, folks.

Therefore, instead of watching Roscoe's truck travel closer and fretting about what was going to happen this weekend every time I accidentally-on-purpose popped up wherever he happened to be, I flipped open my latest copy of *Journal of Forensic Sciences* and scanned the table of contents.

Forensics instead of fretting.

Two articles immediately caught my attention. The first dealt with obtaining DNA from fingerprint lifts, and the second was entitled, "An Exceptional Case of Acute Respiratory Failure Caused by Intra-Thoracic Gastric Perforation Secondary to Overeating."

What the heck?

Morbidly curious, I immediately found the second article and glommed the entire thing, happy to be distracted from my maddeningly contradictory thoughts and feelings for Roscoe Winston.

But when I glanced up some time later, my gaze focusing on the GPS coordinates of Roscoe's current location, my heart faltered. His truck had driven past his family's house, past Green Valley, and was now headed up the mountain.

Where is he going?

Grabbing my gear, I gave myself a pat-down—keys, gun, flashlight, phone, tracker—and left the safe house. One eye on the tracking screen and one eye on the road, I followed his path up the mountain, frowning when I saw he'd stopped some forty minutes outside of town.

Wracking my brain, I almost pulled over so I could check Google Maps, cross-reference his position. However, in a moment of acute clarity, I realized where his little dot resided.

He'd gone to Hawk's Field.

In the fall, after high school football games, the field would be crawling with teenagers, making out in their cars or holding an impromptu bonfire, or both. It had the distinction of being privately owned by the Cooper Family. They also owned Cooper's Field closer to town, which made things confusing at times. Regardless, Bell Cooper had never been especially good at keeping the gate locked at Hawk's Field.

Then again, Bell Cooper was a frisky older lady whose exploits were legendary. She and my grandfather lived in the same "mature adults" village in town, and I'd had to suffer through their flirting often when I visited.

Actually, I thought it was cute. But I'd never tell my grandpa that.

This time of year, it was too cold to park, therefore the field was typically vacant. So of course, my mind leapt to the absolute worst conclusion.

The Wraiths must have carjacked Roscoe and have taken him to the field to work him over and/or murder him.

This was why I would never make a good field agent. To a hammer, everything looks like a nail. To my brain, everything looks like a precursor to murder. Likely, I was a gothic novelist in a past life.

Pressing my foot more firmly to the gas pedal while attempting to talk myself off the ledge, I reasoned that—statistically speaking— the worst-case scenario was always the most unlikely answer. Plus, if the Wraiths picked up Roscoe, they'd take him to the Dragon Biker Bar, not a field thirty minutes down the road. Plus, Isaac would be the one to pick him up, and Isaac would keep him safe.

Plus, plus, plus.

Despite my attempt at reasoning, my heart continued to gallop, and my jaw hurt from clenching it by the time I arrived to the first fence post of Hawk's Field. The field was vast, several acres, and Roscoe's GPS coordinates had him near the back southwest corner, which made me feel a modicum better.

The southwest corner was mostly flat and open while other spots of the gated acreage were covered in thick growth of both new and old forest. If the Wraiths had him, and wanted to do him harm, they would have taken him to one of the forested areas, not the out-in-the-open area.

But as I neared the entrance to the field, my heart did another jump, this time at the sight of a police car, all lights off, parked along the side of the road just beyond the open gate. A flash of terror, an echo of feeling from my encounter with Officer Strickland last week, had me gripping the wheel tighter as I pulled into the field. I kept one eye on my rearview mirror as I drove—holding my breath—in the direction the tracker dictated.

Luckily, I spotted Roscoe's truck easily. He had the headlights on and, even from a distance, I could see him moving around his vehicle with easy steps. Furthermore, he was alone.

So, not murdered.

I was just breathing out a relieved sigh when I spotted the unmistakable sight of police high beams behind me, some hundred feet or more away. Keeping my speed constant, because I'd reach Roscoe before the police car reached me, I mentally sketched a quick plan of action should the officer be of the Strickland variety.

Roscoe seemed to spot my car and realize I was heading for him, because he stopped in front of his open passenger door, where his features would be bathed in light instead of silhouetted by it. I pulled next to his truck, shut off the engine, and jumped out, my attention split between Roscoe and the quickly approaching police car.

"Simone?" Roscoe was looking between me and the coming vehicle, his attention equally divided.

I'd parked so that my driver's side was along his passenger side and closed the distance between us in two steps.

Peering up at him, I made no attempt to disguise my nerves, mostly because I was too anxious to disguise anything. "Hi, Roscoe."

"What's going on?" In the pale-yellow illumination provided from the pilot light of his car, I could discern that he didn't seem upset by my sudden appearance, but rather looked concerned. "Are you okay?"

Hoping Roscoe wouldn't notice my hand inching toward the concealed weapon at my side, I asked, "Who is that?" I lifted my chin toward the cop car that was slowing to a stop. "Do you recognize the number on the side of the car? Is that Jackson? Or Duke?"

Roscoe glanced between me and the now stopped car. Abruptly, his arm came around my waist and he pulled me closer. I felt his body grow rigid, and I soon knew why.

Officer Strickland straightened from his vehicle. Just like last time, he'd placed his hand on his weapon.

I gritted my teeth, rapidly assessing the situation. This man would not find me as powerless and docile as he had last week. Also, I was a *great* shot. Really, really great. I could hit a mannequin's balls from seventy-five feet with a revolver.

Officer Strickland was less than thirty feet away.

"What're y'all doing out here?" he asked, not kindly. I couldn't be sure, because it was as dark as the inside of a closed coffin out here, but it felt like his eyes were on me.

Roscoe sucked in a breath as though he were going to say something, but seemed to stop himself. He then gave me a squeeze that felt reassuring, followed by another squeeze. I realized he—Roscoe —was waiting for *me* to speak.

Taking the hint, I squeezed him back (because at some point my arm must've found its way around his waist, though I didn't remember that happening) and replied evenly, "Good evening, Officer Strickland. We're setting up camp."

The man said nothing. I couldn't see his face, but I could see parts of his form in silhouette, backlit by the interior of his car. His hand still rested on his weapon.

"Can't camp out here. This is private property." He adjusted his stance. Like before, he placed his weight on his left foot. "Y'all need to leave."

"I have permission from Mrs. Cooper." Roscoe lifted his voice.

"You saying you got permission don't mean much to me, boy. You still got to go."

"I have her permission in writing." Roscoe's voice held just a hint of irritation.

"I'm not interested in no phony—"

"And a picture of Mrs. Cooper holding the letter, giving the camera a thumbs-up." Now Roscoe sounded fierce, angry even, reminding me of last week when he'd argued with his father.

In that moment, I decided I liked fierce Roscoe. I liked him a lot.

And also, a picture of Mrs. Cooper holding the letter and giving the camera a thumbs-up? This was something I needed to see.

Officer Strickland sighed loudly. "Fine. Let's see it."

"I have to reach in my back pocket for my phone," he growled in response, but didn't move.

The man huffed again. "Then git it."

Roscoe gave me another squeeze and I looked at him as he said, "Can't say I feel safe reaching for my phone right now." His profile was grim and his eyes were pointed at Officer Strickland's waist, where his hand hovered over his gun.

"Officer Strickland, do you think you could take your hand off your weapon, please?" I asked, my tone again calm, even. "When you have your hand on your weapon, it's frightening."

Once more, the man said nothing, and his eyes seemed to be on me. I gave him a tight smile.

Finally, *finally* his hand fell to his side, and he braced his feet apart.

"You frightened, girl?" He sounded amused, pleased even.

I had the sudden urge to shoot him in the balls.

But I also sensed a change in Roscoe, his frustration multiplying into rage. If this had been the Roscoe of my childhood, then I would have known what to expect. Kid Roscoe always grew quiet in his rage, turned it all inward, and worked through his anger privately. But this adult Roscoe was unpredictable and might possibly have a crush on none other than *moi*.

I'd seen both men and women lose their temper in a fit of possessive rage before. Not that I thought Roscoe was on the precipice of doing that, or that his alleged crush on me ran deep or crazy enough to inspire a sense of possession. But—that said—I didn't know what adult Roscoe was capable of.

So I spoke before he could, "Yes, sir. You frighten me. If that was your goal, you've achieved it."

Roscoe turned his head in my direction and he released a quiet, restless sound, as though my words pained him, like he couldn't abide the thought of me frightened. The sound caused an answering flutter in my heart, which honestly made no sense to my brain.

Hearts are weird, best to ignore.

The officer appeared to consider my words, like they were a puzzle, or I was trying to trick him, and silence stretched.

Then a thought occurred to me, and I said, "When I worked at the Virginia Department of Forensic Science, I interacted with hundreds of police officers. My degree was in law enforcement, and my graduate degree is in forensic chemistry. I interned there, helping officers —such as yourself—solve crimes. But none of those fine men and women in blue frightened me. You have the distinction of being the first."

Officer Strickland shifted, seemed to rock back slightly on his feet, his chin lifted a notch. The three of us passed another long moment, during which Roscoe continued to look at me, some of the tension leaving his body, and the officer stood eerily still.

Strickland was the first to move, placing his hand on the top of his car door. "I have things to do, can't be out here all night." His tone was stiff, gruff, but neither aggressive nor threatening, and his fingers drummed distractedly on the metal frame. The man didn't move to leave otherwise, giving me the impression he wanted to say something else.

He didn't.

He slid into his car, shut the door, turned the engine, and left.

When his taillights were out of sight, Roscoe released me, his arm sliding away as he turned. "That was . . ." He shook his head, pulling his fingers through his hair. "That was impressive."

I swallowed, my fingers and toes tingling with the ebb of adrenaline, my gaze still focused on the distant spot where Officer Strickland's car had disappeared.

"Are you okay?" he asked, his hand coming to my shoulder and sliding down my arm, his voice soft.

It was the softness of and palatable concern in his voice that drew my attention. I found him studying me. He appeared deeply concerned, and that's when I noticed adult Roscoe Winston was exceptionally handsome this evening, his eyes exceptionally entreating, his mouth exceptionally alluring. This last thought was a bizarre thing to note as I'd never considered a man's mouth to be alluring before.

Who am I kidding? Noticing anything enticing about Roscoe Winston, especially after what had just transpired mere moments ago, was incredibly bizarre.

Nevertheless, my heart did another little flutter thing while we swapped stares, causing me to wonder if maybe I had a heart murmur . . .?

I should go see a cardiologist and increase my electrolyte intake.

"Hey." He entwined our fingers, releasing an audible exhale. "Are you okay?"

"I'm fine." I nodded absentmindedly.

Relative to the context of Roscoe's question, I was okay. But I was also not okay, because I needed to see a cardiologist about this odd, aching flutter.

The right side of his alluring mouth tugged upwards. "You sure about that?"

I nodded again, but said, "I think I need to go to the doctor."

His frown was immediate. "What? Why?" Roscoe's hand squeezed mine and he gained a half step closer.

Dammit. Freaking heart flutter explosion.

"Nothing. Never mind." I pulled my hand from his and laughed, hoping it didn't sound uneasy as I waved away his concern. "It was a joke, but it came out weird and wrong and . . ." I sighed, placing my hands on my hips, peering up at him and his partially concerned, partially confused, but all handsome expression. "I don't think Officer Strickland likes me."

Roscoe crossed his arms and his eyes seemed to heat and harden. "I think Officer Strickland is an asshole."

I laughed again.

Roscoe added, "To put it lightly."

I nodded, chuckling, and glanced over Roscoe's shoulder to the dark field, peaks and branches of the trees outlined by pinpricks of starry light. I also spotted the small, two-person tent he'd set up just a few feet from his truck.

"How was your week?" I asked. I didn't particularly want to talk about Officer Strickland, so a change in subject seemed in order.

"Just fine." I sensed his eyes still on me, the way his gaze leisurely traced my features. My mouth was suddenly dry.

Heart palpitations and dry mouth, those sounded like adverse side effects in a pharmaceutical commercial, right? I'd changed my birth control seven months ago, but maybe I was having a delayed reaction.

"How about you?" he asked.

"How about me, what?" I looked at him, losing my place in the conversation.

He flashed a smile—there and gone—and glanced at his feet. When he looked up again, his expression looked patient, but also interested. "Do you want to talk about what just happened?"

"With Officer Asshole?"

"Yes."

"No," I said. Firmly.

"Are you going to tell your family?"

"No."

"Why not?" he asked, his voice hard, frustrated.

"I just said I didn't want to talk about it," I said on a rush, hoping he'd let the issue drop.

He stared at me. I stared at him. Crickets chirped. Wind whistled through nearby trees. Seconds ticked by.

After staring—intently and *at length*—he finally said, "Okay," nodding once.

I released a silent sigh of relief.

Roscoe continued scrutinizing me as he leaned a hand against the roof of his truck and asked, "What are you doing out here, Simone?"

I was definitely coming down with something. It was not normal for the sound of my name on a man's lips to set my lungs on fire. An upper respiratory infection. That's what it was.

"Oh, well, you know—" *Now, ladies and gentlemen, we have reached the half-truths portion of the evening.* "—Shelly and Beau mentioned that you like to camp one night a week."

Roscoe seemed to straighten, grow taller at this news, least I forget how deliciously tall he was in the first place. "You were looking for me?"

"Yes." I glanced at him, watching him react to my half-truth. Seeing that this news seemed to inspire conflict within him, I shrugged and glanced at the interior of his truck. "So, you're camping? Tonight? Out here?"

"I am—"

"Why not just camp in your backyard?"

"Because Cletus—"

"Isn't it kind of cold outside to go camping? And where's your sleeping bag?"

"It's in the—"

"Are you sleeping in your clothes? Did you already eat? Do you really have a picture of Mrs. Cooper holding a letter of permission and giving the camera a thumbs-up? And what about—"

Roscoe clamped his palm over my mouth, his other hand coming around my neck to hold the back of my head. He smiled, a closed-mouth smile warm with affection, his eyes seeming to reflect the twinkling of the stars in the sky.

. . .

Seeming to reflect the twinkling of the stars in the sky? What the what? Did that thought come from my brain?

Great. Now I'm having delusions of grandeur.

I knew why he was smiling. He'd covered my mouth often growing up, when I'd get stuck in a "curiosity loop" as he called it. No mystery there.

But why all my symptoms chose that moment to flare together—heart flutter, dry mouth, lungs on fire, delusions of grandeur—a trifecta plus one of adverse reactions, I had no idea.

No idea.

No idea, at all.

Adult Roscoe Winston still smells good.

Also, I was dizzy.

But my ailments did not prevent me from noticing how Roscoe's smile faded by degrees; or how his eyes dipped, grew hooded and hazy as they focused on the hand covering my mouth; or how his breathing changed. I also didn't miss how strong and—yes—delectably tall he was.

No, I did not miss these details. But I was also forced to add *feverish* and *confusion* to my list of symptoms.

So, basically, I was dying. Probably of a brain disease.

Roscoe gathered what sounded like an unsteady breath and released me, averting his eyes as he turned and walked around the open door of his truck and to the tent pitched in the dark field. He cleared his throat once, twice, three times while he fiddled with the stakes anchoring the poles.

"To answer your questions, I am camping. Tonight. Out here." He sounded funny, like he'd lowered his voice, firmed it or something. "I don't camp in the backyard because, when I tried doing that, Cletus woke me up before sunrise, complaining that I was in his yoga spot. It's not too cold to go camping if you have the right gear. My sleeping bag is in the bed of the truck, all set up. I will be sleeping in these clothes. I already ate, but I have supplies for breakfast. And yes, I have a picture of Mrs. Cooper holding the letter and giving the camera a thumbs-up on my phone."

This time the flare of feeling I experienced was easily identifiable. Nostalgia.

"You just answered all my questions. In order."

He paused in his work but didn't look up. "Yeah. So?"

"You still do that."

"Yep." He exhaled as he stood, still not looking at me, and walked to the driver's side door. He opened it.

"I always thought it was cool, when you did that," I admitted quietly, mostly to myself.

I couldn't see his expression well, since he was moving and it was dark, but I thought I saw a small, fleeting smile curve his mouth.

"I always thought it was cool, when you could remember a series of numbers after reading them a few times," he said, just as quietly.

"Yeah, but I used mnemonic devices and practiced. You never had to practice. If you heard something, you could always repeat it, word for word." At one point I wondered if he had a photographic memory. He definitely didn't. His ability to retain facts read—or even pictures seen—had never been as good as mine, especially once I started working on my memorization skills.

Roscoe shrugged, pulling out two pillows from the cab and closing the driver's side door.

I walked around to the bed of his truck, inspecting this sleeping bag he claimed he had. Reaching inside, I discovered it was more than just a sleeping bag. He'd placed a wooden board on the bottom, followed by a foam mat, an air mattress, a sheet and that wool blanket, and topped it off with a sleeping bag.

"You're sleeping back here?" Look at him, a regular princess and the pea.

He nodded, adding the two pillows to his bed, and moving to place a battery-operated camping lantern near the tailgate.

Studying what I could see of Roscoe—which wasn't much—I wondered what he was thinking. This was a novel experience for me. It had once felt like we could read each other's minds. When he disappeared, I didn't care what he thought or felt.

But now . . .

"What are you thinking about?"

Roscoe's steps faltered as he walked along the side of the truck to the back, but only for a second. I heard the pause more than saw it.

"How are you getting home?" he asked.

Immediately, I understood his meaning. Did I feel comfortable driving home, in the dark, forty minutes on mountain roads, with Officer Strickland somewhere out there?

To my credit, I thought about telling the whole truth, that I didn't feel comfortable, but that I would deal with it.

But before I could, he offered, "I could pack this up and follow you home, make sure you get there safe . . . if you want."

His chivalrous gesture had me saying without thinking, "Or I could sleep out here with you."

Dammit.

My body was covered in hot chills and my heart was fluttering on overtime. Dammit. I hadn't meant to say that, and I had *no idea* from whence it had emerged.

There's that brain disease acting up again.

Again, his steps faltered. But this time he didn't move for a long moment. He didn't seem to be breathing either.

If I didn't know myself better, I would have sworn this was an attempt at flirting. But I did know myself. Since I knew myself, I knew I wasn't of the flirting species. It's not that I couldn't do it, it's just that—like pep rallies and barking orders—what was the point?

My moves were more like, "Hey. Let's go have safe sex, and I'll leave before breakfast so we don't have to make awkward eye contact in the morning or pretend to be interested in each other."

And then we did.

I was just on the cusp of turning the suggestion into a joke when Roscoe said, "Okay."

"Pardon me?" I almost choked on air, I was so shocked.

"Okay," he repeated, louder this time. "Sure, why not. Sleep out here with me."

CHAPTER NINE

"We all have our time machines, don't we. Those that take us back are memories...And those that carry us forward, are dreams."

— H.G. WELLS

Roscoe

SETTLING IN, I took my spot on the left side of the bed and looked up at the night sky. There was no moon, therefore the sky was teeming with stars. I saw nothing. I was too busy calling myself every word I could think of for idiot.

When she'd suggested staying, my immediate reaction had been violent panic. But once that had cleared and I gave myself a moment to think the idea over, it had struck me as an excellent—if not drastic—opportunity to practice being within close proximity of Simone while maintaining platonic intentions and reflections. This was an opportunity for me to make a new memory with her where I'd be in control.

Plus, it was dark. Even to my super night vision Winston eyes, it was dark. Which meant I'd be making a new memory with one of my five senses at a disadvantage.

I'd considered it to be an excellent idea for exactly two minutes, just long enough to settle on the scheme and congratulate myself. Not a minute later, I experienced an avalanche of regret as I watched her climb into the bed of the truck and snuggle under the covers.

Roscoe, you're a dummy, a voice repeated in my head, one that sounded suspiciously like my brother Cletus.

"Hey, I have some questions."

Simone and her questions.

Sighing, I asked, "Such as?"

"So, what's going on with your dad?"

I started, staring forward and frowning at her subject choice. "My dad?"

"Darrell."

"Yes. I know who my father is." I ground my teeth.

Where we were sitting, our backs were to the spot where Darrell had dropped me off when I was twelve. This was why I always camped here, in this spot. I camped here once a week to bury the memory of being abandoned under a pile of new, better, benign ones.

"Do you want to talk about your dad at all?" Simone sounded like she was choosing her words carefully. "I mean, it looks like he came out of nowhere last week. You didn't seem happy to see him."

"I wasn't."

"Has he tried to make contact with you? Since last week?"

Now I was scowling. "No."

"Hmm . . ."

I felt her eyes move over me while I continued glaring at the constellations. The night sky felt three-dimensional in Tennessee, as though you were a part of, and adrift within, the heavens. With most other places, it was easy to believe the sky was merely the flat interior surface of a sphere.

"Are you really going to sleep in your jeans?" she asked apropos of nothing. "I can't sleep in jeans."

My attention drifted to where her legs—encased in jeans—were stretched in front of her under the covers. "What are you going to sleep in then?"

"I usually sleep in the nude."

I choked, my eyes bugging out of my head, her statement leaving me drenched in a cold sweat of panic. And lust. But before I could sputter a thought, she laughed.

"I'm totally kidding. I'm fine to sleep in these clothes, I just need to message my mom and let her know." Simone pulled out her phone from somewhere behind her and unlocked it. "You know, she caught me last week coming in after midnight, and she did that appearing thing she used to do to Daniella."

That had me smirking and breathing out a quiet sigh. I told my heart to calm down.

"You know," I said, connecting the dots of the Big Dipper with my eyes. "It's warm for this time of year, but I only have one sleeping bag and a blanket."

"I don't mind lying with you, it'll be just like old times."

I had to tell my heart to calm down again—reminding myself that I was in control here, I could leave at any time—as I rasped out, "Yeah, right. Exactly the same."

Apparently finished typing a message to her mother, I perceived the light of her phone's screen extinguish and felt her shift slightly, presumably to put away her phone. We were both quiet for a stretch.

She broke the silence, asking, "So, what's the tent for?" Simone was employing a voice I recognized from our shared past, one she put on when she wanted to sound casual.

She'd never been a good actress, never been gifted at hiding her feelings from folks who took the time to study her mannerisms. I still knew them all by heart, and likely always would.

"I pitch the tent in case it rains," I answered. Not for the first time since she appeared, I wondered why she was here. She'd admitted she'd been looking for me, but why? Why would she do that? Why seek me out?

"Is rain in the forecast?" Her tone was still forced nonchalance.

I glanced at Simone where she sat next to me, just about a foot away. We were under the same covers and she was using one of my pillows behind her back. But what captured my notice was the way her profile was painted in a silvery outline. I could distinguish each of her eyelashes, the graceful slope of her cheekbone, the line of her jaw, the shape of her lips. The sight stole my breath.

She was beauty.

An unforeseen gratefulness settled over me, a gladness and peace, easing the constant sorrow I associated with her memory. Maybe because, in that moment, I wasn't remembering our past.

"No, no rain in the forecast." I had to clear my throat before continuing, my gaze still on her, "But once, I was camping—somewhere else, not here—a few years ago and the weatherman promised no rain."

"And it rained?" She grinned, her face turned up to the stars.

I nodded. "Buckets."

She laughed, stealing a glance in my direction. The sound of her laughter and the brightness of her smile made me laugh, too.

I'd always have heartache with Simone. But now, I'd have this new moment, too.

"The sky opened up and it was like being caught under a waterfall."

She laughed harder, her eyes closing.

"I packed all my gear in the cab, and drove home soaking wet. Ever since, I bring a tent."

"That makes sense." She turned her grin on me, nodding. "So, why do you camp out here? Why do you camp at all?"

Telling her the truth—that though I'd been camping once a week for years, I'd been coming out here for just over a year in order to confront a traumatic childhood memory—wasn't an option.

So I responded to her first question with, "I couldn't say," tilting my head to the side as I considered how to answer her second question honestly. "I guess I got used to camping when I was traveling with Drew."

But it was more than that. I also liked the quiet, the lack of people. Being around animals and nature didn't tax me the same way being around people did, which was why I'd decided to become a veterinarian. I didn't want to be in a general practice for much longer. I wanted to do work with the national parks, where I'd be off on my own.

But I'd still donate my time to shelters at night. I'd never stop doing that.

"When did you go traveling with Drew?"

"I took a semester off during undergrad."

"Where did you go?" Her voice sounded natural now, no longer forced-casual, just plain casual and curious.

"Lots of places. All over the US. The Grand Canyon and Yellowstone were my favorites here. After that, we went to New Zealand for a stretch, and I think I liked that best of all."

"Why?"

"Lots of reasons," I said, struggling, irritated with myself for my reticence. I never had a problem talking to folks when I was around them, never been shy or at a loss for topics if I elected to engage in conversation.

But with her, the one person to whom I used to confess everything, the words stuck in my throat.

"Give me one reason," she requested softly, in that gentle way of hers.

I glanced at Simone, found her turned toward me, her head resting on her arms which were resting on the tops of her bent knees. She wore a soft smile, but it was her eyes that made the difference. Looking into them now felt like such a luxury. They beseeched me to continue.

So I gathered a deep breath, brought forward the sights, sounds, and smells, and I gave her my reasons. All of them.

I told her about my favorite places, The Otago Peninsula with the yellow-eyed penguin reserve and the forest of trees that looked like how I imagined the Ents would in The Lord of the Rings. The white sandy beaches that were too cold for sunbathing, but sea lions did so anyway, and the cloudy aquamarine color of the Pacific Ocean. I told her about the Catlins, the hidden old forests that plunged into caverns, trees with bark that shredded from the trunk like sheets of rust-colored paper, and trees with umbrella shaped canopies, like something out of a Dr. Seuss book.

I told her about "Niagara Falls of New Zealand," which had turned out to be a lark on tourists, an innocuous trap set by locals. I also told her about the best cup of pea soup I'd had at the Niagara Falls Café and how they served their tea with little kiwi bird bag holders, where the long beak clipped on the side of the cup.

I described the boat, then bus, then boat trip to Doubtful Sound. How the water was like a mirror, reflecting the snowcapped mountains rising out of the fjords, with waterfalls cascading to the earth and rainbows reaching to the sky.

"I'd forgotten how you . . ." she trailed off, her chest rising and falling with a large breath. She'd lifted her head during my story about Niagara Falls and her gaze held mine squarely.

Abrupt awareness of how close we were had me leaning away, as though to get a better look at her. "Forgotten what?"

"I'd forgotten how good you are at telling stories," she admitted slowly, like it was a confession. "You make me feel like I could be there. I always thought you'd be a writer."

I gave her a half-smile but said nothing. It was getting late. The frantic cricket chirps and frog croaks of twilight had now faded, replaced with the mellower melody of night, like the darkness was a real blanket, softening and obscuring even sound. A gust swished the trees still devoid of leaves at the north end of the field. The wind sounded like a faint whistle instead of the typical rustling breezes in the summer.

Straightening her legs and resting her back against the pillow again, she turned away, her face once more in profile. "I think I'd like to go there."

"You should." I bumped her shoulder with mine without thinking, the movement reflexive, and liking the thought of Simone making happy memories and exploring my favorite places. I liked the idea even more of being the one to take her there, but I quickly dismissed the thought.

"I think I will." She bumped my shoulder back. "In fact, I will. It'll be my next vacation."

I gave her a sidelong look. "Aren't you kinda on vacation now?"

She grew exceptionally still, but she didn't look put off by my question. Rather, she seemed to be considering how best to answer.

"It doesn't feel like a vacation," she finally said, giving me a slight smile and a shrug, adding quietly, "I can't wait to go home."

"Home? You mean DC?"

She nodded, looking up at the stars. "Yes."

"You know, I thought about moving to DC."

"You did?" She looked at me, surprised.

"Yeah. I was offered a job by their zoo. I liked the idea of taking care of unusual animals—well, not unusual. Just not the typical pets seen in practice."

She studied me, then asked, "Have you been to DC?"

I nodded. "Once. With Drew, a few years back."

"What did you think?"

"I really liked it," I answered honestly. "It's not too far from here, and I like the history. And the food."

"You should come visit me," she said, quickly amending, "I mean, if you want to visit again, you should visit me." She then ducked her head, giving me the sense she'd spoken initially before thinking the words through and they left her a touch embarrassed.

I watched her, appreciating the beauty of her profile while I swallowed around a knot of unease, curiosity driving me to ask, "You got people in DC?" I was careful to keep my voice light.

Again, Simone seemed to debate how best to answer, and the air between us shifted. What had been easy and natural before now felt charged and uncomfortable.

"No one with whom I'm dating or having sex, if that's what you're asking," she said, brazen as sunlight. She settled her gaze on me before continuing, "But I do miss my friends, and my Nancy."

"Your Nancy?" I asked, buying myself some time to process the earlier part of her response, and irritated because the news—that she was single—filled me with something akin to both satisfaction and hope.

"Nancy makes me enchiladas on Tuesdays." Simone's stare flicked over me, turned probing, and she asked, "How about you?"

"Me?"

"Yes. You 'got people' in Nashville?" Now her eyes narrowed.

We traded stares for a few seconds while I fought the urge to smile, and my chest grew hot with pleasure. It was a surreal moment, having Simone ask me if I was dating anyone. I knew what the question meant. Single folks of a similar age only asked other single folks of a similar age if they were in a relationship for one reason.

Because they were *interested*.

Now that might mean interested in just hanging out, or interested in just hooking up, or interested in more. Regardless, the interest gauntlet had been thrown.

Ignoring the alarm bells in my head that I was losing control of this situation, and whatever memory would be created as a result, I responded, "No."

Her pretty lips curved, her gaze seemed to soften and grow more intent at the same time.

Satisfied the joke-trap was set, I followed up with, "I have no one to make me enchiladas on Tuesdays in Nashville."

Simone made a strangled sound and her jaw dropped open with mock outrage, but she was also smiling. "Roscoe."

"Simone."

Her grin wavered as I said her name, and she blinked, shaking her head. "You know what I'm asking."

"Do I though?" I scratched behind my ear, trying to fix a serious expression on my face. "Us Winston boys are pretty slow on the uptake. You might have to spell it out for me."

She gave me a pointed look and made a show of flexing her fingers. "I have ways of making you talk."

Plainly put, she meant she would tickle the truth out of me. For us both, this had always been the most effective way to force an answer out of the other.

I leaned further away at her threat and my grin broke free. "Fine, fine. No need for violence."

"Answer the question."

"There is no one," I said evenly, surprised at how light and benign the words sounded when, in fact, the truth of them was considerably more complex and clumsy.

There is no one.

There's never been anyone.

There's only been you.

"There. Was that so hard?" She patted my shoulder. "Okay, tell me, *why* isn't there someone?"

Now I made a strangled sound. "Excuse me?"

"Do you fear commitment? Because that's my reason."

That had me straightening. "You fear commitment?"

"Not really. *Fear* isn't the right word. It's more like, why would I want to do that to myself?"

"Commit to someone?" I asked, suddenly aware of how fast my heart was beating.

All those years ago, when she'd been drunk and given me her answer, "Not anyone, and least of all you," I'd always wondered about the *not anyone* part. She didn't return my feelings? Okay, fine. But the fact that she planned to live her entire life without returning *any* feelings?

Why?

"I don't see an upside, to be honest." She sighed, nodding at her own assertion. "Yes, there's the consistency of sex. However, there's everything else. The demands, the fights, the *drama.*"

I was so confused. "What are you talking about? Look at your parents, they're the calmest, most drama-free, happiest—in marriage—people I know."

"Exactly." She turned to me, giving me a look as though I'd just proven her point. "I've never seen anyone as happy as my parents. They set unrealistic expectations that can never be met. The world is . . ."

"What?"

"The world is full of crazy, selfish, freaky people. Statistically speaking, the chances of finding the wrong person and falling in love are much, much higher than finding the right person. Why do you think the divorce rate is so high? If you factor in failed unmarried relationships plus people who stay in unhappy marriages for lack of options, then I estimate we're talking about a mere five percent of the population who are happily committed, maybe even less. With stats like that, it's a miracle *anyone* gets married at all." She paused here to take a deep breath and sounded distracted as she added, "And if you fall for the wrong person, what can you do? You're already in love, and your heart wants what it wants, and everything is a mess."

I had a suspicion, regarding this last part, Simone was talking about someone specific.

"Did that happen to you?"

"Did what happen to me?" Her gaze darted over me.

Again, my throat felt tight, but when else would I have an opportunity to ask these questions?

So I forced the words, "Did you f-fall in love with the wrong someone and then—"

"No." She waved her hands in front of her, as though to disperse the horrid thought. "No, no, no. I would never do that. That's never going to happen, because I'm never falling in love. Period."

I stared at her, disbelieving—and a little angry—that she'd never once been tempted to fall for someone, that she'd never met someone who recognized how amazing she was, how smart and hilarious and strong and kind and once-in-a-lifetime. That she'd never found someone worthy of her. How had she made it to twenty-six without someone wanting to cherish her? Not once?

You wanted to cherish her.

Swallowing around a painful thickness—which seemed to be happening a lot this evening—I struggled once more to find words, when she asked, "So how about you? Why haven't you been committed?" She grinned at her own joke, looking silly and gorgeous.

Shaking my head, I dropped my eyes to my hands and made a show of studying my fingers.

I chuckled at the absurdity of the situation, because nothing had changed. She didn't want anyone, least of all me. I'd told myself I wasn't in love with her anymore, but that didn't matter much when I remembered pristinely and precisely what it had felt like when I did.

I didn't want to lie, or make up some half-truth, so I looked up and responded to her question with one of my own, "Why are you here?"

Simone twisted toward me, resting the side of her head against the back window of the truck's cab. "Are you asking me why am I in Green Valley? Or are you asking me why I'm here, now, in Hawk's Field? Because we already covered the latter and, honestly, I don't want to discuss the former."

I lifted an eyebrow at her slippery response. "No. We did not cover the latter."

It seemed to me like she didn't wish to discuss anything of substance except how much she hated the idea of falling in love.

"Yes, we did cover it." Her eyes were on my raised eyebrow and her lips pressed together, like she was combating a grin.

"No. We didn't. I asked, 'What are you doing out here, Simone?' And you said—" I paused here to lift my voice and imitate hers, Yankee accent and all, "'Oh, well, you know. Shelly and Beau mentioned that you like to camp one night a week.'"

"Roscoe." She laughed, hitting me lightly on the shoulder with the back of her hand. "I do *not* sound like that."

I caught her wrist so she couldn't hit me again, she was a double hitter. "So then I asked, 'You were looking for me?' And you said, 'Yes.' And then you asked a hundred questions in order to change the subject—"

"I was not trying to change the subject," she hollered.

The uneasiness and charged atmosphere from moments prior had dissipated, and I breathed in a full breath, rolling my eyes with a great deal of exaggeration. "As I was saying, in order to change the subject and distract me from the fact that you never answered my original question."

"I'm sorry"—she put on a mask of confusion, the effect mostly ruined by the cute and mischievous smile she was attempting to iron from her features— "what was the original question?"

I wasn't going to ask again, but I didn't need to. As she'd alluded earlier, there were other ways to get answers out of her, tried and true methods.

My eyes dropped to her neck. A tick of meaningful silence passed, during which I questioned myself and the wisdom of what I was doing—teasing her, threatening to tickle her, which would necessitate putting my hands on her, disregarding the levelheaded precautions I'd put in place to maintain the essential barrier between us in order to avoid making new memories I couldn't control—but I actively decided to ignore wisdom and good sense.

Just for a minute.

Just for a moment.

Just to be with her again, like this.

Simone gasped, breaking the silence and yanking her hand away. "You wouldn't dare."

I grinned, my eyes still on her neck, where she was most ticklish.

She covered each side of her throat with her hands, a preemptive defense strategy, but she was giggling.

Lifting my eyebrows, I tilted my head to the side and braced my hands on either side of me, preparing to launch myself if necessary. "Answer the question."

Now she was laughing again, watching me, as though waiting to see if I did dare.

I pushed myself up and she squealed, her hands bracing against my chest. I easily captured her wrists with one hand, wrapped my other arm around her torso, and brought her back down on the bed. Straddling her thighs and sitting on her knees, I lifted her arms over her head while she focused her defensive efforts on tucking her chin to her chest.

Between gasping laughter, she said, "I should have worn a turtleneck."

"Poor planning, princess." I laughed, trying to get my fingers under her chin, and had to work to keep my seat because she was now bucking her hips and trying to bend her knees, proving herself to be stronger than I'd assumed.

No matter. Pulling her arms to the right, I maneuvered her on her side and found the sweet skin at the back of her neck.

Simone bucked again, but this time it was a reflexive response, because I'd found her spot. She shrieked as I tickled her.

"Oh my God, I can't breathe."

I stopped. "Answer the question."

She panted and gasped, shaking her head, and giving me a big, teasing grin. "Never!"

Squinting in suspicion, I studied her twisted form. She wasn't struggling, her wrists in my hands were slack, her body was both relaxed and clearly bracing for another attack, like she anticipated it, like she wanted it, like she was having a good time and wanted it to last.

Despite the chill, I was getting hot under the collar. My eyes moved over her prone form, traveling from her beaming smile to her neck, the swell of her breasts, the indent of her waist, the generous curve of her backside. The urge to do something—to her, with her, inside her—seized my lungs and nerves and muscles, a blazing flare of carnal *want* shot down my spine.

Yeah, I'd definitely lost control of this new memory.

Breathing out at the dizzying instinct, I moved completely off her body. I released her wrists—releasing her—as I averted my eyes and backed away to gather my wits. She sat up, reaching for me. I twisted away. The bed of the truck was too crowded, so I turned to jump down. Before I could, she caught me by the arm.

"Hey." Her grip was tight and she tugged. "What's wrong?"

I shook my head, tossing my thumb over my shoulder. "Just remembered something."

"Roscoe—"

Pulling my arm from her fingers, I hopped over the edge of the truck and walked toward the tent. I reached the first post, I walked beyond it, my direction aimless.

I suspected it wasn't like this for most folks, but this sporadically cruel and often inconvenient time travel to my past was all I knew. Therefore, I dealt with it the only way I knew how.

I retreated.

Maybe it was the unanticipated force of desire, but sour memories—ones I was typically able to bury under new, better memories and distraction techniques whenever they surfaced—flooded my mind. Tortured nights spent awake, thinking, wishing; half-formed fantasies from years of wanting her; and again, as usual, the night of her rejection.

I'd made progress this week. Reliving that moment in particular, voluntarily bringing it forth. This had dulled some of the sharper edges, but the pining and longing and craving remained. The combination formed an untenable maze of unwelcome emotions fashioned by hedgerows of unwelcome recollections.

Endeavoring to dwell on a happier time, I winced, because I'd voluntarily shared my first choice—kayaking in Doubtful Sound, New Zealand—with Simone earlier. Now she was part of it, a shadow in the background.

Dimly, I became aware of footsteps behind mine, crunching through the dried grasses.

She called out, "I know you can see in the dark, Roscoe Orwell Winston. But some of us can't. Would you please come back?"

She'd said these words to me before—usually without the *please* —many, many times after I'd stomped off, mad after a fight. But this time there was an edge in her voice. Not fear, but concern, and it sobered me.

Gathering several bracing breaths of the cool night air, I pulled off my sweater—because I was still hot—and returned to where she waited. Her arms were folded. She was standing next to the tent. The way her brows knotted confirmed she was worried.

"What just happened?" she demanded, taking a blind step forward.

"It's getting late. We should get some sleep." I moved to walk past her. She caught my arm, held me in place until I looked at her.

"Talk to me." Her voice was full of pleading, feeling, and she shifted closer. Her chin lifted and I could tell she was searching for my eyes in the darkness. "Why did you stop talking to me?"

"Simone—"

"You disappeared." She sounded hurt, and I wasn't sure if she was referring to just now, or what happened a decade ago.

Part of me suspected she didn't know either.

Her fingers tensed, as though worried I'd disappear now, muttering under her breath as though talking to herself, "Why can't I get past this?"

Those words intrigued me, curiosity pushing me to ask, "Get past what?"

"I biked over to your house every day for two months," she said, still talking to herself, her eyes coming back to mine. "Then I was done, I was so done. I was done missing you and I moved on."

Unsure what to say, how I could get this situation back in hand, I could only watch her. I knew about her biking over, and I remembered, and it still hurt to think about.

"But clearly I'm not done, because it still pisses me off that you switched out of shop class," she said accusingly. "Why? Why did you do it? You were my *best friend.*"

I covered her hand with mine and removed it from my arm. Threading our fingers together, I pulled her back toward the truck. "That was ten years ago."

I said this to remind myself as much as her. I often reminded myself that ten years should have been plenty of time to get over a heartbreak, because everyone told me so.

"Then why are you still avoiding me? What did I do wrong? What made you stop wanting to—"

"You didn't do anything wrong," I growled in response, acutely exhausted.

"You're bitter about something," she said to my back. "Best friends don't just ghost best friends."

"I'm not bitter."

I loved her and she didn't love me, but I wasn't bitter. I didn't resent her, I didn't wish her ill. Her happiness mattered to me, it always had. But what could I do? Every time I saw her face, heard her voice—or worse, her laugh—everything I'd wanted resurfaced.

The memory played again, taking me on an involuntary roller coaster ride, the rise of hopes, the fall and crush of rejection.

I just want . . .

Maybe making new memories with her was a mistake. Maybe what had worked with Hawk's Field wasn't going to work with Simone. Or maybe, if I wanted her to stop mattering, more structure was needed, exposure in smaller increments. Or maybe more avoidance was the solution, not less.

Whatever the answer, I wanted—needed—to move on. I'd never forget her, but I needed her to stop mattering so much.

"If you're not bitter, then you'll stop avoiding me?" she challenged. "We'll be friends again? I'll call you on Tuesdays and describe my enchiladas and you'll take the call?"

No. *No way.*

Friendship would never be possible.

I rubbed my forehead, my stare falling to the ground. "I have enough friends."

Simone made a sound, tugging me to a stop. "You are *such* a liar." Her tone was frustrated as she came around to stand in front of me, holding my hand with both of hers. "Whatever it is, why can't you tell me? Tell me what it is and we'll fix it so we can both let it go."

"I have let it go." I glanced over her head, moving my attention to the bed of the truck.

"You have not." I felt her eyes on me and I pushed the awareness of that away. But then she said, "You can't even look at me," like she was thinking it and saying it at the same time.

I closed my eyes and breathed out. "It's late—"

"I hate that this matters to me, but inexplicably it does." She sounded fraught, so unlike herself. "Unfortunately, I can't ignore and avoid like you can. I have to know."

"Simone—"

"What did I do? Please, just tell me." Her words were rushed, nervous, and a little breathless, like she was afraid of the question, or maybe my answer.

Her tone reminded me of so many other times, so many other questions, and a collection of scenes from our shared moments arranged themselves, a spectrum of spectral sights, sounds, and emotions.

The time she asked me if I would teach her how to fight. We'd been ten. She'd been wearing a red shirt and blue jeans, her hair in a ton of long braids. Her forearm was bruised just below the elbow and she wouldn't tell me who'd done it.

The time she asked me to identify a snake within striking distance of her bare foot. We'd been twelve and it was the last time she'd gone barefoot in the woods.

The time she dared me to go skinny-dipping in Bandit Lake. We'd been fifteen and her daddy interrupted us before any clothes had been removed.

The time she asked me to be her cotillion escort. We'd been sixteen and I'd just given her my chocolate milk in trade for her Gatorade.

That time she asked me to teach her how to kiss. . .

The side of my mouth tugged upward, an involuntary response.

"I need . . ." she whispered, and I sensed her move before I felt her hand on my cheek.

I opened my eyes just in time to see a stunning mix of emotions behind hers, the most prevalent being confusion and desire.

Shocked speechless, I held completely still as she stepped forward, closed her eyes, pressed the warm length of her body against mine, and lifted her chin.

And then she kissed me.

CHAPTER TEN

"The pleasure of remembering had been taken from me, because there was no longer anyone to remember with. It felt like losing your co-rememberer meant losing the memory itself, as if the things we'd done were less real and important than they had been hours before."

— JOHN GREEN, THE FAULT IN OUR STARS

Simone

I KISSED HIM.

Placing the blame on my pretend terminal brain disease non-diagnosis wasn't an option this time.

I kissed him because he was just so damn soulful, and sexy, and funny, and sweet, and smart, and cool, and did I mention sexy? *Dammit.*

So, yeah, I kissed him because I wanted to. Because apparently I missed this man who I didn't know anymore, and being with him this evening had been equal parts confusing and wonderful. It had been like lying on a raft, floating on a body of water beneath the stars, and trusting it would always carry me safely.

Many, many questions.

Why had I felt safe? I shouldn't have, but I did. *He* made me feel that way.

I'd been myself, truly myself, in ways I'd forgotten existed, in ways I'd only experienced when I'd been with Roscoe. I felt relaxed and *known* and understood.

And, dammit, I just really freaking liked him. I wanted to touch him. *With my mouth.* I wanted him to touch me. *Also with his mouth.*

But my kiss had clearly surprised Roscoe. When our lips met, I felt him start, like I'd given him a shock. When my arms twisted around his neck and I pressed my lips more insistently to his, I felt his body go rigid.

Eh . . . Not a good sign.

However, when I lifted to my toes, my body shifting against his, a slight friction, and touched his lips lightly with my tongue, the world tilted on its axis.

Because Roscoe kissed me back.

And *boy oh boy oh boy oh boy* did he kiss me back.

His strong arms came around my torso and crushed me to him; one hand slipping into my back pocket and cupping my bottom; the other fisted in my hair and tugged, opening my mouth so he could taste every inch of my mouth. His hot tongue swept inside and—I know this sounds totally silly—claimed me.

That's right. Claimed.

Another Neanderthal display that I actually felt . . . really, really good about. Like, if our high school had held pep rallies for Roscoe kissing me like this? It would have made sense. I wouldn't have spent one second daydreaming about my science fair project. The cheerleader mania would've been completely understandable and justified. Heck, once it ended, I might cheer.

Goodness gracious, this kiss.

And it went on. It went on and on, and I loved it. He lifted his head once, then twice just to come back and capture my mouth at a different angle. Releasing my hair, he stroked his hand from my shoulder to my backside, up to my hip, his fingers digging into and kneading my body. Roscoe hooked his thumb into the waistband of my pants, touching the bare skin of my stomach, igniting sparks within me. I melted.

I was left clamoring, wanting to be closer, needing to feel more of him. That's what I felt, need and hot, pooling tension low in my belly. Everywhere he touched, need and shivery goose bumps. Each pass of his lips and tongue, bursts of aching, straining, scorching, mindless, chaotic feelings.

And need.

Reaching for his belt buckle, I slid a finger inside and unhooked the prong from the strap, sliding the leather through the metal frame. I was having crazy, freaky, awesome thoughts about logistics, like whether or not I was wearing my nice jeans and whether kneeling in the grass would leave stains. I also wondered if he was one of those guys who wore socks during the deed, and if so, I didn't think I'd mind.

I usually minded.

But not with Roscoe.

He could put on a second pair of socks and I'd probably think it was sexy. Okay, I'd think it was weird, but as long as the rest of him was naked, and he was touching me with his mouth, I'd learn to live with it.

Unexpectedly, suddenly, horribly, we were no longer kissing.

His hands were on my shoulders, and he was far away, and I was confused, so I opened my eyes and I cursed the darkness. I could make out the line of his neck, jaw, and hair; his actual features, however, were mostly a mystery.

I sensed his attention; I felt his grip, firm but not punishing; and I heard his breathing, hard and labored. The taste of him still on my tongue, I licked my lips, finding traces of him there as well.

A sound, beginning as a groan and morphing into a growl, rumbled from his chest, and his fingers flexed on me. For a second, I thought for sure he was going to pull me in, kiss me again, let me unbutton and unzip his pants, touch him, continue what we'd started. I was so sure, I'd even call it a hunch.

Instead, I was set further away and he turned, stomping around the back of his truck.

"What . . ." The word slipped out, the beginnings of, *What are you doing?* But I stopped myself because I soon realized what he was doing.

He jumped on the bumper, reached under the layers of mattress, blanket, and sleeping bag, pulled out the wooden board in an impressive show of strength, and placed it on top of everything. Jumping down, he reached into the bed of the truck, pulled the pillows free and opened the driver's side door. I watched, completely caught off guard as he stuffed the pillows in the cab. He then moved to his tent.

"You're leaving."

"I'm escorting you home," came his gruff reply.

A short laugh of disbelief burst past my lips, and all those aching, straining, scorching, mindless, chaotic feelings (and need) turned cold and clammy, swirling in and upsetting my stomach.

Inexplicably, I felt like crying. I wouldn't cry, but I felt like doing it, which was enough of a shock to snap me out of my stupor. My mouth was hanging open, so I snapped it shut. Ignoring the hot blush that had crawled up my neck and over my cheeks, I reached into the bed of the truck near where I'd been sitting earlier.

"What are you doing?" he asked, pulling up the stakes around his tent.

"Getting my phone and keys." *And gun.* "Don't worry, I'm not putting a snake in your bed." *This time.*

He sighed. Loudly. And he stopped his work dismantling the tent. "Simone—"

"No need to *escort* me home. I know how you like to pretend I don't exist, so . . ." I marched to my car, blinking furiously, because —dammit—it hurt. I hurt. But I was not going to cry over Roscoe Winston.

He caught up with me before I'd managed to get the driver's door all the way open, his hand pushing it closed as he caged me in with his arms. "Don't be angry."

"I'm not angry."

"You're—"

"I'm *pissed.* There's a distinct difference." I tried to pull my door open again but he held it closed.

"I can't—I can't kiss you."

Ugh. . . wow.

"Fine. Whatever."

"I can't—"

"Multiply large numbers in your head, balance on Tanner's junkyard wall, do a backflip off the Bandit Lake diving platform, put a worm on a fishing hook, or kiss me. I got it. Now move." I didn't turn, though I felt him behind me, the length of his body a hair's breadth from mine made infuriating pinpricks of awareness rise on my arms and the back of my neck.

Great. Now I was cold and clammy and hot all at the same time.

He was hesitating, thinking too hard, undecided about what to do next. His breathing gave him away.

"Just . . ." I shook my head, my upset stomach now spreading to my heart, my chest feeling too small. "It's fine," I lied. "If we run into each other, we'll be pleasant, polite. That's what we agreed to, that's what we'll do. Now, please move."

I tugged on the door again, and this time—after a brief reluctance —he let me open it.

Taking my seat, I shut myself in and wasted no time starting the engine. Twisting on my high beams, I pulled onto the gravel road and drove to the gate, careful to keep my speed below fifteen miles per hour, even in my disordered mess of feelings and unfulfilled—no, *rebuffed*—need.

But really, what had I been thinking? Kissing him? Chasing him? *You like him.*

Yes, but that's a bad reason to act like a fool and—

You care about this man. You care deeply.

I grunted in frustration, a breath hissing between my teeth, because I DIDN'T WANT TO CARE ABOUT ROSCOE WINSTON.

. . . too bad.

Dammit.

Force of habit, I flipped the turn signal and paused just beyond the gate, looking left then right for approaching traffic. Noting that Officer Strickland must've moved on, because he was nowhere in sight, I turned left onto the winding road that would take me in the direction of home.

I'd just decided I would go through my bedroom, hunt down the rest of my Roscoe-related memorabilia from childhood and incinerate it all as soon as I made it home, when I spotted headlights behind me. My heart plummeted. I gripped the steering wheel tighter with abruptly sweaty hands, sending a prayer upwards that the car in my rearview mirror wasn't Strickland's.

I then realized the vehicle wasn't a car, but a truck, and I exhaled equal parts relief and frustration. Stopping at a stop sign, I glared in my rearview mirror as the truck also came to a stop behind me. The truck was, without a doubt, Roscoe's.

Gritting my teeth, I turned right, not signaling this time.

He followed.

He escorted me all the way home.

* * *

SINCE I'D TEXTED my mother earlier and told her I would be camping with Roscoe at Hawk's Field, I wasn't strategizing being-scared-out-of-my-wits avoidance tactics when I opened the front door. I was thinking about my kiss with Roscoe, and how he'd kissed me back (eventually), and how it had never been like *that* when we'd experimented together at fifteen.

I was also pondering how he'd followed me home, stopping halfway down our driveway. When he saw me walk up the steps and into the house, he turned and left.

Which was why I was scared out of my wits when I shut the front door behind me.

But this time the scare-er wasn't either of my parents. It was my sister Dani, wearing a green beauty mask on her face and a streaky pale-yellow conditioning mask in her hair, looking like something out of a *Mystery Science Theater 3000* episode.

I jumped, gasping, my hands coming to my chest in startled fright, but so did she.

"Dani," I growled, leaning forward to place my palms on my knees, breathing deep and shaking my head. "You scared the shit out of me. You look like an alien had a slimy baby with mayonnaise."

I glanced up and found her leaning one hand against the wall, her shoulders shaking with silent laughter.

Three seconds later, we were both laughing. Two seconds after that, neither of us could catch our breath.

"You should have seen your face." She pointed at me, holding her stomach with her other hand. Her features moved behind the mask, allegedly attempting to recreate my scaredy face.

"What? What are you doing there?" I sniffed, wiping at my eyes. "Is that your impression of Munch's *The Scream*? Is that what you're doing?"

She shook her head. "No, gorgeous. That was you."

"I would try to imitate your face"—I made a show of patting down my sweater and jeans—"but I don't have any alien sperm on me. Sorry."

Now she laughed harder, which made me laugh again. Those chaotic and troublesome *feelings* I'd been stewing in since leaving Hawk's Field dulled, chased away by laughing with my big sister.

Once I was able to form words again without breaking into a fit of giggles, I asked, "What are you doing here? I mean, other than *that*." I flicked my wrist toward her face.

Dani lifted an eyebrow at my wrist flick. At least, I thought she lifted an eyebrow.

"I was just about to wash it off, actually." She darted forward, maneuvering around me to grab her purse from the closet, which must've been her intention before I walked in. "Don't go to sleep," she called over her shoulder as she jogged out of the entranceway. "I have questions for you."

With that, she left me.

I took a seat on the bench near the door and pulled off my boots. Tucking them inside the closet along with my bag, I locked the front door and ambled to my room.

Plans to incinerate my Roscoe-related memorabilia abandoned— for now—I crossed to the open suitcase on the floor and rummaged through my packing pods, looking for pajamas while swatting away thoughts of Roscoe Winston's lips and hands and tongue and—

"Nope, nope, nope." I shook my head, resolved to not think about him.

Skipping over the unknowns—such as, if Roscoe had a crush on me, why didn't he want to kiss me? And why did I want to kiss him so, so, so badly? And why couldn't I just let go of the unknowns surrounding his sudden disinterest in me ten years ago? And why was my body and heart conspiring against me by arranging intricate feelings fireworks displays whenever Roscoe and I were in close proximity?—I decided instead to make a beeline for a comprehensive listing of facts, which would lead to levelheaded action items.

His father hadn't made contact with Roscoe since last week and clearly Darrell was still a sore subject, completely understandable. As such, it was doubtful I'd gain much intel by interacting with Roscoe further or attempting to gain his trust. Better to clandestinely follow him, wait for the Wraiths to make their move, and allow myself to be abducted/taken at the same time.

This would achieve two aims: keep Roscoe safe, and minimize time spent in his company. He wanted to avoid me? Fine.

"Fine, fine, fine, fine, fine."

Fine with me.

New list. Once all this is over, I'll go back to DC, get laid, make brownies, and return to an existence where I never think about Roscoe's soulfulness, height, or touching him. With my mouth.

"What are you doing in here? And you still haven't unpacked?"

Dani's questions had me turning over my shoulder and straightening from my suitcase, holding my pajamas to my chest.

She stood in the doorway, wearing a plastic grocery bag over her hair which was still drenched in the conditioning mask. But the green slime had been washed from her face, revealing gorgeous, smooth, glowing skin.

My sister really was stunning. Ever since I could remember, she had always received compliments on her looks, and not the garden variety *you're so pretty* ones. More like, *Are you a model? No? Do you want to be?*

"Why wouldn't I be in here?" I glanced around my space. "It's my room." I didn't answer her second question purposefully. The truth was, I didn't want to unpack because I didn't want to stay in Green Valley. I wanted to be ready to go home as soon as the case was done, *which will hopefully be soon.*

"No. I mean"—she crossed the threshold, pausing near my dresser—"why aren't you in the kitchen?"

"Uh . . ." I moved my eyes from side to side. "Because I don't sleep in the kitchen?" Although, with a cot, that could be easily rectified, *and think of the convenience.*

"Are you okay?"

"Yes," I responded immediately.

Mostly.

Eventually.

"Are you sure?" She came to stand directly in front of me.

"Yeah, why?"

"Because you always go to the kitchen looking for leftovers when you come home late."

I made a face at that. "No, I don't."

"Yes. You do."

About to protest again, I snapped my mouth shut as I considered her statement and found it wasn't entirely without merit. In fact, it was correct.

Chuckling lightly at the discovery, I shrugged. "You're right. I guess I do."

"And Dad made low country shrimp tonight, so you don't want to miss that."

"You were home for dinner?"

"Uh, yes." She picked a nonexistent piece of lint off the arm of her silk pajamas. "I was."

"How long are you in town?"

"Just through Sunday." She took several steps toward my desk and sat on the edge of it.

"Are you here to see Billy?"

Dani's reluctance to respond was obvious.

When she did, she offered a cagey, "No."

"Does he . . ." I studied her, took note of the way she'd cleared her face of expression. "Does he know you're in town?"

"No. He's busy—at the mill. Also, government is in session this week—I didn't want to interrupt." She sounded so blasé about this, like it was a perfectly adequate excuse.

"Interrupt?" I snorted. "Dani, you're getting married to the man."

She crossed to my dresser and opened the top to my jewelry box. "What are you doing home tonight? Mom said you were camping with Roscoe." Then, quieter, as though she were speaking to herself, she added an amused, "Dad almost had a heart attack when he found out, he was so happy."

A pang of residual discomfort tightened my chest, a virtual potpourri of inconvenient thoughts and emotions. Yeah, I'd been embarrassed when he'd rejected me, but that was honestly the least of it.

I was . . .

I was so . . .

I just wanted . . .

"Simone?"

I sighed. "I decided to come home."

She was watching me, examining me in that uncanny way of hers. My sister could read people like most folks read the newspaper. She knew when to act, when to chill, and how to outmaneuver at precisely the right time. If life was one big game of Clue to me, then it was a game of Chess for her, where she was both the queen and the king.

When she continued examining me in silence, I gathered a bracing breath and met her penetrating gaze.

Her expression shrewd, she tilted her head slightly to one side. "Please don't tell me you and Roscoe, that you—"

"What? No!" I made a sound of protest, like a *pshaw*, and shook my head. "That's *never* going to happen."

Not adding the rest of my thought, *Even though, if it did happen, it would be totally hot and awesome.* Somehow, I knew this. It would be life-changing. Which was why it could never happen. I didn't want to change my life.

Now she looked doubly suspicious. "You like him."

I found I had to swallow against a sudden dryness in my throat. "I don't- I don't like him." *I really, really like him against my will. Big difference.*

"You're lying."

"I'm not—" I covered my face with my hands and released a short breath. "Can we talk about this tomorrow?"

"Simone, what are you thinking? He ghosted you. You were inseparable and he just"—I heard her snap her fingers—"dropped you, acted like you didn't exist. You shouldn't even give him the time of day. Plus, you could do so much better than Roscoe Winston." She made a face as she finished her tirade, as though Roscoe smelled like dirty socks.

Dropping my hands, I rolled my eyes, expecting to say, *Can we not talk about this?* But accidentally said instead, "What's wrong with Roscoe? I mean, besides him ghosting me over ten years ago."

"First of all, he's a flirt and a *huge* player."

My first instinct was to defend Roscoe, to tell her she didn't know what she was talking about. But searching her face, I saw she believed this to be true. Now I was officially curious.

"What makes you say that?"

My sister arched an eyebrow. "Have you seen him out and about town? It's ridiculous. He flirts with everybody, he's flirted with *me*, and I'm getting married to his older brother."

"Yeah, but—"

"No. No buts. Just last month, I went grocery shopping for Mom and he was flirting with Mrs. Townsen behind the deli counter, who is at least thirty years his senior and in a wheelchair. And then he flirted with one of the stock girls—I forget her name, one of the Pattersons, awkward with braces—and *then,* he flirted with Kimmy Jones at the register. The girl was a flustered, giggling mess the entire time she rang me up." Dani huffed a sour sounding laugh, shaking her head, like she thought his behavior shameful.

Meanwhile, I was back to stewing, because I'd witnessed what Dani described. Roscoe had flirted up a storm with Charlotte last week at Genie's, but he hadn't flirted with me.

That's right, I was feeling cranky because the guy I liked against my will had never flirted with me. Another fine example of feelings-fail.

"Roscoe is just like Jethro, when Jethro was that age." Dani pressed her lips together, giving me her you-know-what-I'm-talking-about glare. "Careless, thoughtless. Just look at how he treated you."

Again, I wanted to defend him, to tell her she was wrong, that he hadn't treated me poorly.

But I couldn't. Because she was right.

Since I had no thoughtful response to offer, I set my PJs on the bed and pulled off my shirt. Those earlier unknowns that I'd skipped over resurfaced as I dressed for bed.

What I knew about Roscoe Winston, what I'd experienced tonight, and what my sister suspected to be true—about him being a shameless flirt and player—weren't adding up. My Simone-senses told me there was more to him than that, and I refuse to believe it was just wishful thinking.

"I just wish . . ." Dani started, the wistful unfinished thought drawing my attention.

She was gazing at me with affection and concern, and that combination always made me apprehensive. It was the I-want-to-give-you-a-makeover look, and I couldn't handle another makeover from my sister. I just couldn't. My eyebrows still hadn't recovered from last time, and neither had my—sorry if this is TMI—my furry lady closet, which hadn't been furry after the last makeover day was done.

"What?" I asked, the word infused with caution.

"I *see* you," Dani said softly, gently, and with a slathering of sympathy.

"I can see me, too. There's a mirror right there." I gestured to the mirror over my desk.

"No, I mean, I see *you*, Simone." She drifted closer, the slathering of sympathy had now saturated her features and she whispered, "I know you have these . . . worth issues, about how you look. But you shouldn't. If you would see yourself how I see you, then you'd never give someone like Roscoe Winston the time of day."

Oh dear Lord. Not this again.

"No. I don't have 'worth issues.'" I couldn't help the hard edge in my voice as I turned from her, deciding that leftovers sounded like a splendid idea.

"Fine. You don't." She followed me out of my room and I could almost hear her roll her eyes.

"That's right, I don't. My self-worth isn't based on what I look like."

My sister and I only seemed to fundamentally disagree on three things in life: how potato salad should be made, the best method to bring about positive change in the world (I said roll up your sleeves and dig in, she said power and influence meant no sleeve-rolling was necessary), and whether or not lack of attention to my appearance meant that I had self-worth issues.

Dani made a soft noise with her tongue from behind me. "You have no idea how beautiful you are. I just wish you could see how gorgeous and—"

"Or maybe I don't care," I harsh whispered as I opened the refrigerator door.

"Come on," she whispered as well, since our parents were asleep down the hall. "Everybody cares."

Frustrated, I shut the fridge and spun on my sister, loud-whispering, "No. *Everybody* doesn't. I honestly do not care. Why is this such a difficult concept for people to grasp? I don't go around saying, 'Dani, you clearly have self-worth issues because you have no idea how good you are at word searches and jigsaw puzzles. If you knew how great you are at puzzles, a magical world of opportunity and self-confidence would open up to you!'"

She crossed her arms as her gaze grew hooded. "It's not the same, the world we live in doesn't put the same focus on word searches and jigsaw puzzles, and you know it. Why do you think you like Roscoe? He's not good enough for you. If you would just see that you're one of the most stunning—"

"Then maybe society should stop judging people for their DNA and start judging them for their inability to solve logic-based, combinatorial number-placement puzzles."

She blinked, her forehead wrinkling. "What?"

"Sudoku!"

Throwing my hands in the air, I marched out of the kitchen and back to my room, shutting the door firmly—but quietly—behind me, and making a point to turn the lock.

I understood, on a theoretical level, why she continued to bring this up, I did. How she looked, how others looked, was important to my sister. She placed value on taking great care with her exterior. It *mattered* to her on a fundamental level. I estimated at least half of her self-worth was based on her appearance.

Therefore, it must've been disorienting that appearance didn't matter much to me. Just like, it was disorienting for me when people didn't base most of their self-worth on the abilities of their brain.

Liking Roscoe, caring about Roscoe, *wanting* Roscoe had nothing to do with how I viewed myself, or a supposed lack of worth or lack of confidence, and everything to do with . . . him.

Dammit.

My mother used to tell me that (most) people value what they have in abundance *and* what they lack in abundance. If a person didn't value the strengths and interests they had in abundance, then they would have no self-worth. My strengths and interests were book and brain related.

Conversely, if a person didn't place value on what they lacked, then they would never strive to be better. I lacked—among other things—the ability to make friends easily. Therefore, when I made a good friend, I poured a good deal of energy into maintaining that friendship.

Everything else, all that stuff in the middle—including how I looked—which was neither a strength nor a weakness nor an interest, didn't occupy my thoughts or take up self-worth shelf space.

For some reason, this topic had me thinking about Roscoe again and our kiss. I had a hunch my thoughts would be boomeranging back to this topic often over the coming weeks. It would be difficult, but that was okay. The memory would fade.

In the meantime, I would just have to ignore these messy feelings.

Fact: I would always care about Roscoe Winston. I accepted this. Nothing I could do about it, as frustrating as it was.

Also fact: Caring about someone didn't mean I had to let that someone keep hurting me.

He wanted to shut me out? So be it. Fine. Following him, tracking his movements didn't mean I had to interact with him. Caring about him from a distance, without getting involved, was entirely possible. I could keep him safe from the Iron Wraiths without speaking to him.

So that's what I decided to do.

Simple, right?

Right?

. . . *Right.*

CHAPTER ELEVEN

"Do not let the memories of your past limit the potential of your future. There are no limits to what you can achieve on your journey through life, except in your mind."

— ROY T. BENNETT, THE LIGHT IN THE HEART

Roscoe

SIMONE PAYTON WAS following me.

She was either terrible at it if her goal was stealth, or tremendous at it if her goal was being conspicuous.

I first caught sight of her Friday morning. She was sitting in her car in the parking lot outside the Starbucks in Maryville, the one on Lamar Alexander Parkway, near Target. She'd backed into the spot and had her head down as though she was reading something on her lap.

After what had transpired between us the night before, I wasn't sure what to do.

On the one hand, we'd promised to interact, be friendly and polite if we happened to run into each other.

On the other hand, she didn't seem to notice me. And I hadn't moved on from that kiss. I didn't know if I'd ever move on from that kiss. Everything about it—and about being with her last night—was branded on my brain. Concentrating on anything else would be a labor for the rest of the day, which was why I'd left the house early this morning and driven all the way to Maryville for decent coffee.

Plus, I hadn't been able to sleep. I couldn't stop thinking about things between us, the reality of what it had been like to hold her in my arms.

I'd been open to spending time with her, making new memories of us together in the hopes that she'd matter less. But now the opposite had happened. Problem was, I couldn't seem to bring myself to care.

I want . . .

I wanted to see her again.

I wanted to talk to her, to touch her, kiss her, more. The pull toward her was irresistible, and so I made excuses, reasoning that if she did notice me in the Starbucks parking lot, if she caught sight of me now and thought I was avoiding her again, then that would make me a liar.

After all, I did promise to be friendly. My momma taught us never to break a promise.

My heart in my throat—where it seemed to have taken up permanent residence—I strolled up to her car. While crossing the lot, I realized a startling fact. Her rejection hadn't been the first memory (and accompanying time machine of emotions) to surface when I'd spotted her just now. The first memory to come forward was of us kissing last night.

Basically, I'd traded one unwieldy memory for another, but at least this new one included me grabbing her ass and her unbuckling my belt.

Simone glanced up when I was a few feet away. She did a double take, setting whatever was on her lap to one side. Her features seemed carefully stoic as she opened the door and stepped out of her car, watching my approach.

I stopped at the hood of her car, my gaze moving over her from behind my sunglasses. Last night she'd been in jeans and a sweater. This morning she wore different jeans and a different sweater. Her clothes last night had been baggy. Her outfit today fit considerably better, showing off her shape in a way that was difficult to ignore.

So I didn't ignore it.

I appreciated it.

"'Morning," she said evenly. But her hands fisted at her sides. She then crossed her arms, paused, and then dropped her arms again and stuffed her fingers in her pockets.

"Good morning." I gave her a single head nod, knowing I sounded more formal than the situation merited. But—damn—the feel of her body arching and rubbing against mine, the heat of her mouth, the soft sounds she made were all on repeat in my mind.

Not that I was complaining, far from it. But keeping things formal was a good idea if she didn't want me mauling her in the parking lot.

"What are you—what are you doing here?" she asked, promptly grimaced, and gestured to the coffee in my hand. "I mean, obviously you're getting coffee. But what are you doing here, in this parking space, at the place where my car is parked? Do you need something?"

I gave her a tight smile so I wouldn't lick my lips and try to taste her there again. "I promised you last week at Genie's that if I saw you I'd be polite." I motioned behind me to the Starbucks. "I saw you as I was coming out. So here I am, being polite."

It wasn't even a half-truth. It was a lie I'd told myself to justify seeking her out. But I couldn't seem to care about that either.

Simone frowned in response.

No. Scratch that.

Simone *scowled.*

But her angry expression was soon replaced with a sarcastic one. "Well, goodness gracious me." She adopted a saccharine sweet southern drawl, her voice light and breathy, and pressed one set of fingers to her chest. "I don't know how I'll recover from this gentlemanly kindness."

I held in my laugh, barely.

"Thank you, good sir, for condescending to come over here and bequeathing your politeness upon me."

Sliding my jaw to one side, I took a step forward. "Simone—"

"Oh no, no." She fluttered her hands before her. "I won't keep you another moment from your busy schedule of chivalry and valiant deeds, certainly you have maidens aplenty waiting in rapturous verisimilitude."

"Verisimilitude?"

She shrugged and switched to her real voice. "I know, it's the wrong word and it doesn't fit in the sentence. But it's fun to say and I couldn't think of anything else. Speaking like that is exhausting, but I was determined to use it. That and *bequeathing*."

I laughed.

She did too, but it sounded reluctant.

Looking toward the Target, she crossed her arms. "All right, well . . ."

"Well?" I prompted when she didn't continue, hopeful that maybe she'd suggest we grab coffee together, or maybe breakfast.

Her stoic expression was back when she returned her gaze to mine. "Enjoy your coffee."

Staring at her, I did my best to ignore the disappointment of her dismissal and considered asking her to come with me to breakfast. As I considered, her glare grew even more remote.

Even so, I found I wasn't ready to leave, not if she wasn't coming with me somewhere.

"You got any questions for me today?" I asked, hopeful.

She shook her head. "Nope."

We stared at each other and I decided to take a chance. "Are you hungry?"

Her standoffish expression didn't alter, but she said, "I'm always hungry, you know that."

I smiled, just a little. "You want to go get breakfast? With me?"

Some of the frost behind her eyes thawed, but not much. "No, Roscoe. I don't."

Swallowing what felt like rocks, I nodded, my eyes and my stomach dropping to the ground. Instinct told me to push, to coax, to win her over, to fight for her affections, to ask until she relented. But my momma and my sister always told me that when a lady says no, a gentleman listens and believes her the first time.

If Simone wanted to see me, she knew where I lived. If she didn't want to see me, I would respect that.

"All right then," I said to my shoes before lifting my eyes. "I guess I'll see you around."

I didn't expect to see her again, not for a while, so I allowed myself another lingering look from behind my sunglasses before turning and strolling to my truck.

The rest of the morning was spent in a distracted and depressed haze, endeavoring to settle into the idea of letting her go again, distracting myself by reciting more of the dictionary, and swallowing around the persistent rocks in my throat.

I'd avoided her once. I'd moved on reasonably well. I could do it again.

Therefore, imagine my surprise when I spotted her car later that afternoon when I accompanied Cletus to Big Ben's dulcimer shop after running errands with him in Knoxville.

Once again, she was sitting in her car, in the parking lot, staring at her lap. This time, based on her frosty reception this morning, I made no attempt to intercept her or make polite conversation. Instead, I left with Cletus and his new book of music.

"Hey," he said, lifting his chin toward her car once we were back in my truck. "Isn't that Simone Payton?"

I nodded, grinding my teeth and putting the truck in gear. "Yep."

My brother stared at my profile as I pulled out of the lot. I ignored his stare. I could always tell when Cletus was looking at me because his stares carried a certain weight and were heavily fortified with either disappointment or insinuation.

"You should ask that woman out on a date," he said, speaking his mind.

"Oh? You think so?" I didn't roll my eyes because, if I did, he'd likely exact some small revenge. Cletus despised few things more than an eye-roll.

"No. I know so." He turned his attention to the passenger side mirror. "And do you want to know what else I know?"

"Do I have a choice?"

"Fine, surly britches"—he sniffed—"I won't tell you."

We drove in silence all the way to the Piggly Wiggly, completed our grocery shopping with as few words as possible passing between us, and when we left the store he insisted on pushing the cart because I *pushed it too loudly* over the asphalt.

I wasn't three steps out of the store when I spotted Simone's car again, and my feet slowed to a stop.

"What the hell?"

"That's what I was going to share in the car, but you were too busy sassing me." Cletus had stopped at my side and he was looking where I was looking. "She's been following us all day."

A small sound of confusion escaped my throat. "What is she up to?"

"She's tailing you."

I gave my brother a flat look. "Yeah, thanks so much, Sherlock. I figured that out."

He huffed. "Then why did you ask?"

"It's called a rhetorical question, Cletus."

"Well then, it was a gross abuse of the English language, Roscoe. You only use a rhetorical question in order to produce an effect or to make a statement. It's a question asked to further a point, to persuade, or for literary effect, none of which were required or relevant in this situation."

A deep, frustrated growl erupted from my chest. "You are so freaking frustrating."

"Because I'm correct? Or because you're incorrect?"

"Just—just let's get to the car." I stomped away from my brother, tired of his company, while he trailed after pushing the cart ostensibly much quieter than I would have.

When we arrived at the house, I helped unload the groceries and put things away, but left through the back door at the earliest possible opportunity, needing quiet and space and time away before dinner with my family.

I walked for miles, through paths I'd traversed as a kid, usually with Simone close by. I visited memories I'd sought to abandon years ago, many of which involved my mother.

Why in the world would Simone be following me? She'd made it clear this morning even my politeness was unwelcomed. Then why spend the morning making a point to show up everywhere I went?

By the time I made it home I was tired, brain tired and bone tired, and I still had no idea why Simone would be tracking me all day. After the poor sleep from the night before, I was ready for bed.

But Ashley, Drew, and Beth had arrived while I was out walking, as had Beau and Shelly, and Jenn. So I ate with my family and I made an effort.

After dinner, while I was in the kitchen helping Beau with the dishes and discussing the plans for the family's trip to Italy this summer, Cletus walked in.

He stood in the middle of the kitchen, his hands on his hips, and asked, "Why is she still tailing you?" Then, giving me a meaningful look, he promptly left. But not before calling over his shoulder, "Let the record show, that was proper application of a rhetorical question."

Beau glanced between me and the doorway to the living room, where Cletus had just disappeared. "What is he going on about?"

I didn't answer Beau because I was too focused on what Cletus had just said, and what it meant. Skipping around the counter and jogging out of the kitchen, I caught up with my schemer of a brother just as he made it to the landing at the top of the stairs.

"This way." Cletus motioned for me to follow, which I did as he navigated down the hall and into our momma's room.

The light was off. He made no move to turn it on, instead

walking straight to the picture window. It faced the long driveway leading to the house from Moth Run Road.

"There." He pointed to a spot in the distance, on the other side of the road, partially obscured by tree trunks and a flowering quince bush just beginning to bloom scarlet red. Anyone paying attention who looked at the road from our house would see the car.

"Huh." I folded my arms, shaking my head, disbelieving the vision in front of me.

"Want to bring her some coffee? Or maybe one of Jenn's tarts? Simone is definitely tart-worthy."

Frowning at the sight of Simone's car, I exhaled a heavy sigh. "She probably thinks we can't see her."

Cletus scratched his neck through his bushy beard. "I don't know. She's smart. If she didn't want to be seen, I reckon she'd make herself invisible."

I nodded at that, because he was right. Which begged the question—not rhetorical—what the heck what she up to?

"You want to ask her inside? You know she's always more than welcome here."

"It certainly would be the polite thing to do . . ." I muttered under my breath, staring at the mystery that was Simone Payton.

* * *

SATURDAY MORNING SHE followed me to Cades Cove. She couldn't follow me into the back trail area where Drew and I were checking traps, but she was still there in the afternoon when I left for home, her car parked three spots down from mine. She wasn't inside her car but rather was sitting at a picnic table several feet away.

Also, Cletus had been right. She definitely wasn't trying to hide the fact that she was tailing me. When I spotted her at the picnic table, she looked up, gave me a dispassionate stare, and turned her attention back to whatever magazine was sitting on the table in front of her.

Perplexed, I left.

I drove home.

I washed up in a hurry.

I returned to my momma's room to look out that big picture window.

Sure enough, Simone's car was sitting in the same spot it had been last night. I released an incredulous exhale, shaking my head at her odd behavior, but also feeling lighter because of it and having no idea why.

Rationally, I knew her actions were strange. If it had been anyone else following me around like this, I would've found it alarming to say the least. But Simone wasn't anyone else, and what might've been alarming from other folks was . . .

It was . . .

Well, it was almost romantic coming from her.

Clearly, she was trying to make a point, but what was it? Was she trying to say that this time she wasn't going to let me disappear from her life? That she wasn't going to let me forget about our kiss? That I meant something to her? That she wanted to be with me?

But that couldn't be right. If she wanted to be with me, then why not take me up on my offer of breakfast on Friday?

Oscillating between optimism and confused frustration, I pulled together a quick dinner for me and Billy—who, according to his text, was coming home from the office—and made a third plate for Simone. Opening the fridge, I skipped over the beers, and grabbed her a bottle of water.

Then I walked down our driveway.

Moth Run Road was never busy. An hour or more might go by with no cars passing in either direction. Even so, I made a show of looking left and right, giving her ample time to spot me before crossing. She must've seen me coming, because as soon as I stepped onto the road, she opened her car door, just like yesterday morning.

This time, she leaned against the closed driver's side door, watching me come.

Today she was wearing Converse, a black skirt with black tights, and a maroon fleece zip up. Keeping my eyes on her, I didn't stop until I was close enough to hand her the plate and water.

"Hey," I said, my heart beating fast. "Are you hungry?"

Simone glanced between me and my offerings, her gaze distrustful. "I'm always hungry. What is it?"

"Tacos."

She immediately took the plate. "Thank you."

I grinned, watching as she lifted the tinfoil wrap and smelled the contents within.

"You know, you could join me inside the house"—I tossed my thumb over my shoulder—"if you want."

She lifted an eyebrow, her lips twisting to one side. "What would we talk about?"

Now my heart galloped excitedly. "Anything you want."

"Anything?" Her eyes narrowed.

"Anything," I confirmed, thinking, *just please come inside.*

Simone seemed to consider this information before asking, "Will you tell me why you ghosted me in high school?"

I stared at her, clenching my jaw so I wouldn't wince, and spoke without thinking, "So that's what this is about?"

She said nothing, just returned my stare, hers hard as the rocks that had been clogging my throat.

Taking a step back, I exhaled a bitter laugh. She was unbelievable.

"You've been following me around for two days because you want me to tell you why I disappeared when we were sixteen, is that it?"

Still, she said nothing, just gave me one of her stubbornly patient looks, the kind that always made me crazy.

Shoving my hands in my pockets, I turned and left her on the side of the road, stomping toward home and—just for the hell of it—reliving that terrible moment.

She swayed a little, laughing, and shaking her head. "Why'd you let me drink so much?"

"Let you?" I laughed, too. "Nobody lets *Simone Payton do anything."*

"Damn straight." She slurred the word straight *and sat on the grass in an ungraceful heap.*

I vacillated a second, sat next to her, wanting to put my arm around her shoulders, to support her, hold her close, but I didn't know how she'd react to that.

More and more, I'd wanted to touch her. And she'd been letting me. We'd always hugged, but now holding hands wasn't unusual, and —I reminded myself—she'd been the one to pat my backside first.

"Simone."

"Yes?" She had her eyes closed, her dark lashes against her cheeks, her head lolled to one side, long braids spilling over her shoulder.

She was so pretty.

I wondered if she'd remember this tomorrow. I knew I would.

"What would you say if I told you I love you?" I was so nervous. Even drunk as I was, I was nervous. But the liquor helped.

A laugh, a wide grin, exquisite amber irises moving over my face. "I love you, too. Of course I do."

"I mean"—I reached out, my fingers closing gently over her wrist and a thrill shot through me to see my hand on her skin—"what if I told you I'm in love with you?" My voice cracked a little on the last three words.

Her smile fell as understanding sharpened behind her eyes, disappointment, dismay.

She covered my hand with hers, prying away my fingers.

"Roscoe . . ." She'd never said my name like that before, like it was a word to put distance between us. She blinked like she was trying to bring me into focus. "No. No, no, no."

I studied her, holding my breath, feeling like my life and heart were balanced on the edge of a knife.

"Why no?" I whispered.

Her head swayed a little, and she blinked, and I saw she was real drunk. I cursed. Guilt had me gritting my teeth and shaking my head at myself. I was drunk, too. But I wasn't as drunk as she was.

"We'll talk about this later."

"Still no."

I swallowed a lump in my throat, her words like a punch in the stomach. "Let's get you home. I'll call Billy. He'll drive us." I stood, offering her my hand.

"No. Never." She didn't seem to be speaking to me, but rather to a conversation going on in her head.

"Come on." I shook my hand, gesturing for her to take it. "Tomorrow, when you're sober, we'll talk." And I'd make a romantic declaration, not take the chickenshit, coward way out and try to pry answers from her while we were drunk.

"The answer will still be no," she said, loudly.

I winced, my hand dropping.

"I'll never love anyone that way." Simone frowned at me, then at the hand at my side. "Especially not you."

She wanted to know?

Fine.

Reaching the gate on my side of the road, I turned and called, "Hey."

She'd just opened her door, so she looked up from the car, her eyes growing wide and expectant at my shout.

"I'm going to Genie's tonight."

Staring, she waited, like she expected me to continue. When I didn't, she called back, "Thanks for the heads-up."

"I'll make you a deal. If you dance with me—one dance, whatever song I want—I'll tell you why."

Simone's eyes narrowed. She seemed to be searching my words for hidden tricks and traps. "You'll tell me why you disappeared," she clarified, her stare pointed. "You promise?"

"I promise."

"Deal," she responded immediately, though the look she gave me was full of distrust. "But you also have to answer all of my follow-up questions."

I shrugged at that, my expression flat, and turned back to the house.

"I mean it, Roscoe," she yelled after me. "You have to answer all my questions."

I didn't turn and I didn't respond, just kept walking because there weren't likely to be any follow-up questions.

CHAPTER TWELVE

"Memories warm you up from the inside. But they also tear you apart."

— HARUKI MURAKAMI, KAFKA ON THE SHORE

Roscoe

SATURDAY NIGHT AT Genie's was typically the busiest night of the week, with most folks showing up around 10:00 PM and heading out around 1:00 AM.

I left my house at 12:30 AM and, sure enough, Simone followed me the whole twenty-minute drive there. I parked my truck and exited, spotting her pulling into a space near the front of the lot. Gathering my nerve and the figurative suit of armor I'd been working on all evening, I walked over to her car and opened the driver's side door just as she turned off the engine.

Not looking up, she reached for her phone on the passenger seat, and unlocked it. "Hey, I'll meet you inside. I just need to send a message real fast."

Smothering a flare of aggravation, I said, "Fine," and shut her door.

Then I walked to the front door of the bar, gritting my teeth and fighting the petty urge to turn, get back in my truck, and drive home while she was busy sending her messages.

I mean, what the hell? She'd been sitting in her car all day, and now—as soon as we're here—she needs to send a message?

Whatever.

Determined not to let this hiccup ruin my plan, I strolled into Genie's and hung my coat up on the wall of racks by the entrance, noting there were less coats left than usual for this time of night. Good. I'd chosen 12:50 AM on purpose.

Genie had an unwritten policy. All the line dances and fast songs played until 12:30 AM. After that, until 1:30 AM closing time, it was nothing but slow dances and ballads. She told me once fast music sold drinks, but slow music helped folks wind down and pair off— i.e. leave and get laid.

This information had made me blush at the time. I'd just turned twenty-one and had kissed a total of two girls, Simone and a girl I'd met in college named Elaine. Since then, I'd kissed two more.

But despite my lack of experience, Genie's vulgar talk didn't make me blush anymore. This was mostly because, like most folks, Genie told the same stories over and over, and I'd only been embarrassed during the first telling.

Stepping up to the bar, I motioned for Patty—Genie's daughter, and apparently the bartender for the evening—to bring me a beer. It was my first of the evening, and I wouldn't have another, but I didn't feel right using Genie's dance floor without providing patronage first.

"Roscoe?"

I turned at the sound of my name and discovered Hannah Townsen standing to my left.

"Oh, hey Hannah." I gave her an easy smile and nodded to Patty as she handed me my Heineken, mouthing a quick *thank you.* Patty winked in response and moved on to another thirsty customer.

"Everybody is here tonight," Hannah said cheerfully, grinning as her eyes swept over me. "I have got to get over here on Saturdays more often."

"You should," I agreed, tipping my beer toward hers and giving it a clink. "Speaking of which, what are you doing here? Don't you usually work on Saturday nights?"

I'd gone to high school with Hannah Townsen. Everyone thought she'd be a doctor by now, or a lawyer, or something else high-powered. But her mother had gone through a spell of bad luck and Hannah had dropped out of college after just one year.

Now she had two jobs, a stripper at the Pink Pony Thursday through Saturday, and a hostess at the only steak restaurant in town, the Front Porch, during the rest of the week. I never saw her here or anywhere as it seemed she never had a night off and slept during the day whenever I was in town.

In fact, now that I thought it over, the last time I'd seen her was at the Front Porch two and a half years ago, when Billy had taken me out to dinner randomly, just the two of us.

Hannah's grin faltered a little, but she was quick to resurrect it. "Hank gave me tonight off, said I needed some rest."

"So you came here." My grin widened.

"Yes"—she nodded firmly—"I came here. Because I need fun more than rest."

"And did you have fun tonight?" I asked, interested, because Hannah was a good person who had been dealt a shitty hand.

She gazed at me thoughtfully, her features seeming to grow determined the longer she stared.

Without warning, she took a step forward into my space and said low, so only I could hear, "I'd have fun if you asked me to dance."

Oh jeez.

Okay.

This situation was going to require some fancy sidestepping. As I mentioned, Hannah was a good person, she deserved some fun, and the last thing I wanted to do was ruin her first night off in forever by making her feel rejected.

I let a slow grin claim my mouth and I sighed, making a show of sounding and looking regretful. "I'm actually meeting somebody tonight."

Her lips parted and her eyes rounded in surprise. "Oh. I'm sorry." Hannah's gaze dropped to the bar and she began backing away, "I'm so sorry—"

I caught her hand, stopping her retreat, which caused her to lift her chin.

Gazing deep in her eyes, I said sincerely, "Never apologize for giving someone the honor of asking for a dance."

She gave me a tight smile and nodded; some of her embarrassment seemed to ease, but not all of it.

"Only apologize if you use a cheesy pickup line first, like"—I frowned, patting down my shirt front like I was looking for something—"Wait, I seem to have lost my phone number. Can I have yours?"

Hannah wrinkled her nose, but also laughed. "That is cheesy."

Seeing her smile made me smile, so I gave her another one. "Are you a parking ticket? 'Cause you've got fine written all over you."

"Oh my God, that one is even worse!" She covered her face, peeking from between her fingers.

"Are you from Tennessee? Because you're the only ten I see."

She groaned through giggles. "Oh no."

"Yeah, that one is pretty bad." I nodded. "How about this: do you know what my shirt is made of?" I pointed to the flannel I was wearing.

Letting her hands drop, she glanced between me and my shirt. "Cotton?"

I lifted my eyebrows, gave her a pointed look, and said with flourish, "Boyfriend material."

That made her laugh-snort. "No more!"

"One more." I laughed. "Just one more. I hate this one so much, and I actually heard a guy try to use it over the summer. It was brutal."

"Okay, fine." She nodded, her grin immense. "Give it to me."

"Would you grab my arm"—I held out my elbow—"so I can tell my friends I've been touched by an angel?"

She swatted my arm away, laughing again, all awkwardness forgotten, and I laughed with her.

A voice from behind me—dry as a desert—said, "You've certainly been touched by something."

Simone.

I stiffened, my smile morphing into more of a grimace. The first memory that came to mind at the sound of her voice was her stand-offish dismissal of me on Friday morning when I'd asked her to breakfast.

Hannah leaned to the side to peer behind me and her eyes widened again with surprise. "Simone Payton?"

I turned toward the bar and backed up a step, so the two women could see each other.

"Hey, Hannah." Simone gave our former classmate a little wave and a small genuine smile.

"I haven't seen you in forever!" Hannah appeared to be both shocked and excited. "How have you been?" She reached forward, gave Simone a quick hug, and stepped back. "How long are you here for? What are you doing in town?"

I glanced at Simone just in time to find her gaze moving over me. We both looked at Hannah, and comprehension—or more accurately, miscomprehension—passed over the blonde's features.

Hannah alternated between gaping at me and Simone, visibly nonplussed, and said, "Oh my goodness. You two are together?"

I lowered my attention to the barstool tucked under the counter and waited for Simone to correct Hannah's misunderstanding of the situation. I wasn't going to do it. If she expected me to do it, we'd be waiting here all night.

The next thing I knew, Simone had slipped her hand into the crook of my elbow, moved closer to me, and said brightly, "Yep. We're together."

Shocked, I turned my head to look at her. Her smile was pointed at me.

No. Not smile. *Smirk.*

"I know what you're thinking," Simone continued, giving her attention back to Hannah, "It's about time, right?"

Hannah nodded enthusiastically. "I just, I mean, I can't believe it finally happened. It's so great, so great."

"I reckon I can't believe it either," I said, rubbing my chin and earning me an elbow in my ribs. The elbow didn't hurt, but it did make me grin for some reason.

Simone twisted toward the dance floor, as though something had caught her notice, and said to me, "I think that's our song."

I listened as the opening bars of "Marry Me" by Thomas Rhett played over the speaker, lifting an eyebrow at the maudlin yet ironically appropriate song.

"Oh, yeah." Hannah shooed us toward where the other couples were already swaying. "You two go dance." To Simone, she said, "How can I reach you? Should I call your house?"

"Stop by the diner." Simone tugged on my elbow, pulling me away from the bar. "These days, I usually work Monday through Thursday, and Sunday mornings. Come see me."

"Okay, I will." Hannah waved and Simone grinned.

Meanwhile, unable to walk backward anymore without knocking into someone, I turned and covered Simone's hand on my arm with mine, taking the lead and guiding her to an empty corner of the dance floor.

Her gaze focused beyond my shoulder, her expression impassive. I encircled her waist, and her arms lifted on autopilot to twine around my neck. Soon we were swaying to the music and I marveled at how natural it felt to hold her like this, like we'd danced together a hundred times even though this was officially the first.

Or maybe I was just suffering from a serious case of wishful thinking.

But then she looked at me squarely and I saw a crack had formed in her impassive façade.

Simone cleared her throat, saying, "Of course you had to be a good dancer. Of course," as though this both frustrated and flustered her.

I moved my palm to the center of her back, bringing her closer. She let me.

"If you recall, my momma taught all us boys to dance."

I felt her nod, her temple brushing against my jaw, her arms relaxing. One of her hands slid from my neck to my shoulder. "I remember. She used to make you take turns with each other."

"And Cletus wouldn't let anyone else lead," I said dryly, still irritated by the memory.

Simone leaned just her head away, capturing my eyes. "Neither would you."

I shrugged, grinning a little, because she was right.

Quiet stretched between us, during which we looked, just looked, at each other's faces. She didn't seem to be wearing a mask, or any expression at all. I was grateful for the chance to memorize her face, as she was now, completely. Especially while I held her close.

This was why I'd made the deal. I wanted this memory—dancing with her, gazing at her, feeling her body move against mine—before I answered all her questions and probably never saw her again. Simone wouldn't understand why I'd had to disappear from her life.

But that was okay, most people wouldn't understand. That was because most people's memories didn't work like mine.

Her sudden frown broke the moment, and I felt her chest rise and fall with a huge sigh.

"What is it?" I asked.

The frowned deepened, her eyebrows drawing closer together. "Can I ask you a question?"

Great. Here we go.

I shook my head. I wasn't ready. I wanted the dance, just one dance. Afterward, she'd have a chance to ask all her questions.

"No, Simone. After we—"

"I know I just asked you a question. But I want to ask another question."

"The deal is—"

"Actually, don't answer that first question. Answer this next question."

"Simone, you promised me a dance, and—"

"How come you've never flirted with me?"

I blinked, staring at this amazing woman in my arms. I didn't try to stop my brows from pulling low in confusion or the curving of my mouth, mostly because I was too surprised by the question to do anything about the expression it elicited.

She hasn't changed a bit, I thought as I traced the line of her upturned face, her cheekbone to her jaw, her lips. My gaze rested there as the memory of our kiss resurfaced for the hundredth time in the two days since it happened; how she'd felt in my arms; how hungry her mouth had been; how she'd arched and rocked against me; how a handful of her luscious body stoked my desire hotter rather than satiated it.

The recollection caused me to amend my earlier thought, *Well, maybe she's changed a little.*

"Are you going to answer my question?" Simone's uneven tone drew my eyes back to hers. She regarded me with wary curiosity. "Or is this you flirting with me right now?"

The music changed to "How Do I Live," the remake by Claire McClure that was currently burning up the charts.

"This is not me flirting with you," I responded honestly, my voice gruffer than I'd intended.

It couldn't be helped. Holding her here, now—the teasing, swaying touches, feeling her hips move beneath my hands, joined but not touching how I wanted, how my skin and body craved—was driving me crazy.

"Then why are you looking at me like that?" The question was rushed, and sounded nervous. It was that voice again, like she was asking me things she wasn't sure she wanted an answer to.

But it was too late. She'd asked the question. She couldn't take it back.

"Because this is how I look at you."

Simone's intelligent eyes held mine for a long moment, her brain working. Then she blinked, as though realizing something big. Her breathing changed, turned shallow, anxious. Her gaze dropped to my neck. She swallowed with visible effort.

"You liked me," she said, like she was solving a mystery aloud while we danced, her hands sliding down and around my torso. "You liked me and you knew me well enough to figure out that I wasn't going to return your . . . that I wasn't *capable* of returning your feelings. So you dropped me."

"No." I shook my head, my lips curving into a rueful grin, my hand sliding lower on her back. This would be the last time she'd let me hold her. "That's not what happened."

Her eyes snapped to mine. "Then what happened?"

"I loved you." I took a deep breath, ignoring the stab of pain in the center of my sternum, determined to speak plainly. "I loved you and I told you."

"No, you didn't. I would have remembered that."

"I did."

"Oh, yeah? When?"

"The night you got drunk at Kelly Winters's party."

She flinched, pressing her lips together as her eyes grew wider. I saw denial there, and I could almost hear the workings of her mind, the arguments forming. "I don't remember that happening."

Unable to hold her gaze any longer, I looked over her head. "Do you remember anything from that night?"

"No. Not after . . . not after doing shots with Hannah Townsen in the kitchen. But—"

"Don't tell me I was too young to have feelings that big. You knew me, you knew me better than anyone."

I felt her head nod before she spoke, and when she did her voice was hoarse. "I did. I did know you. You were . . . " She cleared her throat again and I looked at her. Her attention cut away to some spot beyond me. "You were excessively sensitive."

The way she said this, like my being sensitive was a source of great frustration for her, made me want to laugh, because it definitely had been. Me being too sensitive and her being too pragmatic had been the source of all our disagreements.

"But you also knew me," she continued, her voice now a harsh whisper as she returned her stare to mine. "And so you knew *I* was too young to have feelings that big."

Movement behind her drew my notice and I spotted Grady and Pamela giving us curious looks, clearly picking up on some of the heavy vibes between us.

I glared at Grady and Pamela until they averted their gazes. Still, it was a good reminder that right now was a terrible place and time to be having this conversation.

Holding Simone closer, I dipped my lips to her neck and felt her shiver, but she also held me closer in return.

Hoping to disperse the tension between us before we had the attention of the entire dance floor, I whispered softly in her ear, "It doesn't matter, it was—"

"It does matter."

"Simone—"

"It matters to me." Her fingers tightened on my back, grabbing fistfuls of my shirt. "Don't say it doesn't matter."

I sighed, frustrated. If we were going to do this now, well, then I guess we were doing this now.

"Given how well you knew me, I guess you understand why I disappeared."

"No. I don't. I don't understand." She leaned her head back, ensnaring my gaze. I noticed with a pang of remorse that hers was glassy. "I don't understand why you did that to me, why you dropped out of my life like that, if you—if you—"

Her chin wobbled and my lungs ignited with hot regret.

"Simone."

She shook her head, looking overwhelmed, her eyes darting everywhere.

I stopped swaying and cupped her cheek, bringing her chin up and forcing her to look at me. "Please."

"Please what?" she croaked, and then pressed her lips together in a stubborn line.

Please forgive me.

The words were on the tip of my tongue, but I couldn't say them. The truth was, knowing what I knew now, the only thing I would have done differently was leave her earlier, before I'd fallen so completely.

I would have guarded myself better, I would have offered less to her, and I would have saved my heart for someone who wanted it.

Nope. You wouldn't have done that, because there's only one her.

Her eyes moved between mine as she waited. When I said nothing, she nodded, her gaze falling away.

"Right," she said, letting me go and stepping out of my arms, her hand coming to her forehead.

Turning without giving me another look, Simone maneuvered through the couples. She made a beeline for the exit. She left me standing on the dance floor.

CHAPTER THIRTEEN

"If you wish to forget anything on the spot, make a note that this
thing is to be remembered."

— EDGAR ALLAN POE

Roscoe

H ER CAR WASN'T in the lot when I left Genie's after paying for
my beer.

The next morning, I checked Moth Run Road from the big
picture window in my momma's room, unsurprised when Simone's
car was nowhere to be seen. Now she knew the truth, now she'd be
avoiding me like I'd avoided her.

I wouldn't be seeing her again.

Now, my brother Cletus had a habit of fixating on things he had
no desire to think about, and Beau's lady friend for the last five
years, Shelly Sullivan, had an obsessive-compulsive diagnosis. They
each had a different coping mechanism for dealing with invasive
thoughts.

Cletus made lists, lists and lists, to distract himself in the moment, until he could think clearly again.

Shelly confronted the obsessions in the moment using logic, tried to think about them from a completely rational perspective in order to disarm their power, so the obsessions wouldn't lead to compulsions.

Watching and observing my family, I'd adopted these strategies to help me manage invasive memories, reasoning that memories are basically just thoughts and therefore one or the other coping mechanism—distraction or confrontation—should work depending on the situation and the memory.

I tried to focus on the present and the mundane task of getting ready for church. I couldn't, my mind in chaos. Memories of last night transposed on memories of us kissing at Hawk's Field on top of memories from my father leaving me mixed with memories of my mother's death along with memories of Simone and I as kids.

I tried distracting myself by reciting the dictionary. I even pulled it off the shelf and read it aloud. It didn't help. Nothing helped. The idea of never seeing Simone again, after what had passed between us over the last few days, made my brain want to go through each memory of her and relive them all. I didn't know if the rest of me would be able to handle it, especially not while sitting in a church pew surrounded by my family.

It was no use. Distraction wasn't working, which meant I'd need to retreat for the day and set my mind in order.

Changing out of my Sunday finery and into hiking gear, I sent a group text to the Green Valley family members—Ash and Drew, Billy, Cletus and Jenn, Beau and Shelly—that I'd be missing church this morning and breakfast after.

Cletus quickly responded,

Cletus: *An email would have sufficed. We all check ours.*

With Ash chiming in,

Ashley: *Leave Roscoe alone, Cletus.*
I hope you feel better, Roscoe. <3

Campsites at Cooper Road Trail were usually empty this time of year, partially because it was still cold, partially because no one but the locals could find the trailhead. I parked in the small lot at the base of an incline leading up to the ranger station, allowing my mind to run through the events of last night.

Indulgently, I hit pause and repeat a few times on the moment where we'd looked at each other, how her hand had rested on my shoulder, the heat of it seeping into the skin beneath my shirt, and the forthright, open quality of her expression and eyes.

Unfortunately, the memory continued, and the next part wasn't so good. I rubbed my chest as I left my truck, wincing at the pain there and distracted by the bruised and tattered organ. I made a promise to myself I'd take better care about making new memories moving forward.

And yet, even though I'd been reckless with Simone and would now pay the price for a lifetime, I couldn't bring myself to wish I'd done anything differently.

Because now I had that first hug outside of Daisy's; the conversation, laughter, and kiss at Hawk's Field a week later; and the dance last night. If I'd continued avoiding her, giving the woman one-word answers and cold shoulders, my heart might've been better off, but I doubted—overall—my life would have been.

These were my reflections, the lens through which I was visiting the past, when I felt a heavy hand shake my shoulder followed by a gruff, "I said, turn around."

Startled, I looked at the hand and the arm attached to it, finding both covered in leather. Frowning, I turned completely around as the hand dropped and its owner took a step back, crossing his arms.

It was Twilight—aka Isaac Sylvester, Jennifer's brother turned Iron Wraiths member—glaring at me with his arms now crossed. Several parking spots away, next to a black SUV with the back passenger door open, was Catfish, highest ranking lieutenant of the

Iron Wraith's MC. Or as I'd known him years ago, Curtis Hickson. Catfish was also looking at me. But he wasn't glaring. His features were more cautious and thoughtful than aggressive.

"Did you hear me?" Twilight asked, his purplish-blue eyes flicking down and then up, as though reassessing my person. "You deaf? Or just stupid?"

"Leave him alone," Catfish said evenly, still holding my stare. Then to me, "Time to go."

Time to go?

"Where're we going?" Stalling, I crossed my arms, quickly estimating how long it would take Catfish to sprint from the SUV to where I stood, should I decide to punch Twilight and escape.

Taking down Twilight wouldn't be a problem, but Catfish . . . that was a different story. The man was huge, smart, and strong. I didn't like my chances.

I didn't know how much Catfish—Curtis—remembered about me, but I remembered *everything* about him. Especially the night he'd returned Simone's older sister to her family after having run away with her for the two months and five days prior.

He'd been twenty, already a recruit of the Wraiths. She'd been eighteen, in her senior year of high school. General consensus was, Curtis Hickson had no business getting involved with someone like Daniella Payton. Smart, sweet girl from old, local prestigious family falling for a con man. Folks said it was like my parents—Darrell Winston and Bethany Oliver—all over again.

Personally, I didn't think Curtis was anything like Darrell. I'd been a kid when it all happened, so maybe I'd been mistaken, but I didn't think that was the case.

Darrell never loved my momma, nor did I think he was capable of loving anyone.

I knew for a fact Curtis Hickson had been head over heels in love with Daniella. Why else would he have walked away?

Your heart wants what it wants . . .

Simone's words from Thursday repeated in my mind, and I saw her sitting next to me in the bed of my truck beneath starlight.

She paused here to take a deep breath, sounded distracted as she added, "And if you fall for the wrong person, what can you do? You're already in love, and your heart wants what it wants, and everything is a mess."

I had a suspicion, regarding this last part, Simone was talking about someone specific.

"Did that happen to you?"

"Did what happen to me?" Her gaze darted over me.

Again, my throat felt tight, but when else would I have an opportunity to ask these questions?

So I forced the words, "Did you f-fall in love with the wrong someone and then—"

"No." She waved her hands in front of her, as though to disperse the horrid thought. "No, no, no. I would never do that. That's never going to happen, because I'm never falling in love. Period."

I didn't get much time to reflect on the memory, because Twilight was speaking at me again.

"Your daddy wants a word." Twilight sounded bored. Bored and impatient.

Glancing between the two men, I widened my stance, preparing for Twilight's inevitable advance. "What does Darrell want?"

"A word," Twilight repeated, over-enunciating. "And that's all you gotta know."

He advanced on me again and I tensed my right arm in readiness. Twilight made just one step before stopping, turning over his shoulder as the sound of an approaching car met our collective ears.

Actually, the Audi wasn't just approaching. It was speeding over the gravel road, kicking up a quantity of rocks and dust in its wake while its shocks took a beating.

Simone.

My stomach fell.

What in the hell? How could she possibly know where to find me?

Speaking of which, how did she find me last week at Genie's?

And how did she know the exact spot where I'd be at Hawk's Field on Thursday? And Starbucks on Friday?

I glanced at my truck, a suspicion taking hold.

. . . No.

She wouldn't.

Yes. She would.

My brother Cletus had placed an over-the-counter car tracker on someone's car once (once that I know of), and he was just a sneaky bastard.

Whereas Simone had a bachelors in criminal justice, and a master of forensic science in forensic chemistry. The woman might've been unemployed in her field, but she was a modern-day Sherlock. I couldn't believe the possibility—that she'd been tracking my truck—hadn't occurred to me until now.

"Son of a—" Twilight stopped himself, his lips pinching as an expression of intense frustration claimed his features.

His unfinished thought was my sentiment exactly.

"Okay, well." I locked my truck, walked past a distracted Twilight toward where Curtis stood by the SUV. "Let's go."

But I wasn't fast enough. Simone pulled her car—recklessly, I might add—between my truck and their SUV, blocking my path. Undeterred, I set my jaw and walked around her car just as she jumped out of it.

"Thank goodness you haven't left yet," she said, sounding breathless and ridiculously cheerful, her hand grabbing my arm and yanking me to a stop.

I spun on her and shook her off, giving her a warning glare. "Go home."

"I just got here," she said, her tone hard and determined, as were her gorgeous eyes.

"Simone, I swear to God—"

"Listen to Roscoe, Simone." Curtis's boots crunched over the gravel, the big man strolling toward us and drawing her notice.

I watched as she did a double take, presumably recognizing him. A hint of fear or astonishment sparked behind her eyes and she took a half step back. Almost immediately, she straightened her spine, lifting her chin as renewed defiance blanketed her features.

"You don't tell me what to do," she spat at the big man, raising a finger.

He seemed unaffected by the vehemence in her tone, but his steps slowed, like he was recalculating what to do next.

She spun on Twilight, finger still raised. "Neither do you, My Little Pony. And"—she turned to me, the gold in her eyes flashing, her lips a grim line—"neither do you."

"Fine." I seethed. "Goodbye."

She caught my arm again, her gaze darting between Curtis's slow-motion approach and me. "Don't go with them. Stay here. With me. We'll go on that hike, like we planned."

I shook my head, confused by the words—lies—spilling out of her mouth. "What are you talking—"

"They can't take both of us," she said on a rush, her eyebrows lifting meaningfully. "That would be kidnapping."

"Yes. We can." Curtis's deep voice was closer now, but he still moved at a snail's pace. "And we will."

"I prefer the word *detain* to kidnapping," Twilight said. The comment was clearly meant to be sarcastic, but he didn't sound too happy about it. "Baby Winston here is coming with us willingly."

"That's right," I said through clenched teeth, "I am. And you're staying here."

"No." Her hand slid down my forearm to tangle our fingers together. "Please." She brought our hands to her chest, worry making her eyes bright. "Please don't go. You have no assurances that you'll come back, that they'll let you leave."

At these words, Curtis stopped moving.

But Twilight stepped forward, leaning in close. "All your daddy wants is to talk to you, that's it. You got my word that you can leave as soon as Darrell is finished."

Simone shook her head, not releasing my gaze.

My chest constricted in response to her plea and the worry I saw in her eyes for me. But what could I do? Her sudden appearance had tied my hands.

The Wraiths were a mixed bag of human garbage and salvageable souls.

Darrell Winston and Razor Dennings—the club vice president and president, respectively—were human garbage.

Curtis I trusted. Maybe I shouldn't have, but I did.

Twilight was anybody's guess. How he treated his sister, his momma, the choices he'd made, he hadn't made any sense in years.

There were a few other recruits there—two guys I'd gone to high school with in particular, and Drill, a big bald dude who sometimes went fishing with me and Beau on Bandit Lake—who were not human garbage. If I needed to get out of a bind, they'd help me escape and make it look real.

But I had no idea if the same could be said for helping Simone. These MC guys, they were encouraged by senior members to view women differently. Women to them were property, used and disposed of, subhuman submissives kept around to meet physical urges.

Maybe Darrell would let me go once he had his say, maybe he wouldn't. One thing I knew for sure, with Simone here as potential leverage, any chance I'd had of fighting my way out or escaping this mess was gone. Curtis and Twilight were taking me with them one way or the other, and I'd never forgive myself if they took her, too.

So I shook her off, grinding my teeth and shaking my head. "Goodbye."

Worry gave way to fury and she glowered at me. I could almost hear the parade of expletives marching through her mind.

Turning to Curtis, I nodded and walked past him to the open door of the SUV. I slid in. I buckled my seatbelt. I waited. Curtis and Twilight lingered where they were for several seconds, but then eventually moved to the black vehicle.

"If there's no danger, then I can come along too," she said to their retreating backs.

"Simone. You're not coming." I shot her another glare.

She shot me one back, following in Curtis's footsteps. "I'm coming."

"You are not." Curtis spun, blocking her path.

Lifting her chin and meeting his towering gaze, she crossed her arms. "If you don't bring me, I'll call the police and say Roscoe was man-napped."

"Then, when they show up"—Curtis crossed his arms, too —"Roscoe will explain the situation and they'll leave."

She smirked. "Then I'll skip the police and call Congressman William Winston. Or better yet, Cletus Winston."

Curtis stood exceedingly still, staring down Simone, obviously considering the merit of her threat. It was a great threat, maybe the most effective one she could have made. I think I knew before he did what his decision had to be because I cursed under my breath and my vision clouded with red.

"Simone," I hissed, but it was too late.

"Fine." Curtis turned, stomping back to the SUV, his mouth a wrathful, frustrated slant. "We bring her, too."

CHAPTER FOURTEEN

"Touch has a memory."

— JOHN KEATS

Simone

I SANG **"IT'S** a Small World After All" and Roscoe paced.

Pacing, pacing, pacing. Back and forth, back and forth. Prowling the medium-ish room we'd been deposited and locked in.

The room held barely any furniture. No windows, one door with two locks from the outside, cement walls with no pictures; a gray metal desk and chair sat against one wall next to a neatly made twin bed with a white bedspread and gray metal frame; a wooden footstool with an embroidered cushion was on its own near the center of the space; three folding chairs were leaning against the wall near the door. A huge, pristine-looking oriental rug covered the floor—red, dark blue, and light green—and felt soft and clean beneath my feet.

Oh yeah, they'd taken our shoes and socks. They'd also taken Roscoe's sweater, whereas I'd been allowed to keep my jacket. Which meant he was prowling the room in bare feet.

189

This—bare feet, clothed only in a black T-shirt and tan hiking pants—added to my impression of him as a caged cheetah. Not a lion, or a tiger, or a jaguar. A cheetah.

A lean, strong, restless, and extremely pissed-off cheetah.

His pissed-off-ness, I assumed, had begun as soon as I'd arrived at Cooper Road Trail. Allegedly, it was threefold:

1. We'd been abducted by the Iron Wraiths
2. I'd insisted on being abducted right along with him, and
3. I currently sang his least favorite song in the universe

I was fine with his pissed-off cheetah status because nothing I currently felt was as neat and tidy as being pissed off. I was angry. I was also not angry, which was confusing. Additionally, I was having strange thoughts about Roscoe and me and the past and the future.

Resentment stew had been simmering since Thursday night when I'd kissed him, he'd kissed me back, and then he'd pushed me away. However, last night during the dance floor incident, the resentment had ceased to simmer and had morphed into anger. Red, hot, boiling anger.

Now, pay attention, because here is where things get interesting.

After leaving Roscoe at Genie's, driving home in a wrathful tizzy, and parking in front of my parent's house, I cried. I cried and cried, and at the time I didn't know why I cried. Not only were there tears, there were also soul-wracking sobs. So many sobs. And pain. In the chest, stomach, behind my eyes, and chest again.

I imagined the tears came from within my bones, marrow deep, because even my bones hurt.

Once the tears were spent, I went into the house—grateful I'd texted my mom a heads-up early so I wouldn't be subjected to an apparating attack—and collapsed on the couch in the living room. I slept there in a dreamless sleep, waking up disoriented much later than I'd planned.

My first thought upon waking, before realizing I was on the couch and not in my bed, was of Roscoe.

He loved me, my brain thought in wonder, dumbfounded but not displeased.

My heart answered, *You stupid, wonderful, brilliant fool. You loved him, too.*

That, ladies and gentlemen, was the reason I'd cried in the car.

Slowly, I became aware that I was on the couch, still in my black skirt, leggings, and black shirt from the day before. My shoes were still on. Glancing at my watch, I realized I'd overslept, and I panicked. Frantically reaching in my bag, I pulled out the tracking screen just as Roscoe's truck left the Winston house. I rushed through a quick bathroom visit and was once more on the road.

Also, of note, my hair was a disaster. I mean, I can't even with the succubus on top of my head right now.

But back to Cheetah Roscoe, the medium-ish room, and my superior singing.

Let the record show, I was not singing at the top of my lungs.

Oh no.

I was singing his most hated song a la opera style. I'd already done a Beyoncé rendition, Adele, Gloria Estefan, James Brown, Weird Al, and Cake. After opera, I would move on to Kanye—which required a mirror if I was going to do it right—Alicia Keys, Broadway, Britney Spears, Snoop Dogg, Sammy Davis Jr. or Frank Sinatra—depending on my mood—and then, my personal favorite, Elvis.

Old, gross Las Vegas Elvis, not alarmingly attractive young Elvis. Young Elvis smiled too much and moved his hips in ways I wasn't sure I could imitate without sustaining a back injury.

I'd just finished my operatic rendition and was searching for a mirror in the metal desk—if you're going to Kanye, you *must* commit—when Roscoe snarled, "Are you finished?"

"I'm looking for a mirror."

A noise emerged from him, deep like a growl, but short like a grunt.

"Not the Kanye."

"Yes, the Kanye."

Another growl, longer this time, as fingers pulled through his thick, black hair. More pacing.

Watching him prowl, I set my hand on my hip. "If you would talk to me, I wouldn't have to serenade you."

"You don't want me to talk to you." Roscoe glared at me through slitted eyes.

"Why not?"

"Because I'm so angry right now, I'm liable to start yelling."

I shrugged. "Then yell."

"Are you fucking crazy?" he exploded, finally. "What the hell is wrong with you, demanding that they bring you, too?" He pointed at the door. "These are bad guys, Simone. Dangerous, evil, fucking nightmare, dumpster fire, human garbage assholes."

I bit back a smile and the urge to say, *Tell me how you really feel,* or, *So. . . take them off the Christmas card list?*

Instead, I hazarded three steps toward him. "That is exactly why I came. Strength in numbers."

Plus, as I'd suspected would happen, no one had thought to frisk me. They'd frisked Roscoe, but not me. Therefore, I still had my gun.

Roscoe scoffed, shaking his head and kicking the embroidered footstool, sending it flying across the room to the far wall.

"Kicking isn't talking."

Although . . . I could see how it might be gratifying to kick random furniture.

"Fine. You want me to talk?" Roscoe wasn't yelling anymore, but the quality of his voice made it obvious none of his fury had dissipated. He was simply doing a better job of controlling his temper.

As I reflected on it, I'd never seen Roscoe lose his temper. Therefore, the last half hour had been a revelation. When we were younger, he'd always stomped off to be alone whenever he was mad, sulking and sullen. He couldn't do that now.

"Tell me why you've been following me," he demanded, his blue eyes heated, his posture and the angle of his head giving the impression of a cat ready to pounce.

He looked quite intimidating, but I didn't believe he had any intention of frightening me. Rather, Roscoe was clearly at his wit's end and incredibly angry. Nor was I intimidated by his demanding tone or loss of temper. I found it was easy to take both in stride.

Maybe because you've loved him.

Not a hunch, not a hypothesis, not a theory.

A law.

I'd *loved* him.

But what I'd told Roscoe on the dance floor last night was also true. I'd been too young, too immature to deal with feelings that big. I hadn't been ready at sixteen, or eighteen, or even twenty-two. There existed the possibility I still wasn't ready now.

I mean, loving someone is a big fucking responsibility. How could I love someone if I couldn't even decide between Chinese or Thai food when ordering takeout?

I loved my family. I loved myself. I loved my neighbor—especially my Nancy—but the nature, requirements, and demands of those relationships were different than what he'd wanted from me. Could I love, really, truly love someone as remarkable as Roscoe, and all his soulfulness, how he deserved? Was I ready? Was I capable?

And did I want to?

As an aside, assuming I couldn't figure this out on my own, I made a note to ask my mother if my qualms were normal—a la, was it normal to worry whether one is capable of loving another person how they deserved? If anyone could shed light on the situation, help me dissect it, and reach a satisfactory conclusion, it would be her.

I must've taken too long to answer, because Roscoe made another frustrated growl, asking again, "Why have you been following me? The real reason this time."

I shrugged, trying to look bored. "Where I go and what I do is none of your business."

Roscoe's features darkened. He wasn't having my answer.

In the next moment, he strolled forward with determined, menacingly slow steps. He didn't stop even as he entered my personal space, forcing me to shuffle backward until my back was against a wall, literally.

Lowering his voice to a whisper, he glared down at me. "You knew the Wraiths were going to pick me up. How did you know?"

"I overhear things at the diner," I whispered in return, impressed with the reasonable sounding half-truth, and definitely not noticing again how tall he was.

Have I mentioned that Roscoe was tall? Because he was really tall. Also, even angry, his eyes were still soulful. *How does he do that?*

"What did you overhear?"

I glanced at the ceiling. "I heard one of the Wraiths talking about how Darrell wanted to speak to you."

"Why didn't you tell me? Warn me?"

Shaking my head, I moved my attention to his neck while I searched for a reasonable sounding lie. "I couldn't be sure."

I felt his eyes on me, assessing. "You're lying."

Lifting my gaze to his, I feigned impatience. "About what?"

"I don't know." He shifted back a step, scrutinizing me. "Why are you lying?"

"Maybe I don't trust you."

That gave him pause, his stare growing hazy. "You don't trust me?"

Twisting my lips to the side, I stalled, studying him for several seconds before admitting, "I do trust you, but I'm angry that you don't trust me."

He made a face of confusion. "What are you talking about?"

"You wouldn't let me come, here, to keep you safe."

The confusion became vexation and he regained the step he'd ceded. "What is wrong with you? Me not wanting you here has *nothing to do* with not trusting you, and *everything to do* with wanting—no, *needing* you to be safe. I can't—"

Roscoe turned, shaking his head and grabbing fistfuls of his hair as he paced away. I thought I heard him mutter, "Unbelievable."

I followed him. "Okay, so maybe you trust me. But clearly you underestimate me."

He shook his head faster, his glare darting to the door and then to me. "Simone, this is not one of our adventures from when we were kids. This is not finding Blithe Tanner's cat. These men are *murderers*, drug dealers, thieves."

"I know." Boy oh boy, did I know. I didn't want to be here anymore than he did. I was frightened. Yet allowing Roscoe to be taken on his own hadn't been an option. "I can handle myself, and I can provide backup for you, if you need it."

Roscoe gripped my shoulders. "Nothing can happen to you, do you understand?" His words were emphatic, his gaze disoriented, desolate, frantic. "If anything happens to you, I'll . . ." He swallowed, apparently unable to finish the sentence.

My heart twisted to see him like this. I wished there were some way to show him what I could do, what I was capable of, so he would stop seeing me as a liability.

Well, why can't you?

"Huh."

Now there was a thought.

Stepping out of his grip, I walked backward to the other side of the room and took a deep breath. "Okay. Come at me."

He blinked. "What?"

"I want you to come at me."

"Simone," he seethed.

"Come at me, bro." I did that little movement with my fingers, my palm turned upwards. "Come at me or I'll start singing again."

"I'm not doing this."

"Fine." *Frustrating.* "I'll come at you."

He stood there, features set, looking raw.

Moving quickly forward, staying light on my feet, I faked right and then went left, hooking him behind the back of his leg, catching his arm to twist behind his back, and sending him to the ground— face-first—with a thud.

I winced as he grunted, my knee at the base of his spine, his arm restrained behind his back. "Sorry! But you wouldn't listen to me." Leaning forward, I whispered in his ear, "Are you okay? Did I hurt you?"

Roscoe's back and shoulders rose and fell with an expansive breath, like he was about to respond, but in the next moment he'd spun his legs to the right, leveraged my knee on his back to throw me off-balance, and slipped his wrist from my hold.

In my defense, my grip had been lax as I was purposefully trying *not* to injure him.

The next thing I knew, Roscoe had me pinned to the ground, air knocked out of me, him hovering above, and my gun digging into my ribs beneath my shirt. He'd been careful to subdue my legs, likely so he wouldn't end up with a bruised ballsack.

His stare more probing than angry—which I took as a good sign —he said, "I didn't teach you that. Where'd you learn that?"

Even though I was still coughing, I smiled and rasped, "Since college, take judo."

He nodded faintly, his eyes moving between mine, looking concerned. "Are you okay? Did I hurt you?"

"No." Endeavoring to catch my breath, I said, "I took it easy on you because I didn't want to hurt you either, but I'm an asset, not a liability."

"You're definitely an asset." Roscoe frowned, his gaze dropping to my mouth. "And a distraction," he said, his voice rough.

"I'm a distraction?" I asked, my words still breathy.

I bucked, but he held me fast.

"Yes. . ." His stare turned inward. "You are most definitely a distraction."

Even though I'd had plenty of time to recover and we'd been holding still for close to a minute, I was still breathing hard. This might have been because of my lingering irritation. Or, maybe it was because the length of Roscoe's lean body was lying on mine. He held my hands on either side of my head, our faces even, his mouth just inches away.

Was it insane that I hoped he kissed me?

Yes?

No?

Let's go with no.

He gave me his eyes again and I saw something there, a battle. He looked undecided, at war with himself, straining against something I couldn't see.

"Roscoe?" I whispered.

Roscoe closed his eyes, and I thought he was going to let me go, but in the next second his lips descended, capturing my mouth in a tender kiss.

I moaned.

I kissed him back.

That's what one does when Roscoe Winston kisses one. Moan and kiss. Repeat. Because not doing so would be a travesty.

His hold on my hands slacked, his fingers seeking and threading with mine. He settled his hips between my legs, his form relaxing. The weight of him was different now, warmer somehow. At least I felt warm. I also felt cherished as his tongue sought mine, again tenderly, stroking, causing my abdomen to twist and tighten into delicious knots.

He broke the kiss and a protest died on my lips as his mouth trailed down my jaw to the sensitive skin of my neck, sucking, licking, savoring me. What had felt warm and cherishing heated, and my hips tilted reflexively as he nibbled on my ear, cradling his rapidly growing erection.

We both gasped as his hips rocked in an answering yet inelegant movement. It felt perfect and essential in the moment.

"Oh God." His hot breath spilled against my jaw, a ragged sigh. "What are we doing?"

"I don't know, but don't stop."

I tilted my hips again because I needed to, because I needed him hard for me. I needed his heat and touch and taste. My body demanded it, a rising frenzy that felt like silk and sandpaper beneath my skin. I craved, yearned, wanted him, the feel of him, in a way I'd never experienced with anyone else.

I didn't know what this was, but it was all-consuming, a special kind of madness, an abandonment of logic and reason, a possession of my mind by my body.

His mouth continued devouring the ticklish places on my neck as his hips rocked again, a rhythmic rubbing this time, up and down, up and down, and I moaned in response because it felt so right, he felt so good, and I wanted . . . I wanted . . .

"Please." My breath hitched, and I tugged against where he held my hands captive, needing the movements of his body beneath my palms and fingers, his bare skin.

That's when I heard a noise like distant approaching footsteps. At first I considered ignoring the sound. I'd noticed footsteps approach and walk past the door twice since we'd been locked in this room. So why would I stop this epically awesome moment if I didn't have to?

But then I stiffened, straining my ears. The approaching footsteps hadn't walked past. Roscoe must've sensed a change in me, because he abruptly ceased loving my neck and moving his body, lifting just his head to peer at me.

"Are you okay? Did I do something—"

"There's someone outside the door," I mouthed, knowing the wideness of my eyes would communicate my alarm.

The sound of the first lock turning was like a cannon blast. Roscoe flinched, immediately pushing up and off of me, standing lightening fast. He reached a hand down to help me, but I was already on my feet.

He stood in front of me just as the second lock turned, his hand on my thigh as though to keep me in place. I didn't fight him on this for a few reasons, but mostly because the element of surprise was my favorite, even if it wasn't on the periodic table.

My second favorite was potassium, mostly because of its freak show reaction to water.

But I digress.

The handle turned, the door opened, and Isaac Sylvester was revealed. He stepped to the right, toward the folding chairs. I exhaled

a relieved breath, hopeful he was here to give us a heads-up about
what to expect, or help us escape, or—

Or, maybe not.

Darrell Winston appeared in the doorway, and I frowned at the
sight of him, confounded. I'd only heard one set of steps. At least, I
thought I'd only heard one set, but now I couldn't be sure. Having a
Roscoe Winston on oneself—kissing and loving and doing delicious
things—made a difference in attention to details.

Strolling through the door, a pleased-looking smirk on his face,
Darrell seemed to be holding Roscoe's gaze.

"Son," he said, a smile in his voice, a *knowing* smile.

That gave me pause. How could Darrell have known what we
were doing? The first thing I'd done upon entering the room was
check for cameras and microphones. There were none that I
could find.

My attention shifted to the doorway. A Wraith I didn't recognize
stood with his arms crossed, staring forward, looking aggressive. . .
ly constipated. When the man continued to just stand there, Isaac
moved around the room, setting up the folding chairs.

"What do you want?" Roscoe asked, getting to the point.

I placed my hands on his waist and tucked myself more fully to
the length of him, silently communicating that I had his back. His
hand on my thigh gave a small squeeze.

"To chat. Sit." Darrell gestured to one of the folding chairs Isaac
had just placed near where the footstool had been (before Roscoe
kicked it).

"We can listen just fine from here." Roscoe's tone was flat, indo-
lent, and he shifted his weight, bracing his feet apart like he planned
to remain standing. This was a smart move. We were more vulnerable if we sat, and it would be easier to divide us. Whereas standing
together like we were, our—defensive and offensive—position was
much better.

Darrell did a thing with his mouth, a half-smile, half-considering
pursing of his lips that reminded me of Billy Winston and the way
he'd look at his brothers. Actually, everything about Darrell's expres-

sion in that moment, everything about him other than his clothes, looked so much like Billy. I stared in astonishment. He could have been the second oldest Winston's brother rather than his father.

"Fine. Stand," Darrell finally said, taking a seat for himself. He turned just slightly over his shoulder, giving Isaac and the constipated Wraith his profile. "Leave us," he ordered.

They did. Not ten seconds later, Roscoe and I were left alone with Winston. I couldn't believe it. The bureau had been trying to get their hands on this guy for over two years, and here he was. With me.

I needed to make the most of this. But I had to do so without arousing suspicion from Roscoe or his father.

Presently, the two men seemed to be sizing each other up. I couldn't see Roscoe's expression, but I imagined his was more of a glare than a stare. Meanwhile, Winston's was a cross between calculating and hopeful.

"What do you want?" Roscoe was the one to break the silence, his words exasperated.

Winston considered his son for another few seconds, then asked softly, "How have you been?"

Roscoe shook his head. "Nope. We're not doing this."

"Doing what?"

"Pretending to play catch-up, pretending like you care two shits about me." More exasperation, but also some antagonism, too.

"Now Roscoe—"

"What do you want?" It sounded like Roscoe had said these words through clenched teeth, a little louder, a whole lot angrier.

Now, I decided, was as good a time as any for me to intervene.

So, on a hunch, I peeked further around Roscoe's shoulder and asked quietly, "How are you, Mr. Winston?"

His gaze flickered to mine, and the persistent, charming grin he'd been wearing since entering waned. His gaze sobered. He swallowed.

"You always were perceptive, Miss Simone." The smile he wore now looked weary. "Smart girl."

I didn't cringe at the *Miss Simone,* even though I'd always hated it growing up. Though, I imagined, I would've hated anything Mr. Winston called me. He was a bad man, and I didn't need to be smart or perceptive to know that. All I had to do was look at the bruises on Bethany Winston's face.

The older man sighed, his eyes lowering to where one of his legs was bent at the knee and crossed over the other. "The truth is, Miss Simone, I'm dying."

Winston held my gaze for a long moment. He glanced up at his son. He waited.

Dying?

Roscoe's breathing changed, came faster. He was struggling with this news.

"What?" he finally asked, the single word clipped, impatient. "What do you mean you're dying? What are you—"

"I have cancer. Cancer in my blood."

Roscoe straightened, then seemed to rock back just slightly on his heels, as though he were absorbing this news.

Winston inhaled a large breath, uncrossed his legs, and leaned his elbows on his knees. His hands were folded together in a way that reminded me of how religious folks prayed.

"It runs in the family, on my side, in case you didn't know. My daddy died from it real young. I need your help," he said, his voice raw. "Son, if you don't help me, I'm going to die."

CHAPTER FIFTEEN

❈ ❈ ❈

"You can accept or reject the way you are treated by other people, but until you heal the wounds of your past, you will continue to bleed."

— IYANLA VANZANT, YESTERDAY, I CRIED

Simone

ROSCOE DIDN'T SPEAK. He didn't move. I knew him well enough to know he was overwhelmed, couldn't speak, couldn't move.

The older man leaned back in his chair, watching Roscoe intently. He fidgeted, scratching his jaw, his arm, twisting his fingers, his eyes growing dark, hooded with what looked like misgiving. The longer Roscoe said nothing, the more sour and impatient Darrell's mood turned.

"Did you hear me?" Winston stood, his shouted question tight, laden with emotion. "I'm dying and you have nothing to say?"

My quick assessment of the situation was as follows: Roscoe was in shock, overwhelmed, unable to answer. Winston wouldn't care or understand this about his son. But based on the wild look in the older man's eyes, if someone didn't show some empathy or interest—and soon—the situation was likely to get ugly.

"He's in shock, Mr. Winston." I stepped around Roscoe with the intent of standing between the two men. Roscoe caught my hand, preventing me from moving forward.

Winston shifted his glare from me to Roscoe and must've seen the truth in my words because his features relaxed.

He breathed out. "Yes, I see. Of course he is." To me he gave a tight smile. "Worried about his daddy."

Yeah, no. Not so much.

"How long do you have?" I asked, lacing my fingers with Roscoe's and giving them a squeeze.

"If I don't get a marrow transplant, not long. A year, maybe two." Winston's gaze slid back to Roscoe's. "And that's why I needed to speak with you, son."

I glanced at Roscoe. He looked pained, as though he were suffering from persistent heartburn.

"You want him to get tested?" I guessed. "See if he's HLA compatible?"

"HLA?" Winston looked confused.

"See if his marrow can help you?" I simplified.

"Oh no, he don't need to be tested. Doctor told me he's already been tested, all the kids were, by some miracle. Roscoe here is a match. Him and Billy both are. But ain't no way Billy gonna help." Roscoe's father shrugged, giving me a look as though to commiserate. "That one would dig my grave sooner than lift a finger to help me."

There was no arguing with that. Billy Winston would not just dig his father's grave, he'd push the man into it with relish (and I don't mean the pickled kind).

I leaned closer to Roscoe and held his hand with both of my own. "If or when Roscoe helps, how and where? Because if you're asking him to go to some shady backroom doctor, then that's not going to work. The procedure is incredibly dangerous as it is."

Roscoe released an odd-sounding breath, like he couldn't believe I'd asked the question. I ignored him. Even though we'd been making out hot and heavy on the floor moments prior, and I wanted to be making out hot and heavy with him *elsewhere* ASAP, I still had a job to do.

This situation had landed in my lap, and I was going to make the most of it.

"No, no. No backroom doctor. I got a real good doctor, a team who does work in blood cancers and they think mine is interesting. They're ready to help at a big-name hospital in Texas. MD Anderson or something like that."

"I don't mean to be a Debbie Downer here"—I tried to keep my tone gentle, not wanting to aggravate an already tense situation—"but how are you going to get treatment without attracting the attention of law enforcement? No offense meant, but won't you be arrested? And Roscoe will be arrested for aiding you."

He sighed, seemed to ponder my question, or maybe how best to answer. After a time, he glanced behind him to the door and took a half step forward, leaning in close.

"I have a plan for that." His voice was barely over a whisper.

"How to evade law enforcement?" I whispered in return.

He shook his head. "No. I have- I have it worked out. I'll be turning myself in."

"Bullshit." Roscoe finally spoke. "You would never do that."

"I would, if you help me."

"That's a lie." Roscoe shook his head firmly. "You wouldn't."

"I would if I knew I wouldn't be locked up for long and if I had a plan to get out," he said defensively, his eyes narrowing.

"Your plan is to escape?" I asked, trying to parse through the tangle of his words. "After the treatment? When you're well again?"

"There's other ways to get a get-out-of-jail-free card that don't include escaping, Miss Simone."

Other ways to get a get-out-of-jail-free card . . . Escape he'd already dismissed. A not guilty verdict wasn't going to happen; Darrell had jumped parole; there'd be no trial or verdict.

Which left what? A pardon? A deal?

A hunch, a strong one, had me studying Winston anew.

Winston's eyes grew shifty as I examined him, insomuch as they likely ever grew shifty, and he scratched his neck, glancing behind him at the door again. I grappled with what I was seeing. Darrell Winston nervous? Afraid? Since when?

Based on our intel and my own understanding of the Iron Wraiths dynamics, the only person that Winston had ever shown any deference to or fear of was Razor Dennings, president of the Iron Wraiths. That was because Razor was one seriously bad dude. It was also because Razor controlled his cash flow and ultimately decided Winston's fate within the organization, just as he decided everyone's fate.

The title president was a misnomer. Despot would have been more fitting.

A deal.

He wanted to make a deal.

"Who else knows you're sick?" I asked, trying to sound sympathetic and not ecstatic. My guess was that no one here knew, and that was why he wanted to talk to us alone.

Winston's eyebrows pulled together, and his gaze moved over me, confusion and a hint of suspicion—just the barest hint—turning his blue eyes hazy. "Why do you want to know?"

"I just meant"—I rushed to add, thinking on my feet, and lying my heart out—"if you're sick, do you have anyone to look after you? Who is helping you through this difficult time?"

I felt Roscoe's gaze on my profile and my neck heat. Roscoe would know I was lying, because he knew me so well and because I wasn't a great liar. I just hoped Winston wasn't as perceptive as his son.

Roscoe's father shook his head, still looking a touch confused and doubtful of my intentions. "No one needs to know except my doctors in Texas and Roscoe here."

"You're afraid of looking weak in front of your brothers," Roscoe muttered, drawing the older man's attention away from me.

"That's how it works here. If they smell blood in the water, it's over for you."

I tried not to grimace at Roscoe's words, because even to me they sounded like a threat. Which, given the fact that we were trapped in this room with no windows and no shoes, wasn't a great way to endear us to our captor.

Confirming my worry, Darrell Winston straightened to his full height—FYI, not as tall as Roscoe—his eyes flashing. "Is that a threat?"

Roscoe smirked. "No, sir. Merely an explanation for the lady. She's not been touched by the filth of this place, doesn't know how your stupid shit works."

I felt certain at once that Roscoe was purposefully trying to draw attention away from me and my poorly timed question. Even so, I was glad I'd asked it.

Darrell made like he was going to push Roscoe and I held out a staying hand, pressing it against his chest. "Hey, stop. Stop. Roscoe is going to help you, remember?"

Roscoe made a scoffing sound. "Yeah. That's why we're here. To help."

"You are helping your daddy," Winston said firmly, looking torn between wanting to punch Roscoe's lights out and hope that he actually would help.

Roscoe didn't say anything at first, glaring at his father and looking torn as well. I couldn't speak for him, or distract Winston with more questions. Roscoe had to answer for himself.

Oh please oh please oh please, just tell him what he wants to hear so we can leave.

At length, Roscoe released a bitter sounding laugh, shaking his head, then his gaze shifted beyond Darrell to the door behind him.

"I honestly don't know," he said, his voice rough with emotion.

I tensed, bracing myself for a tirade from his father.

It didn't come.

Winston nodded, his eyes glassy as they moved over his son's features. "I suppose I can understand you need some time. I wasn't

—" He stopped himself here, his voice breaking. He inhaled a shaky breath, as though needing to steady himself. "I wasn't there for you like I wanted to be. Your momma kept us apart, and—whatever you decide—I want you to know that missing out on watching you grow up has always been my biggest regret."

Wow.

I mean, holy freaking wow. I almost clapped, that's how good of a performance Darrell was giving. He was laying it on pretty thick, sure. But still, I almost believed him.

Roscoe withdrew his hand from mine and slid it around my waist, pulling me close. "Thank you for telling me that. It means . . ." He paused here, glancing at his shoes, and then back to his father. "It means something." His voice was all quiet solemnity, and I had to work to not gape.

Again, the urge to clap was intense. I didn't think I'd ever get a chance to see a bullshitter bullshitting another bullshitter at this level. The bullshit was strong with this family. We're talking bullshitting Olympics, and they'd both tied for first place.

But then I watched as Winston searched his son's face, and that's when I knew Roscoe had been the one to win the gold. There was no mistaking the hope on the older man's features.

In that moment, I realized something interesting: in a battle between two bullshitters, the one who cares about the outcome will always lose to the one who doesn't care at all.

* * *

LET ME BREAK down this awkward situation for you.

Roscoe and I were escorted out of the Wraith's compound and returned to our cars by: a) Isaac Sylvester, who was working under-cover, acting like an asshole, and technically Roscoe's brother-in-law through Jennifer Sylvester's marriage to Cletus Winston, and b) Curtis Hickson, an actual asshole who'd taken my sister away from her family when she was in high school and broke my parents' hearts (and my heart, too).

Green Valley was entirely too small.

Nothing was said while we were escorted or chauffeured until the tail end of the journey, when Isaac pulled next to Roscoe's truck and placed the SUV in park.

I opened my door, ready to get as far away as possible from the pretend asshole and the actual asshole. I didn't know how Isaac had managed it, day in and day out for years. The man deserved a medal when all this was over, maybe even a bullshitter gold medal.

Roscoe placed his hand on the door handle, but didn't open it, instead saying to Isaac's reflection in the rearview mirror, "Your sister misses you."

I glanced between Roscoe and Isaac, both men so incredibly honorable, but one having to hide it so completely. I wondered if Isaac missed his sister, if he ever thought about her, if he wished things were different, and swallowed around a sudden thickness in my throat.

"I don't have a sister," he finally said, his voice emotionless. "Now get out."

Sigh.

Roscoe shook his head and exited the vehicle, walking around to my side and shutting the door as soon as I'd cleared the SUV.

Isaac backed out of the gravel space and drove away down the dirt road. As I watched him go I knew—without a shadow of a doubt —undercover work would never be for me. Lying to people, pretending to be something I wasn't, it felt impossible.

"We all got tested five years ago," Roscoe said, pulling me out of my contemplations.

"Pardon?"

He gave me his eyes for a split second before dropping them to the gravel at our feet. "Darrell had another son. He lived in Texas. Cletus found out after he'd already died."

I had a hunch, but I asked anyway, "How did he die?"

"Cancer." Roscoe shook his head, huffing a humorless laugh. "Probably the same type of cancer Darrell has."

I closed my eyes, absorbing this information. If they'd known about their brother, if Winston had told them, they might've been able to save him.

"I'm sorry." Opening my eyes, I studied this man next to me, still staring at the ground. He was beautiful, in so many ways, and the pain he felt for a brother he didn't know endeared him to me even more.

Endear? Is that what we're calling it?

"Oh yes, I *esteem* him greatly," I muttered to myself, feeling ashamed for ogling his beautiful soul and face and brain and body and person while he was obviously going through a difficult time.

Determined to give him support, I placed a hand on his shoulder. He grew still.

I slid my hand from his shoulder to his fingers and squeezed; we'd squeezed each other quite a lot today. He exhaled.

"Roscoe, if you need—"

"You can't tell anyone about what happened," he said, shaking his head.

"Uh . . . what?"

He gave me his eyes; stubborn determination shone back at me. "I don't want anyone to know about Darrell. My family has been through enough."

"You're not going to tell them?"

"Nope."

Incredulous, I asked, "You're going to give him your bone marrow and not tell them?"

Now his expression turned hard. "What makes you think I'd give that man anything?"

"I- I don't understand."

He turned to face me, withdrawing from my grip and placing his hands on my shoulders. "Promise me you won't tell anyone. Promise."

My mouth opened, closed, then opened again, because I was struggling to give him an answer that wasn't a lie—I couldn't lie—but also wouldn't piss him off.

"I'm sorry, I can't make that promise."

Roscoe's eyes narrowed. "Simone."

"No." I shook his hands off, taking a step away. "No, I can't promise that. What if he takes you again? You want me to, what? Not tell your family what happened?"

"That's something different. I'm not in any immediate danger."

My jaw dropped. "Are you joking?"

"He won't—"

"Yes. He will. He most certainly will. He'll come for you again. That man is desperate and he believes you are his only chance at survival."

"Then it would be a dumb move to hurt me."

Oh for fuck's sake!

Stubborn, stupid man.

"Roscoe." I found I needed to take a breath, to calm down, because my blood pressure had just launched itself into the atmosphere. "Take a minute to think about what just happened. Fact, Darrell believes he is going to die if you don't give him your bone marrow. Also fact, a desperate Darrell Winston is a dangerous Darrell Winston. He is not above abducting you and sucking those cells out of you, one way or the other."

He shook his head. "All I have to do is tell Catfish, or Drill, or one of the other guys that Darrell is sick, that he's dying. Like I said, a hint of blood and they'll swarm."

I licked my lips, my heart racing, because I could not let Roscoe do that. If Roscoe did that, then Winston wouldn't turn himself in, he wouldn't ask for a deal. My Simone-senses told me Darrell Winston knew something big, something that would help us break this case, stop the murders, maybe take down the entire organization.

And then Isaac could see his sister. And Nelson would be free of the G-Spot. And I could stop lying to everyone. But most importantly, justice would be served.

"Don't do that. Don't tell Catfish or Drill anything. Don't."

"Why not?" he demanded, his words dripping with aggravation. "Let his precious Wraiths take him down. It's what he deserves."

"Promise me you'll wait."

Gritting his teeth, Roscoe shook his head. "Like you'll promise not to tell my family what just happened?"

Shit.

Shit shit shit shit shitter shiticker shite shoot shat shit.

Shit.

"Fine." I crossed my arms, lifting my chin. "You promise not to tell anyone about your father being sick, I'll promise not to tell your family what just happened."

He also crossed his arms. "And no one in your family either. Or anyone who might tell my family."

"Deal."

I stuck out my hand.

He shook it.

He dropped it.

He turned and stomped away.

I frowned at his back. "Where are you going?"

"To Nashville." He opened the door to his truck. "I have work tomorrow. Early."

"Well, okay then," I shouted at his back.

"Don't follow me," he growled in response.

I snorted. "I won't."

I won't need to. Bwahaha—

"I hope you aren't too attached to that tracker you put on my truck"—he turned, his eyes flashing blue lightening, his words catching me completely off guard—"Because when I find it, I'm going to feed it to a black bear."

CHAPTER SIXTEEN

"There was a long hard time when I kept far from me the remembrance of what I had thrown away when I was quite ignorant of its worth."

— CHARLES DICKENS, GREAT EXPECTATIONS

Simone

"YOU HAVE TO go to Nashville."

I stared at Nelson, saying nothing. Lundqvist was giving me a sympathetic look. I suspected I'd bought his sympathy with doughnuts.

Nelson's glare moved over me and she grunted; it was an impatient, unhappy sound. "Payton, time is running out."

"I know."

She met my stare with one of her own, clearly waiting for me to continue speaking. When I continued my silence instead, Nelson stood and paced the length of the small kitchen, her movements restless. "Okay, so, let me break this down. The Kentucky Derby is next weekend. According to your contact in the Wraiths, Razor Dennings will be there, reasons unknown."

"Right."

"Lundqvist's intel from the Black Demons and my information from the G-Spot point to Razor Dennings as the perp. All the local clubs believe he's the one behind the murders. We have circumstantial evidence, but no smoking gun."

Or knife. Razor carried knives, all the dead bodies we'd found had been stabbed to death, but we'd found no murder weapons.

"Three weeks ago, you believed Winston wanted to make a deal, that he has information about—as you said—'something big' and seemed nervous during your meeting. He's looking for a trade, an exchange for cancer treatment."

"And a get-out-of-jail-free card," I added, the reminder a warning.

She waved my comment away. "He gives us definitive evidence on Razor, he's got his ticket out."

"Right." I tried not to grimace.

"But Winston needs his son's—Roscoe's—bone marrow."

My heart twisted. "Right."

"And you haven't made contact with Roscoe in three weeks. Which—and I don't think I'm making a huge leap here—is probably why Winston hasn't approached us about a deal."

I sighed, resting my elbow on the kitchen table and rubbing my forehead, combating a whole lot of feelings. Roscoe hadn't found my tracker yet, so I was still monitoring his movements. Over the last several weeks, he followed a similar schedule to the first week I'd watched him, but with one big exception. He'd remained in Nashville Thursday night through Sunday instead of coming home to Green Valley.

Initially, I'd been relieved by his absence. Nashville, though not far in the scheme of things, was likely too far for Darrell Winston to arrange another abduction, especially if Darrell was trying to keep a low profile within the Wraiths.

But then, after one week became two—BAM! Feelings.

Always with the feelings.

This time it was longing. I missed him. I'd started missing him the day after he left, but I'd been able to reason through the foreign musings. Heck, I'd gone years without thinking about Roscoe, why should I think about him now?

So what if we'd kissed? (twice, on two separate occasions)

So what if we'd made out? (on the floor of a cell in the basement of the Dragon Biker Bar)

So what if it had been fan-fracking-tastic? (so much so, that—in retrospect—being abducted by the Iron Wraiths ranked among my top ten best dating/romantic experiences . . . who am I kidding, it was number two, right after dancing with Roscoe in Genie's bar and right above kissing him at Hawk's Field)

Three weeks later, I was missing him, thinking about him, *wishing* for him constantly. I found myself daydreaming, his smile, the cadence of his voice, how he looked at me, his body over mine, our hands woven together, how he'd devoured my neck, the deep growling groans he made, his tender—and not so tender—kisses.

Time and distance, which I'd hoped would clear my head, had only accomplished the opposite.

"Agent Payton."

I glanced at Nelson.

Her eyes were wide, her eyebrows suspended on her forehead. "You need to go to Nashville."

The rest of her instructions were implied: you need to go to Nashville and convince Roscoe to give Darrell Winston his bone marrow, so Darrell will turn himself in before the Kentucky Derby, so we can arrest Razor *at* the Kentucky Derby.

Just the thought of suggesting Roscoe help Darrell made my stomach turn.

My features must've communicated my displeasure, because she rolled her eyes, her palm hitting her thigh. "What? What is it?"

Lundqvist spoke around a huge bite of doughnut. "I've been to Nashville. It is a nice place."

"I'll go," I said, glancing between Lundqvist and Nelson. "Nashville isn't the problem. But Roscoe is. Like I told you weeks ago, he won't give his father a bone marrow donation, and nothing I say or do will convince him."

Nelson crossed her arms. "Then who can convince him? Who will he listen to?"

I shook my head. "His brother Billy—but that's no good. Billy wouldn't help Darrell either. Maybe Ashley."

"The sister," Nelson explained for Lundqvist.

Lundqvist picked up another doughnut, his third. "Yes. I've seen her. She's an efficient and competent nurse."

I gave Lundqvist a double take, because most men commented on Ashley's stunning looks, but then I remembered Roscoe's sister donated her time to a free clinic in Knoxville, which was where most of the Black Demons biker club went for health services.

"Anyone else?" Nelson pushed. "Anyone else he'll listen to?"

My dad.

I shook my head again, huffing in frustration. This conversation was pointless. I couldn't tell Billy or Ashley or even my dad because I'd made a promise to Roscoe.

Nelson considered me, her jaw ticking. "Payton, you're killing me here. You need to do something. Lundqvist and I can do nothing. We have evidence, but nothing concrete and only hearsay as motive. You're going to have to make it happen. Winston doesn't have forever, and neither do we. The Derby is—"

"Next weekend," I finished, rubbing my sternum and glancing behind her to the kitchen wall.

"You'll go tomorrow."

My heart gave a sudden leap in anticipation, and then promptly deflated with dread. Closing my eyes, I nodded. I would go. I would see Roscoe. I'd figure out how to convince him to help Darrell, even if it made me sick to my stomach, because catching bad guys was my job.

I would . . . think of something.

* * *

THERE WERE A few places I avoided whenever I was home in Green Valley. The library was number one on that list, ever since Ms. Julianne MacIntyre—the head librarian—accused me of using one of the library's desktops to look at porn.

I wasn't looking at porn, okay? It was a crime scene photo. A guy had gotten his junk trapped in the muffler of a car, a car I suspected he'd stolen, and I was squinting at the screen in an attempt to verify the license plate. But all she saw was his muscular back, bottom, and thighs. It was like I'd set loose Satan himself in the library.

Anyway, for the record, I suspect she'd been looking for a reason to toss me out ever since we'd entered into a yelling match about whether or not an op-ed was considered news and therefore belonged with the periodicals.

I maintained not. Obviously.

The second place I avoided in my hometown was the Donner Lodge and Bakery, because I loved cake. I could control myself around my mother's doughnuts and pie, but Lord help the poor soul who tried to get between me and a Donner Bakery cake. This was because Jennifer Winston—previously Jennifer Sylvester—made the world's best cakes.

Unfortunately for my strict workout program, I was presently on my way to the Donner Lodge and Bakery.

After a night of internal debate, I decided Jennifer Winston was the best person to enlist in my pursuit of tracking down Roscoe in Nashville. With congress in session, Billy wasn't in town. Jethro wasn't in town either, he and Sienna were off somewhere with their kids while she filmed her latest blockbuster. Also, I didn't know Billy or Jethro all that well, so they were out in any case. Beau and Ashley would ask too many questions, whereas Shelly and Cletus had an uncanny ability to see through a ruse without asking any questions at all.

Therefore, Jennifer Winston was the only choice for what I required and that meant I'd be doing cardio daily for the next two weeks. As much as I hated cardio, and as much as I needed to pass the bureau's PFT, I loved Jennifer's cakes more.

The Donner Lodge and Bakery sat on a gorgeous piece of property overlooking the main valley and the gently sloping mountains beyond. Spring had finally sprung, which meant the rolling greens were a vibrant emerald and the blue haze—which had earned the national park its "smoky" designation—hung over the distant landscape like a delicate, gauzy veil, especially now in the early morning hours.

The chilly morning air smelled like spring rain, pine needles, and freshly cut grass as I stepped out of my car, twisting at my waist to stretch and take in the surroundings. Slashes of sunlight filtered through the trees, abrupt beams dotting the well-maintained parking lot and surrounding flower-lined footpaths. Early birds sang their song overhead, a cacophony of sweet trills and noisy squawks that reminded me of an orchestra warming up before a performance.

Years ago, when I was a kid, the lodge had languished, falling into disrepair. But then Jennifer had been crowned the Banana Cake Queen after winning the state fair blue ribbon for her confectionary concoction at the tender age of fifteen.

Overnight, the Donner Bakery had become a novelty, with Mrs. Diane Donner-Sylvester, Jennifer's mother, capitalizing on her young daughter's success. Soon, the novelty became a sensation and word spread throughout the valley when it was discovered Jenn was by no means a one-cake wonder.

Over the years, she'd won the state fair baking blue ribbon again and again and again, until a few years ago when she'd stopped entering the contest. There was no need. Jennifer's cakes were now infamous, having been featured in national and international magazines and TV shows.

The Donner Lodge was now run by a distant relative of Jennifer's. I'd heard through the grapevine that she had no interest in the day-to-day management. But still, she owned the property outright. And because the bakery was now a destination hot spot in the area, so was the lodge. It had been updated to modern standards some time ago, and the line for the bakery typically ran out the door and around the building.

Which was why I'd arrived so early in the morning.

Word on the street was, Jennifer still made all the cakes—every single one—herself. Locals knew, if you wanted something from the Donner Bakery, you emailed a minimum of two days prior and arrived before posted hours to pick it up. What I'd said I wanted was one of Jennifer's compassion cakes—dark chocolate with dark chocolate coconut meringue frosting—but what I really wanted was a few minutes of Jennifer's time *and* one of Jennifer's compassion cakes.

As I approached the bakery, I hesitated. No lights were on and I perceived no movement. Gingerly, I tested the door and was surprised to find it unlocked. I opened it.

A bell jingled overhead, the only sound in the dim space. It was a Monday, which meant the bakery was only open a half day, and I began to worry that I was too early.

"Simone."

The sound of my name made me jump and I searched the far-left corner of the bakery. A light flipped on, a little one, but enough to illuminate my companion. Jennifer stood at a curved entryway that presumably led to the bakery kitchen. She wore a black baseball hat over her hair, a Smash-Girl superhero apron, and what looked like a T-shirt and jeans beneath. The front of the apron was covered with patches of flour. She also had a little flour dust along her jaw and just under her right eye.

I couldn't see her shoes from where I stood, but my guess was that they were Converse.

"Hey, Jennifer." I gave her a smile. "Am I too early?"

"Not at all. I'm just toasting the coconut for your cake. Come on in here and keep me company." She waved me forward, and I followed her.

The curved entryway did lead to the kitchen. When I closed the door behind me, I took a moment to study the space. A large stainless-steel counter ran along the wall with three industrial sinks. Set in the center of the space were two large butcher block islands. On one of the islands sat a six-quart KitchenAid mixer, a smattering of ingredients, and a chocolate frosted cake, three layers high. The room smelled like cocoa powder, vanilla, and faintly of coconut.

My mouth watered.

"How's your momma? I haven't seen her in an age." Jennifer slipped on an oven mitt as she spoke and turned from me toward one of four large ovens along the side wall. Reaching inside, she pulled out a cookie sheet and jostled it a little, nodding. "Just right," she murmured to herself.

I took a stool on the other side of the island from where most of the mess was spread out, not wanting to get in her way as she set down the cookie sheet, the tasty aroma of toasted coconut now smacking me in the face. She was right, the tray of shaved coconut was a gorgeous golden brown. Just right.

"Mom's fine." I faltered a minute as I watched her, because the proper thing to do here would be to ask after Jennifer's mother in return. Jennifer's mother, Diane Donner-Sylvester (who many folks had nicknamed *The Dragon Lady*) had been missing for years, on the run from the law for the murder of Jennifer's father (profligate and cheating jackass, Kip Sylvester).

Therefore, I didn't ask after her mother.

Instead, I asked, "How are things with you?"

"Oh, right as rain, I suspect," she said distractedly, poking just the tip of her tongue out as she concentrated on pressing the toasted coconut to the chocolate frosted cake.

I watched her, mesmerized by the procedure, knowing I was watching a true master at work. My mouth continued to water, necessitating a quick glance at the front of my shirt to ensure I hadn't drooled.

If that cake lasted the drive to Nashville, it would be a miracle. Of course, I'd need to wait until the grocery store opened so I could buy some milk. Cake without milk is like drunk without disorderly. Where's the fun in that?

"So, why're you here?" she asked, yanking me out of my musings.

"Pardon?"

She lifted her eyes from her work. "Why're you here?"

I sat straighter in my stool, confused by her question. "For cake." *Obviously.*

Jennifer gave me a small smile, one of her sculpted eyebrows lifting just slightly higher than the other as she turned her attention back to the coconut. "I've never received a cake order from you—not once—my entire life. Your daddy? Sometimes. Your momma? Twice a year. Judge Payton, one a month. Even your brother orders when he's in town. So, what're you really doing here?"

"I guess I was in the mood for—"

"Nope." Jennifer peeked at me again, her gaze pointed, sharper than I'd expected as she said flatly, "This is about Roscoe."

CHAPTER SEVENTEEN

"It is strange how we hold on to the pieces of the past while we wait for our futures."

— ALLY CONDIE, MATCHED

Simone

I FLINCHED. **"OH, no.** No, not at all. I- uh- I mean—"

"You want to know why he hasn't been home."

"What?" I croaked.

She smirked. Then, she laughed lightly, shaking her head at me, and sighed. "You want to know what y'alls problem is?"

"Problem?"

"You're trying to bake a cake without preheating the oven."

I glanced at her askance. "I- I don't follow."

She considered me for a moment, still looking amused. "You're a chemist, right? You work in a lab?"

My eyes shifted from side to side. "Yes . . ."

"You're running your electrophoresis backward."

My lips parted in surprise and I blinked at Jennifer, dumbfounded.

I mean, you think you know someone, and then one day out of the blue, they accuse you of running your electrophoresis backward. How the heck did she even know what that meant?

Jennifer, Roscoe, and I were the same age, but she'd lived an extremely sheltered life. Homeschooled from kindergarten to twelfth grade, never allowed playdates or friends, the only time I caught sight of her was during Roscoe's church choir performances in middle school.

My mother had fretted to Bethany Winston—Roscoe's mom—on more than one occasion that she worried for Jennifer. Diane Donner-Sylvester had forced her daughter into child beauty pageants at a very young age, but had stopped once Jenn had shown promise as a baker.

"Huh." I crossed my arms as I studied Jenn, feeling as though I was seeing her for the first time. And here I'd come to her because I thought she was the least likely to figure out my ulterior motives.

As a teenager and young adult, Jennifer used to prance about town in stilettos and those 1950s housedresses. Her clothes were always yellow with her hair dyed to match. However, since getting tangled up with Cletus Winston about five or so years ago, she now dyed her hair all kinds of colors (most recently red) but typically wore jeans and T-shirts.

I assumed her mother had been to blame for her previous fancy outfits, but I'd never questioned Jenn to confirm nor deny this suspicion. This was because I never spoke to her except polite chitchat in passing. I'd just always assumed she and I had very little in common. Truthfully, when I'd heard Cletus and Jennifer were getting married, the union had confused me. The two couldn't be more different.

But something I'd once eavesdropped Cletus saying about his wife, years ago on a Sunday morning at my mother's diner, came back to me.

He'd said, *"Astute woman is astute."* Which was Cletus Winston speak for saying a person is brilliant.

Presently, the side of her mouth curved higher. "Roscoe told Cletus three weeks ago that he'd be staying in Nashville for the remainder of the spring, only coming back the first weekend in June."

I couldn't stop the small sound that emerged from my throat, half alarm, half protest. "First weekend in June? But that's another five weeks from now."

"He appeared to be in a state of severe agitation," she added, turning back to the cake.

My heart hurt.

Another five weeks without seeing Roscoe? *Unacceptable!*

Not to mention, the first weekend in June would be too late, lest I forget the—you know—minor issue of a serial killer on the loose who only claimed victims beginning in June.

She pressed more coconut to the frosted cake, sighing. "And he's only coming back in June because we're all going to Italy once Jess and Duane have their baby. Roscoe'll be coming home so we can all fly out together from Knoxville."

"Roscoe is leaving? In June?" I didn't even try to disguise the crack in my voice. What was the point of hiding anything from her? Clearly, astute woman was astute.

I stared at a spot beyond Jennifer unseeingly and realized my mouth had stopped watering. In fact, I was no longer hungry for anything, not even this decadent, singularity of a cake.

He's avoiding me again.

The realization made my heart hurt anew. Here I was, missing him, *longing* for that asshole, daydreaming about him, and there he was in Nashville, avoiding me.

AGAIN!

"But, if you happen to know anyone going to Nashville . . ." she started, recapturing my attention as she tilted her head to the side, her gaze focused on the coconut. "Our dog, Pavlov, needs his yearly vaccines and a checkup."

Staring at Jennifer Winston, I huffed a small laugh of disbelief, uncertain what to say. I'd come here, looking for information on

Roscoe, with a big master plan on how to pry it out of Jennifer without her realizing I was prying, and then she volunteers everything I need to know plus offers me her dog as an excuse to see him.

Stepping back from her cake, she dusted her hands off on a towel. "There," she said, turning to a shelf and pulling out a white cardstock rectangle. In less than five seconds, she'd turned it into a cake box. In another five, she'd placed the cake inside and sealed it up.

Then and only then, she lifted her gaze to mine. "I used caramel, coconut, chocolate walnut icing—like the stuff used for German chocolate cake—instead of the meringue because it's Roscoe's favorite. I asked your daddy yesterday if you'd mind and he said you liked walnuts."

"You asked my father about whether I liked walnuts," I stated, shaking my head, deciding I'd never be surprised by anything Jennifer Winston did or said ever again.

Clearly, she was exactly like Cletus Winston, just with less facial hair and a sweeter—appearing—disposition.

"That's right." She passed me the box as I stood from the stool, turned and walked to the back door. She opened it. "Come out this way. If there's anyone in the lot out front, I don't want them to know I'm here yet."

I stumbled after her reluctantly, frowning at her back, because she was confusing me. "But won't they see me carrying the box? And what about the cake? Don't I need to pay you?"

"No charge for the cake," she said, standing in the doorway after I walked past her to the back lot. "You're taking my dog to the vet, right? So I'd say we're even. I'll text Cletus and say you're coming by to pick up Pavlov. Oh! And you know your momma sometimes stocks my tarts in the spring. I'm hoping folks will just assume you came by for a box. In any case, I'd be real obliged if that's the story you told should anyone see you leaving and ask."

I gaped at her. "You want me to lie?"

She blinked at me, her eyes wide and innocent (appearing). "I could pack you some tarts, if you like."

I laughed again. "Oh good Lord."

She grinned, stepping forward hurriedly to give me a one-armed hug. "Be gentle with yourself, Simone. These Winston boys can try a saint's patience." Stepping back, her hand lingered on my arm and she tightened her fingers. "Don't give him any more chances than you'd expect him to give you, whether that number is two or ten or a hundred."

Sighing, I glanced at the box in my hands, and then back to her. "Then I guess I'm giving him a hundred and one chances."

Jennifer gave me a look of amused commiseration. "And after he uses all those, it'll be another hundred and one. I feel ya there."

Laughing at that, I shook my head. My goodness, Jennifer Winston was the bomb dot com (to borrow my Aunt Dolly's phrase). Anyone who knew this woman would be crazy to—

Poor Isaac.

A mild pang of sadness seized me and I swallowed it, glancing at the ground to hide the sudden melancholy. I mean, how badly must it suck for him? To have his awesome sister in the same town, to be alienated from her so completely without her ever knowing or understanding why.

And how awful must it be for her? He was her only family, so close and yet so far. It must've been terrible, especially with people like me in town, misunderstanding from a distance and never caring to look closer.

Thank goodness she has the Winstons.

I was just going to have to seek her out more often, perhaps even thrust my friendship upon her, if she'd have me.

Heck, maybe I'd request that she teach me how to bake cakes.

No, no. That's a bad idea. Remember your fitness test.

"Seriously, though. Roscoe is so sweet. Solemn, serious, but a real sweetheart. You're the only girl I've ever seen him with where he wasn't putting on his flirty-face act, so you'll have to forgive us for staring at y'all last month at Genie's. It was such a shock. I hope things work out with you two."

"Yeah, well . . ." *Me too.* "Thanks for the cake."

"Thanks for taking Pavlov to the vet." She winked, waved, and shut the door.

Blowing out a breath, I turned, a ball of lead in my stomach. Actually, it was more like searing hot lead, and I swallowed stiffly as I debated what to do next.

I had cake.

Now, presumably, Cletus would be waiting for me at his and Jenn's house so I could pick up their dog and drive to Nashville. And then . . . what?

I wanted to see Roscoe, I *longed* to see him, but clearly he didn't wish to see me. But, oh well. I had a job to do. Whether he wanted to see me or not was immaterial.

If he doesn't want to see me, then I'll be fine. I was fine before, I'll be fine now. Eventually.

I reasoned, as I rounded the corner of the bakery, that I would just have to focus on the mission. Somehow, I'd ignore all these feelings and figure out a way to stem my nausea whenever I thought about helping Darrell Winston and convince Roscoe to donate his bone marrow to—

I stopped.

I stepped back.

I blinked.

My stomach dropped, as did my jaw.

I blinked again, unable to believe my eyes.

"What the hell?" I muttered, unable to move, because my sister was there—*right there*—standing off the parking lot not fifty feet away, just inside one of the flower-lined footpaths.

She didn't see me, *nah-ah.*

Likely, she was out of her damn mind.

Because Dani was all wrapped up in, and kissing, Curtis Hickson.

* * *

ON THE ROAD to Nashville, after picking up Pavlov—who was

appropriately enough a Central Asian shepherd—I sent my sister a text.

Simone: *I need to speak with you about a MOST URGENT MATTER.*

She responded twenty minutes later, and I pulled to the side of the highway to read her message.

Dani: *Are Mom and Dad okay?*

Simone: *Yes. We are all fine. The real question is: ARE YOU FINE?*

Dani: *Quit shouty capping me. I'm boarding a plane to London, will be hard to reach for a few days. If this isn't an emergency, send me an email sis. *eye-roll emoji**

I gasped at the eye-roll emoji and quickly typed out a new message. A long one. Chock-full of emojis of an equivalent obnoxiousness as the eye-roll emoji. I expressed my outrage, reminding her of the damage she and Curtis had done to my family, reminding her that she was engaged to Billy Winston, and explaining to her that this loser had abducted me—her own sister—less than a month ago, just in case he forgot to mention it.

I also added quite a few *WHAT ARE YOU THINKING* with varying amounts and kinds of punctuation.

But as I typed, my brain caught up with my thumbs, and I stopped.

I closed my eyes. I opened them. I sighed. I turned off my phone and set it to the side. I glanced in my rearview mirror at Pavlov.

"What is she thinking, Pavlov?"

He panted, his tongue hanging out one side of his mouth.

I nodded. "That's exactly right, Pavlov. She's not thinking.

Clearly, she's not thinking at all. In lieu of using Google Maps or a Sherpa, my sister is *feeling*. That's her problem."

Pulling back into traffic, a two-ton weight on my chest, I flipped on the radio and determined to push her and her bad choices from my mind, muttering to myself, "That's her problem, not my problem. She is a grown-ass woman, and I can't make this my problem. I won't. I won't do it."

I would concentrate on driving to Nashville.

Instead, unsurprisingly, I mentally ranted at imaginary versions of my adversaries for four hours.

I mentally fought with my sister about her terrible choices. I mentally fought with Roscoe about his penchant for avoiding me. I mentally fought with myself (i.e. my feelings) for still wanting anything to do with him.

By the time I pulled into the vet clinic where Roscoe worked, I was exhausted. I was tired of fighting. I just wanted everything to get back to normal. My research work was waiting for me in Washington, DC, my apartment, and last but not least, my Tuesday enchiladas with Nancy.

I didn't belong with Roscoe any more than I belonged in the field as an undercover agent. Love wasn't for me. The odds weren't in anyone's favor, least of all mine.

A plan formed, one devoid of feelings. A pragmatic plan, one where I'd walk Roscoe through all the reasons he should save his father's life. I would swallow my bile and try to convince him, assuming he'd listen to me at all. I would do my job, but accept that ultimately it was up to him. I would then leave and I'd stop tracking him, I'd stop seeking him out.

I was officially letting go of Roscoe Winston.

After parking under a giant oak tree, I twisted in my seat and clipped the leash to Pavlov's collar. Threading it around the headrest, I encouraged the big dog to climb into the front seat and exit out the driver's side with me.

Once outside the car—as Cletus had predicted—Pavlov would need a good stretch and pee. He quickly accomplished both, and promptly pulled me toward the door of the vet office. I followed reluctantly, as though I were the one getting my annual shots and checkup instead of him.

Gathering a bracing breath, I opened the clinic door, prepared to encounter a receptionist, or a vet tech, or an admin, or someone other than Roscoe Winston covered in puppies.

I encountered Roscoe Winston covered in puppies.

Stopping dead in my tracks as the door swung shut behind me, a kind of *well, of course he is* despair cinched my heart, because the scene was—bar none—the most adorable thing I'd ever witnessed in my twenty-six years on this earth.

He was in faded greenish-blueish scrubs, his long form lying on the floor, allowing at least twelve happy, fluffy puppies to crawl all over him, wagging their fluffy tails, licking his face and forearms while he laughed and they yipped and growled playfully. His eyes were closed, but he reached for whichever one was the least wiggly and snuggled it to his chest, kissing it on the head, scratching its ears, and nuzzled it with his beard.

Oh for fuck's sake!

I gritted my teeth, demanding my heart not explode with warm, gooey, shock waves of swoony hearts and flowers and stars.

. . . Too late.

It exploded.

I rocked back on my heels as the blast overtook me, closing my eyes at the impact of feeling and strangely biting back tears.

"Can I help you, ma'am?" someone asked, probably that receptionist, or vet tech, or admin for which I'd been prepared.

I shook my head, slowly at first, and then faster, because my chin wobbled.

Why? Why did I feel like crying? Why all these emotions? Why? Why? WHY?

More importantly, why did Roscoe have to be a vet? Why couldn't he be a . . . a . . . a mortician? He wouldn't look quite so stunningly and alluringly gorgeous covered in dead bodies, now would he?

I can't do this.

Wordlessly, I turned and opened the door we'd just entered, shortening Pavlov's leash in order to pull him through.

I'd made it completely out, and Pavlov was reluctantly following me, when I heard Roscoe say, "Simone?"

Sucking in a breath, a new shock wave seized me, urging me faster. I jogged to my car, fumbling with the leash and my keys, determined to slow time and space and leave before Roscoe unbridled himself from the puppy brigade.

Sadly, time and space were not under my control, and a hand caught my arm when I was only three steps from my car, spinning me around.

I turned, lifting my chin, because I was prepared for a fight. I mean, I'd spent one-third of my trip to Nashville arguing with an imaginary Roscoe. I was ready.

"Where did you get this dog?" he demanded, his eyebrows drawn together, his eyes unreadable chaos.

"I borrowed it," I yelled so I wouldn't burst into tears.

"You borrowed Pavlov?"

"Yes?" I answered, unsure why I sounded so unsure.

He looked thoroughly confused. "Why are you here?"

"I wanted to see you," I said without thinking, because it was true.

"Why?" Roscoe shifted closer; he'd said the single word as though he was out of breath.

"Because . . ." Kissing!

Don't say that!!

"Because you're avoiding me—" I held up a finger. "Don't try to deny it."

"I'm not going to deny it. I am avoiding you."

"Why?"

Roscoe swallowed, and he seemed to do so with effort, his eyes darting over my face. As though suddenly deciding something, he slid a hand against my jaw, the other coming to my waist.

He pulled me close.

He kissed me.

Our lips met. Soft, hot, yielding, sudden, urgent, sweet. I moaned, or he did. Whatever. And apparently Roscoe did control space and time, and sound, because everything stopped and faded. There was only him and his lips moving against mine.

I became aware that he'd backed me against my car because he was leaning against me, his teeth nipping at my bottom lip just before he gave it a sensual lick, slipping his tongue into my mouth and stealing my breath.

Stars, flowers, hearts, puppies, fireworks, Roscoe. I was drunk, liquid heat in his arms, his embrace, his strong hands reforming me, twisting my insides until I was sure I would dissolve, an amorphous puddle of *feeling.*

He pulled away—maybe hours, maybe minutes later—breathing hard as his lips came to my neck, kissing me there, his beard tickling me.

I gasped for breath, my mind a fog, trembling in his arms.

That's right, I freaking *trembled.* My body felt like the physical manifestation of aroused and pining Jell-O. Wrap your mind around that! Because I certainly couldn't.

"I missed you," he said, his arms now tighter. "God, I missed you so fucking much."

Blinking against a stinging behind my eyelids—the good kind this time—I snuggled against his chest, felt the heavy and fast beating of his heart against my cheek, and smelled him. He smelled like Roscoe. And dog. And antiseptic.

I didn't care.

Unthinkingly, forgetting all the reasons I was furious with this man, I admitted, "I missed you, too."

He huffed a laugh and it sounded relieved.

"Don't leave," he said, kissing my forehead and then my cheek with more fervent urgency. "Don't go."

I shook my head, ready to say, *I won't.*

But he spoke again, "Let me take you out. Tonight. I know a

233

place, a great restaurant. Stay and let's- let's do this- let's go- let me—"

"Yes." I lifted my chin and pressed a quick kiss to his lips, leaning away just in time to see his mouth part with surprise and his eyes widen with hope.

"Yes?"

I nodded. Another wave of emotion, several I couldn't name because they felt so foreign and new, crashed over me. "Yes."

Happiness that seemed too immense for him to contain brightened his eyes. I couldn't stop my grin.

And Roscoe? Roscoe kissed me again. Again and again, kisses that were 100 percent inappropriate for a veterinary parking lot. It was wonderful. His ravenous mouth and covetous hands gave me the time necessary to place and name these emotions that had seized me, so foreign and new.

Elation.

Euphoria.

Ecstasy.

The three Es.

Forget Google Maps and Sherpas.

Feelings for the win!

I was so screwed, and I couldn't care less.

CHAPTER EIGHTEEN

❤ ❤ ❤

"I don't want to repeat my innocence. I want the pleasure of losing it again."

— F. SCOTT FITZGERALD, THIS SIDE OF
PARADISE

Roscoe

Roscoe: *Pavlov is spending some time in the puppy yard this evening.*

Cletus: *How long?*

Roscoe: *I don't know yet. A few hours.*

Cletus: *Overnight?*

Roscoe: *I don't know.*

S etting my cell on the sink counter, I returned my attention to the collar of my shirt. Catching sight of my image in the mirror, I frowned, wondering for the tenth time if this was what I wanted to wear for my first date with Simone.

Picking out clothes was a problem for me. Since I remembered what I wore on each occasion, I didn't want the clothes to define the event by being the wrong choice—too casual or too fancy, an out-of-date style or color, a previously unseen tear or hole—which was why I was careful about the clothes I bought and my appearance whenever I was in public.

My phone rang, yanking my thoughts away from worries about my light blue shirt and to the screen of my cell.

It was Cletus.

Since he wasn't here to see, I rolled my eyes as I answered. "Hello?"

There was a pause, then a deep breath. "You better not've just rolled your eyes at me."

"What?"

"Roscoe."

"I didn't." I lied, laughing. Man, I loved that he'd never know whether I was telling the truth.

Cletus grunted. "Eye-roll notwithstanding, let me see if I've got this straight. You text your auspicious older brother to inform him that you've abandoned his pride and joy to a cage, and you can't even tell said brother how long said pride and joy canine will be there. For shame."

I rolled my eyes again. "It's not a cage. It's the puppy yard. He has plenty of space and you know he likes playing with the puppies. Hell, whenever you bring him down, you leave him in the puppy yard for as long as possible."

"That's not the point. You don't just drop a person's beloved animal off for an unknown stretch of time and follow up with a text message. How long will he be there?"

The sound of my apartment's front door opening and closing

made my heart jump. I switched the cell from my right hand to my left as I left the bathroom.

When I'd first spotted Simone this afternoon, the first memory that had come to mind had been of us dancing at Genie's, of holding her close, and how her eyes had shone with hurt. I didn't want to hurt her, I never wanted to do that. So, unlike my foolish non-action that night, this time I'd chased her out the door.

Maybe the best decision I've ever made.

"I told you, I don't know." Poking my head out of my bedroom, I caught Simone's eye as she set a shopping bag on the kitchen counter.

My breath caught because she gave me an easy smile, and because she was here and real and gorgeous. Seeing her in the parking lot earlier, and now, after missing her desperately over the last three weeks, I knew it was now or never. I had to try. I had to give this thing between us everything I had. If I didn't, I'd live in a constant limbo of regret and wondering what could have been.

Tonight or never.

I was all in.

"You're telling me you have no idea?" Cletus released a frustrated huff. "Days? Weeks? Can I expect to see Pavlov again before I die?"

I glanced at the ceiling, shaking my head. "You're being ridiculous and you know it."

Movement in my field of vision snagged my attention. Simone was moving closer, a question behind her mesmerizing eyes. Have I mentioned how beautiful her eyes were? Because they were. They were so very *her.* Bright and engaging, belying her devastating intelligence and wit. I loved her eyes.

"You look great," she mouthed. Lifting her chin toward my phone, she whispered, "Who is that?"

"It's Cletus," I said, not bothering to whisper in return. "He's got his panties in a bunch about Pavlov."

"Who's there?" Cletus sounded like he was on high alert. "Is that Simone? Is Simone there? Put her on the phone."

"She doesn't want to talk to you," I grumbled. "We're getting ready to go out."

"Put the lady on the phone," he demanded.

"I'll talk to him." Simone held out her hand, pressing a quick kiss to my lips when I passed her the phone. "All I need is ten minutes and I'll be ready. Go finish up," she whispered soothingly, indicating with her chin toward my room as she brought the cell to her ear. "Heya Cletus."

She stepped back and shuffled unhurriedly to the kitchen counter, leaning a hand against it as my eyes moved over the shape of her. Simone was in jeans and an artfully faded button-down shirt, sleeves rolled up her forearms, sneakers on her feet, a few bracelets on her wrist. I glanced at my slate gray pants and blue suit shirt, deciding I was overdressed.

"Uh-huh," she said, nodding, clearly listening to Cletus's nonsense with admirable patience. She dug inside the bag she'd placed on the counter and nodded at something he'd said. "Right."

"I'm going to go change," I whispered. Her eyes cut to mine and I tossed my thumb over my shoulder. "I'll put on something more casual." I didn't know what I'd been thinking, getting all gussied up.

She frowned, shaking her head and covering the receiver with her fingers. "No. Wear that. I love that color on you."

Hesitating, I glanced at my clothes again, taking in the shine of my shoes. I was definitely overdressed.

After she'd shown up this afternoon and I'd kissed her like I'd been dreaming about for weeks—and years—I'd brought both Simone and Pavlov back into the waiting room. Introductions were made, and I'd done my best to ignore the knowing smiles sent my way by our receptionist, the two veterinary technicians, and my colleague, Dr. Yi, who'd come out of the charting area to see what all the fuss was about.

Once Pavlov's checkup had been complete and he was safely—and happily—tucked away in the puppy yard, Simone had followed me to my apartment in her car. But as soon as we arrived, she told me to go inside and get ready, that she needed to run a few errands first.

I might've grown uneasy at this point, except she'd also asked for a key to my apartment, which I'd handed over. She then tugged on the front of my scrubs, pulling me down to her window for more kisses, and I'd enthusiastically obliged. When I straightened, she handed me a Donner Bakery box, told me it was a cake for later.

Her gaze seemed a little hazy, extremely happy, her eyes on mine with a promise to return.

So I didn't grow uneasy. I trusted that she'd return, especially since she'd left the Donner Bakery cake behind.

I'd showered, trimmed my beard and shaved my neck, applied aftershave and cologne, and dressed.

Now, my momma had always said—when on a date—it was the woman's job to dress like the painting and the man's job to dress like the frame. Our mother had some hokey sayings, some poignant, some out-of-touch and definitely old fashioned, but I could usually find some kernel of truth in all of them.

However, if Simone wanted me to wear what I was wearing, who was I to argue? She'd said I looked great, didn't she? And besides, as far as I was concerned, no one could ever outshine Simone.

I moved my fingers to the buttons of my shirt as she said to Cletus, "At least eighteen, maybe forty-eight, possibly sixty, but I'll bring him over here tomorrow morning."

I stilled, straining my ears, my gaze moving to her profile.

Eighteen, forty-eight, sixty? Was she . . . did she mean hours? Was she planning to stay here with me for days?

Before I could think too much about that, she pulled a length of purple fabric from the bag on the counter. Sluggishly, I realized it was a dress. She then absentmindedly pulled out a few other items and my brain catalogued them before I could comprehend their meaning: toothbrush, underwear, a bra, a satin scarf, lotion, a shoebox, a black lace something.

Holy shit. . .

And

FUCK YEAH.

And

Holy shit.

At that moment, her gaze swung around and connected with mine. Something about my expression had her lifting her eyebrows in confusion. She looked down at the pile of items on the counter and when she lifted her eyes again, they were wide with what seemed to be embarrassed alarm, but also amusement.

"Shoo!" she said, fighting a smile, flicking her wrist and shaking her head at me. "Stop being so nosy and go get dressed."

"Yes, ma'am." I grinned, feeling dichotomously ten feet tall, nervous as hell, and more than happy to do as I was told.

Tonight was the night, and I was all in.

* * *

THERE WERE TWO kinds of dresses: dresses, and *dresses.*

Simone was wearing the latter—a thin-strapped dark purple slip of a thing that left nothing and everything to the imagination—which meant my collar and pants felt too tight, and my neck was hot.

Eighteen, forty-eight, sixty.

She was touching me while letting me touch her. I held her hand on the way to my truck, I held her hand in the truck, I slipped my arm around her waist on the short walk to Rene's Bistro while she tucked herself close to my side. She smelled fantastic, *like night jasmine.*

I struggled for words while I struggled to hold back memories. All the times I'd wanted to be with her like this, on a real date, on the same page, just she and I, but with the obtuse and chaotic force of a teenager carrying around unrequited feelings.

I struggled because I wanted this memory to be perfect, unspoiled by thoughtless or inane conversation. I wanted everything to be meaningful.

"Relax," she said, her arm squeezing my waist as we followed the maitre d'. "It's just me."

"You'll never be *just* anything," I murmured.

Her hand came to my chest as we stopped at our table and she pressed a soft kiss to the underside of my jaw. "Relax or I'll hum 'It's a Small World After All' all through dinner," she whispered.

Before I could respond, her arm fell from my waist—followed by a quick, sneaky smack to my backside—and she slipped away, taking the chair the maitre d' held out for her.

Dammit, I lamented, *I should've pulled out her chair*, even as I grinned inwardly at her clandestine backside pat, making plans to return the favor.

As I took my seat adjacent to hers, I consoled myself with the possibility that she'd have to stand at some point, maybe to use the ladies' room, and then I would pull out her chair. I'd be ready next time. . .

The man rattled off the specials in French while placing our napkins on our laps. He then departed, wishing us a pleasant evening, also in French. As soon as he left, Simone picked up her menu and began humming my least favorite song.

I grinned at her nonsense, breathing out some of my nerves. "Do not, please."

"What?" She gave me a wide-eyed, guileless look while she seemed to be battling a smile.

"You know what," I responded, low and deep, my attention dropping to her luscious mouth, and I remembered in a vivid flash kissing that mouth earlier today. I swallowed. "Thank you for coming to dinner."

She sat a little straighter. "Thank you for inviting me."

"You're—" I had to clear my throat and try again, forcing my eyes back to hers. "You're beautiful."

A slow grin claimed her features as she gazed at me and it took me a few seconds to realize my error.

"I mean"—I rolled my eyes at myself—"you *look* beautiful. Tonight."

Simone leaned her elbow on the table, her stare moving over me. "Why can't it be both? Why can't I be beautiful and look beautiful?"

I returned her grin. "Well of course it's both. But I wanted to make a special point of verbalizing my admiration for that dress."

"Oh yeah? Why is that?" Her index finger dropped to the low cut of her neckline, tracing the edge of the fabric over the swell of her breasts.

I didn't take the bait, but I wanted to.

Keeping my eyes on hers, I leaned forward an inch. "Because I'd like to see you wear it again. On another date. With me."

"Hmm . . ." Simone considered me, tilting her head to the side, but her eyes gave her away. My words made her happy. "I thought you wanted to stay for dinner."

Confused, I nodded slowly. "I do."

She leaned back in her chair, returning her eyes to her menu. "Your flirt game is very strong, young Winston."

"I'm not flirting with you." I wasn't. Flirting was meaningless fun. No part of tonight with Simone would be meaningless to me.

"If you continue being so sexy and alluring, I shall have to cut the meal portion of tonight's evening short and seduce you in your truck."

It was a good thing I wasn't drinking anything, because it would have gone down my windpipe.

As it was, I choked on nothing. "Excuse me?"

"What's good here?" She frowned at the menu. "It's literally all French to me."

I covered her wrist and held it until she gave me her eyes. "I'm not flirting with you." For some reason, it was important to me that Simone understand this.

She gave me a look as though she didn't believe me, but still found me cute.

"Simone—"

"There's nothing wrong with flirting, Roscoe." She covered my hand with hers, her eyes full of her soft smile. "And I think maybe you do it without realizing, it's just second nature. Also, do you speak French? If so, would you mind ordering for me? I know what fromage is, but everything else might be endangered turtle soup and I'd have no idea."

I frowned, not ready to move on from the flirting issue, but then the waiter arrived, interrupting us.

"Do you like wine? Or cocktails?" I asked her.

"Wine. Red."

Good.

It was easy to plan a meal around a bottle of red wine.

Turning to the waiter, I ordered for us both. "Hello, thank you. We will begin with the escargots de Bourgogne, two petit bucherondin de chèvre to follow. The lady would like the duck confit for her main, and I'll take the tartare de boeuf. To drink, let us have your house Bordeaux."

The waiter bowed, collected our menus, and left.

I returned my attention to Simone and found her watching me through narrowed eyes.

"What?"

"Do you speak French?"

I shrugged, told a white lie. "Just a little."

"But you said all those words, like *butcher-rodan* and *bord-doh* like you know how to speak French." Her gaze sharpened. "Could you have ordered entirely in French? If you wanted to?"

"Yes." I took a sip of my water, replacing it on the table exactly where it had been.

"Then why didn't you?"

"Because you just said you didn't speak French."

"All the more reason. Think of how impressed I might have been."

I shook my head, giving her a face. "Uh, no. You wouldn't have been impressed. You would have been annoyed."

A small smile danced behind her eyes. "You think so?"

"I know so. You would have thought me pretentious and made fun of me all night. No, thank you. Plus"—I straightened my fork so that it was perfectly parallel to the plate—"what's so impressive about leaving a person out? If someone doesn't know a language, and you knowingly speak that language in front of that person, well, I think that's pretty rude."

"Yes. Thank you. I agree," she said, leaning toward me like this was a major issue with her. "It's like, I'm happy for you that you speak another language. But how would you feel if I launched into a diatribe using a plethora of terms specific to forensic science research, knowing full well that you'd have no idea what I was saying?"

I was nodding before she'd finished speaking. "Yes. That drives me nuts. Like, why am I here? Just to listen to someone talk at me about shit I don't understand. If I wanted that, I'd hang out with Cletus and ask him about his tractor engines."

Simone chuckled. "Oh good Lord, is he still fixing up old tractors?"

"Sure is. He bought a stretch of land near the homestead, you know the old Coleman place? Well, he removed that trailer, demolished the foundation."

"Holy cow, the Coleman trailer is gone?"

Our waiter returned and unobtrusively opened our wine, pouring it for me to taste while I caught Simone up on Cletus's latest machinations, which turned into a story about her brother's adventures in California teaching astrophysics and working at the observatory, which flowed into swapping stories about our respective college years and the horrors of finals week.

We finished our escargot, our salads, and had just poured the last of our wine when our waiter brought out Simone's duck and my beef tartar, conversation never slowing, time passing at a steady, easy pace. Everything was so easy between us, and I found myself laughing more than I had since . . . well, since I was twenty, right before my momma died.

I indicated to the waiter that we'd need another bottle of Bordeaux while Simone popped a roasted potato into her mouth, making a pleased sound as she chewed.

"This is really good."

"I like this place," I said, glancing around the interior. "I never get a chance to go, only when Dr. Yi wants me to take out a client, or for the office Christmas party."

"This is where you have your Christmas party?"

"Yep. Dr. Yi is from France, or her parents were, so she favors the food."

"Huh." Simone ate another bite of potato, her gaze moving over me. "So, by clients do you mean pet owners?"

"Uh, no." I sighed, moving the pieces of beef around on my plate. "Dr. Yi is an equine specialist. There's three of us in the practice. Dr. Tucker is the boss, it's her practice, but she's basically retired. Though she does come in for a tricky or interesting surgery if she has the time. I focus mostly on domestic animals, cats, dogs, birds, turtles, and such. Dr. Yi travels a lot, meets with breeders in the field, makes house calls to some of the big horse folks in Tennessee. It's those horse folks we sometimes have to take out to dinner, wine and dine them as it were."

"That's interesting. Have you ever had an interest in working with horses?"

"No. Not full time. They're beautiful animals, but—hey, speaking of which—" I sat up straighter as an idea occurred to me. "You want to come to the Kentucky Derby with me this weekend?"

Her eyes widened and she stared at me, like a stunned doe in front of an approaching truck. "Kentucky Derby?"

"That's right." I examined her closely, searching my earlier words for anything that would explain the odd alteration in her demeanor. "Unless . . . are you afraid of horses?"

"No." She shook her head quickly, picking up her napkin and touching it to her lips. "No. I'm not afraid of horses. And, y-yes," she stuttered. "I don't- I mean, I would really like to go. With you."

She seemed flustered.

"Are you sure?"

"M-hmm." Simone reached for her wine glass with one hand and scratched her neck with the other, peering at me while she took a gulp.

I thought about giving her another out, or suggesting we do

something else the following weekend. Before I could think of a way to steer the conversation, she said, "So why don't you want to work with the horses full time?"

"Oh, uh, well." I picked up my earlier train of thought. "Interacting with the breeders requires too much schmoozing."

Simone grinned at her plate, setting her wine glass on the table, and when her eyes lifted to mine they were full of mischief. "I would have thought you'd enjoy schmoozing."

"What? Why?"

"Because you're so good at it."

I smiled, but I didn't mean it, and took a bite of my broccoli.

"Hey." She placed a hand on my arm, her thumb sweeping a caress on the inside of my wrist. "What's wrong?"

Cutting into my beef, I shook my head. "Nothing."

"Liar."

I smiled again, but this one was sincere.

"Tell me," she said, sliding her hand down to mine. "I said something I shouldn't have. Tell me what it was so I don't repeat the mistake."

I shrugged and gave her my eyes. "Just because you're good at something, doesn't mean you like doing it, and it definitely doesn't mean it defines you."

A wrinkle appeared between her eyebrows. "I don't think of you as a schmoozer."

"Don't you?" I kept my voice gentle, because I wasn't upset. I was honestly curious. "If not, you'd be one of the only ones. But I'm not bitter about it, even though it's just people looking at me through the image of those who came before. Jethro, Beau, even Billy and Cletus sometimes, they're all charmers, just like our dad."

"But not Duane?" She gave me a sly smile that—paired with her question—made me laugh.

"Oh God, no. Not Duane. It's like our daddy saved all his surliness and poured it into Duane."

Simone chuckled, tightening her fingers over mine, and then

releasing me. "Don't sell yourself short. You have your fair share of surliness, too."

"Well, thanks."

She laughed harder and her smile captivated me, held me suspended in the moment. I sighed.

Her smile waned.

We swapped stares.

Somewhere in the restaurant, someone laughed loudly, breaking the moment between us. Simone glanced at her plate, blinking as though trying to find her way back to the present, or clear her mind.

"Uh, what were we talking about?" she asked, laughing a little.

"You were calling me surly." I took a big bite of my food, watching her as she tried to find her place in the conversation.

"Wait, no." She shook her head, placing her fork on her plate and pushing both forward. "We were talking about you and how you're not a schmoozer, even though you schmooze all the ladies at Genie's."

That earned her a look, and when I'd finished chewing my food I asked, "What are you talking about?"

"Charlotte? Hannah? Ring any bells?"

"Charlotte Mitchell?"

"Yes."

I felt my forehead crease further. "Are you accusing me of schmoozing Charlotte Mitchell?"

"I am. Or"—she lifted a finger—"more precisely, flirting shamelessly with her."

"Ahhh." I leaned back in my chair, folding my arms as understanding dawned. Studying Simone as she studied me, I detected a hint of something—not jealousy, not anger—rather, an edge of mistaken conviction. "You are right. I do flirt shamelessly with Charlotte Mitchell. But I've never schmoozed her."

Simone picked up her wine glass—which was now full again, even though I hadn't noticed our waiter return with the new bottle— and examined me. "Please explain the difference between flirting and schmoozing."

"Well, you schmooze someone when you want something. Like my father, he's a schmoozer, always looking for the con. But flirting"—I shook my head—"that's just meaningless fun. You flirt to make someone feel good, to put a smile on her face, to give her a warm feeling about herself."

Simone continued to scrutinize me over her glass. "You mean—let me see if I have this right—you flirt with women to make them feel good about themselves, not because you want anything from them."

I nodded once. "Exactly."

The wrinkle between her eyebrows was back. "Then why were you so insistent earlier—when we first arrived to the restaurant—that you weren't flirting with me?"

"Because I wasn't."

Now her nose wrinkled. "So you're saying you want something from me?"

"I most certainly do," I said darkly, my gaze moving down to her lips, chin, neck, and chest in a meandering perusal. Maybe it was the three glasses of wine, but I said these words with every ounce of conviction I felt on the matter.

Her mouth fell open, drawing my eyes back to hers. "You were schmoozing me?" she asked quietly.

"Nope."

Simone returned her glass to the table and leaned her elbows against the edge. "Then what was that earlier? All that talk about me being beautiful and my dress."

"Sincerity."

We swapped stares again as all traces of humor dissolved from her features. But this time I could tell she was thinking, her mind working through possibilities, making me feel like I was one of her puzzles that needed solving.

So I pushed my plate forward and mimicked her posture, leaning my elbows on the edge of the table, bringing us closer.

"Simone," I said, just above a whisper. "Do you know what I want from you?"

She shook her head, but her eyes told me she had a hunch.

Simone and her hunches. The thought made me smile, and something about my smile made her eyelashes flutter, her breathing change.

"Roscoe," she whispered hoarsely, and then cleared her throat. "I have some questions."

I felt my smile deepen.

Simone and her questions.

"Ask me anything." Unable to stop myself because she was so close, I trailed the back of my knuckles along the smooth skin of her arm. But I did stop short of placing a biting kiss where the strap of her dress lay against her collarbone.

Maybe later.

She cleared her throat and leaned an inch closer. "They're standard first or second date questions, nothing wacky, but they're topics we haven't touched on yet, so . . ."

"Okay." My smile lingered. For the first time this evening, she seemed a little nervous. I found myself looking forward to these questions.

Her eyes moved between mine and I could sense her hesitation. "The thing is, they're usually brought up with a great deal of finesse. But as you know, I suck at finesse."

I nodded once. "Yes. You do."

She pressed her lips together, her nose wrinkling slightly. "Well, thanks."

"Hey." I grinned. "I suck at forensics. It's important to know your limitations."

Simone rolled her eyes and grinned, but even in the cozy lighting of the restaurant I perceived a slight pink hue claim her cheeks. "I will make you sorry for teasing me, Roscoe Winston."

Nudging her shoulder with mine, I whispered, "I'd certainly like to see you try."

"Fine." She looked at me squarely, lifting her chin, no longer whispering. "How many relationships have you had?"

My mouth dropped open, but she wasn't finished.

"And did you always use a condom? Even so, when was the last time you were checked for STDs? Are you clean? And are you currently seeing anyone else right now?"

"What? No!" I shook my head vehemently. I was so shocked by her last question, it was the only one I could focus on.

"Any children?"

"Simone—"

"I like children, I think they're great. I just like to know ahead of time if there are kids, because that usually means birthday parties, which might mean clowns, and as much as I like children—"

"You don't like clowns," I finished for her, looking at her sideways. "Do you really ask all these questions on the first or second date? Is that what people do?"

"I do," she sighed. "Or, I used to, when I dated."

That had me sitting up straighter. "*When* you dated? You don't date anymore?"

"Not recently, not since undergrad."

I did the math in my head. "That's, what, three years?"

"Yes. But my last 'relationship' was my junior year of college. So it's been four years since my last boyfriend, but "—now she seemed to be doing the math in her head—"six months since my last hookup."

At some point I'd leaned away and crossed my arms. Now I was watching her through narrowed eyes, debating whether or not I wanted to know more about this part of her history. I thought about her questions.

How many relationships have you had?

Did I want to know how many relationships she'd had?

No. It didn't matter.

Did you always use a condom? When was the last time you were checked for STDs? Are you clean?

Those three sounded important, but only the last one was actually important.

So I asked, "Are you clean?"

She nodded, seemingly unperturbed by my question. "Yes."

"So am I," I mumbled, hedging, my palms suddenly itchy.

"You're not seeing anyone else right now," she said. "And I'm guessing you don't have any children."

"Correct on both accounts." My response was distracted.

"Same for me. And I'm on birth control," she said quietly, her attention moving from my arms, which were crossed over my chest, to the posture of my shoulders. "Why do these questions bother you?" The question was gently asked.

Because they're irrelevant to how I feel about you, I wanted to say, *and because they shouldn't be irrelevant to how you feel about me.*

But that wasn't the whole truth, and Simone deserved the truth.

So I exhaled, my eyes dropping to my half-eaten dinner. I was no longer hungry.

"There's something you should know about me."

I sensed her shift in her chair, her interest piqued. "Yes?"

"My last relationship—"

"Yes?" She leaned forward.

I shook my head, laughing at myself. For someone who carried every memory of his life around with him like baggage, it occurred to me in that moment that I hadn't done a whole lot of living.

Her hand came to my arm, a tender touch, drawing my eyes to hers.

"Whatever it is, you can tell me. I'm not going to judge you for choices you made in your past." Her words were solemn, sincere.

I covered her hand with mine, plucked it from my arm and held it between my palms. "See, that's just it." My smile was wry, wary. "I . . . I didn't make many choices in my past. Always the same one."

Her gaze moved over me. "I don't understand."

I winced. I hadn't counted on this being so difficult, or such a big deal.

Just say it.

Tell her.

It shouldn't matter.

Leaning forward, still holding her hand in both of mine, I took a deep, bracing breath and confessed, "Simone, there's been nobody."

She watched me, her gaze patient, waiting. When I didn't continue, she blinked, her head moving back an inch, confusion clouding her brilliant eyes.

"What are you . . ." She blinked again, a reluctant conclusion sharpening her expression. "Are you saying—are you—" she cut herself off, pulling her hand away while leaning all the way forward. Her eyes darted between mine.

"You're a virgin?" she whispered on a rush, just like she always did when she asked a question without truly wanting to know the answer.

CHAPTER NINETEEN

❦ ❦ ❦

"Remember tonight... for it is the beginning of always."

— DANTE ALIGHIERI

Simone

S HORTLY AFTER THE "revelation" we left the restaurant.
We drove back to his place in near silence.

We entered his apartment, Roscoe holding the door for me just as he'd done each time we'd encountered a door, and he hung his keys by the hook just inside.

I watched his back as he moved about the space, flipping on a light here, going through his mail there. I watched him, the graceful confidence of his movements. I watched him, the stoic, unperturbed expression masking his features.

He's a virgin.

To say I was shocked would be an understatement, but not as much of an understatement as saying I was curious.

Man oh man oh man, I was so fucking curious. And nervous. And therefore tongue-tied. I mean, what does one say to a smokin' hot, gainfully employed, super smart and kind, educated, with a nice family, didn't live with his parents, wasn't addicted to World of Warcraft, no arrest record virgin of twenty-six?

Excuse me, but I have a few questions. How the hell is it possible that you, Sir Roscoe the Soulful, are a virgin?

I shook my head, my mind a mess. I was so confused. I was also ashamed, because along with the confusion and nervousness and shock and curiosity, I also wondered, *what is wrong with him?*

My eyes dropped to the front of his pants, where his virginal penis resided, all locked up in its ivory tower, a fair . . .

Wait. What was the male equivalent of a maiden?

I wracked my brain, trying to come up with a word or phrase. An untried youth? That didn't quite fit. Eventually, I abandoned my search and just decided to coin a phrase.

Roscoe was a man-maiden. That's what he was. A fair man-maiden, with a beard so dark and eyes so blue, a tall specimen of manly greenness, innocent and untouched.

A virgin.

A mother-non-fucking virgin.

How would this even work?

So. . . what does one do with a man-maiden? I mean, I'd read historical romance novels before (Beverly Jenkins and Lisa Kleypas were my homegirls), so I had some idea about how a virgin was debauched, or deflowered, or whatever it was called. Basically, a big four-poster bed was involved, and a coverlet, a duke, stays, and a chemise that is peeled back to reveal an expanse of smooth, virginal skin.

I didn't know where we could find a chemise at this time of night, so his T-shirt would have to do.

Also, the debaucher would need to take control of the situation and ensure the debauchee (that is, the deflowered) was left gratified. Usually, penetration occurred twice—the first time to get the virgin accustomed to the invasion by taking things slowly and gently, and the second time for the virgin's pleasure, again slowly and gently— because satisfying the virgin was of utmost importance.

Also, the deflowered virgin often felt sore and "twingy" in new, unforeseen places afterward.

Two consecutive penetrations wouldn't be a problem. If I had him lie on his back during the first round, then he wouldn't have to think about much else other than enjoying himself. Perhaps we'd go cowgirl for the second round of plucking his petals (i.e. deflowering), and move on to doggy style for times three and five. Maybe have him stand at the edge of the bed while I lie upon it—if his bed was tall enough—for times seven and ten, to give him a sense of gradual control. I felt confident, after some instruction, we could eventually move on to sitting face-to-face if—

"Want any coffee?" he asked, breaking me from my musings, his tone distant. "If you're planning to leave any time soon, the drive back home feels twice as long this time of night without it."

My eyebrows shot up, his cool, insinuated dismissal catching me off guard, and I fought for a moment to find clarity of thought. I was disappointed by his demeanor.

And yet, at the same time, what had I expected? A ballooning burst of shame crashed over me, sobered me from my stunted shock. I'd told him I wouldn't judge him for the choices of his past, and here I was, doing exactly that.

Breathing out, I glanced around the apartment, waking from my daze.

Yes. Roscoe is a virgin.

So what?

He's still Roscoe. And you're still Simone.

Clearing my throat, because my heart was suddenly there, beating against my larynx, I hazarded two steps toward him, deciding that my plans for his gradual debauchery would have to wait. I had feelings to consider first.

As Jenn had said, I was trying to bake the cake without preheating the oven. *Wise woman.*

"I have questions."

He made a scoffing sound, not looking up from his mail, and muttered something like, "Of course you do."

I didn't let his salty tone deter me, because I had a hunch. And this hunch fueled my bravery in the face of his alleged aloofness.

Therefore, gathering a breath specifically for bravery, I asked, "Do you want to be with me?"

Stillness settled over him, his eyes staring forward. I watched his chest expand and my hunch told me that Roscoe was also breathing in bravery.

He blinked. He looked at me, his eyes and expression stark.

"I want to be with you. Always." He sounded sad, resigned.

I smiled, because I couldn't help it, and because his answer aligned with my hunch. I never get tired of being proven right.

The three Es returned, and they brought butterflies with them, depositing the Rhopalocera low in my belly where their wings fluttered and warmed me from the inside out.

Closing the rest of the distance between us, I covered his hand holding the mail and took the envelopes, tossing them to the coffee table. Entwining our fingers, I gazed up at him, at my spectacular man-maiden, and my feelings warmed me, unfolded, bloomed.

Perhaps I'd been a green bud as well until this moment, blossoming under his stern admission, because my heart swelled even as my breath was stolen.

Everything became clear, and fuck it all, I loved him.

I loved him.

I loved this man.

I wanted him, to be with him, always.

It was *him*. How he touched me, looked at me, held me, *knew* me, accepted me. His gentleness, his ferocity, his sweetness, even his caution. I loved his reluctance, how earnestly and sincerely he approached every situation, with heart and soul over mind and matter.

I loved him.

"I want to be with you, too," I said, my gaze dropping to his lips, my voice unsteady, because this was both scary and wonderful. "I want to be with you always. And, Roscoe, I—"

That's all I got out, because he captured the words, fusing his mouth to mine, ensnaring my body, just as he'd ensnared my reason, and feelings, and heart.

My hands—smart, useful hands—were unbuttoning his shirt as he untucked it. He didn't wait for me to finish before pulling it over his head, his undershirt following, leaving him bare-chested, somehow taller than before, and so fucking magnificent.

I mean, *ladies*.

Holy cow.

Get thee a Winston, stat!

His hands came to my waist, flexing on my sides as his mouth hungrily devoured mine. His fingers dug into my ribs, giving me the sense—now that his lack of experience had been revealed to me—he wanted more. He wanted to touch me, but he didn't know how to take what he wanted.

Reaching for his hand, I slid it higher to my breast, moving his fingertips to the edge of my neckline and encouraging him to push his hand inside. He did, shuddering even as he turned us both and surged forward, backing me against a wall in three large steps.

My head tilted back as he massaged me, a ragged breath torn from his lungs, the rock-hard length of his erection pressing against my belly.

Yes. Yes. Yes.

Prior to now, I'd taken male arousal for granted. A given. A necessity to get where I needed to go. But not with Roscoe. Watching him now, his mindlessness and loss of control, his confusion and uncertainty, it was a beautiful, pure thing. I felt a pang at the rawness of him and at my own envy.

I wished, so badly, that he'd been my first. That this sweet, sexy man and I could have taken this journey together, fumbling, failing and falling, rising and learning from each other. But I couldn't change the past, and nor would I want to, because everything that came before had brought me—had brought us—to right now.

I love him.

His hips rocked, grinding in a thoughtless movement, one of pure instinct and need, somehow both innocent and carnal.

Scratching my nails down the lean muscles of his chest and stomach, I cupped him over his pants, stroked, and watched, captivated as he stilled, seemed to hold his breath. His eyes scrunched shut, restless energy pouring from him in tsunami-sized waves. If I didn't know any better, I'd think he was in pain.

Maybe he was.

"Roscoe."

He made an unintelligible sound and my chest expanded, a tight, aching flare. I stroked him again and his hands came to either side of me, caging me in as he leaned heavily on the wall.

"Don't," he said, shaking his head. "I'm so close."

I rolled my lips between my teeth, because he didn't need me laughing right now, and removed my hand from his pants, instead arching my back and unhooking my bra. His eyes opened, collided with mine as I peeled one strap from my shoulder, and then the other, tugging my dress downward. His eyes lowered, as though mesmerized, wide and focused on my chest and I let my dress drop, my bra falling next to it.

He sucked in a shaky breath, his eyes wavering but not blinking.

"Kiss me," I said, not recognizing my own voice.

A thrill, a shock passed through me as he lowered to my breast. I felt his hot breath before his hotter mouth closed over the peak, kissing me there as he'd kissed me so expertly on my lips.

I moaned, threading my fingers into his dark locks and anchoring my nails into the short hairs at the back of his neck. My sound of pleasure must've unleashed something within him, because his movements grew more certain, demanding. He cupped my other breast, twisting the center between his thumb and index finger, tugging it sharply.

I gasped.

He stilled.

"Don't stop," I breathed, holding him more firmly in place. "Just . . . just keeping doing everything you're doing."

So he did. He feasted on my skin as I watched him, until I grew restless, tightness coiling in my belly. Until I *needed* him to touch me lower, deeper.

"Roscoe," I panted, grabbing his wrist and directing it downward. "Use—use your middle finger to—to—oh God."

His hand was in my underwear, his warm palm against my abdomen, his middle finger separating me, tracing the swell of my clitoris. This time we gasped in unison.

"You're so hot . . . and soft," he groaned, trailing wet, biting kisses from my breast to my neck, swirling his tongue against the sensitive skin.

God.

If he did that *elsewhere*, just like that, I'd lose it.

A shudder claimed me at the thought. I moaned again as he discovered me with his fingers, gently probing, caressing, stroking. He explored lower, finding my entrance, his other hand smoothing from my shoulder, down my back to dip into my panties, grabbing a handful of my backside.

"I want to bite you," he whispered roughly against my neck, sucking my earlobe between his lips. "Taste every part of you. I want you everywhere."

His words inebriated me, pulling me under the surface of reason, cutting the air supply to sanity and filling my lungs with reckless desire.

This was not how I'd imagined things between us would progress.

I was losing control. I couldn't remember what to do next, how to ensure his first time was gratifying. A chemise, and then skin, and something about double penetration . . .

No.

I made a face.

That's not right.

But I couldn't think. His exploring fingers where stroking and teasing me perfectly; and his mouth was at my neck sending jolts and spikes of ticklish sensation radiating along my nerves in all directions; and his long, lean body was pressing me against the wall. *He was everywhere.*

Suddenly, I was the one being seduced.

"Let me . . ."

Abruptly, his fingers left my body, and I became aware he'd hooked them into the waist of my underwear. He was pulling them off, down my bare thighs, his fingers skimming the back of my legs. Maneuvering me away from the wall, he captured my mouth again, his hands wrapping around my thighs and back, lifting me from the ground. His movements were bolder, more certain.

We were moving. Vaguely, I was aware he'd taken me into another room. His bedroom. The light was off but then he flipped the switch and all was illuminated. But I only saw him.

Roscoe placed me on the bed and released me, stepping away. I reached for him, irrationally heartsick at his departure. But then he was unbuttoning his pants. I watched him over the canvas of my naked body. His pants dropped, his eyes on my skin hot and ardent and dazed.

I was extremely thankful he'd turned on the light. *Wise man.*

He came back to me, his hands braced on either side of my head, careful to avoid my hair. He kissed me, his body pressing me against the bed as our bodies rubbed together in a slow, torturous rhythm.

But it wasn't right. His boxers were still on.

"What—what are you doing?" I couldn't breathe, I wanted him so badly. I was mad with it. Reaching for the only remaining barrier between us with shaking hands, I felt him suck in a breath.

"Wait. Wait. Not yet." He shook his head, tucking his face into my neck. "Let me—I want—God, I've wanted you, this for so long."

His hot breath tickled my skin as he nipped and licked and bit his way down my body, lavishing everything between my shoulder and stomach with sultry kisses, groaning as he explored me with his mouth and hands. His hips rocked in unpracticed movements, first against my hip, and then my thigh. By the time he reached my legs and spread them wider, I was covered in a gloss of sweat, my body shaking.

"Roscoe, what—what—"

And then he was there. Right *there*.

My hands flew to my face and I felt the first uncontainable ripple of pleasure-pain radiate outward, seizing my limbs, curling my toes.

He parted me with his lips and tongue, all slippery friction and sensation. He made a *Mmm* sound and it rumbled against me, his arms wrapping around my thighs and pulling my body across the bed towards him like I was a doll, a plaything.

Nothing about what he was doing was skillful or rehearsed, but everything about it was honest, and that made all the difference. I *believed* he loved this, he loved licking me slowly, savoring strokes of his tongue and lips, he loved the taste of me. He was ravenous yet tender—entirely too tender—and with each pass of his mouth I sunk deeper and deeper into madness.

"Your hand." I swallowed the last word, besieged yet wanting to give voice to my desires.

His eyes lifted to mine, a shock of blue flame. Distrustful and greedy, they dared me to tell him to stop. I huffed a startled laugh at the ferocity there, like he'd found his favorite toy—or a slice of his favorite cake—and I'd just suggested he release it.

"Give me your hand," I said, finally finding my voice. It held a tremor.

Reluctantly, he released my thigh, his tongue still lapping too slow, and caressed a path from my stomach to my breast, at last offering his hand.

I grabbed it, lifting on an elbow and brought his middle finger to my lips. Sucking it inside, I rocked my neck slowly at first, and then faster, setting a pace for him, teaching him how to increase tempo, which he did. His pace mirrored mine until I could no longer hold on and I fell back on the bed, my body arching uncontrollably as a soundless scream echoed and rippled, a shock wave, and I fell, gripping the comforter for purchase.

I hadn't quite recovered, tremors still seizing me at intervals, when I became aware that Roscoe was trailing kisses along the sensitive flesh on the inside of my thigh. I couldn't handle it. I felt as though I'd break in two.

"Please," I said unthinkingly.

He looked at me, still ferocious, but also a little smug. The smugness made me chuckle.

"Please," I tried again. "Please come, please lie down with me."

"Why?" He sounded curious, cautious.

"Because I want you to hold me." It was a half-truth, but it worked.

Not one second later, he'd stretched out, gathering me to his chest and holding me close, kissing my jaw and cheek and hair. A sound of contentment slipped past my lips, and I felt his chest rumble.

"Did you just purr?"

I snuggled closer. "Maybe."

His hand slid down my back to fondle my bottom. "You just did it again." He sounded pleased.

But I could also feel him, the press of his length against my hip. It felt large, and I imagined it was painful, and there was nothing I wanted more in that moment than to offer relief.

So I wriggled in his arms, shifting myself to my side and pressing my hands flat against his chest until he lay on his back. Skimming my nails down his body, enjoying the angles and ridges of his form beneath his hot skin, I slipped my hand inside his boxers.

He sucked in a breath between his teeth, his eyes closing as his head fell back. I watched with fascination as his Adam's apple bobbed, a thick swallow, his muscles tensed everywhere as I encircled his length, stroking down, and then up.

"Simone." It sounded like a plea and a warning.

A new thrill shot through me.

"Shhh," I whispered next to his ear, releasing him and kneeling to pull off his boxers.

He lifted his hips, helping me, even as his eyes remained closed, his jaw clenched. I licked my lips, the anticipation of seeing him—all of him—causing my heart to quicken, to gallop, to fly.

Quite suddenly, he was naked.

My heart squeezed as I looked at him, at this beautiful man. His beauty, his nakedness seemed somehow both vulnerable and domineering, overwhelming to my eyes. Even his cock was beautiful, thick and gorgeously proportioned to the rest of his long body, jutting straight up as though issuing me an invitation.

Or a dare.

I let the boxers fall from my dangling fingers and I climbed back on the bed, straddling his hips, wanting the feel of his hot skin against mine, wanting to be filled, claimed, and to claim him in return.

His eyes flew open, wide, rimmed with something wild. "Simone," he repeated, but different this time. His hands lifted to my thighs, digging into my skin.

Yet, he made no move to stop me as I reached for him.

"Do you want me?" I asked, trying not to sound coy, but knowing I kinda did. I couldn't help it, he got me so hot. Apparently, I turned into a sex kitten with Roscoe, and—you know what?—I was really okay with that.

He made a sound, something helpless, fierce and primal. In the next moment, a hand slid to my waist, gripping me, impatient. I rocked my slippery center against him, rubbing my softness along the hardest part of him.

He gasped, cursed through clenched teeth, his fingers flexing restively, his eyes flashing again like they'd done before, a hint of possession. Or maybe more than a hint. And, again, I was really okay with that. Likely because I was looking at him with more than a hint of possession as well.

Because he's mine.

The thought didn't bother me now, and I wondered half-heartedly if it would bother me later.

Positioning his gorgeous cock, I slid him inside me, taking him slowly, watching with rapt fascination as he pressed the back of his head against the bed, his lips parted in a slight snarl, his hips tilting, trying to give me more of himself, trying to take me faster.

I grinned wickedly, sliding a hand up to his lips as he lifted to his elbows. He took two of my fingers into his mouth and rocked his head up and down, showing me as I'd showed him how to set the pace. I obliged, rolling my hips slowly at first, and then faster, matching the rhythm of his mouth.

God, I'd never witnessed anything so overwhelmingly sexy as Roscoe Winston sucking on my fingers while I took him within my body. I'd never felt anything so perfect as when I rode him and I felt my stomach coil and twist, preparing for another shock wave and accompanying release.

But then he grabbed my wrist and pinned it to my side as he surged up, wrapping his arms around me as he strained beneath, his breathing ragged and labored. Roscoe's eyes caught mine, attempting to focus through chaos as he came.

He pressed upward unevenly once, twice, and then three times more, a desperate sound wrenched from his lungs.

And then he fell back, taking me with him, still wrapped in his arms. His mouth sought mine and I capitulated, giving into his urgent, greedy kisses, his heart beating against my breast, a thunderous and harsh drumbeat, reminding me that we were still joined, and that every inch of him felt amazing.

"I love you," he said between kisses, pushing my hair from my face and turning us on our sides. "God, how I love you."

"Roscoe—"

"Don't. Don't say anything." He kissed me again on the lips and then lowered his mouth to my neck, nipping at my chin and jaw on the way.

"But—"

"Let me have this." His mouth was at my ear, his words landing hot and urgent. "Give me this." Another kiss. "Give me this memory."

CHAPTER TWENTY

"Let us hope that we are all preceded in this world by a love story."

— DON J. SNYDER, OF TIME AND MEMORY: MY
PARENTS' LOVE STORY

Simone

KISSES WOKE ME up.

Kisses on my stomach and ribs, followed by caressing strokes of big hands touching my shoulder, breast, knuckles brushing against my back, bottom, and thigh.

Roscoe.

I smiled. All of my thoughts were selfish, every single one of them, and I stretched, nestling my backside against his groin and grinning wider at his state of readiness.

His lips were at the back of my neck now, his hand audacious as it slipped between my legs, encouraging me to lift one so he could touch me.

"What time is it?" I asked, my voice raspy.

I felt him shake his head in the darkness. "Doesn't matter."

"You'll care in the morning, when you're too tired to work." My breath hitched as he rubbed and stroked and played with my body.

Was I really trying to talk him out of this? Good Lord. Get a grip Simone.

Reaching behind me, I closed my fingers around his cock, giving it a rough tug. He released a hissing breath, the heat of which sent a wave of goose bumps along my back, shoulder, and arm.

"I want to be on top," he said, nipping my ear.

I thought about that, about the wisdom of moving to missionary so soon, and I frowned.

After our earlier lovemaking, I'd left him in the bed, opting for a quick shower before round two. But when I came back, I found he'd passed out. Naked. Delightfully, deliciously naked.

Therefore, I'd wrapped my hair in the silk scarf I'd bought earlier, brushed my teeth, turned off the lights, and crawled into bed next to him, snuggling close. Content for now that my virgin debauching—part one at least—had been a success, I promptly fell asleep.

But missionary? For his second time? *Eh, no.*

This might not be a popular opinion, but I considered missionary a PhD level sex position, one of the most difficult to perfect, which was why I'd never had any interest in it.

I mean, just think about the logistics.

Firstly, it was one of the least athletic, which meant lack of skill was difficult to disguise. Form, angle, and rhythm had to be just right. Secondly, the woman had little control over her own pleasure. She couldn't touch herself, she couldn't rock her hips with any reliability, she had to rely solely on her partner's dexterity and expertise. Basically, she was completely vulnerable and at a very real danger of never reaching orgasm, or even getting anywhere close.

Meanwhile, the man was guaranteed a good time, which made the position dangerous as a second-time deflowering. Bad habits are difficult to unteach. It would be a disservice to Roscoe to go full missionary without first explaining potential pitfalls.

Also, I needed some time to mentally prepare.

I doubted I would ever enjoy missionary. But—at the same time —I didn't want to dismiss it out of hand without giving Roscoe a chance to prove me wrong. Then again, I didn't want to doom him to failure by encouraging him to jump into the deep end without giving him the option of floaties first.

His breathy laugh brought me back to the present and he placed a tender kiss on my shoulder. "What's going on in your head right now? You sure are thinking hard."

"Your deflowering," I muttered.

He grew very still behind me. "My what?"

"I have a hypothesis. I think we should map out an ideal progression of sexual positions in order to maximize competency and acquisition of abilities, each offering new skills which build upon each other. A forum for feedback is also important—for both of us— where we can compare findings and modify our approach. I just don't want you to draw any false conclusions due to lack of appropriate specific aims or deficiencies in sample size."

Roscoe was silent, and then I felt the bed begin to shake behind me. Turning my head, I peered into the darkness, searching for him. After a few seconds, realization dawned. He was laughing.

Twisting to face him completely, I placed my hand on his chest over his heart; he couldn't see it, but my smile was self-deprecating and mild embarrassment heated my neck and cheeks. "Okay. Right. That might be *too* scientific of an approach. But—"

"Oh my God, I love you." He sniffed, his arms coming around my body.

"You love me and you're laughing at me."

"Yes." He kissed my lips. "Please, never stop defaulting to the scientific approach. Never change that about yourself."

"Oh? What should I change?"

"Na-ah," he said, laughter in his voice. "That's a trap."

I leaned away, trying to make out his face but deciphering only shadow. "It's not a trap."

"Oh yeah? Fine. Then you tell me what you'd change about me. Then maybe I'll tell you what I'd change about you."

I scoffed, because that was easy. "First of all—"

"First of all?" His voice cracked. "You mean there's a second of all?"

"And a third of all, but let me list them in order."

He laughed again, closing the distance between our mouths for a quick kiss, and then settling on his back, bringing me to his chest. "Okay, let's hear my list of deficiencies."

I shook my head, sighing loudly. "They're not deficiencies. They're things I wish would change."

"Fine. Let's hear it."

"As I was saying, first of all, I'd like your zip code to be closer to mine."

Roscoe's chest rose and fell with an expansive breath. "You mean you want me closer to Green Valley? Because I could apply for a position with Drew, at the Park."

Oh . . . right.

Shit.

I grimaced, my stomach dropping, because I'd meant Washington, DC, and my cozy apartment, and my Nancy, and my job at the bureau's forensics research lab.

My job.

My grimace deepened. I exhaled, my lungs filled with remorse and fiery frustration. I hadn't precisely forgotten why I'd come to Nashville, but I'd allowed Nelson's orders and the case to take a back seat. That wasn't like me, not at all. Work came first, duty came first, catching bad guys came first, because saving lives came first.

I still needed to talk to Roscoe about Darrell. Allowing my feelings to guide me meant I'd neglected my mission, and that was unacceptable.

But your mission makes you want to vomit.

"Simone?"

I cleared my throat, blinking as I gathered my thoughts. "We should—we should get some sleep and . . ."

Straining my ears, I tensed. My phone was ringing. But not just any ringtone, it was my mother's ringtone.

"Oh shit!" I shot up and scrambled off the bed, grabbing for my bag by the door to the bathroom. I found my phone and noted with a great deal of dread that I'd missed ten text messages, all from my mom.

"Shit, shit, shit—" I danced in place and swiped to answer my cell. "Hello? Mom?"

A dangerous pause, and then, "Where are you?"

"I'm so, so sorry. I—"

"Where are you?" Her voice was like hoarfrost.

I gripped my forehead, my throat a vise. I paced the bedroom. "I'm still in Nashville."

"For work?" she asked, snapping, and I tensed.

My mother had never been truly angry at me. Disappointed? Yes. Irritated? Certainly. But pissed off? Never.

How could I be so thoughtless?

"Yes, it's for—I mean, no. Not—not for . . . that." God. This was the worst.

Roscoe had also stood from the bed. He'd flipped on the lamp and was now hovering nearby, his hands on his hips, concern etched his features.

He mouthed, "Is everything okay?" I could only look at him helplessly.

"Simone Payton." I listened as she gathered a deep breath and I knew I was really in for it.

So I blurted, "I'm with Roscoe!" I scrunched my face, physically bracing for the impact of her words even though I was hundreds of miles away. "I'm with Roscoe. We went on a date and then we came back to his place and—Mom, I'm so sorry. I—I love him. I love him so much and I wasn't thinking rationally, I was just thinking I wanted to be with him and I couldn't see past that want, and I'm so, so sorry."

She said nothing. I couldn't even hear her breathe, but that might've been because my heart was hammering between my ears.

Forcing myself to take a calming breath, I said again, "I'm sorry."

"Roscoe? You're *with* Roscoe?"

I opened one eye, peeking at him and discovering that he'd moved away. He was now sitting on the bed, gaping at me.

"Yes," I said.

I could almost see my mother thinking. "Roscoe Winston? You two are . . ."

"Uh . . ." I swallowed, my attention affixed to the stunned expression on Roscoe's face, trying to remember what I'd just blurted to my mother.

But then she gasped. And then she laughed. And then she said, "Oh my!"

"Mom."

"Trevor!" I heard her yell excitedly, "Simone is in *Nashville*."

And then my father's voice, "She better have a good—"

"With Roscoe!"

I rolled my eyes. My cheeks burned, because I was standing in Roscoe's bedroom, disrobed, telling my parents that we'd just slept together while he sat on the bed staring at me like I'd grown a leg out of my head.

Lovely.

I pressed my palm to my jaw.

"With Roscoe?" my dad asked. Another pause, during which I'm sure my mother made some very interesting hand gestures, because my father then said, "Praise Jesus!"

My palm moved to my eyes. "Mom."

"Tell him he should take the Payton last name. Your father did it."

"Oh my God!"

"You stay as long as you like, and give Roscoe our love." She sounded like she wanted to get me off the phone. "Have fun," my mother sing-songed much to my mortification.

In the background, just before she clicked off, I heard my father say, "Now *that* will be a nice wedding. We'll do it in the fall, when the leaves change, and Poe can—"

"Ahh!" I dropped my phone like it burned and walked to the far corner, hiding. I mean, not really hiding since I was in the buff, showing the room my bare ass, but I was hiding my face.

A minute passed, maybe more, maybe less, and all I could do was try to calm my pulse and endeavor to cool the hot embarrassment that burned every inch of my body.

I felt a hand on my shoulder and I jumped, releasing a small squeak, having not heard his approach. But I wasn't ready to face him yet, so I pressed myself more fully into the corner and groaned.

"Just let me die here."

A pause. "Why would you die here?"

"Irreversible cessation of respiratory function due to mortification."

His warm, rumbly laugh was an unexpected balm to my frazzled senses and I allowed him to pull me away from the wall and wrap me in his arms.

Roscoe kissed my forehead, his hands smoothing down my back, one stroking from my shoulder to my bottom.

"I love you, Simone Payton," he said quietly, and I noticed the earlier starkness was missing this time. The words sounded just as certain, but also warmer, softer.

I liked the difference.

"I need to tell you something," I said, snuggling closer, ever closer. I sighed, releasing the remainder of my hot embarrassment in favor of his hot, comforting embrace.

"What's that?" His hands continued to pet and stroke, making me want to arch and curl against his palm. Or climb him. One or the other.

But I had words to say, an admission to make, and I wanted to look at him while I did.

Therefore, I pulled a little away and lifted my chin, looking at my former man-maiden square in the eye. "I wanted to tell you earlier, when we got home from dinner, but things got . . . busy."

The corner of his mouth hitched, as did one of his eyebrows, giving his features a smug and yet exhilaratingly sexy appearance.

"The thing is, the truth is . . ." I wavered, my breathing coming faster. I was a little frightened, but not because I was uncertain of how I felt. Rather, I was exceptionally certain. Loving Roscoe wasn't a hunch, or a hypothesis, or a theory.

I loved Roscoe, and that was a law.

His smirk waned, his eyes moving over my face with a cherishing intensity as he waited patiently, giving me the sense he would wait forever, if necessary.

So I licked my lips, gathered a deep breath, and said, "I love you, Roscoe Winston." Suddenly, my chin wobbled for no reason, and my eyes stung, so when I spoke again my voice was unsteady, "I love you."

A small smile curved his mouth and he closed his eyes for the briefest of moments, breathing in, as though inhaling my admission, taking it deep within himself.

When he opened his eyes, they were brilliant and clear, happy, so happy, even though he was giving me a frowning-smile.

"Why are you crying?" he asked gently, cupping my face and wiping my tears away with his thumbs. Roscoe kissed the wet tracks on my cheeks, and then brushing his lips against mine, whispering, "Don't cry."

"I'm just—" I sniffed, kissing him back before stepping away to wipe my eyes with the back of my hand. "I'm just having a lot of feelings right now."

He chuckled, flashing a big smile, and so did I.

He hugged me again, pressing my head to his chest where his heart beat, and I clung to him. So many emotions swirled within me, but vulnerability struck out as the strongest. It was a strange sort of vulnerability, one I'd never recalled experiencing before.

Because instead of making me feel weak, it made me feel powerful.

* * *

I DON'T THINK either of us fell back asleep. But neither did we make a move on the other, content to lay together, talking infrequently. Kissing sometimes, but mostly just being still.

The earliest rays of sunlight filtered through his blinds and a solitary bird heralded morning's arrival. Chirping a solo song, the optimistic bird would pause at intervals, as though waiting for a response.

Roscoe shifted, sighed, and I lifted my head to look at him. Something about his movements and sigh felt different than even an hour ago. My hunch was, Roscoe was about to get up for the day, and I felt an abrupt pang of distress.

I wasn't ready for our night to be over. I wasn't ready for daylight and responsibilities. I wasn't ready for him to leave.

"Don't get up," I said, softly brushing my lips over his. "It's not day yet."

He tilted his head, his eyes caressing my face. "You don't hear that bird? That's a horned lark."

"That sound you heard was the nightingale," I said with confidence, giving him a sweet smile. "The lark sings in the morning, the nightingale sings at night."

Roscoe pulled a face, laughed, and spoke through his mirth, "It was the lark, the bird that sings at dawn, not the nightingale. Look, my love"—he cupped my cheek, his voice now tender—"what are those streaks of light in the clouds parting in the east?"

I blinked at him, frowning my confusion, because now he sounded like he was quoting something.

"Uh, pardon?"

"'Night is over, and day is coming.'" He kissed me. "'If I want to live, I must go. If I stay, I'll die.'"

"What?" I sat up. "You'll die? What?"

Roscoe was still grinning, his expression warm. "It's from *Romeo and Juliet*," he replied. His palm moved down, up, down my arm, a leisurely touch. "I thought you hated that play."

"I do." I wrinkled my nose in distaste. "Why would you quote it to me?"

"Because you just quoted it to me."

That had me rearing back even further. "I did?"

He nodded. "Yeah. You don't remember? When they wake up the next morning? After getting married, and being together, Juliet tells Romeo that the bird outside their window is a nightingale, sitting on a pomegranate tree, and that dawn has not yet come."

I blinked at him, dumbfounded, because he was right.

What was happening to me?

I clutched my forehead and released a humorless laugh. "I can't believe I just did that."

His fingers encircled my hand as he sat up, pulling it away from my face and placing a kiss on the inside of my wrist. "Memory is a strange thing." He pressed another kiss to the soft skin of my interior forearm. "An endless reminder of the past, revealing itself—as a cannon blast or a whisper—when you're least prepared for it."

Studying him, an odd, unsettling sensation settled in my abdomen. "Was that a quote, too?"

"What?" He blinked at me.

"What you just said, about memory. Were you quoting someone?"

He shook his head, his soulful eyes lowering to my arm, bringing it to his mouth for another taste. "Nope. That was just me."

I watched him, sighing fretfully, uncertain how to manage this beautiful man and the weight of his words. I mean, was it just me? Or did he sound like a poet half the time? And here I was, one of the least romantic people on the face of the earth.

Right?

Right??

"What's wrong?" he asked, his gaze scrutinizing.

That's when I realized I'd been frowning. "I'm not . . ."

"What?"

"I'm not sentimental."

Roscoe smirked—like he'd done last night—and I glowered at him. I liked his smirks. They were sexy even if they were also smug.

"Why are you smirking?"

"You forget"—he leveraged his hold on my arm to draw me

closer—"I've known you since we were kids."

"So?"

"So, you are sentimental."

"Oh, really?" I cocked an eyebrow at that. "Well, please, do tell me all about myself."

"All right then." Roscoe nodded once and cleared his throat. "When we were eight and your dog died, you made your folks hold a funeral."

"That doesn't make me sentimental."

"And you wrote a eulogy."

"That doesn't—"

"And a poem."

I shook my head, but I did not roll my eyes.

"That same year, you found a four-leaf clover in the patch of grass near the fairy meal drop-off point at the back of our property."

My eyes narrowed into a glare. How could he possibly remember all of this?

"You pressed the clover between two sheets of wax paper, put it in a box, and buried it on top of your dog's grave, 'To give him luck in doggy heaven.'"

"I was eight. I was mourning. Have some respect for the dead."

"When we were nine, you wrote a poem for your grandfather and had your momma take a picture of you giving it to him. I suspect you still have that photo on your nightstand?"

"I will neither confirm nor deny your suspicion." I pulled my arm from his grip so I could cross it over my chest.

"That means you still got it there." He sounded as though he were confirming this fact for himself. "Two months later, when y'all moved to the bigger house up on the hill, we'd go visit your old house once a week—usually on Fridays after school—to make sure the new owners were treating it right."

I lifted my chin. "Those Wilkersons always rubbed me the wrong way and they neglect home projects until they become emergencies. If they'd replaced the roof three years ago then they wouldn't have the mold problem now."

"When we were ten you—"

"I was a kid. All kids are sentimental."

"You still have Eugene the Dinosaur on your bed?" he asked, his eyebrows ticking up.

I searched for an excuse, hastily choosing, "Stuffed animals make great back support pillows."

"You still keep all your concert tickets?"

"I like evidence."

He chuckled a little at that, shaking his head at me like he thought I was cute.

But when he spoke, there was a worrisome edge in his voice. "You are sentimental. You have a big heart. You just don't want to admit it."

"Why wouldn't I want to admit it? If I had a big heart, I would admit it."

His eyes drifted beyond me and lost focus, like he was watching a scene unfold beyond my shoulder. "My best guess is . . ." He continued staring, and now it looked like he was staring into a crystal ball or reading the answer off a cue card. "My theory is that you watched what happened with Dani when we were kids and decided you didn't want any part of that."

I blinked, honestly stunned. "You have a theory?"

Roscoe's gaze came back to mine, and held. "She made some pretty bad decisions, with Catfish—sorry, with *Curtis*—when they were teenagers, decisions that shaped your ideas about love and sentimentality. I get that."

"You *get that*?" I stiffened, breathing harder than warranted while sitting still in bed. I clutched the bedsheet to my chest, feeling oddly raw, exposed.

"I have five older brothers and an older sister." His voice gentled and he sighed. "Watching them make stupid choices, hurt the people around them, made an impact. The course of their lives changed the course of mine. I'll never use folks like Jet did, or have drive and ambition like Billy. What has that ambition brought him?"

Much of my rash defensiveness diminished as he shared about

his family, and we exchanged a commiserating look at the mention of Billy's ambitions. But neither of us said what was on our minds. I appreciated his forbearance. I wasn't ready to tell anyone about what I'd witnessed at the Donner Lodge between Dani and Curtis, I needed to talk to her first.

He continued, his stare dropping to where I clutched the sheet, "I'll never be a schemer, like Cletus. That man frets and worries more than the rest of us, and his schemes make him restless, bring no peace. Nor will I leave my family for years without making contact, like Ash. I saw how her absence affected my family. I forgive her, and I know why she did it, but I'd never do that to them. See, Duane." Roscoe grimaced. "He takes people for granted, their affection for him. He can be careless, thoughtless, like Jet was, like Ash was when she left us. That's just Duane, how he's built, but I'll never do that. Now Beau . . ."

Pausing, he took a deep breath and leaned back against the headboard, his eyes losing focus once more. "Beau set a good example on how to do things right, how to be conscientious and honorable. He treats folks—everyone—with kindness and respect. That's why he's so well-liked, not 'cause he's good-looking, or does people favors all the time. It's because he makes everyone he meets feel special."

Enraptured by this conversation and these revelations, I nodded. Because Roscoe was right.

He was exactly right about each of his siblings. Seeing how their choices impacted him made me question how Dani and Poe's choices had impacted me, likely without me even realizing it.

Roscoe released a little laugh, scratching his jaw. "He told me when I could be sure about a woman."

"Who? Beau?"

He nodded, giving me his eyes, which held an edge of circumspection.

So I narrowed my gaze on him. "Enlighten me, how can you be sure about a woman?"

Roscoe held my stare for a beat, and then said plainly, "She makes you a priority."

CHAPTER TWENTY-ONE

"Memories are dangerous things. You turn them over and over, until you know every touch and corner, but still you'll find an edge to cut you."

— MARK LAWRENCE, PRINCE OF THORNS

Roscoe

SIMONE STOOD AND walked out of the room, but not before I caught the shadow of unease pass over her expression.

I waited, counting the seconds until I reached ten. I also stood while trying not to think about why she'd left so abruptly. I'd just have to trust she had her reasons.

She loves you, I reminded myself, and I wasn't going to jump to conclusions. I didn't like jumping to conclusions. Truth was, I couldn't afford to jump to conclusions, if I could help it. Overreaction muddled experiences, clouded what might otherwise be a sunny memory.

So I waited, clearing my mind and focusing on the good, the night before, her declaration early in the morning, lying with her until sunrise. When I finished, I remembered it all again, cognizant of the fact that recollections involving a naked Simone were likely to get me hot and bothered.

I'd have to be careful, in the future, about not allowing those memories to pop up—literally and figuratively—at inopportune moments.

Pulling on boxers, I twisted at the sound of her reentering the room. She walked straight for me, her amber eyes dampened by worry.

"There's something I need to tell you." She stopped at my elbow and I saw she'd dressed, once more wearing her jeans, but instead of the button-down, she wore a white tank top with no bra.

I glanced at the clock on my nightstand, figuring we had a good twenty minutes before I absolutely had to take a shower if I wanted to make it to work on time, which was negotiable.

"Oh?" I asked, looking her over again.

She crossed her arms. "Don't look at me like that when I am trying to confess something important."

"How am I looking at you?"

"Like you want me. For breakfast."

"Can't be helped." I shrugged. "Unless you're offering yourself for lunch? Maybe dinner?"

She rolled her lips between her teeth even as a reluctant smile brightened her eyes. "How about a midnight snack?"

"Deal." I reached out my hand and she took it, shook it, and made to release me. I didn't let her, instead bringing her knuckles to my lips so I could kiss them. "So what do you need to tell me?"

Now her hand tightened on mine—like she didn't want to release me—and she shifted her weight back and forth on her feet. "First, I have some questions."

"Okay."

"Really, just one question."

I glanced between her eyes and where she held my hand captive. "Shoot."

"Why?" All the humor left her features and her gaze turned prob-ing. "Why were you a virgin? What haven't you been with anyone?"

I debated on how best to answer, because there were many answers, but finally settled on the most precise response, which also happened to be the least likely to cause either of us awkwardness. "I have a really good memory."

"What? That's it? You've stayed a virgin because you have a really good memory?"

"That's right."

"No." She was looking at me sideways, suspicion lacing her tone. "That doesn't make any sense. If anything, shouldn't that make you want to have *more* sex? So you have more sexy memories?"

"It does make sense, if you think about it."

I paused here, because a scene played in my mind's eye, a complete moment of the first time we'd kissed. I felt, with breath-stealing palpability, how badly I'd wanted to kiss Simone again, and again. The visceral, starving feel of it. The times after when we'd fooled around, when touching was a curiosity to her, but a building, swelling, proliferation of longing in me.

But how could I communicate this to her without the risk of making her feel guilt? She shouldn't feel an ounce of guilt for feel-ings she didn't feel, or amorous attentions she didn't want.

As my momma would say, *"Sometimes hurt ain't nobody's fault. It just is."*

"How good of a memory are we talking about here?" Simone asked, pulling me from my recollections.

"Really, really good."

From the internet searches I'd done and the books I'd read, I knew I was unusual. I knew it wasn't normal to experience time travel, or have periods where controlling memories—a flood of them —was difficult.

I'd read about folks with time-space synesthesia and I didn't think I had anything like that. I didn't see time as a grid laid out before me, and behind me, with myself at the center of a Möbius strip. I was no better or worse than the average person at marking dates in a future calendar.

From everything I'd read, it seemed I had an eidetic memory, just situationally focused. That said, I'd never taken the time to seek a diagnosis. Nor had my momma. A diagnosis wouldn't change the recollections or lessen them. It might give me a label, but so what?

Plus, and maybe it was selfish of me, but I didn't particularly want anyone to know. Correcting folks' stories irritated them, pointing out discrepancies won me no friends. Maybe my situational memory skills could be used as a parlor trick, but that didn't interest me any. I didn't want the attention or the memory that went along with it.

Perhaps it made me strange, but I didn't want to become a research subject, I didn't want to know more about how my mind worked, or why it worked this way. Content with who I was, I just wanted to live my life.

Simone frowned, looking distracted even as her eyes moved between mine. Shaking herself suddenly, she glanced at the clock next to the bed, restless. My answer didn't satisfy her, I could see that, but her attention appeared to be tangled in a more pressing issue.

"I have more questions about this topic," she said, like a warning, looking at me squarely again. "But I know you need to get to work, so it'll have to wait."

"Fine." I scratched my jaw in a show of nonchalance. But the fact was, sooner or later I'd have to sit Simone down and explain the full depth and breadth of the matter. If she truly wanted to be with me always, as she'd said last night, then it was only fair she understood what that meant.

She gave me a tight smile, which I returned.

But then she blurted, apropos of nothing, "Everything I've told you, since I arrived yesterday, has been true."

My eyebrows shot up and I arm-wrestled my urge to jump to conclusions. "Okay . . ."

"But I also came here on a mission." Her tone grew forlorn.

"A mission?"

"Yes. Roscoe." She now held my hand gripped between both of hers and she looked deeply, searchingly into my eyes. "Don't be upset."

I blinked. "Why would I be upset?"

"Because I need to talk to you about your father."

Flinching, I rocked back on my heels and lifted my chin, an automatic defensive posture as I braced for the memory of him leaving me behind, of him trying to take Ashley and Billy after our momma's funeral, unsure which would play first. Instead, the memory that surfaced was Darrell as he was now, asking me to give him my bone marrow, and the desperation behind his request.

"Is this about his cancer?" I guessed, asking around the rocks in my throat. "Because I haven't changed my mind."

"What I'm about to tell you, you can't tell anyone. Promise?" Simone licked her lips and took a large breath, like she always did when she was about to tell me something big, like she'd done early this morning before admitting she loved me.

"I promise." Once more, I wrestled with my fears, suppressing them, determined to let her explain.

"I have a friend with—with the bureau, and there have been some murders over the last two years, bikers, or associates of bikers. Their family members. But only in June."

"The bureau?"

"Uh, the FBI."

"Ah." I nodded. "Yeah, I know about this, about the murders."

"Did you read about it? In the paper?"

"No, I haven't seen anything about it in the papers. I overheard something at the jam session last year."

Sheriff James had been talking to Simone's cousin, Officer Boone. They'd been in the back row of the bluegrass room, just behind me, and had mentioned that the body count had reached over twenty. Cletus was playing the banjo on the right side of the makeshift stage, glaring daggers at Beau in the audience for finishing off all the coleslaw earlier, and I was wearing a green flannel shirt. Beau made Cletus more coleslaw that Saturday and all was forgiven.

"The thing is, my—my friend believes that your father knows information which he will share, probably leading to the capture and conviction of the murderer, in exchange for cancer treatment."

Her eyes were beseeching, near frantic, and I could tell she believed what she was saying. I could also tell there was a lot she wasn't saying; which meant she had her reasons for withholding details; which meant there was a lot I'd have to guess.

"You don't want to endanger your friend," I said, examining her closely.

She neither confirmed nor denied my theory, merely watching me.

"Is this someone you knew in DC?"

Simone remained motionless, her eyes communicating only that she hated not being able to answer me.

I sighed. "Are you in danger?"

Her attention dropped to the floor and panic speared me right through the heart.

"Simone—"

"Please don't ask me that."

I didn't know where to look, I could hardly breathe, but I did huff a frustrated laugh. We'd just found each other, we'd just started living a shared life, talking about moving closer, her parents prob-ably already planning a wedding—which I, for one, would encourage —and now this?

I tried something else, something I considered fairly obvious. "You want me to donate my bone marrow so your friend can get Darrell's information about the murders."

Even before I'd finished speaking, she began nodding, but she also looked a little green, like this entire conversation was making her nauseous.

"Yes. Yes, that's exactly right. I would *never* ask you to recon-sider helping your father. I remember—I remember . . ." Now she was breathing hard, her eyes full of sympathy. "Well, let's just say, I remember."

I nodded faintly, thinking this information over, wondering briefly if she'd answer any of my other questions, but I knew at once she wouldn't. Or rather, she couldn't.

She wanted to keep her friend safe, and I respected that. I respected the badge, the good folks who kept us regular folks safe, and I'd always thought I'd do anything in my power to help, if I was ever called to.

A long-buried memory surfaced, one I'd worked tirelessly to forget, playing in my mind as clear as the walls of the bedroom I stood in now, one of my mother unable to get out of bed after a visit from our father. I'd been five. I hadn't made it to kindergarten that day.

And Billy . . . *Billy.*

I winced, swallowing, closing my eyes and turning from Simone. She released her hold on my hand, but almost immediately after she wrapped her arms around my middle, placing her cheek on my back.

"I'm so sorry to ask this." Her voice was thick with the truth of her words. "God, I am so sorry. If there were any other way."

Keeping my eyes closed, I nodded. "If I help, will you be in less danger?"

She didn't answer, instead pressing her forehead against my back and taking a breath that sounded suspiciously like a muffled sob.

Christ.

"How long do I have?"

Simone didn't answer right away, giving me the sense she wasn't sure how to answer the question, which was all the answer I needed.

"The sooner the better," I guessed, placing my hands over hers.

"Correct." The word was quiet, and she added bleakly, her voice watery, "June is next month."

CHAPTER TWENTY-TWO

❦ ❦ ❦

"If you erase all of your bad memories, you erase all of your wisdom."

— MATSHONA DHLIWAYO

Simone

AFTER MAKING ME promise to stay at least one more night with him—like I was going home anytime soon, *puh-leez!*—Roscoe left for work. Before he left, we made plans to meet for lunch at the vet clinic. As I promised Cletus the night before, I would also pick up Pavlov and bring him back to Roscoe's apartment.

The moment Roscoe's front door shut, because I didn't want to give myself a chance to second-guess anything, I picked up my phone and texted Nelson.

Payton: *R says he'll do it.*

That done, I collapsed on the couch, stared forward, and allowed the reality of what I'd just talked Roscoe into—i.e. helping his scummy father—wash over me. I felt sick.

I belong in a lab.

My phone chimed, pulling me from my miserable reflections, and was surprised to see that Nelson had already responded.

Nelson: *Meet me at Biscuit Love Gulch for breakfast in 45 min, I'll send the address.*

Startled to discover Nelson was in Nashville, and queasy at the prospect of breakfast, I forced myself to finish dressing, gathering all my gear, and reassembling my gun. Less than fifteen minutes later, I was on my way to meet her. I was also fretting and owning my guilt.

So. Much. Guilt.

Closets and basements and storage units full of guilt.

I belong in a lab.

What if Roscoe was only donating his bone marrow because of me? Because he believed I was in danger? I was in danger, as all undercover agents are, but in an indirect, roundabout sort of way. Maybe my non-answers had ultimately manipulated him into agreeing?

That was not okay with me.

Also not okay, I couldn't tell Roscoe that *I* was "my friend the FBI agent." It was a fuzzy lie, but it was still a lie.

You belong in a lab.

A sour taste on my tongue, I parked, walked across the street to Biscuit Love Gulch, and easily spotted Nelson sitting in a booth inside. Her elbows on the table, her eyes presumably on the screen of her phone, she was dressed in all black—leather—and dark, dark sunglasses. Inside.

So, you know, casual breakfasting attire for a badass.

Looking up nonchalantly, she waited until I was a few feet away before lifting her chin in greeting. "You hungry?"

I shook my head, slipping into the bench seat across from her.

I felt her gaze move over me from behind her sunglasses. "You sick?"

"I feel sick."

Glancing at something off to the right, she slipped her phone in a pocket and removed her sunglasses. "You feel guilty."

It wasn't a question, so I didn't answer it.

Crossing her arms, she brought her gaze back to mine. "How did you get him to agree?"

The question gave me pause and I gathered a deep breath as a stalling strategy. I didn't want to tell her how I'd convinced Roscoe. I didn't want to tell her I'd given him half-truths, which might've jeopardized the security of the mission and undercover agents (but I didn't think so).

I'd done it.

I'd done what she asked.

He'd agreed.

Why did she need to know *how* I'd accomplished this despicable Herculean task?

She didn't.

So I mirrored her posture, crossing my arms, and said, "I did what I had to."

Her ebony eyes drilled into me, twin obsidian probes of suspicion and intelligence. I cleared my mind and met her gaze evenly—imagining a future happy time when all of this was over, Roscoe and I were settled in Washington, DC with our three-bedroom apartment and German shepherd named Cletus Maximus, and we were having enchiladas with Nancy on Tuesday—bracing myself for a chew-out or a set down or whatever was coming.

But then Nelson sighed, the stiffness in her shoulders easing. "Okay."

I was surprised, obviously, and relieved.

I worked frantically to hide both, saying, "Okay."

Giving me another once-over, she sipped her water. "Want to watch me eat?"

"That's fine." I reached for my water glass, pulling it and the square napkin it sat on closer to me. "I have more to tell you, if you think now is the time and place."

"Tell me." She returned her glass to the table.

"Roscoe invited me to the Kentucky Derby."

"Hmm." Nelson examined me. "Do you have a hat?"

"Not yet." *Dammit.*

I made a mental note to figure out what to do about a hat, and what to do about putting a hat on my hair, and all the nightmare logistics involved with that. *I bet my sister would know what to do . . .*

"Why is he going?"

"One of the vets in his office works with horse breeders. She's an equine specialist, and has tickets."

"Does your contact still believe Razor will be present?"

"My contact hasn't given me any reason to doubt it." I knew better than to ask what the plan was for apprehending Razor at the Kentucky Derby, having resigned myself to the fact that I was more or less an information mule at this point. It was need-to-know information and I didn't need to know.

"Are you meeting Roscoe at the Derby? Or driving separately?"

I gave her an eye-squint. "Why?"

"I'd prefer you to arrive separately. Then, you'll drive in with us and go through the law enforcement entrance, keep your gun and gear on you. I hadn't planned on you being there, but if you are, you might as well come prepared."

This earned her my crazy eyes—as in, I was looking at her like she was crazy. "Does this mean you're bringing me into the loop?"

"No." Nelson eyed her water. "You'll be backup."

"How can I be backup if I'm there with Roscoe? I'd blow my cover."

She shrugged. "I doubt it'll come to that. But if you're going— with Razor Dennings there—you should be in gear. We're talking about a serial killer."

"Fine," I said, resigned to the fact that I'd have to carry my weapon, handcuffs, phone, flashlight, et al. all day. Carting my gear around wasn't a problem—occupational hazard—but hiding it under a dress would be.

"What is it?" Nelson was peering at me funny.

"Do you have any tricks for hiding your gear under tight clothes? Or dresses?"

She rubbed her chin. "Where do you usually carry?"

"Back, left side."

"What about when you wear a dress?"

"I don't usually wear a dress." Last night, I'd left my gear hidden at Roscoe's place for our dinner date, pieces of the gun scattered all over the kitchen since I couldn't figure out where to put it on my person.

Nelson's expression seemed to relax, and she leaned forward as she spoke. "You know those conceal-carry thigh holster shorts? The ones that sorta look like SPANX? Those are perfect for dresses. If you add a second thigh holster—buy it with the garter, otherwise you'll be yanking it up all day—you can use the second one for your additional gear. Carry on the front, inside of your thigh—both thighs—so you can sit comfortably. Oh, and definitely bring a hat. You can set it on your lap to hide any bulk. Better yet, get a dress with tulle beneath, so it's already fluffy in the front."

Halfway through her instructions, I'd pulled out my phone and began to take notes.

"The field office here only stocks the external thigh holsters, which are useless for undercover work," she said irritably. "I'm sure you can find what you need at a gun store in Knoxville. You can also get everything online, but make sure to rush the shipping."

"I will," I responded distractedly, still typing.

She said nothing for a few seconds as I finished, but when I looked up she was smirking at me. "Have fun with your boyfriend."

"I will," I said again, more firmly this time.

She lifted an eyebrow. "Oh? So now Roscoe Winston is your boyfriend?"

"Yep." I turned off my phone and slipped it back in my bag.

Agent Nelson studied me, her eyes once again probing. "You

know you can't tell him. You can't tell him about what you do, why you're in town. Not even when all this is over."

"I know."

Still looking wary, she reached for her glass again. But instead of picking it up, she pushed it to one side because a waiter approached with her food. After ascertaining that she was pleased, and that I was fine with the water already in front of me, he promptly left.

I glanced at Nelson's plate, wrinkling my nose slightly at the sight of her egg white omelet with spinach, sliced tomatoes, and air. I wouldn't judge her for the world's most tasteless breakfast, even though breakfast food was my favorite, but I did send a little prayer upward in thanksgiving that I wasn't the one working undercover as a stripper.

Seriously. The woman needed her own series on TNT. She was dynamite.

"Anything else you want to share?" she asked, reaching for the hot sauce and dousing the contents of her plate with it. My eyebrows inched up with surprise and approval. The tangy aroma of Tabasco hovered between us.

"Yeah," I said, "I'll be staying in Nashville through tomorrow."

Her hand paused, mid-douse, and her eyes cut to mine. "No. Now that you have Roscoe's agreement, you need to be back in Green Valley."

"What? Why?"

"What if your contact needs to reach you? So close to the Derby, what if you're not at the diner when she or he shows up?" Nelson leaned closer. "You need to tell your contact about Roscoe agreeing to the treatment, so we can make plans to extract Winston and get his statement. The sooner this loop is closed, the sooner this will be over."

I breathed out through my nose and glared at Agent Nelson, hating the fact that she was right even as my brain clamored to find an alternate solution.

Maybe . . . maybe I could hire some white dude to drive me back to Nashville every night? Deveron Stokes was a shady character, but he was always looking for more work. Or maybe I could talk Roscoe into meeting me halfway? At least for one night, because four days —four miserable days—separated us before the Derby and I didn't know if my heart could make it that long without seeing him. Kissing him.

And debauching him.

"Shit," I muttered under my breath, my rib cage squeezing my lungs painfully. I hadn't meant to say the word aloud, but it was perfectly reflective of this shitty situation.

Shit.

Shit shit shit shit shitter shiticker shite shoot shat shit.

Shit.

"I'm sorry," she said, looking sorry, and the show of sympathy caught me off guard. "But think of it this way: thanks to you and your boyfriend, we might be able to wrap this up by next week. Lundqvist might have to stay put until the trial, but the rest of us will be able to move on to new assignments."

Nodding faintly, I reluctantly abandoned thoughts of meeting him halfway and instead turned my energy towards working through the ramifications of leaving Nashville today. What version of the truth could I share with Roscoe? Was it possible to salvage my integrity while also keeping the case confidential and my colleagues safe?

"What are you going to tell him?"

"I was just thinking about that." I tapped my fingers against the top of the table, working through possibilities in my mind and trying to guess Roscoe's reaction to each.

"Not the truth."

I gave Nelson a flat look. "Obviously."

"A family emergency?"

"No." My flat look persisted. "Everyone in Green Valley knows everyone. He'd know I was lying as soon as he called a member of his family." Plus, I didn't plan on lying.

Something that's not the truth, and not a lie either. . . *help me out here, God. I don't ask for much, just racial equivalence, new episodes of Shonda Rhimes's canceled period drama* Still Star-

Crossed—*and yes, I understand the irony—and Roscoe Winston's eternal love and soulful devotion. Oh! And occasionally a good hair day, but I understand if this last one is too much to ask.*

We sat in silence for a bit while Nelson inhaled her hot sauce with egg whites and veggies, and I said my little prayer. I'd just decided to tell Roscoe a version of the truth—that I needed to get back to work in Green Valley at the diner, even though it sounded weak—when my contemplations were interrupted by the buzzing of my phone.

Retrieving the cell from my bag, I glanced at the screen and immediately checked the time. It wasn't yet 8:30 AM.

Swiping to the right, I answered, "Roscoe?"

"Hey," he said, using his regular voice, and my heart did something unexpected. It became the figurative equivalent of that hearts-eyes emoji, you know the one with the big stupid grin? Sighing happily, it melted into warm wonderfulness.

I said, "Hi," like a doofus, unable to stop my grin and blush. But at the same time, I was aware of Nelson's eyes on me. Therefore, I strong-armed the grin and the blush into concealment, cleared my throat, and asked, "Uh, what's up?"

How am I going to make it four days without his voice? Impossible!

"Did your momma get a hold of you?"

A fissure of alarm passed through me. "No. Why?"

I heard Roscoe sigh. "I got a call from Cletus. He just made it to the police station and overheard someone say Officer Strickland was fired this morning."

"Oh." I sat a little straighter, my gaze flickering to Nelson for no reason. I hadn't told her about my run-ins with Officer Strickland. I didn't consider them relevant to the case. "What happened?"

"Cletus spoke to Jackson, and Jackson said your grandpa and your Aunt Dolly came in first thing with Bitty Johnson to talk to the sheriff. When they were done, Strickland was called in and fired."

Now I sighed, long and loud and frustrated, leaning my elbow on the table and rubbing my forehead. "Crap."

"My guess is you'll be hearing from your momma any minute now." He sounded concerned.

"What a mess." I twisted my lips to the side, wanting to curse Bitty Johnson, but also recognizing that she likely believed she'd been doing something good. "Thanks for the heads-up."

Roscoe seemed to hesitate for a moment before adding, "If you have to go back home, I completely understand."

"Thanks." I felt my mouth curve into a regretful smile, laughing inwardly—with some bitterness, but mostly self-deprecating amusement—at the timing of everything.

I'd been saved from lying to Roscoe by having to explain to my parents why I'd been lying (or more precisely, withholding information) from them. Now I'd have to tell Nelson the story as well, just in case the attention and scrutiny I would receive post Strickland-gate jeopardized my place on the case, because I would definitely receive attention and scrutiny.

Folks would come into the diner to gossip—to me, about me—and would want the whole story. My earlier low profile was now compromised, at least for a little while. But "a little while" might as well be forever.

I should have known better. God usually answered my prayers, but the prayers always seemed to be answered in the form of a practical joke.

* * *

MY MOTHER CALLED after I briefed Nelson on my interactions with ex-Officer Strickland—and the alleged happenings of this morning with Sheriff James, et al.—but before I'd made it to Roscoe's work to pick up Pavlov. I was just three blocks away when I spotted her avatar flashing on my screen paired with her ringtone.

Bracing myself, I answered the hands-free link. "Hello, Mom."

"Hello, daughter," she said, making me chuckle, because she'd echoed my resigned tone. Seemingly pleased by my light laughter, she continued, her voice full of compassion, "Okay, baby. Tell me what happened."

My eyes and nose stung, so I rolled my lips between my teeth as I pulled into the veterinary parking lot and gathered a steadying breath, prepared to tell her the story.

But then she said, "Don't tell me it was no big deal. Bitty Johnson said he unclipped his weapon and was shouting at you, that he'd shifted back on his foot, like he was preparing to shoot. If Ashley Runous hadn't come running out, she was about to call the sheriff."

The worry in her voice sobered me and I found my composure easily. "Everything Bitty said is true."

My mother made a sound of distress. "Why didn't you tell us? And why didn't Ashley tell anyone? Dolly said Ashley's brother-in-law was harassed by Strickland months ago, and Boone told me Strickland had been on suspension for it until last month. What is going on?"

"Firstly, I specifically asked Ashley to keep it to herself." I put my car in park, but didn't cut the engine as I wanted to keep using my hands-free. "I made her promise to not tell you or Grandpa, or Dolly or Boone, so don't get mad at Ashley. Second—"

"Why would you do that?"

"Because I'm working here." The "undercover" was implied. "You know I need to keep a low profile."

I listened as my mother gathered a deep breath. When she released it, it sounded frustrated. "That man was harassing more than just you, Simone. Your Aunt Dolly said she and Billy have been hearing stories from folks at the mill for the last month, even Eve Templeton was pulled over! Can you imagine? Eve in her Armani suit and BMW? What was she going to do? Give him a paper cut with a hundred-dollar bill?"

I smirked at that, but then immediately sobered, because Eve Templeton was smaller than me, had grown up sheltered, and must've been terrified.

Yes, I was sure she'd received "the talk" when she was a kid, about how us darker-skinned folks must never do anything or say anything that might draw negative attention or suspicion. Green Valley was much more of a melting pot than many places, thanks in large part to the Payton Mill being the major employer in the area as well as the work of my grandfather as a federal judge. We'd felt safe in our small corner, but my parents had to prepare us for the world. Every black kid I knew received the talk, about how to behave around police and law enforcement (outside of our small town) in particular.

Never smile.

Always say, Y*es sir* or *No ma'am.*

Make eye contact, but try not to look threatening or scared.

Keep your hands where they can see them at all times.

Don't move unless instructed, and even then, don't move too fast.

Keep your voice calm, respectful, and even.

Don't say anything more than required.

My father had been careful to tell us that police officers outside of Green Valley were not inherently bad people, but that police and law enforcement in general—those institutions—would not be looking out for our best interest.

My brother had received the same talk, but with one slight variation. My mother, fighting back tears, had told him that when he grew up, the world would perceive him as a big, scary black man. That he must never help anyone stranded or on the side of the road. That he must never leave his car for any reason unless absolutely necessary. That he must be careful about driving or being in public places at night for his entire life.

"It's not who you are, baby," she'd said, her voice shaky, "but no matter what you do, it's who people will see."

Even so, they told us that if we were very careful and always behaved perfectly we would still draw negative attention and suspicion just by existing. We should be prepared for inexplicable hostility. We should behave in a manner above reproach, always with calm reason, and never allow our frustration or emotions to guide our response to irrational aggression.

But most of all, they reminded us that no matter how people saw us, we must never forget that the color of our skin didn't define us.

As a teenager, Dani had raged against this information, but always in the privacy of our home. Her rage became passion, and she vowed to dedicate her life to tearing down institutions and destroying people who perpetuated these injustices. Her weapons of choice were power, money, and influence.

"We have to force them to change," she'd said ardently. "We force them to see us and treat us as equals. No justice, no peace."

That, in a nutshell, was my sister.

Poe's reaction had been to question and research the issue tirelessly. Once he'd researched and felt he understood the phenomenon, he'd followed my parents' advice meticulously. He then moved to an area of California that had the lowest use of force complaints (made by black people per capita) in the country. As soon as he was finished with high school, he left, and he rarely visited. His coping strategy was avoidance.

"I don't like bugs," he'd said pragmatically one Christmas. "Or worrying about being shot on the drive from Knoxville to Green Valley because I'm six foot three and black. If I were shorter, or if my skin were lighter, or if I could fly directly into Green Valley, I'd visit more often."

That, in a nutshell, was my brother.

My response hadn't been to rage and it hadn't been to avoid. I'd been upset, which I think was normal and natural, and I'd researched the issue like my brother. In the end, my conclusions about how to best push positive change differed significantly from my sister's.

I joined the institution.

I *became* law enforcement, which often put me in an awkward position.

Case in point, right now.

Presently, my mother was still speaking. "Billy has already spoken to the sheriff—last week as a matter of fact—and Dolly was planning to meet with him next week to follow up. Sheriff James had been moving forward with the officer's dismissal, going through the proper channels and whatnot. Your cousin Boone said the man wasn't bad, just ignorant. Which, you know what? I don't really care if he was bad or not when the end result is people scared out of their minds just for driving down the road."

"So Officer Strickland was told he was fired because of me?"

"I don't know what that man was told, but Bitty claims the Runous's have the whole thing on their security footage and that Strickland man apparently confirmed her version of events. What happened to you made the process of firing him move faster, and I'm glad."

I grunted, frustrated. "If he was going to be let go anyway, I wish Bitty had kept her mouth shut."

"Don't you get angry at Bitty Johnson."

I continued, undeterred, "And why didn't Aunt Dolly or Grandpa come to me first? Why not ask me what I wanted?"

"Simone Payton, you will not disparage your family members for loving you and watching out for you."

"You're right, I won't. But I do want to point out that no one is talking about a solution to the problem."

She huffed. "He's fired. That's the solution."

"And where does he go? Another town? Where he harasses *those* people? Wouldn't it be better to pair him with someone like Boone or Evans? Make them partners and educate him instead, so we stop the cycle? What if Strickland's parents—"

"Are you saying it's *our* job to coddle and reeducate *adults* like this Strickland man? An *adult* man of thirty-three? You think Boone and Evans have time for babysitting? Or the mental and emotional energy? Good Lord, why should it be their responsibility? It's not. It's not your responsibility, either. The fact is, Officer Strickland failed in his duties over and over, and now he's getting fired for it."

"But—"

"But nothing. If a black officer had done this to a white woman, all hell would break loose and you can be damn sure he wouldn't get a second chance. Giving this individual chance after chance after chance because his parents might or might not have been bigots isn't the answer. It perpetuates the problem. It keeps him in a position of authority where he can continue to do harm."

"It's short-sighted to think—"

She wasn't having it. "We all have to take personal responsibility for our actions, Simone. Black, white, yellow, blue. Expecting a man to behave like an adult—which he is—by taking personal responsibility is not an undue burden. Maybe if someone had held this person accountable prior to now, we wouldn't be having this discussion."

"Mom—"

"You know what? Just you wait. Wait until it's your daughter or son being pulled over for no reason, and the police officer puts his hand on his weapon and threatens your child *with a gun*. Your *child*. Wait until *that* happens. You find me and tell me I'm being harsh and short-sighted. Stop making excuses for him," she said firmly, communicating with her tone that this conversation was now over.

Gritting my teeth, I shook my head and leaned forward, resting my forehead against the steering wheel. My neck and chest were hot. I was frustrated. My mind was going in circles.

On the one hand, I fully comprehended and appreciated my mother's perspective. It made sense. It was fair.

On the other hand, maybe the answer wasn't less chances for people like Officer Strickland, but *more* chances and understanding for *everyone*.

She sniffed, and I heard some papers shuffle, before she spoke again. "Now, tell me when you'll be home."

"This afternoon." Leaning back, I breathed in through my nose and out through my mouth, because staying frustrated with my mother or pushing the issue would lead nowhere productive.

"What?" Her voice was suffused with confusion, and perhaps a little dismay. "Why so soon?"

I couldn't help my little smile. "You don't want me to come home?"

A sound of annoyance, then she said, "You already know I want you home, I always want my babies home, where I can see them and make sure they're getting enough iron in their diets. Stop being cute and tell me what happened with Roscoe."

"Nothing happened with Roscoe." I eyed the front door to the veterinary clinic, wondering if he was inside right this moment, covered with puppies again, just lying in wait for another cuteness attack.

Part of me hoped so. But part of me dreaded seeing him again because it already felt impossible to leave him. I wanted to stay and snuggle. I wanted to force him to talk to me about his theories, argue with me about mine. I wanted him to tell me stories of his travels.

He needed to tell me about each and every one of the places he'd visited. We'd then make a list of all the places we would go. Together. Listening to his recollections of Doubtful Sound in New Zealand, the way he painted scenery in vivid detail, as though I'd been right there beside him, had been as soothing as it had been exciting.

Of course, the deep cadence of his voice didn't hurt either.

Yeah. I loved his voice. In fact, I *especially* loved his voice.

I sighed, a little confused by the intensity of my feelings. Was this normal? To crave and pine for a person who had already given himself to you? To abhor the mere idea of a separation? How did people do this? How did they function, go through the motions of day-to-day with such persistent longing?

"Simone."

My name sounded like a warning.

"Sorry." I shook myself, coming out of my reflections. "Uh, things happened—all good things—but I need to get back to Green Valley."

"What? Why? Stay in Nashville and play house for the week. Good Lord, it's not like you two don't deserve a little happiness. He is the sweetest boy, and your father and I used to hope—"

"Oh no." I stopped her. "Please don't tell me what you hoped. Please don't."

She giggled, sounding pleased by my discomfort. "Fine. I won't.

You can pretend we're very upset and disapprove if it means we'll be seeing you both for Christmas. Your grandfather's birthday is next month. It would be *just terrible* if you brought Roscoe. Please don't bring him. Please tell him not to bring his cornbread for the barbecue."

My grin widened uncontrollably. "I'll let him know and ask about Grandpa's birthday. But let's see what happens before we make plans for Christmas."

"Fine, fine." She sounded unconcerned, giving me the impression she'd already—mentally—added a plate for him to the Christmas table.

Her reaction filled me with a bizarre kind of giddiness. Making my parents proud had always made any success sweeter, but being with Roscoe wasn't a goal I'd tackled or a blue ribbon I'd won. We'd fallen in love. It wasn't an achievement, it was a fact. Being with Roscoe, loving Roscoe, looking forward to our future was awesome. But having my mother excited for us was indescribably awesome.

My mom sighed wistfully. "I am so happy for you. I was worried for a while there, but I knew, eventually, it would happen."

Scoffing, I wrinkled my nose, even though she couldn't see me. "You're telling me you always knew Roscoe and I would end up together?"

"No. I didn't dare count on that. What I meant was, I always knew eventually you'd find someone—someone good and kind and honorable—to love you like you deserve. I've always wanted love for you."

My throat felt scratchy, but I spoke anyway. "You've always wanted me to find someone? But you told me that looking for happiness inside a relationship was a road to disaster."

She barked a laugh. "Oh, my baby, I think you misunderstood your mother."

"No. You said, building your whole world around another person is like building a skyscraper on sand."

"And so it is." She chuckled. "But living a life without love is like living alone in a skyscraper. What good does a solid foundation do if the building is empty?"

I frowned. "You're confusing me, Mother."

She laughed again. "You're smart, Simone. I'm sure you'll figure it out."

CHAPTER TWENTY-THREE

"If only there could be an invention that bottled up a memory, like scent. And it never faded, and it never got stale. And then, when one wanted it, the bottle could be uncorked, and it would be like living the moment all over again."

— DAPHNE DU MAURIER, REBECCA

Roscoe

S IMONE DIDN'T STAY another night. I understood why she had to go, but I missed her like crazy as soon as she drove away.

Knowing she was across the state, that I wouldn't see her for days, amplified an aching emptiness I hadn't acknowledged in years. But since I trusted last night was just the beginning for us, I could admit the emptiness had always been a Simone-shaped space.

She'd texted me when she arrived home, and I texted her when I was finished at the animal shelter I typically visited on Tuesdays. The messages were mostly benign, quick status updates. Even so, I spent an inordinate amount of time staring at the typed *I love you* she'd sent. I remembered her saying it early this morning, recalled the moment, and knew I'd revisit that memory more often than most others.

Nine thirty rolled around and I went through the motions of my routine, going for my run, showering, trying to read before bed. I couldn't read. I couldn't concentrate. Heck, I couldn't breathe, not normally in any case.

My heart kept wanting to race, my skin was overly sensitive, my body restless. The memory of her and me, of us from the night before, held a unique sharpness in my mind. The specter of Simone lingered. I half expected her to walk into the room, or find her trying to hide in the corner, wearing only her birthday suit.

Shutting my book, I clicked off the light and lay back in my bed, trying to catch my breath. Minutes ticked by and I kept chasing it. When I turned on my side, the soft cotton sheets against the bare skin of my legs and chest, paired with the smell of her everywhere, meant I was now painfully hard.

Chuckling at my predicament, I sat up, stood up, and stripped, intent on a cold shower. Sooner rather than later, Simone and I were going to have to live in the same city. This, remembering her here but being without her, was the kind of torture that led to madness.

But then, I stopped on the precipice to the bathroom. Half-turning, my gaze searched for and found my phone.

She wasn't *here* here, yet she was with me. We were together. I wondered if she was up.

Sitting on the edge of my bed, I picked up my cell and stared at the screen for a half second. Navigating to our earlier texts, I scanned them.

Simone: *I made it home in record time! Going to drop Pavlov off to Cletus Maximus and Jennifer Bakeasaurus, and then head to the diner for a dinner shift. I love you.*

Roscoe: *I love you too. Thanks for letting me know you made it. Just got home from the animal shelter, but you probably*

*knew that since I still can't find the tracker you put on
my truck.*

Reading the exchange three times, I decided to send a new message.

Roscoe: *Are you home yet? How was work?*

To my surprise, the three dancing dots appeared almost instantly, indicating that she was already typing a response.

Simone: *Made it home twenty minutes ago, about to take a
shower. Can you talk in ten?*

About to take a shower . . . it was my sincerest regret that I hadn't joined Simone last night in the shower. My cock throbbed at the thought and I gripped it, gritting my teeth and swallowing thickly, a shock of aching longing stealing my breath again. Before I could think better of it, I typed out a quick response.

Roscoe: *Wish I was there.*

Simone: *I promise you, the diner was not someplace you
wanted to be tonight. We wouldn't have been able to talk.
Everyone in town seemed to want pie on a *Tuesday* but
they were just using pie as an excuse to come in and ask me
about Strickland. Let me call you after my shower.*

I frowned, rereading her message, a twinge of guilt cooling some of the heat in my veins. I hadn't forgotten about her trouble with Officer Strickland, but it hadn't occurred to me that she'd be dealing with a gambit of gossipmongers at the diner. Now I wished I'd been there for completely different reasons. Namely, to run interference.

Plus, while I'd been getting hot and bothered, missing her, she'd been dealing with serious shit at home. I shouldn't have been texting, hoping for some sweetness and relief. I should have been texting, looking to provide support.

Lying back against my pillows in the dark, I decided to wait for her call, *and then* I'd take a cold shower, or take care of business for myself. Lord knows, I had enough practice.

True to her promise, Simone called ten minutes later. I'd been trying to concentrate on unsexy memories of my bedroom, like the time I had the stomach flu and threw up all over the carpet on my way to the bathroom. Since I was still holding my phone, I answered almost immediately.

"Simone?"

"Roscoe," she said on a sigh. "It is so great to hear your voice."

"You, too." I grinned, because it was. I'd always appreciated her voice, it was smooth and deep, reminding me of the velvety texture of rose petals. Red rose petals.

My body tightened in response to the sound of her, but I shoved its carnal intentions away. She'd had a bad day. A long day. I would provide support. I would be a perfect gentleman.

"Tell me about your day." I threw a pillow over my erection so I wouldn't have to see it.

I *felt* it of course, but somehow seeing it in the bed where we'd been together last night while listening to her talk in my ear was too much.

"I don't want to talk about that right now. Maybe tomorrow. I mean, what I said in my text summarized the situation, and there's really nothing else to say other than the next few weeks are going to be busier than usual at the diner."

"That's terrible," I said, wincing and closing my eyes at the pithy response. So I quickly added, "I could take some time off work for a few days, if you want, keep folks from bothering you."

I heard her laugh lightly and could picture her face, her nose wrinkled slightly, her eyes bright with amusement, her gorgeous mouth curved in an alluring smile. "What's your plan? You're going to sit in the diner and scare people away?"

I didn't hesitate. "Yeah."

She laughed harder and the sound of it sent a new kind of warmth along my nerves. Not the scorching fervor of desire, more like a languid heat. No less intense, just less urgent.

"I can be scary," I said, hoping to prolong her laughter.

It worked. "Yeah. Uh-huh. Okay."

I imagined she was rolling her eyes.

"My junior year of college, I won an award for scariest Halloween costume."

"What were you?"

"Organic Chemistry final."

She barked another laugh, and so I laughed, too. I rested my arm against my forehead, my palm turned, and stared at the dark ceiling, enjoying the moment.

"Thanks." She sniffed, and I imagined she was wiping her eyes. "I really needed that."

"I have jokes, whenever you need them."

"Tell me, what's your favorite joke these days?"

Oh man, I had so many. One of my patient's owners told me I'd make a great dad because I already had so many dad jokes.

"Okay, you asked for it. Prepare yourself."

"Consider my loins girded."

That made me laugh, which made her laugh again, and I shook my head at us. We'd always shared the same humor, but she was much funnier than me. I'd missed laughing with Simone.

"Roscoe! Tell me your joke."

"Fine, fine. Here it is." I cleared my throat unnecessarily. "What's the best thing about being from Switzerland?"

"What?"

"I don't know, but the flag is a big plus."

"Oh no!" She laughed again, but it sounded like a pity laugh.

"Hey. That joke is funny." I'd thought it was hilarious the first time I heard it from Beau.

"You poor, sad, little man."

I gasped dramatically, and that made her laugh again.

Eventually, our laughter tapered, and she sighed. "Roscoe . . ."

Simone paused, I heard her breathe in and say on a rush, "I feel I should tell you that I'm naked."

My eyes flew open and I groaned before I could stop myself, my dick waking, pressing against the pillow.

She laughed again, but it sounded breathier this time, a little nervous. "So . . . maybe, if you want, you should change so we're wearing matching outfits."

The nervousness seeped into her words and piqued some new instinct in me. The urge to assure her that I *did* want, I wanted very much, for us to wear matching outfits.

So I said, "Done."

She hesitated, and I could tell she was surprised. "That didn't take long."

"Since we're being honest." My voice deepened because it felt right. "I should tell you I was already naked."

"Oh my!" Her excitement and pleasure were obvious. I heard the springs of her bed depress, the click of a lamp. "That is *fantastic* news. Are you in bed?"

"I'm lying in my bed, yes."

"And you're naked."

"Very."

"Are you . . ." More nervousness, but this time it was laced with anticipation. "Are you comfortable?"

Uh, what?

Was I comfortable?

No. Not even a little.

But I wasn't telling her that.

So I took over, because lying here in the dark with her scent all around put me in a bold frame of mind. "I have some questions."

"Hey. That's my line." I could hear the smile in her voice.

"And since we're wearing matching outfits, now seems like a good time to ask them."

"What kind of questions?" Her voice was quieter, interested.

"Do you have any fantasies?"

She gathered an audible breath while I held mine.

"Yes," she said softly, using a voice I didn't have a lot of experience with. "I have fantasies."

Vulnerability.

That's what it was.

Protectiveness flared, an imperative to put her mind at ease. "Will you tell me one?" I asked gently.

"Why?" She sounded wary.

"I'd like to know what you think about when you touch yourself."

Simone made a soft sound, like her breath caught. "You've done this before."

I shook my head even though she couldn't see me. "I haven't."

Simone seemed to hesitate before saying, "Then how are you so good at it?"

"Maybe because I'm honest?"

"You honestly want to know what I think about when I touch myself?" Her voice was thicker, huskier.

"Don't you want to know the same about me?" I wrapped my fingers around my cock. I didn't need to close my eyes to imagine her here, whispering in my ear.

"Maybe." Another soft sound. "As long as it involves me."

That made me chuckle, because how could she doubt it?

"You're here," I began, giving myself a stroke, and she *was* here. "And you're wearing something that's see-through."

"What color is it?" The question was more breath than voice.

"Red." *Rose red.* "And you come into the bedroom while I'm reading. You grab the book and toss it somewhere—to the floor or table, whatever—and take my hands, put them on your ass." I had to stop here to swallow, my throat tight. "You're not wearing any underwear and you ask me if I want dessert."

"Uh, what? I'm baking in this fantasy?"

I ignored her question, lost to my own imagination. "I nod, because I really do. So I lie back and you sit on my face—"

"Oh . . . oh!"

"—and I—" I groaned, licking my lips, wishing they were hers.

"You taste so fucking good. My hands move up your stomach to your breasts while you rock your hips, grinding against my mouth and tongue." I had to swallow again.

She was breathing heavier now, and I could almost feel her racing heart through the phone.

"Okay, okay. Wait," she said, using that new soft tone. "I do have this one- I've *had* this fantasy for a while. But it's- it's cliché and stupid."

I had to blink several times to focus on her words, to pull myself out of my own fantasy. "Does it get you hot?"

"Yes."

"Then it's not stupid."

Her laugh sounded sincere, but still nervous. "We're in high school," she started, and a shock of white-hot longing speared me. I stilled, every muscle in my body tense.

I remembered her in high school.

I remembered wanting her in high school.

I remembered losing sleep over it.

"You know how you played football and I played soccer, and we used to practice on the fields at the same time once in a while?"

"Yes," I said immediately, my eyes wide and staring at a memory of her running after a soccer ball, dressed only in shorts, cleats, shin guards, socks, and a sports bra. It had only happened once, during an unseasonably hot day in the middle of January, but it had made an impression.

"So it goes like this." She cleared her throat. "The boys' locker room is closed. You guys have to use the girls'. Our teams take turns, whatever. But, for some reason, I'm there late, taking a shower. . ."

"Yeah?" I prompted, anxious to know everything. Fucking hell, I was on the edge of my seat.

"Hearing you guys come in, I start rushing through, trying to finish. But then you're there, pulling back the curtain."

All the air left my lungs in a rush and I felt the telltale signs of my orgasm build. I'd barely moved my hand.

"I try to cover myself as your eyes roam over me. You're wearing only a towel."

I groaned, closing my eyes, my hand moving faster.

"You put a finger to your lips, telling me to be quiet, and hang the towel on one of the hooks." Simone's voice had grown dreamy, like she wasn't really talking to me. "We're naked, and you reach for me, kissing me, the hot water between us. You bend to tongue my breast, your hand slipping between my legs."

"Fuck." I was chasing my breath again, my chest too tight, fire in my veins.

"Not yet. That part comes later. First you touch me with your fingers and you tell me you miss me, that I'm all you can think about."

"You *were* all I could think about."

Now she moaned. I listened as she panted. "Roscoe."

"Simone." I growled her name. "I thought about you every day. I wanted you so fucking badly."

"You make me come with your- your fingers." She sounded out of breath. "And you bring them to your mouth and suck them. You bend to my ear and say all these dirty things. Like, you tell me you're going to- to—"

"What? What do I say?"

"You're going to come to my bedroom that night and- and fuck me, but then I have to suck your—"

The rest of her words were lost. I pressed my head back against my bed, my hips jutting forward, and I came. A patchwork of visions flashing through my mind. Simone on her knees, her mouth around me, her eyes on mine. Me waking her, in her bedroom, the middle of the night, her body ready, pulling her shorts down her legs.

"Roscoe," she panted, pleaded. "I'm so close. What would you do to me if you were here?"

"Uh." I shook my head, trying to clear it, but then ultimately decided to tell her my lingering thoughts. "After the shower, I keep my promise."

She moaned.

Her ragged breathing was the sexiest sound in the world.

"I sneak in the window, which you leave open." My heart still hammering in my chest, my hand covered in my release, my brain foggy, I needed to hear her come. "I wake you up by peeling back your covers and sliding up your shirt, exposing your breasts."

Simone made a soft, strangled sound.

"My mouth is on you, sucking. My fingers move inside your underwear and I tell you I'm going to make you feel so, so good. We take off your shorts together."

"Yes."

"I spread your legs—"

"Yes."

"I climb on top and rub my cock against your clit."

"*Yesss*," she cried.

"I ask if you want me to fuck you hard or—"

I stopped speaking, because she was coming.

Closing my eyes, saying no more, I listened, memorizing every moan, sigh, and cry. A symphony of seduction, fireworks in my chest, and an overwhelming sense of arrogant satisfaction.

But then arrogance and satisfaction turned into frustration, because as much as I loved hearing her come and being the one responsible for it, I wanted to hold her afterward. I wanted to stroke her body, feel the fever of her skin cool, watch her stretch and arch.

I wanted her here. Now.

Or I wanted to be there.

I cursed silently, sitting up, listening to her soft sigh and wishing I could capture it with a kiss. This being apart business wasn't going to work. Tonight had been great, no doubt. We'd come together, but we'd be going to bed alone.

Sooner rather than later, no matter what it took, we were moving to the same city.

CHAPTER TWENTY-FOUR

✠ ✠ ✠

"If you tell the truth, you don't have to remember anything."

— MARK TWAIN

Roscoe

I'M NOT GREAT with details, usually by design. Too many details makes for a cluttered memory. This was especially true when attending events with a large number of people.

Approximately one hundred and sixty thousand people—give or take a few thousand—attended the Kentucky Derby. Which meant, on Derby Day, Churchill Downs becomes the third largest city in Kentucky behind Lexington and Louisville (pronounced "*Lou*-ah-ville" for all y'all not from around here).

Speaking of which, now you know how to pronounce the capital of Kentucky . . . Frankfurt. (That's one of my favorite jokes).

Anyway, I'd been told around eighty thousand of the fans entered via general admission tickets and basically threw a huge party on the infield all day. I had a friend from college who attended the Derby every year of undergrad and told me he never once saw a horse, but he did drink a quarter of his body weight in mint juleps.

Simone and I wouldn't be partying on the infield. The tickets Dr. Yi gave me were for a private box in the clubhouse—the covered stands overlooking the finish line—with full access to Paddock Plaza, where folks can watch the horses get prepped for each race.

The original plan was for us to meet just inside the Clubhouse Gate, which I'd been warned had formerly been named Gate 10, around 2:30 PM. But Simone had texted me earlier in the week, requesting instead that we meet past the metal detectors and ticket scanning lines, both new features since the '18 Derby, and we moved our meet-up time to 2:45 PM.

Regardless, I arrived three hours early, anxious to see Simone again. I missed her something fierce, and though my recent memories of us together were vivid, and our nightly phone calls had been spectacular, I went to bed each night far from satisfied.

I wanted her with me. I wanted to have dinner together *every* night. I wanted to hear about her troubles, her worries and fears, and be a big part of her life. I wanted her to be a big part of mine. I'd never anticipated creating new memories so much in my entire life.

Which meant I was also anxious to ensure the day would be a great one, with no hiccups or unforeseen unpleasantness. With all the recent changes to Churchill Downs—from traffic flow to renaming of gates, etc.—I planned to message her ahead of time, providing explicit instructions on how to park and enter the track. So, yeah. I arrived super early to scope out our box, how to get there, and the folks who would be sharing it with us.

I introduced myself, sized them up, and indicated my girlfriend would be joining me later. I did this to make sure they were the right sort, who wouldn't be giving a white boy and a black girl together stares. Maybe it was overkill, but I didn't want any small-mindedness ruining our day.

As it turned out, most of them were veterinarians from out of town, and I was relieved to see two other mixed couples already present.

Breathing easier, I checked out what kind of food was being served and debated whether or not Simone would like it, or would want to visit the concession area instead. There were a few new bars since the recent renovation, all of which had clever names: the Behave Yourself Bar, the I'll Have Another Bar, the Spend a Buck Bar, the Regret Bar, and so forth. I thought it might be a good time to visit each over the course of the evening, when the bar name suited our situation.

Finally, I scoped out our designated meet-up spot—near the mutuel windows where bets were placed—and sipped my newly acquired mint julep while I tried to get a feel for the flow of traffic.

After a short time, or what felt like a short time, I was surprised to discover my drink empty and my attention absorbed with the general ambiance of the event. This was my first time attending the Derby and the people watching wasn't half bad. Or rather, more precisely, the clothes watching.

I didn't have to concentrate on details to notice how many men wore light colored linen suits, with blue and white striped shirts and silk ties, or how many ladies wore fancy dresses and outlandish hats. Both were so plentiful, only those people who didn't subscribe to tradition snagged my attention, sticking out like dark spots against an ocean of brightly colored hat brims, feathers, fabric flowers, and tan suit jackets.

Maybe if I'd been anywhere else, at any other event, the three men dressed entirely in black—each standing in a different betting line—wouldn't have caught my eye, but they did. Instinctively, my gaze lifted to their faces and, mesmerized, I was shocked to discover I recognized them.

Tattoo Mike from the Talons MC club over in Georgia. I'd met him once when I was six, the last time my momma had allowed us to go to a family picnic at the Dragon Biker Bar.

Hawk from the Chains MC club, out in Texas. I'd also met him at an Iron Wraiths family picnic the summer before kindergarten. He had two sons—twins—my age and they'd played too rough.

Gunner from the Snakes MC club in Kentucky. He'd come over

to our house with my father once when I was five. They'd worked on their bikes in the Quonset hut and sent our momma out for more beer when they'd run out.

Those were just the first three. Over the next several minutes, while I stood transfixed, I spotted seven more. Of the ten total, I recognized five, but that didn't matter. It was clear as day, all of them were from a motorcycle club. Without meaning to, I began noticing details, likely because the details formed a pattern.

Each man carried a large bag strapped to his chest. When the man approached the window, he placed a bet quickly, apparently knowing exactly what to say. He then passed over a quantity of cash —by the looks of it, from where I stood and what I could see, it seemed like a significant amount for each of the betting men—and then he collected his ticket, turned, and left.

But none of the men went very far, nor did they cluster together, nor did they watch the races they'd just bet on. Even the two guys from the same MC club—Tattoo Mike and another fella I recognized named Cueball, also from the Talons MC—didn't talk to each other.

However, after each race, one of the men—only one of the ten— approached the window to collect winnings. This part seemed random, not the same man twice, giving me the impression that the betting part had been done in some organized fashion, and that the winner actually won.

I didn't usually have hunches like Simone, but after watching this happen four times, even I—with my tendency to gloss over details— knew something weird was going on.

Which was why, when I became aware of a tall man walking towards me, dressed in a blue suit with a white pocket square, I wasn't as surprised as I should have been to see my father.

A smile curved his mouth and I watched as his eyes moved over me, taking in my attire.

"Nice suit," he said, drawing to a stop a few feet away. He was also holding an empty mint julep glass. Unlike mine, his ice hadn't melted. "Light gray with a matching vest. Is that tie pink?"

Glaring at him, I blinked once slowly, doing my best to suppress the rising tide of aggression simmering in my stomach, along with the parade of horrible memories clamoring to be relived and re-experienced.

I didn't want that.

I didn't want to spend any of my time today fighting against and sorting through shitty memories.

And I'd be damned if this asshole ruined my day with Simone.

Therefore, my tone was cold as I asked, "What do you want?"

His smile didn't waver, but his gaze did seem to sharpen. "Haven't seen you in a month."

"So?" Glancing at my watch, I saw with some alarm that it was almost 2:45 PM. Simone would be arriving any minute. He needed to be gone before she came.

"Roscoe." The edge in his voice had me looking at him again. "Son," he said, and much of his laisser-faire façade had crumbled, leaving his eyes rimmed with fear, the worry lines on his forehead in stark relief.

Scowling at his expression, I took a half step forward and lowered my voice. "Listen, I don't know how this works, but one of my stipulations for helping has to be that you'll leave me alone."

He flinched, like I'd thrown sand in his eyes, and his brow knotted itself into a mess of confusion, followed by relief. "You— you're helping me? You're going to help your old man? My boy—"

"Don't do that, don't fucking do that," I said through gritted teeth. "You know I'm not doing this for you."

Darrell stared at me, watching me closely for several seconds. "Then who are you doing it for? Because you're lying to yourself and cheating us both out of the time we have left if you keep letting Billy—"

I scoffed, shaking my head. "This isn't about Billy. This is about you making a deal with the feds, handing over critical information, if and only if I donate my bone marrow. Like I said, I don't know how any of this works, but you leave my family out of it. I don't want them to know."

"A deal with the feds . . ." My father rocked back on his heels,

319

his features a mess of wonder and curiosity. He looked so much like Ashley—the unaffectedness of his eyes, the shape of his mouth—I had to look away.

I heard him clear his throat and sensed him move closer. He hesitated just a second before placing his hand on my shoulder, blocking our conversation from the rest of the room.

"I haven't made a deal with the feds, Roscoe," he said, his voice an unsteady whisper. "Because I didn't know you'd agreed to help."

I tensed, but I didn't move away, my mind working overtime.

"But now that I know, now that you've agreed, I need you to pass along some information for me to your contact."

Shaking my head, I was just about to say that I didn't have a contact, only Simone's loose connection with a friend, when we were interrupted by someone tugging on my arm.

I turned, finding Simone standing there in a light pink dress. Her eyes, wide and worried, darted between me and Darrell.

She was a vision.

I took in the low scoop of the neckline, the way the material hugged her breasts and torso, and puffed out past her waist to a full skirt that fell to her knees. On her feet she wore pink and white checkered stilettos, on her head a small white hat covered with calla lilies tilted artfully to one side. Her hair had been pulled up and beneath the frothy concoction of fabric flowers, and her lips shimmered pink.

I wanted to lick them.

I wanted to taste the silky brown skin over her collarbone and whisper into her ear, telling her how gorgeous she looked, how much I'd missed her, how I needed her.

But I couldn't, because Darrell was there, and all I could think to say was, "I'm sorry. I didn't know he would be here."

She waved away my apology and asked tightly, "Are you okay?"

Grinding my jaw, I nodded and gently pulled her hand from my sleeve. I kissed the back of her fingers. I then tucked them into the crook of my elbow and faced my father.

"We're leaving. Don't follow us, don't speak to us—either of us—again."

"Wait." His hand on my shoulder tightened, his voice strained and desperate. "You have to pass along a message for me, to your contact at the feds."

I felt Simone stiffen at my side and I grunted, frustrated with my father. I'd been so careful, arriving early to ensure the day would be perfect. Here he was, ruining everything.

"I don't have a contact at the feds," I whispered harshly.

Darrell's eyes narrowed with suspicion. "Then what are we talking about? What did you mean, 'deal with the feds'?"

The urge to shake him off strangled me, and I struggled to remain calm. "Remove your damn hand right now."

"No. Not until you tell me what you know." His gaze floated over to Simone before returning to me. "I have a number of associates here, right now, and I know this track like the back of my hand. We may be in a crowded place, but if you want Miss Simone to leave here as untouched as she is now, then you'll—"

"I told him." Simone stepped forward and in front of me, her hands coming to my thighs as though to hold me in place, perhaps sensing that my control was snapping and I was seconds away from laying the old man out—nearby associates or no.

"I told him about the deal, and that it was unlikely you would cooperate if he didn't offer his bone marrow in exchange for information," she whispered quickly, drawing the full weight of his attention and suspicion.

"And how did you know, Miss Simone?" His tone and blue gaze were remote, and yet both held an unmistakable threat, and both made me want to pound his face until his bones were dust.

"Be-because I have a contact, and that c-contact told me," she said quickly, her voice strange.

Darrell's chin lifted as he regarded her, his cool stare seeming to read her face as though there were words on it. He shook his head.

"No," he whispered darkly. "I don't think so, Miss Simone. I don't think you have *a contact* at all. You've always been bad at lying."

I gripped her shoulders and I tried to move her, but she wouldn't budge.

Darrell's eyes came to mine, held, his features devoid of emotion, and he asked, "Does he know?"

"What are you talking about?" I growled, my patience at an end. "He who?"

But then Simone said, her voice small, "No. He doesn't know," and I realized Darrell's last question had been for her, not for me.

I wasn't anywhere close to recovering from my confusion when Darrell said to Simone, "Here's what's going to happen: you're going to arrest me, right now."

"What?"

"What?"

She and I spoke in unison.

My father ignored me, all his attention focused on Simone. "You're going to arrest me, right here, right now. You're going to flash your badge for everyone to see, real public like, and you're going to take me out the way you came in."

"That's not necessary," she whispered. "I also have associates nearby, and—"

"No, you don't." He shook his head.

Meanwhile, my hands dropped from her shoulders and I tried to take a step back. I couldn't. Her fingers gripped the fabric of my pants.

"Yes, I do," she insisted. "They arrived with me. We all came together hours ago."

"They're after Razor, right?" Darrell's tone had turned businesslike. "Well, he ain't here now, but he was here. You don't think he has eyes and ears in law enforcement? And now he has your *associates* running around on a wild goose chase. None of them are left at the Derby. Why would they be here if he's gone? You're on your own, Simone. It has to be you."

Her grip on my pants lessened and I was able to step away, but I did hear her ask, "Why now?"

Darrell's glare grew intense and his words were clipped, "Because if you don't take me now, I don't know if I'll be alive tomorrow to give you the information you need, given that *my* associates have been watching this entire exchange and—" He stopped, swallowed, his eyes flickering to me for the briefest of seconds before saying, "Razor knows about the cancer and he knows Roscoe is going to donate."

"How could he possibly know that?" I thought and asked at the same time.

"Because I told him," Darrell said through gritted teeth. "He found out and I admitted I was sick, but that I had it covered."

"You're a damn fool," Simone hissed. "You thought he'd spare you? Help you? Take care of you? To someone like Razor, weakness makes you a liability."

I couldn't see her face, her back was to me, but I sensed her hesitate, knew she was thinking over her options, and that's when my brain finally caught up with what was happening.

She's FBI.

Simone was an undercover FBI agent.

I searched my memories, looking for signs, and cursing myself for always endeavoring to avoid details.

The way she'd spoken to Darrell outside of the diner on the last Thursday of March, how she hadn't seemed to care at all that he'd called her Miss Simone.

"Maybe y'all could come in and have some pie?"

The fact that my father had been the first topic of conversation the next day, when she brought doughnuts to the house, followed me out the back door and onto the porch.

"I have questions. Has your father been bothering you?"

I shook my head.

"When was the first time he made contact with you?"

Something about the tone of her voice grabbed my attention, like the question was an official one, and I chanced a quick glance at her.

"Why're you so interested in Darrell Winston?"

How she knew where to find me at Hawk's Field, the first topic of conversation that night had been my father, too.

"Hey, I have some questions."

Sighing, I asked, *"Such as?"*

"So, what's going on with your dad?"

I started, staring forward and frowning at her subject choice. *"My dad?"*

"Darrell."

"Yes. I know who my father is." I ground my teeth.

"Do you want to talk about your dad at all?" Simone sounded like she was choosing her words carefully. *"I mean, it looks like he came out of nowhere last week. You didn't seem happy to see him."*

"I wasn't."

"Has he tried to make contact with you? Since last week?"

How she'd shown up just as Catfish and Twilight had come to take me, forcing them to take her as well. The disarming moves she used while we'd been trapped in the room. The tracker she'd placed on my truck, the one I'd never found.

Of course. *Of course.* How could I have been so blind? Why else would she track me down, follow me around town, suddenly interested?

She wasn't interested. She didn't want to know me. She needed me, *used me* to get to my father. She used me to talk to him, to make contact with him, and now to help him, because she needed the information he had.

Something within me cracked open, fire and ice spilling out of my chest and to the floor. I couldn't breathe. To breathe was to live, and the pain . . . *the pain.*

Urgency in my father's voice brought me back to the present, and I battled my mind, forcing the tsunami of disordered, cutting thoughts and bruising memories back. I had to get out of here. I had to get away, from both of them.

"We got to hurry. You want my information? You want the murders to stop? You take me in now. Once Roscoe has made his donation and everything is set for my treatment, I'll hand Razor Dennings and all his accomplices—because, I guarantee you, there are a lot more than you know—over to the FBI on a goddamn silver platter."

"I'm sorry, Roscoe," she said under her breath, her eyes darting to me and then away. What I saw there sobered my mind, shame quickly eclipsed by inflexible determination.

Simone didn't hesitate this time. Apparently, she didn't require even a second to think. She reached under the front of her dress and withdrew several items, like a magician pulling rabbits out of a hat, tossing something in my direction.

I caught it. Handcuffs.

Disoriented, I staggered to the side three steps as she backed away, out of his reach, and pointed her gun at my father. Peripherally, I was aware of people gasping, staring, gaping at us. I ignored them.

"FBI," she shouted firmly, all grit and intensity and focus, standing there like Lady Justice in her pink dress, calla lily fascinator, and matching stiletto heels. Simone's shoulders bunched, her arms bent at the elbows. She put him in her sights, her face a mask of rigidity, the barrel pointed directly at his chest. A black wallet in her other hand, showing it to Darrell and anyone else nearby, she proclaimed, "Darrell Winston, you are under arrest."

CHAPTER TWENTY-FIVE

❦ ❦ ❦

"It's so hard to forget pain, but it's even harder to remember sweetness. We have no scar to show for happiness. We learn so little from peace."

— CHUCK PALAHNIUK, DIARY

Simone

TELLING THE STORY didn't get easier. If anything, it became more cumbersome each time, with Roscoe's part a leaden albatross around my neck.

I'd told it five times since bringing Darrell into the Western Kentucky FBI field office. First to Agent Lehey, the field office's Special Agent In Charge (SAIC), along with her deputy. Both, I discovered, had been briefed about our operation at Churchill Downs at some point prior to the Derby. As well, Lehey was intimately familiar with the case since three of the victims were found in her jurisdiction last July.

Next, I recounted the tale for Agent Nelson over the phone on her way back to Louisville. After Nelson, I repeated the story to our SAIC down in Knoxville, and once more for his deputy.

And now I was repeating it again to Nelson and SAIC Lehey. Sitting in a small office, still wearing my pink dress and thigh holsters while sipping stale coffee, I spoke into a recorder. It was the middle of the night. My awesome hat was presumably in the locker room along with my shoes.

"It was at this point that Officer Parkland with Louisville PD brought us here." I finished my latest retelling, rubbing my forehead.

"Why didn't you call us?" Lehey asked, watching me closely. "Why not have us pick you up? Why rely on Louisville PD?"

She'd already asked me this question—as had her deputy—the first time I told the story.

"For a number of reasons." I repeated my original answer tiredly, glancing at Nelson, "First, I didn't know if your office had been briefed."

"Payton wasn't part of the apprehension team for Dennings," Nelson said from her spot next to me; she'd arrived at the field office over five hours ago, but had just been allowed to sit with me recently. "I can confirm that she had no knowledge of the information trail between our offices."

Lehey nodded and motioned for me to continue.

"Second, I didn't want to wait for clearance and a car since Winston had mentioned that a number of his associates were present at Churchill Downs. Any delay felt dangerous and it had been communicated to me by Nelson that Winston was a high-profile asset. Louisville PD was already cooperating. As soon as I gave them Winston's warrant number, they offered the car, which was already on site. They asked me only to wait for reinforcements to arrive, which they estimated would take less than five minutes. This proved to be true."

"So, timeliness was the main issue."

"Expediency, urgency," I clarified. "Yes."

"What about the son? Roscoe Winston?" Lehey asked. "Why didn't you detain him as well? Why rely on the Louisville PD?"

My gaze flickered to Nelson again and I sucked in a slow breath as a buffer against the agonizing spikes of pain radiating outward from my chest, cinching my throat tighter and tighter. I rubbed my sternum against the stabbing throb.

The way he'd looked at me, like I'd betrayed him, like he didn't want to know me . . . God. I'd never forget it. Even when Roscoe had ignored me in high school he'd never looked at me like that.

He's never going to forgive you.

I hadn't seen him yet, but I knew Roscoe was here, being held in another office most likely. Lehey had told me hours ago that he'd been picked up by the Louisville PD, that he was safe.

I began again, repeating myself from earlier, "At Churchill Downs, once it was clear to me that the crowd around us wasn't going to panic, I instructed Roscoe to cuff his father. Again, I was acutely aware of Winston's threats about his associates and I didn't want one of them coming at us from a blind spot."

I didn't need some MC recruit trying to be a hero for the Iron Wraiths' vice president and endangering more than just me and Roscoe. I had one hundred and fifty thousand citizens to worry about.

I considered myself proficient and capable, but I doubted even Nelson would have been able to simultaneously cuff Winston and cover all threats.

"Roscoe did as I instructed." *His face like stone, his eyes like granite.* "After, he stepped back and effectively disappeared."

"What do you mean he disappeared?" Lehey asked.

"He faded into the gathering crowd, allowed it to swallow him. I couldn't find him and I needed to move."

"So you asked Louisville PD to step in?"

"Yes. As I've said, as soon as the asset was secured, and we were waiting for transport, I'd attempted to reach Roscoe Winston on my phone." I texted Roscoe. He hadn't answered. I'd called. He hadn't picked up. "Running out of options, I gave his description and picture to the Louisville PD, indicated that he was a person of interest."

"And they stopped him outside the Clubhouse Gate?"

I shrugged, forcing calm in my voice while willing the excruciating twisting of my heart to stop. "I can't confirm that. You know better than I do what happened to Roscoe. The last time I saw him—as I've said—he was cuffing his father."

Lehey nodded thoughtfully, her eyes flicking over my dress. "What is your relationship with Roscoe Winston?"

My chin wobbled because, quite abruptly, I felt all the sad.

All the sad.

All of it.

I wouldn't freaking cry. I wouldn't. Simone Payton doesn't cry at work. Simone Payton gets shit done. Apparently, Simone Payton also talks and thinks about herself in the third person when she has all the sad.

But I digress.

Gathering a deep breath, I held it within my lungs, waiting for them to stretch and expand and relax. They didn't, so I breathed out. I didn't feel better, I felt more numb. But at least I could speak.

"Roscoe Winston and I were childhood friends and recently we've become romantically involved," I said, sounding like a robot.

"I see." Lehey's eyes slid to Nelson. "Did you know about this?"

"Yes. I did," Nelson responded flatly.

"And you approved?"

I studied Nelson's profile as she glared at Lehey. "She got him to agree to help his shit-bag father, didn't she? Of course I approved."

Lehey's mouth twitched, but she quickly tucked her chin to her chest. A second later she cleared her throat and gave me her eyes again. "Payton, prior to your arrest of his father, did Roscoe know you were with the bureau?"

I shook my head, embracing the numbness in favor of crippling sadness, because the way he looked at me was eternally etched on my brain and would forever give me all the sad.

"No," I said, my voice hollow. "He appeared to be completely blindsided."

Unless I was imagining things, Lehey's gaze softened and she looked a smidge—just a smidge—sympathetic.

But then the smidge of sympathy was gone in a flash and she was back to business, giving Nelson a brief head nod.

"We're finished here, unless you have additional questions."

My senior agent stared at Lehey for a long moment, and Lehey stared back. Clearly, they were communicating silently, but since I had no way of knowing what passed between them, I concentrated on keeping it together.

All I needed to do was force Roscoe to talk to me, forgive me, and trust me again. Simple, right?

Right?

It's the end, Simone. He is never going to forgive you. Let a Sherpa be your guide, not feelings.

"There is one issue," Nelson began haltingly, pulling me out of my depressing reflections, her eyes still on Lehey. After a brief pause, she turned in her chair and studied me. "Simone," she said, surprising me with the use of my first name, "tell me about Roscoe's memory."

My eyebrows pulled together. "His memory?"

Crossing her legs, Nelson folded her hands on her lap. "You've known him a long time."

"I've known him his whole life," I corrected her, but then had to amend my statement. "Well, actually, I knew him until we were sixteen. But he—"

Lehey cut in, "Have you ever noticed anything unusual about Roscoe's memory?"

I shook my head, about to say, *No,* but stopped myself. That wasn't precisely true. "I guess, I mean, when I think about it, Roscoe has always been really good at remembering conversations."

"Can you give us an example?" Nelson seemed acutely interested.

I thought back to Hawk's Field over a month ago and countless times during our childhood. "He can repeat, word for word, a list of questions he's been asked. Or even . . ." I blinked, and was startled to discover that, when I really considered the matter, Roscoe did have an exemplary memory.

"Even?" Lehey pushed.

"Uh." I cleared my throat. "I- I can't- I mean, yes. He has an excellent memory. He has repeated conversations back to me, word for word, that occurred years ago." I covered my mouth with shaking fingers, a hot wave of the confusion that follows a sudden—and obvious—realization rushing over me.

"I have a really good memory," he said, like it was a matter of fact and not nonsense.

And then I questioned him further, but I couldn't quite remember what was discussed, something about not believing his memory was why he'd stayed a virgin.

Ah, yes! I told him it didn't make sense.

"It does make sense, if you think about it," he said, his gaze focused on some spot beyond me. He stared silently for a moment, obviously lost to his own reflections.

I gave him a few seconds, and then I interrupted again, asking him more about his memory, about how good it was. . . I think . . . or something like that.

But then, when he looked at me, I was struck once again by how soulful his eyes were. And then I was struck by how achingly handsome he was. And then I was struck by how awesome it was that he'd chosen me as his deflowering partner. If I could have high-fived myself without it looking like applause, I would have.

"Really, really good," he answered.

But I'd already forgotten the question.

"Simone." Nelson was speaking again, bringing me back to the present. "Roscoe told us that he recognized several men at the Derby who were placing bets."

"Okay." I nodded dumbly, trying to follow the conversation.

Nelson's eyebrows pulled together as she studied me. "He said he recognized the men from meeting them just once. When he was a child."

"Okay," I said again, still struggling.

Nelson and Lehey shared another look.

"That shouldn't be possible." Lehey pointed out the obvious. "It's not normal for someone to remember a face or a name after meeting the person just once in passing at five years old. It certainly isn't normal for someone to recall—word for word—a conversation years later."

My throat was dry, so I swallowed. "That sounds about right for Roscoe," I croaked, overwhelmed by my failure to recognize the unusual nature of Roscoe's memorization skills prior to right now. I mean, I knew he had a good memory, but I'd never really thought about it. It was just part of him, like the color of his eyes, or the shape of his nose, or the way he became squeamish about putting worms on fishing hooks.

That was just Roscoe.

"Really?" Nelson's question was higher pitched than normal, her tone laced with disbelief. "Simone, that's- that's crazy. I've heard of super-recognizers—the bureau has a whole fleet of them—but you're talking about someone memorizing conversations *as well as* faces encountered just once. That would mean he has a situational photo-graphic memory. Do you know how rare that is?"

I felt a little sick to my stomach, because she was right. What other explanation could there be? I'd known him my whole life. How could something so obvious have escaped my notice?

Maybe because you've known him your whole life . . . ?

Endeavoring to recall my best childhood memory with Roscoe, I realized a few small parts were vivid—flashes of images, a sense of feeling—but overall it was fuzzy, an impression rather than a scene. I then attempted to bring forth our worst shared memory, one involving his father, and a sense of dread slithered up my spine, cold and clammy and paralyzing.

If he remembered those men today with such precision after meeting them just once as a child, what else did he remember?

Perhaps more importantly, how clearly did he remember it?

* * *

IT WAS PAST 1:00 AM when I finally saw Roscoe. He was asleep on a couch in the break room, his coat hanging on the back of a nearby chair, his pink tie tossed over it. My chest squeezed my heart at the sight of him, like my rib cage was trying to give the organ an aggressive hug.

So many feelings.

But strangely, the strongest and loudest ones weren't about me, my worry that he'd never forgive me, my fear that we were over. The most powerful of my feelings were about him. Worry for him. Fear for him.

"I have a really good memory."

I shivered.

What would that be like? To remember *everything*?

Studying his long form, how his legs dangled off the couch, I thought about how awkward his height must be for him at times. Airline travel was likely a killer, entering rooms with a low ceiling, or sleeping on strange sofas. However, instead of deciding that he was too tall, I decided that the world was too small.

Roscoe was perfect, just as he was. I hoped he knew that.

He stirred in his sleep. The unexpected movement spurred me forward and I placed a hand on his shoulder, lowering to my haunches at the side of the sofa and giving him a gentle squeeze.

"Roscoe," I whispered, moving my hand to cup his face, the short hairs of his beard tickling my palm. "Roscoe," *my love,* "it's time to go."

His eyelids blinked open, his gaze hazy at first, but then sharpening almost at once upon recognizing me. He flinched, sitting up and moving away from my touch, glancing around the room as he pushed his fingers into his hair.

My heart cried out at his withdrawal, protesting the distance he placed between us. But I told my heart to chill the fuck out.

If he didn't trust me, so be it. I wouldn't blame him.

But, dammit, he would forgive me. If I could forgive him for ghosting me ten years ago, he could and would forgive me for doing my job as an undercover agent. He'd see the reason-Sherpa, consult factual Google Maps, and we'd get through this. Guided by logic.

Obviously, he'd never forget about it, but he *would* forgive me.

"What time is it?" he asked, his voice full of sleep.

I sat next to him on the sofa, careful to maintain the distance between us. "It's past one."

He nodded. He swallowed. He stared forward.

"I can leave?" he asked.

"Yes. I'll drive you home."

He shook his head, not looking at me. "I'll call a taxi."

Examining his profile, the firm set of his lips, the tightness of his jaw, I wondered what he was thinking. *Or what he's remembering.*

"I really must insist that you allow me to drive you home," I said as gently as I could muster.

Roscoe continued shaking his head, but then he closed his eyes, resting his elbows on his knees and letting his forehead fall to his hands.

He mumbled something, too low for me to hear.

"What was that?" I asked.

Sitting up, he turned to face me, and I winced at the vehemence behind his stare. It was an echo of the look he'd given me inside the clubhouse of Churchill Downs, when he'd discovered I'd been working undercover.

"I said"—his voice like ice—"I don't want you to drive me."

Gathering my composure, I squared my shoulders and met his stare evenly. "We need to talk about what happened."

He was shaking his head again and he stood, walking toward the door I'd closed on the way in. Jumping to my feet, I darted to the door and inserted myself between Roscoe and it before he managed to touch the knob.

Roscoe cursed, rocking back on his feet, hastily withdrawing his hand, as though I was fire and he feared I might burn him.

"It would be prudent for you to give me a chance to explain," I said, ensuring my tone was level, practical.

He scoffed, his hands coming to his hips as his gaze—ripe with accusation—moved over me, but never quite settled on my face. "What is there to explain?"

"Clearly, a lot. Judging by your tone and the way you can't stand to look at me." My voice cracked. I ignored it.

His shoulders rose and fell in an inelegant movement, and his attention moved over my head. "You're right."

I sighed, relieved he'd at least admitted that we had a lot to discuss, even if the topics were daunting.

But then he said, "I can't do this right now."

I reached for him. "Roscoe—"

"No." He twisted away, stepping out of my reach, his eyes now on the floor. "You don't understand. I can't."

"Can't what?"

He squeezed his eyes shut, pushing the palms of his hands into his eye sockets. "I can't look at you. I can't talk to you. All I see is you lying to me and all I feel is . . ."

I held my breath, willing him to continue, to finish his sentence, and hoping what he felt was something like longing, wishing, pining, or hope. Because that's what I felt when I looked at him.

But he didn't continue.

Even though I wasn't sure I wanted to know, I prompted on a rush, "What? What do you feel?"

"Pain."

I flinched, holding my stomach and chest, because—*damn*—that hurt like a knife to the kidney, and a punch to the throat, followed by a knee to the vag. I lost the breath I'd been holding and sucked in a new one, pressing my lips together because I wasn't allowed to cry.

I wasn't the one who'd been lied to. I wasn't the one who'd been deflowered by the same someone who—days later—had broken my trust. I wasn't the one with a photographic situational memory. Not that I truly comprehended everything that entailed, but the ability to vividly remember precisely when and how I'd lied to him likely wasn't helping matters.

So, no. Crying wasn't on Simone's agenda.

But neither was leaving this room until he agreed to talk to me.

"Fine," I said, my voice shaky, still holding my stomach and chest for fear that my insides—starting with my heart—would all tumble out. "Fine, I'll call you a taxi. But you have to promise me that you'll talk to me later today."

His hands dropped from his face, returning to his hips. When his eyes opened, they remained on the floor. "I can't make that promise."

"Roscoe." I'd tried not to growl, or demand, or raise my voice. Instead, I did all three. I had to swallow before trying again. "Once upon a time, ten years ago, you dropped out of my life. I am *not okay* with that happening again."

He shook his head, but said nothing.

"Promise me you'll talk to me. Promise me you won't disappear. Promise me I get a second chance."

"Why?" His head snapped up, his gaze a chaotic mess of pain and confusion and anger. "You got what you wanted, didn't you? I said I'd help my father. Why can't you leave me alone?"

Oh, for fuck's sake!

"Because I love you," I shouted, taking an instinctive step toward him, still hugging myself. "I love you and nothing has changed, not for me. I love you and I can't see a future for me without you in it. I love you and you're looking at me like I'm a stranger and it makes me want to—"

"Stop," he said, the word choked, his eyes closed tightly once more. "Just, stop. Please. Please stop."

Watching him, his tangible suffering, I wanted to rush to him and hold him and never let him go. But I didn't, because I'd been the one responsible for it.

With my heart at his feet and tears blurring my eyes—which I blinked away angrily, because they weren't on the agenda—I stepped to the side, clearing his way to the door.

"Go," I said quietly, closing my eyes because I didn't want to watch him leave, but I didn't want to prolong his misery either. "I won't stop you."

All was stillness.

I sensed the air shift. I heard him sigh. I felt him move past and I tensed, squeezing my eyes shut tighter, willing myself to remain immobile, to let him go—if that's what he needed—to hold myself together long enough until I could put crying back on the agenda.

But then I felt rough hands on my cheeks, lifting my face until warm lips brushed and pressed against mine, his nose sliding along my nose.

"I love you, Simone," he said, in that same choking way as when he'd pleaded with me to stop speaking.

He kissed me. His lips a brand, his touch a flame. I tilted my chin upwards, straining, wanting more, but then he shifted, pressing his forehead to mine.

Roscoe whispered against my mouth, "I'll always love you," just as his hands fell from my face and I felt the heat of his body withdraw, leaving frost where there was fire.

I opened my eyes. He was gone, but not without a trace. He'd forgotten his jacket and pink tie on the chair.

CHAPTER TWENTY-SIX

"Remembering is easy. It's forgetting that's hard."

— BRODI ASHTON, EVERNEATH

Roscoe

"WHERE'S THE JACKET?"

I lifted my eyes from the newspaper I wasn't really reading and met the glare of my second oldest brother. Arms crossed, eyes narrowed, one eyebrow lifted expectantly. His mouth was in a flat line, which meant he'd already made up his mind about the answer before asking the question.

"You lost it at the Derby," he said, right on schedule.

I shook my head, returning my eyes to the newspaper. It was almost 9:00 PM and I hadn't made it past the front page. I should have been on the road to Nashville hours ago, but I couldn't bring myself to leave. Nor could I bring myself to return Simone's messages with anything of substance.

I was in indecision limbo.

"I didn't lose it," I said, knowing I sounded like Eeyore.

I understood why Billy was anxious. Italian, custom made, silk, which meant leaving the jacket behind had been a risk. A calculated risk, but a risk nevertheless. If Simone had the jacket, then—eventually—I'd *have to* see her. Billy would never let me borrow anything again if I lost that jacket, and he had great taste in clothes.

The tie, however, was mine.

I'd bought it specifically for the Derby because Simone had told me on Thursday, during our nightly pillow talk, that her dress would be pink. I'd wanted us to match. Therefore, in retrospect, leaving that tie behind felt like an even bigger risk than abandoning the jacket of Billy's suit. I wanted that tie back.

I heard shuffling footsteps approach, like he hadn't made up his mind whether to stay or go, and I listened to him exhale a long sigh.

"Okay," Billy said, sounding resigned. "What's going on, Roscoe?"

I shook my head—not in a denial, but because I needed to clear it —and rubbed my forehead. "It's complicated."

Now he scoffed, taking the chair across from mine and entering my peripheral vision. "Oh really?"

"Yeah. Really."

Really, really, really.

My mind wanted to take me back to Churchill Downs, to the moment I'd finally put two and two together and came up with four instead of, *She's the woman you're going to marry.* Two plus two equaled a number and that number was four, not a happily ever after.

Instead of time traveling to that awful moment, I diverted my thoughts and forced the memory of our later encounter at the FBI field office in its place, when she'd told me she loved me.

"Because I love you," she hollered, her voice coming closer. "I love you and nothing has changed, not for me. I love you and I can't see a future for me without you in it. I love you and you're looking at me like I'm a stranger . . ."

I had no idea what to do about Simone. But after reliving that moment over and over all day, turning it around in my mind, studying it from different angles, I decided that I believed her.

She loved me.

And I loved her. I would *always* love her.

But she'd lied to me.

"Try me." Billy tapped on the table within my vision and I blinked him back into focus. His brow was knitted with concern as his eyes—which were exactly like mine—moved over me. "What's so complicated?"

Maybe it was because I was tired, *so damn tired.*

Or maybe it was because, over the course of my life, I'd had several father figures, some good, some bad. But for all intents and purposes, Billy was basically my dad.

He'd been the one to show up to all my sporting events. He coached my soccer team in middle school and was the assistant coach of my varsity football team in high school. He took me around door-to-door so I could sell popcorn and candy bars for school fundraisers. He attended all my Cub Scout camping trips. He was the one to ask for my report card, and sign it, every quarter. He took me shopping for new school clothes, talked to me about the birds and the bees, and put condoms in my wallet when I turned sixteen.

Jethro, Cletus, Beau, and Duane had done similar stuff, but never with the same dedication or consistency as Billy.

Whatever the reason, I found my tongue loose and my mouth speaking before I'd given either permission to form words. "I'm in love with Simone Payton."

Billy smirked, which quickly became a grin, his forehead clearing. "What's so complicated about that?"

"She lied to me," I said starkly, feeling the twist of the knife renew, finding I could no longer hold my brother's gaze. "She lied to me, and I don't know how I can trust her again."

My brother was quiet for a long moment, but I felt his steady gaze, as substantial as a touch.

Eventually, he cleared his throat and I glanced up just in time to watch his chest expand with a deep breath. "Well," he said, nodding faintly, his stare thoughtful. "That's . . ."

Curious how he would finish his sentence, I watched him and

waited, noticing for the first time a few details about my older brother I'd glossed over in recent years.

He'd turned thirty-five in December and now had wrinkles, worry lines on his forehead and between his eyebrows. But he didn't have any laugh lines.

"That's unexpected," he finally finished pragmatically. "Can you tell me what she lied about?"

Deciding that Simone's cover was well and truly blown, and that it was only a matter of time before folks in Green Valley learned she'd been the one to arrest our father, I said, "She's been working undercover for the FBI and arrested Darrell at the Kentucky Derby."

Billy's eyes popped open, wide open, and his eyebrows nearly hit his hairline. "She- she what?"

"She's been working with the FBI, which was why she reached out in the first place. But I thought—"

"Wait. Stop." My brother held his hands up. "You're going to need to start from the beginning."

The beginning? What was that?

Seeing my confusion, he said, "Okay, I know you haven't been enthusiastic about spending time with Simone Payton since high school. Or at least until just recently. Tell me what changed. Why did you two start hanging out again?"

I folded the newspaper. "I'll tell you the story, but you have to promise not to get angry."

His gaze narrowed with suspicion. "Why would I get angry?"

"Promise," I said.

He glared at me, making a deep, distrustful rumbling sound in the back of his throat. "Fine. I promise. Now tell me what happened."

"It involves Darrell."

"Yeah." His blue eyes sparked with hatred and his tone grew hard. "Figured that much out already. Tell me."

Scratching my cheek, I reminded myself not to include word-for-word dialogue, which I sometimes unconsciously did. All Billy needed was the gist of things, not a transcript.

"All right . . . end of March, she started seeking me out," I began, and told the story from there. Going through the events in chronological order made it a bit easier to distance myself from the situation, but I still had to brace myself for the emotional highs and lows that accompanied the scenes—like when Simone had kissed me at Hawk's Field, or when we'd danced at Genie's.

Billy listened patiently as I explained about her showing up everywhere I was and how we'd agreed to be polite for his and Dani's sake. But when I got to the point where Twilight and Catfish picked us up at the Cooper Road Trail on behalf of Darrell, Billy stood, his chair scraping against the floor. He began pacing the kitchen.

I halted the story, watching him prowl back and forth, rubbing his jaw, shoving his fingers in his hair.

"Billy."

He shook his head.

"Billy—"

"I'll kill him."

I winced. Billy didn't make idle threats.

"You promised."

"Cletus should have taken care of it when he had the chance." He seemed to say this mostly to himself.

"Hey." I waited for him to look at me. "You said you wouldn't get angry."

"I'm not angry." He stopped pacing, his eyes wild with fury, though his voice was dead calm. "*Angry* is when my youngest brother forgets my favorite suit jacket at the Kentucky Derby after repeatedly promising to be responsible. I'm not angry." A hint of hysteria had entered his voice, a touch of madness. I'd seen him like this before when I was young, and again when our father showed up after our mother died. But not since then.

For some reason, his words made me smile, but my face felt stretched, my skin too thin. "You might not need to kill him."

"Oh? Why's that?" He began pacing again.

"Because Darrell has cancer."

Billy grew unnaturally still. He stared at me, and I at him, and the fury dissolved into wonder.

"What did you say?"

"It runs in the family, on my side, in case you didn't know. My daddy died from it real young. I need your help," he said, his voice raw. "Son, if you don't help me, I'm going to die."

"Darrell has cancer," I repeated, glancing at my hands. "I suspect the same kind that took our half brother. He needs a bone marrow transplant or he'll die." I eyed Billy, debating whether or not to share more details, specifically that only he and I were a match as potential donors.

Reclaiming his seat, Billy nodded, then swallowed, his voice hoarse. "Okay. What happened after Cooper Road Trail?"

"Twilight and Catfish didn't manhandle us. Other than frisking me on the way in, they didn't touch us." I paused here, re-examining the memory, and realizing they hadn't frisked Simone.

Despite everything, my mouth curved into a small smile. She'd probably been carrying. She'd probably had her badge and handcuffs on her even then, and they hadn't frisked her.

As my momma used to say, *"If a man underestimates a woman, it will be his downfall."*

"What did Darrell want?" Billy prompted.

Shaking myself, I continued with the story, briefly mentioning how Simone and I had tussled and kissed. I saved most of my details for what happened after Darrell showed up. Billy stopped me often enough—asking questions, seeking clarification—that I decided to relate the entire scene with our father word for word.

"He believed you? When you said you'd think about it?" Billy asked.

"Yep." I nodded. "That's why he let us go."

My brother leaned back in his chair, staring at the table. "Why didn't you tell me?" When his eyes came up, he looked more confused than irritated, but he did look irritated.

"Billy," I began quietly, searching for the right words. "I am twenty-six years old. Y'all have done an admirable job of trying to protect me from hardship, from Darrell's crazy, you in particular. You've done—" I couldn't hold my brother's eyes any longer. Frowning at the wood grain of the table, the heat stains left by dishes placed without a potholder and circle stains left by coffee cups, I cleared my throat. "You've done more than your fair share."

"You should have told me. You should have let me handle it."

I shook my head. "It wasn't about you."

"It wasn't about me?" He sounded incredulous. "Everything that concerns you, concerns me. Everything that concerns *any* of you, concerns me."

I laughed my frustration, lifting my eyes to the ceiling and shaking my head. "You know how old I am, right?"

"It doesn't matter if you're ten or fifty."

For some reason, this comment frustrated me. "I know you want to help. But at some point, you need to stop taking on everyone else's burdens. You've already given up too much."

He was quiet for several seconds before asking gently, "What do you know about what I've given up?"

I still couldn't bring myself to meet his gaze, because I knew enough. He'd taken beatings for all of us; he'd given up scholarships to college in order to stay and help our momma; he'd worked tirelessly to make a name for himself, build a reputation, and therefore change how the last name of *Winston* was regarded. He'd made it possible for each of us who came after to succeed.

But what happiness did he have for himself?

The swelling frustration increased, ballooned in my chest, and I grit my teeth. Maybe he was happy being a congressman, on his way to becoming a state senator, but I didn't think so. Maybe he was happy to marry Daniella Payton, but as amazing and gorgeous as she was, I didn't think so. Maybe he was happy to live vicariously through all of us, but I didn't think so.

I didn't answer his question, instead I asked a new one. "Don't you think it's time for me to handle things myself? Don't you think it's time we all did?"

He didn't respond.

Giving him back my eyes, I leaned my elbows on the table and asked plainly, "Who are you living your life for, Billy? For us? Because, if that's the case, you're done. Look at this family you built." I motioned to the house around us.

"You're my responsibility. You all are."

"No." I huffed a laugh. "We're not. We haven't been for a while."

His features grew stern. "Roscoe—"

"Jethro isn't a worthless bastard anymore, in case you didn't know. He hasn't been for a long time. He's a stay-at-home dad who freaking *knits* matching sweaters for his family and builds folks houses in his spare time. Cletus is crazy, but he's happier than he's ever been. Yeah, he's had his rough patches, but the Winston Brothers Auto Shop is franchising this year, they can't keep up with demand. Jennifer is the weirdo yin to his yang. One can't live without the other.

"Speaking of soul mates, Ashley and Drew were made for each other, like they were carved from the same block of marble. They're living their best, peaceful life with Bethany and talking about having another. Beau has Shelly and she has him, his work and her work, our family and her family. His cup *runneth over* with blessings. Duane and Jess are married, expecting, and they're living in freaking *Italy*. He works on Maserati and Formula One racing cars. For *fun*."

I stopped there and studied my brother, at the stubborn set of his mouth. But his eyes gave him away. He was listening, and he seemed conflicted.

Quieter, kinder, I said, "You are the reason. Never doubt that. You and Momma. She did the best she could. With seven of us she couldn't do it on her own. She needed you. We all did, and you stepped up. Your sacrifices, and I'm sure there are a ton I don't know about, made this family possible. But brother, it's time for the sacrifices to end."

"Roscoe—"

"Why are you avoiding living your own damn life? What are you so afraid of? Of failure? Of making painful memories you can't forget? If that's the case, I've tried that. I'm here to tell you that no matter what you do, shit is going to happen. You can't avoid heartache without also leaving out the love."

His frown intensified, the deep grooves on his forehead and between his eyebrows making an appearance, and he opened his mouth as though to speak.

But I wasn't finished. "You deserve more than a life of work and nothing else. You deserve more than being a politician when I know you hate it, no matter how well-regarded you are, and marrying a woman you don't love, no matter how much you respect her. You've lived your life for country, for work, for family. For Bethany, Jethro, Cletus, Ashley, Beau, Duane, and Roscoe. But your hiatus is at an end. Go take some risks, go find your purpose. The time has come to live your life for Billy Winston."

I hit the surface of the table with my fist as I finished because . . . *there*. I said it. I didn't regret it. It had been on my mind for a long time. Dammit, but someone had to let Billy off the hook.

"Are you finished?" he asked softly, a whisper of a smile behind his eyes. "Because I think that's the most I've ever heard you say all at one time."

I shrugged, my heart beating fast and continuing to accelerate as all the words I'd just said to my brother boomeranged, repeated, an echo in my head.

Why are you avoiding your own damn life?

No matter what you do, shit is going to happen.

"Do I get to speak now?" he asked.

Leaning back in my chair and crossing my arms, I tried to focus on his words and not mine. I couldn't. Not quite yet.

I was having an epiphany.

You can't avoid heartache without also leaving out the love.

Well . . . shit.

I'd missed out.

I'd had my memories of Simone, of us, growing up. But I'd missed out on everything that came after. Taking a moment to look at my choices through the lens of who I was now, I wished I'd done things differently. As Beau had said in his drunken wisdom, if you love someone, you make them a priority. That meant you took risks, you made the bad memories trusting that you'd be making sublime ones in between.

"Roscoe?" Billy's smile now encompassed his mouth, but he looked uncertain, as though he were a smidge concerned by my silence.

Standing from the table, I pointed at my brother and announced, "I know what I have to do."

"About Darrell?"

"What? No. Were you even listening? I'd already decided what to do about Darrell last week." I shook my head at my brother. "About Simone." *Obviously.*

Billy also stood. "Wait, I thought we were talking about Darrell."

"No. This was never about Darrell. None of this has ever been about anyone or anything but Simone. All this shit happens, all these people get in the way. They're clutter, they make a mess. We make things complicated that shouldn't be, and we want things to be simple when they're not. Sometimes we'll disagree, but so what? It's not about them, or her job, or my job, or our past. None of that matters. She doesn't need my forgiveness. She needs—we need— each other. The only thing that matters is- is now, and . . ."

Simone. And me.

Billy's eyes were wide as he stared at me, apparently at a loss for words, or waiting for me to finish my thought. No matter. Like I'd said, I knew what I had to do.

Before he could question me further, I was out of the kitchen, making a beeline for the front door.

"Wait, Roscoe," he called, and I could tell he was following. "Where are you going?"

"To find Simone." As an afterthought, I added, "And to get your jacket back."

CHAPTER TWENTY-SEVEN

"Our memory is a more perfect world than the universe: it gives back life to those who no longer exist."

— GUY DE MAUPASSANT

Simone

REBECCA, THE DINER'S longest serving employee, kept a monthly calendar behind the counter next to the cash register. She used a black Sharpie to X out each date as it passed. Not purple, not green, not blue. Black. The X was always drawn carefully, meticulously, two lines extending from one corner to the other of each date's small box.

I'd asked Rebecca once why she did it, whether she was counting down to something good. I'd been twelve and I think I'd been drinking a milkshake or eating a hamburger. As far as I could remember, we were the only two left in the diner and my brother was on his way to pick me up, or maybe it was my dad.

Rebecca looked up briefly and said in her flat, matter-of-fact southern drawl, "Time passes and people don't notice. I want to be sure I take note of every moment I'll never live again."

She promptly went back to filling the salt containers.

I didn't know what to make of Rebecca's X-ing out habit at the time, or her grim philosophy, but now I think I finally understood. Things will happen in your life and they will make you question where all your time has gone.

All is well. Life is going swimmingly. Or maybe it's not. Maybe you're frustrated by the day-to-day doldrums, the infinite tasks, the seemingly endless list of shows to binge on Netflix.

How will you ever catch up?

How will you ever get it done?

But then something happens. Doldrums, tasks, and Netflix shows become—literally—nothing. In one single instant, POOF! They're gone.

The only *things* left are what really matters. The bare essentials. The people you love.

I hadn't tried calling Roscoe since he left the field office in Louisville, but I did text him when I made it home. He'd messaged me back, letting me know he'd also made it home—to the Winston house—safely.

I texted him once more this morning, that I was spending the day with my grandfather, but that I'd be at the diner later for a shift. That was it. He hadn't responded. I still had all the sad.

Other than a short phone call with Nelson earlier, during which she'd given me more info on what Roscoe had seen at Churchill Downs prior to my arrival, I'd stuck to my plan for the day. I suggested that they review the security footage of the Derby for the past few years, to see if there was a trend. Was this the only year the MC members gathered to bet on races, or how long had they been doing it?

Nelson also mentioned two local police officers had been assigned to watch me for my safety, now that my cover was blown. Furthermore, tomorrow I'd be meeting via teleconference with our

East Tennessee's SAIC as well as my old boss in DC about my future on the case.

So much was up in the air. Not just with me and Roscoe, but with my job. Obviously, I was no longer viable as an undercover agent. Soon everyone in the Valley would know—including all the MC clubs—that I was FBI. Maybe they already knew. I assumed Isaac would need a new contact, but that was up in the air, too.

Was the case over? Roscoe had said he would donate bone marrow, but had he changed his mind since the last time we'd spoken? If he hadn't changed his mind, did that mean Darrell would give us what we needed on Razor? And how would we capture Razor even if Darrell turned state's evidence? Would the bureau send a team into the Dragon Biker Bar compound and try to extract him? Why had Razor said he would go to the Derby only to draw all agents away from it? Did he know Isaac was undercover?

That seemed unlikely. If Razor knew Isaac was undercover, Isaac would be dead.

And what the heck was with all the MC guys making bets at the Kentucky Derby?

This last one I had a hunch about at least. I had questions, but without knowing more than what Nelson had conveyed over the phone—i.e., the transcript of Roscoe's interview with Lehey from last night—my preliminary theory was that the MC guys had been laundering money. If each person placed the same bet for each race, they would see a return of approximately the same amount.

But one thing in particular didn't add up. The guys were all from different motorcycle clubs. So whose money were they laundering?

Maybe Darrell knows.

Regardless, we were running out of time. Things needed to be decided. June was approaching quickly.

Bethany Winston once told me that time was like a closet. No matter what you do or how good your intentions are, you will always fill your time and closets with things that don't matter.

"That's why funerals are so important," she'd said. "They force you to clean out closets and reevaluate how you spend your time. Without death, we'd never have empty closets."

I'd been thinking about Bethany all day, but I didn't realize why until I caught sight of today's date out of the corner of my eye on Rebecca's calendar.

Today was the day Bethany discovered she had cancer, six years ago. She hadn't told her family. Instead, she'd invited Drew Runous out for a margarita since it was Cinco De Mayo and told him about her diagnosis over a salted rim and nachos.

After Bethany's death, he'd told my mother the story, and she'd told me.

I stopped what I'd been doing—which was closing the cash register and zipping the money bag—and for some reason, did the math in my head. Like both me and Roscoe, her birthday was in February. She would've been fifty-two this year.

I was twenty-six, which meant I was the same age she'd been when she had Roscoe. Staring forward, my eyes lost focus as I found myself adrift in the overwhelming nature of my thoughts. I couldn't imagine having seven kids by the age of twenty-six. In so many ways, I was still a kid myself. Still fumbling and failing, still trying on thoughts and emotions to see if they fit, discarding those that weren't right and hoarding those that had clicked seamlessly into place (and made my ass look good).

Until recently, trying on thoughts and emotions had been mostly a leisurely activity. Meaning, I'd done it at my leisure. If a situation made me uncomfortable or challenged me, I simply avoided it.

Falling in love had taught me more about myself in six weeks than I'd taken the time to learn in ten years. I discovered that I did want to fall in love; I would make someone a great partner and that person was Roscoe Winston; I was up to the challenge and responsibility, and I was ready to meet both head-on.

But I'd also learned that—in love—nothing makes sense. I didn't make sense. I didn't understand myself. Down is up and up is purple. The sky is drawer. The moon is goat.

In love, everything was nonsense.

But maybe that also means anything is possible.

Shaking myself out of my bizarre reflections, I finished zipping the money bag and turned to the kitchen. After I put the money in the safe, I could leave for the night and throw myself a pity party with my constant companions: all the sad.

The sound of someone aggressively knocking on the front door had me stopping and turning, frowning at the darkness outside. Setting the money just inside the kitchen entrance, I dragged my tired feet out from behind the counter and shuffled to the front, prepared to mime and shout, *We're closed.*

But then I saw who it was, and my feet were no longer dragging.

Roscoe stood at the door, his hands cupped around his face, which was pressed to the glass, his eyes on me as I approached.

My heart leapt. To my throat. It remained there, unwilling to behave no matter how I chanted for it to calm down, because down is up and up is purple. The sky is drawer. The moon is goat.

With no hesitation, I speed-walked to the glass door and hastily unlocked it. He pushed inside the second the lock released. In the next second, his arms were around me. He walked me backwards, into the diner, his lips on mine. Kissing. Devouring. His tongue in my mouth. His hands roaming over my body, as though to convince himself that I was here and real.

I was . . . confused. Because so much was unsaid between us. But kissing him felt good. Too good. Great. Exceptional. Heavenly. But again, so much was unsaid.

What the heck?

If the moon was goat, then kissing Roscoe made sense, right?

I went with it. I kissed him back. I gave him my tongue, I sucked on his, I arched against him, I pulled his shirt from his jeans, lifting the offending garment so I could touch his bare skin, his back and sides and stomach.

I was hot and breathless in a matter of seconds, my mind frantically trying to figure out *where* we could go.

The kitchen?

No. Our food safety rating wasn't anything to mess with.

The back office.

Yes!

I pulled my lips from his, specifically to communicate this extremely viable and brilliant plan, when Roscoe cupped my face and pressed his forehead against mine. He was breathing heavy and so was I. He laughed, more air than sound.

"Simone," he said, leaning away so his eyes, both soft and ardent, ensnared mine. "Simone, I love you. And, yes, we need to talk about what happened. But I know you. I know you and I trust you. I carry you with me, I always have." He pressed a quick kiss to my lips, whispering against them, "You are in my heart. You have shaped my soul. Nothing—*nothing*—will change that for me."

Grinning like a doofus, I tried to find some worthy response, but what could I possibly say to that? Everything melted. Every corner and crevice warmed with happiness and relief and more happiness and . . .

And yet, I was a creature of reason. Even in this gift of a moment, I couldn't turn off my misgivings. The logic-Sherpa told me there was too much left unsaid.

"This is very sudden." I closed my eyes, breathing him in, and whispered what was in my heart. "I love you. But before we move forward, I need to know you forgive me."

"If there's anything to forgive, I forgive it." His hands slid down my neck to my shoulders and he covered my mouth with an achingly tender kiss, withdrawing to say, "I can't miss out on any more time with you. I want all your moments, I want every memory."

"They won't all be happy," I warned, tilting my head back. "A lot of them will be boring."

He grinned, his eyes conducting a cherishing sweep of my face. "I seriously doubt that."

"It's true. And I have questions," *so many questions*, "about your memory."

Roscoe blinked, his gaze flickering to my lips, then back to my eyes. "My memory?"

Gripping his shirt front, I blurted, "Do you have a photographic memory? I mean, how much do you remember? Do you remember everything? About me? About us? Even that one time you walked in on me going to the bathroom? Please tell me you don't remember that."

Roscoe rolled his lips between his teeth, his eyes shining brightly as his shoulders shook with silent laughter.

And I had my answer.

"Oh God." My forehead fell to his chest and I groaned. "You should have knocked."

"You should have locked the door."

"I'll never win an argument again," I said with more dismay than I felt. Mostly, I felt wonder. I was curious. So, so curious.

But my questions could wait. We *literally* had a lifetime.

And just like that, I was grinning again.

"Hey." His hand came to my cheek, encouraging me to give him my eyes again. "Come with me."

"Where?"

"Anywhere."

I sighed, lost in Roscoe's soulful eyes, and nodded. "Okay."

"Okay." He nodded too, threading our fingers together. "Let's go."

Floating on a cloud of thoughtlessness and euphoria, I took three steps forward, allowing him to lead me to the door, when I remembered a few critical details.

"Wait, wait." I pulled him to a stop.

He turned, giving me a small expectant smile.

"I- I—" *Damn, it was hard to think when he was so close and so very, very Roscoe, and I loved him so much.* "I have to go put the money away." I tossed my thumb over my shoulder. "I was just about to when you knocked on the door."

His attention drifted over my shoulder; when it returned to me, he still wore his small smile. "I'll wait."

"Okay," I said, obviously still in a daze. There were so many other details for us to discuss. Such as the two police officers parked in the lot who would follow me wherever I went tonight, and the fact that no matter how much my parents loved Roscoe, they would not be okay with me having him stay over.

Stepping forward, he gave me another sweet kiss, released me, and stepped back. "Go on. I'll wait here."

I nodded and turned quickly, speed-walking to the kitchen entrance. "I'll be right back."

"Oh, and I'll message Billy," he called to my back, laughing lightly to himself. "He insisted on coming along."

I'd just moved to slip through the counter opening when I heard the bell above the front door give a jingle.

"Billy," Roscoe said, "I was just about to text you."

Out of the corner of my eye, I saw Roscoe start to turn, and I gave the brothers a cursory glance, my mind on the bag of money sitting in the kitchen and calculating how quickly I could stash it and get out of here. But then I did a double take.

Because that wasn't Billy.

Oh my God.

A man in black. Long black hair. Tall and thin. Knife raised. Eyes on me. I'd never seen him in person, only his picture.

Only his picture.

My heart thudded painfully against my rib cage, a shot of pure terror and adrenaline had me reaching for my gun before my mind fully comprehended what was about to happen, because I couldn't fathom it. I couldn't accept it.

"ROSCOE!" I yelled, aiming, but I had nothing to shoot.

Razor Dennings had already brought his knife down, following Roscoe's body as it crumpled to the floor, out of my sight.

Roscoe.

He didn't make a sound. Not a sound.

Or maybe I hadn't heard his scream. I didn't know. I didn't know.

Move!

I moved. My heart wrestling with my training, I slipped back through the counter opening and ran towards the front of the diner, my weapon ready.

Shots. Bullets breaking glass. I grunted at an unexpected impact and collapsed to the floor.

My brain told me someone was shooting into the diner from the parking lot, but all my heart could see was Roscoe's boot from where he lay on the ground.

Someone screamed. A sound of anguish, of heartache, and I was moving again, on my belly, crawling on the floor, on the glass, trying to get closer. Sharp, excruciating pain in my side, searing, wet.

I ignored it.

I ignored everything as Roscoe's legs came into view. His torso. His shoulders. He was blurry. I blinked, clearing my vision.

The bullets stopped just as Razor came into view. Crouching, his back pressed against the front wall of the diner, just below the window, his hands up as though he surrendered, a small smile on his face.

His mouth moved. He was speaking. Asking me a question. I raised my weapon, and aimed.

His eyes grew large and he shook his head, waving his hands, and I heard his voice. "I'm unarmed! You can't shoot me, fed. I'm unarmed!"

I hadn't made up my mind about what I could do and what I would do before another shot rang out, followed closely by another. A revolver this time. Razor flinched, twisting away, covering his head, as though he thought I'd been the one to shoot.

Shouting followed. Voices grew closer. My eyes darted to Roscoe's body, lying there, just lying there. I saw no blood, but he didn't look like he was breathing. He was still, so still.

Another scream of anguish, and I realized—as Razor opened his eyes and looked at me—that I was the one screaming. He blinked, smiling his small smile, and I lifted my weapon, aimed, seeing only Roscoe's unmoving body and a barren, meaningless future before me, one without Roscoe. One without his smile, and stories, and soulful eyes.

I'll never see them again.

I pulled the trigger. If I could have done it a hundred times, I would have. But once was all that was needed.

Razor's body jerked as the bullet hit its mark, he fell to the side clutching his wound between his legs. And this time, he was the one screaming.

"Agent Payton!" Someone yelled, the voice close. "It's Officer Evans. We've subdued the gunman. Are you injured?"

"Call 911!" I yelled, or I tried to. But my voice sounded wrong, quiet. I coughed, and the hot, metallic taste of blood burned my throat. Even so, I tried again, "Help Roscoe. Call . . . 911."

I was tired. So tired.

But I couldn't rest, not yet, because Razor's eyes locked on mine, wild with pain. Or was that madness? He was struggling to stand, his attention dropping to something I couldn't see. More voices close by, but I couldn't understand what they were saying, everything was garbled, dulled. I could only see Razor and his insanity and determination.

He lunged forward, grabbing for the object. Once he had it in hand, he immediately lifted to unsteady knees. It was a knife. It was *the* knife. It was covered in blood.

Roscoe's blood.

Rage and grief pumped through my veins, and all I could think was, *Now he is armed, and now he'll die.*

But this time, when I tried to lift my weapon, my arms didn't work. The pain at my side had become a void. I couldn't feel my legs. My vision turned gray, like I was peering through a screen, and I narrowed my eyes, willing myself to live long enough to kill Razor Dennings.

Suddenly, he was there. Over me. He snarled, growled. A sound of wrath. He lifted the knife and part of me was glad.

I would follow Roscoe. Where he went, I wanted to be. I didn't know how to be Simone without "and Roscoe," and I didn't want to find out. Not this time. Not ever again.

I carry you with me. You are in my heart. You have shaped my soul.

I stared directly at this man, this murderer, unwilling to meet death with my eyes closed. I was not afraid.

But then, just as suddenly, he wasn't there. I blinked, ink filling the edges of my vision, and the last thing I saw before succumbing to darkness was a pair of frantic, soulful blue eyes.

CHAPTER TWENTY-EIGHT

❦ ❦ ❦

"When he shall die,
> Take him and cut him out in little stars,
> And he will make the face of heaven so fine
> That all the world will be in love with night
> And pay no worship to the garish sun."

— WILLIAM SHAKESPEARE, ROMEO AND JULIET

Simone

WAKING UP IN the hospital was like waking up in a Salvador Dali painting. At least at first.

I know now that I'd been dreaming. But at the time, I was convinced I was in a desert. It was cold, and someone was pouring sand down my throat when all I wanted was water. Coughing, I tried to turn my head away from the funnel filled with sand and the cold heat of the blinding, rolling dunes. I couldn't. A bird overhead chirped. Or beeped. Its irises were red.

Do birds beep?

"Simone. . ."

Did that bird just say my name?

"Simone!"

I opened my eyes, or tried to, but someone had poured sand in them as well, and the bird was now sitting on my chest, definitely saying my name.

"Simone, baby, open your eyes, open your eyes," she said. My mother, the bird.

My mother isn't a bird.

"What? What?" the bird demanded. "She's awake. Can we give her water?"

Abruptly, the sounds of my surroundings filled my consciousness —machines, TV, a door opening, soft murmurs of people—chasing away the false reality of the desert-like smoke rings rising into the sky.

"Mom?" I tried to say, my voice a croak.

"Thank you, God. She's awake." My dad was there, next to me, his hand in mine.

I tried to open my eyes again and mostly succeeded, but everything was too bright.

"Ms. Payton," someone was saying, a voice I didn't recognize. "Can you hear me?"

Nodding, I swept my tongue out to lick my lips, but it was just as dry as my throat. "Yes."

"What is your full name?" the voice asked.

"Is this really necessary?" my mother asked, sounding agitated.

"Yes, it is," another voice said, this one further away. "We're looking for neurological impairment. The sooner we identify an issue, the better her prognosis."

Neurological impairment.

"Where am I?"

My father's hand gave mine a squeeze and I turned my head towards him, trying again to open my eyes. "Dad?"

"You're at the hospital. There was a- an accident." He hesitated here, but only for a second before continuing, "You were shot, but you're out of surgery and the doctors say you're going to be fine."

"You lost a lot of blood." This came from my mother, her voice wobbly. "We all donated."

"Who . . ." I shook my head, confusion tangling with something else. Dread. Fear.

My mind was in disarray, and I didn't understand what they were telling me, so when the first voice began asking me questions again, I responded in rote, clinging to each and breathing easier when I found the answers came quickly.

By the time she'd finished—the nurse—my eyes were open, thanks in large part to someone dimming the lights. I blinked around the room.

The nurse checked something by my bed, giving me a reassuring smile. "I'll be back with the doctor. She'll want to know you're up." To my family, she said, "Ice chips only. And please keep her calm. Say nothing to upset her."

She left.

My eyelids felt heavy. Even so, I forced them open, greedy for details.

Daniella stood at the foot of my bed, staring at me, and I gave her a frown. "You're not wearing any makeup."

My sister lifted a tissue to her eyes and laughed, so did my parents.

"Is that your way of saying I look terrible?" Dani asked, grinning and sniffing.

"No. You're always beautiful. I'm just . . ." I shook my head, blinking heavily. "I'm sorry, I'm really out of it."

"You're on painkillers." My mother touched my cheek, drawing my attention to her comforting gaze. "Poe is on his way. His plane should arrive any minute." She grinned, her eyes seemed to shine. "Oh, my baby. I'm so happy you're alive."

"Poe is on his way?" I tried to follow the conversation, my head wanting to fall back against my pillow. The lead weights attached to my eyelids forced them closed. "But where is Roscoe?"

"Go to sleep," my dad whispered, his lips close to my temple. "You're safe."

"Is he here?" I asked, but could no longer keep my eyes open or keep my head from the magnetic cushion of the pillow.

"Tell him I love him," I said, or I think I said. But maybe I didn't, because I was already asleep.

* * *

The second time I awoke, I knew where I was.

I'm in the hospital.

When I tried to open my eyes, they worked. The room was dim, but not dark. Lights from machines, a panel light against the wall, and lights coming in through the window illuminated enough of the room that I could see my mother sleeping in a second bed against the far wall, my father asleep in a recliner near the door, and another figure sitting in a wooden chair next to my bed, not asleep, staring forward in thought.

I frowned at this third figure while I waded through sleep inertia and drug-induced grogginess.

At first glance, I thought the figure was Roscoe, and hope sparked feebly in my chest. Almost as soon as I had the thought, I dismissed it. The man wasn't Roscoe. He didn't *feel* like Roscoe.

While I was staring at him, the man looked up and our gazes clashed.

Frantic. Blue. Soulful.

"Billy," I whispered, shifting as much as I could in the bed to get a better look at him.

He stood, presumably so I wouldn't have to move, and reached for a paper cup from the table hovering over my bed.

"Do you want some ice chips?" he asked, already digging into the cup with a spoon.

I nodded, and he fed them to me, our eyes meeting again over the paper cup. He couldn't seem to hold my gaze and his fell away to my mouth, watching the progress of the spoon.

The ice was ambrosia, and I sighed, my head falling back to the pillow as a shadow began to surface in my mind. I closed my eyes, looking deep within, chasing the phantom memory.

Roscoe.

"Where's Roscoe?"

Billy had been digging in the cup again. At my question, the sound ceased. I opened my eyes. His were still on the paper cup.

"How much do you remember?" he asked.

My heart rate increased. I know this because the heart monitor over my bed told me so. Billy glanced at me, the monitor, then back to me.

"Is he dead?" I asked, not immediately knowing or understanding why, just that it was a possibility.

However, after the question left my mouth, I remembered—I remembered it all—and I began to shake. The room blurred. Oh God.

Oh god oh god oh god oh god.

"He's- he's dead, isn't he? Isn't he?"

Billy was there, his hands on my shoulders, his face in mine, and I knew with no doubt in my mind that the face I'd seen right before passing out had been his, not Roscoe's.

"He's not dead, Simone. Roscoe is not dead," he said, his fingers flexing on my arms. "Calm down."

The big man's eyes darted to my heart monitor, and the machine began to beep, an alarm, a warning. My mother stirred.

"Calm down. You need to calm down." Billy gently gathered me to his chest, as much as was possible, and stroked my cheek. "Roscoe is alive. He's alive. Calm down."

Thank God.

Thank god thank god thank god thank god.

I nodded, sucking in a shaky breath and wincing at an answering pain in my side. It was then that I became aware of a dull, persistent ache in my lower rib cage.

"I was shot," I said, not remembering being shot, but remembering my father telling me. "Where was I shot?"

"Your chest. You came through surgery just fine." Billy's deep, rumbly voice soothed me. I listened to the rhythm of the monitor slow in one ear and the beat of his heart in the other.

Roscoe's older brother continued to hold me, caressing my face, until the cadence of my pulse returned to normal. I felt his chest expand against my cheek just before he pulled away. Carefully, gently, he helped me settle back against the pillows and pushed my hair away from my face.

"If anything happened to you, if I upset you," he said, his attention on my hair, "there'd be a hundred people in line, ready to maim me."

"Tell me what happened. Where is Roscoe?" I asked again, my tone watery this time, because the question was a plea. I needed to know.

Billy gathered a deep breath, a flash of pain behind his eyes, and he nodded. "I'll tell you. But if your heart goes rock-n-roll again, I'll stop."

I nodded, taking a careful, slow breath, frustrated when I encountered what felt like a block in my airway.

"Roscoe wanted to see you Sunday night, right away, and he was acting a little, uh, manic. Like how Cletus used to get, in high school. Agitated." His gaze moved over me as though continuously assessing my fitness for this conversation.

Staying completely still, I waited with an outward show of patience for him to continue.

He finally did. "We got to the diner and he told me to leave, that he'd catch a ride with you. I told him I was going to stay, just in case things didn't work out according to his grand plans. So he left me in my truck, jogging for the front door. I watched him knock, then you showed up, then he went inside."

I remembered all this, too. I remembered his speech and us kissing.

"When I saw that you two were right as rain, I decided to leave, figuring you'd drop him back off at home when y'all were done. I pulled onto the Parkway and wasn't even a tenth of a mile away when I heard the gunshots." He paused here, swallowing, and when he spoke again his voice was thick with emotion. "I got there just as Evans shot Strickland, and I jumped out of my—"

"Wait." I shook my head, closing my eyes so I could imagine the events better. "Strickland was there?"

"Yeah. He was the one shooting into the diner."

"Oh my God," I breathed, or tried to. But when I heard the monitor betray the rhythm of my heart, I forced my mind to clear, breathing in through my nose.

"You have oxygen here," Billy was saying, and I felt him press a mask into my hand. I took it and he helped me guide the cone to my face. I took a breath. Another.

"He's dead," the second oldest Winston said, his voice devoid of emotion. "Boone shot him."

I nodded, indicating that I understood, though the information did not make me feel better. "He was working with Razor?"

"I'm sorry, I don't know. I assume he must've been, the timing is too convenient, but the sheriff is being tight-lipped about it and says he can't share any details."

That gave me pause, and I had to wonder if the reason Sheriff James wouldn't talk about Strickland's role was because of the bureau's case and the ongoing investigation into the murders.

"What about Razor? The last thing I remember is him coming after me with a knife. And what about Roscoe?"

Billy didn't respond right away, so I opened my eyes, seeking some sign in his expression.

His jaw was set, and his eyes were narrowed into angry slits. However, when he spoke, his voice was eerily calm. "Your cousin and Evans didn't know Razor was even inside. So they called 911 and checked the perimeter. When they weren't looking, I ran inside to check on you both. I found Roscoe on the ground and Razor stumbling over to you with that knife. And I—uh—stopped him."

"Billy, where is Roscoe?" I asked for the third time.

He sighed and gave me a small, sad smile. "They flew him to Nashville three days ago, to the Vanderbilt Trauma Center." His gaze held mine for a moment. It dropped to the floor. "He had his third surgery today."

"His . . . ?" I swallowed, my throat like sandpaper, my eyes stinging, a rush of hot, prickling anxiety passing through me.

Third.

Surgery.

Dear God, I'm going to ask you for something, but I really need you to take this request seriously and not play a joke on me.

Save Roscoe. Make him whole. Bring him back to me.

I carry him with me, in my heart. He has shaped my soul. Make him well.

Billy sniffed, not looking at me, and the sound pulled my attention. "He woke up yesterday, just for a minute"—the big man's voice cracked, he cleared his throat firmly—"and made me promise to come look after you."

I tried to swallow again, my eyes now blurry, and I nodded, because I understood. I understood that Roscoe's status was by no means stable.

"Razor got Roscoe on the left side," Billy said, his Adam's apple bobbing once, twice, his voice gruff. "Aiming for his heart."

I continued to nod, because I couldn't do anything else.

No. That's not true.

"What happened to Razor?" I asked, tired and yet somehow galvanized. Electrified. Determined. Because Roscoe *would* recover. I would force him to recover.

Billy's eyebrows hitched up an inch and he blinked several times. "Well, it seems you—uh—you shot him in the balls. Blew his bits clear off."

A second of silence ticked by before Billy lifted his eyes to mine, peeking at me. I twisted my lips to the side, debating what to say.

"Did I do that?" I finally spoke, lying easily for the first time in my life. "My gun must've misfired."

I didn't feel *better*. Rather, I simply couldn't feel badly about my vengeful decision in the moment of crisis. Another good reason why I belonged in a lab. If I had to do it over, I would have shot Razor

Dennings in the balls one million times. Thirst for vengeance was not a good character trait for a field agent.

A small, slowly dawning smile brightened his expression for just a moment. He nodded once, an acknowledgement. But then the smile fell away, the haunted, tormented shadow returning.

Eyeing Billy, I asked, "What did you do to him?"

His eyes lost focus as they moved to some point beyond me. An odd look claimed his features, like he was recalling something particularly upsetting, but was working to distance himself at the same time.

"Did you kill him?" I asked quietly, worried for the big, sweet man, for what he must be going through. "If you did, it was self-defense. You saved my life."

"I didn't kill him, I knocked him out." Billy shook his head, the words distracted. Abruptly, he blinked, his gaze cutting to mine, growing sharp. "If I was going to kill Razor Dennings, I'd want him to be awake for it."

* * *

AGENTS NELSON AND Lundqvist stopped by for a visit a few days later.

I'd just come back from my walk around the floor, making three laps before running out of breath. When I walked into my room, they were both there, standing by the window and wearing black suits with white shirts, their badges prominently displayed on their belts.

Nelson, unsurprisingly, was wearing sunglasses.

TNT. Dy-no-MITE.

"You are stronger than you look," Lundqvist said, crossing his arms. "You must have Viking blood."

Nelson and I shared a look and she rolled her eyes, ignoring our colleague.

"Actually, no. My people come from Wakanda."

He frowned, his eyes narrowing, like he was trying to figure out where Wakanda might be.

Meanwhile, I glanced at Nelson and found her pulling off her sunglasses, fighting a smile. "I'm glad you're alive," she said, successfully subduing her grin.

"I'm glad I'm alive." I walked slowly to the recliner and carefully lowered myself into it. "Tell me what's going on."

I hadn't seen or heard from anyone at the FBI since the day after waking up from surgery. My SAIC at the East Tennessee office and my old boss from the research lab in DC visited me for exactly a half hour, and only to record my statement. They'd told me nothing, but that might've been because my mother, father, sister, brother, and Billy Winston had all decided to hover nearby, sending them dirty looks.

Nelson glanced at the door, then back to me. "Where's your family?"

"My parents finally went home yesterday to sleep in their own bed. My sister left yesterday for New York and my brother leaves tomorrow for California. He'll be back this afternoon."

She nodded absentmindedly, sliding her eyes to Lundqvist and indicating with her chin that he should close the door. He did. He then turned, facing the room, and crossed his arms.

I guess we won't be disturbed.

"We're not here in an official capacity." Nelson leaned back against the windowsill. "But, knowing you, I figured you were probably going crazy with curiosity."

Holding her gaze, I didn't respond. I hadn't been going crazy with curiosity. I'd been going crazy with worry for Roscoe. I hadn't spoken to him yet because he was still in the ICU. Billy gave me verbal status updates, but that's all I got.

Curiosity about the case wasn't even a blip on my radar.

Nelson must've taken my silence as agreement, because she said, "You were right. The MC guys at the Derby were laundering money. We caught up with all of them and two turned on the others. They'd been recruited by someone claiming to be an associate of Razor Dennings for a cut of the winnings."

"Huh." *An associate.* "Any idea who?"

Nelson shook her head. "We don't know. Razor isn't talking much. He's, uh, going through psych evaluations and his injuries are extensive."

I was careful to keep my face impassive at the news of Razor's injuries, which was a major accomplishment given the way Nelson's gaze probed and prodded.

"I read your statement," she said finally. "You were aiming for his leg and missed, huh?"

Nodding just once, I said nothing.

She pressed her lips together and glanced to her right. "Okay. What about his hands?"

His hands?

"What about his hands?" I sounded confused, because I was confused.

Her attention moved back over me, prodding and probing. "How did he injure his hands?"

Frowning at the question, I glanced at Lundqvist for a clue as to what she was talking about. He seemed to be watching me with interest but gave nothing away.

"I don't know what you're talking about." I gave her back my eyes. "My recollections from that night are fuzzy. But why all the questions? I thought you weren't here in an official capacity."

She studied me for another moment, her words reluctant. "Okay. Fine. Where were we?"

"Razor's associate," Lundqvist supplied.

"Right." The suspicion behind Nelson's expression cleared, getting back to business. "Your contact from the Wraiths—Isaac Sylvester—said he had no idea who the associate might be."

My eyes bulged. "You know about Isaac? Isaac is out?"

"Yes." The answer came from Lundqvist. "According to Sylvester's debriefing statements, his position within the organization was no longer secure and the organization was in chaos. Razor suspected a mole when his scouts detected FBI presence at the Derby. No one was pointing the finger at Isaac, but higher-ups at both the B and the DEA agreed it was time to get him out."

"Is Isaac safe?" I didn't know the guy—I doubted anyone did—but I worried for him.

"His cover is intact, if that's what you're asking. But he's given his notice to the Wraiths. He maintains the MC club is fractured and his departure will not be noticed." Nelson shrugged. "With both Razor and Winston out of the picture, it's a power grab over there."

"So, to be clear, the Iron Wraiths still don't know that Isaac was undercover?"

"Correct. Sylvester said in his interview that his exit story was accepted as truth. Several members have left the club, looking to join other organizations now that Razor and Winston are in custody. Sylvester has no reason to believe they suspect him as the mole."

I nodded, marinating in this new information. This was great news for the government. Conceivably, Isaac could slip back into his undercover role with the Iron Wraiths, or any other MC organization, whenever needed. But this was not great news for Jennifer, Isaac's sister. She still believed, and would likely continue to believe, her brother was lost to her.

"There's something else," Lundqvist said.

I glanced at him, taking in his unusually somber expression. "What is it?"

"Actually, there are a number of things." Nelson crossed her arms, her gaze steady. "First, and thanks to you, in reviewing the footage from the Kentucky Derby over the last several years, we finally figured out what all the murder victims have in common."

"What's that?"

"The victims from two years ago are the same MC members who were present at the Derby two years ago, placing bets and laundering money. Same is true with the victims from last year."

My mouth fell open, because one of the biggest missing pieces in the case clicked together. "Razor was using them to launder his money but then he killed them afterward?"

Lundqvist nodded, his features stark. "It seems so."

A sound of disbelief escaped me as the full ramifications of this information snapped into place. "But- but why would these guys agree to help Razor? I mean, you'd think they'd see what happened to their colleagues who helped him in the past and never agree to it. If helping Razor launder money means you die, why would you do it?"

Lundqvist exhaled an audible breath. "I can't answer that, because it doesn't make sense to me either. But I can tell you that no one in my club knew about Razor's method for laundering money or how the murders were connected. They suspected he was making a power grab, and that's it."

"So, so strange." I made another sound of disbelief. "These guys should unionize. Or have an annual conference, or compare notes. Jeez, talk to each other, use the buddy system. Something."

Nelson smirked, standing away from the window where she'd been leaning and crossed her arms. "Razor is in custody, we have him for attempted murder, so he'll be staying put for a while. Which brings us to Strickland."

Leaning forward in the recliner, my hand instinctively coming to the bandages at my side, I asked the one question I had been curious about, "How long had Strickland been working for Razor?"

Nelson's eyebrows pulled together and she shook her head. "We have no idea. Again, Razor isn't talking. Isaac said, if Strickland had been working for Razor prior to the attack on the diner, none of the Iron Wraiths had any idea. According to Isaac, most of their rank despised Strickland as he had a habit of targeting minority members of the local clubs." She shrugged, looking frustrated. "Sorry. Maybe we'll find out more when Darrell Winston fills in the blanks."

I sighed, grimacing. "Darrell fucking Winston. Man, I hate that guy."

"Yeah, well, he knows where the bodies are buried. So the original plan stands. He's getting treatment in exchange for testifying."

Scoffing, I glared at Nelson. "What? Are you serious? You still expect Roscoe to donate bone marrow?" My voice was dangerously close to becoming a screech, but I didn't care. A flood of anger and resentment sent heat up my neck and cheeks. "And how do you propose he do that when he's fighting for his life?"

Lundqvist stepped away from the door, came to stand next to me, and placed a hand on my shoulder. "Shh. Calm down. You shouldn't—"

"Fuck off, Lundqvist." I shook him off, tears gathering in my eyes as I raised a finger. "You—either of you—even try to *talk* to Roscoe, I swear I'll—"

"Whoa. Okay, you misunderstand." Nelson lifted her hands, her voice gentle. "Roscoe won't be donating his bone marrow. We know he's still very ill, we wouldn't ask him to do anything that would jeopardize his recovery."

"That's right, you won't," I said through clenched teeth. Scowling at Nelson and Lundqvist in turn, I sat back in the recliner, taking a slow breath to calm down.

I pictured a scene, at some point in the future—hopefully soon—where Roscoe and I were at my Nancy's place, eating enchiladas. We'd go home after helping her with the dishes, and we'd snuggle, and he'd tell me stories about our shared past. He'd paint me a picture with his soothing, sexy voice and I'd listen to his strong heart, and I'd never take the sound for granted. *Ever.*

I'd give anything just to talk to him.

"We found another donor," Lundqvist explained, his voice also gentle.

"Good," I ground out. But then an immediate hunch had me stiffening and I looked to Nelson, my mouth dropping. I blinked. "Wait, wait a minute. You mean . . . you mean—"

"Congressman Winston volunteered, so we could make the case against Razor Dennings and his accomplices, if there are any left alive, and discover Strickland's role. He asked that we not tell his family—his brothers and sister—about his decision." Nelson said this quietly, reverently, and with a decent amount of awe. "He flew out to Texas earlier today for the procedure."

Honestly, I was in awe as well. And speechless for several minutes.

"That's—that's incredible," I finally said, the words tumbling out. "I can't believe it."

"Yeah, well." Nelson sighed, rubbing her forehead. "Someone should send him a fruit basket."

A knock on the door had all three of us stiffening and looking at it. I leaned to one side, to look around the wall that was Lundqvist, and spotted a nurse poking her head inside.

"Sorry to interrupt." She looked at little awestruck as her gaze moved between Lundqvist, Nelson, and me. "But I have a call for Ms. Payton that I don't think she'll want to miss."

I sat forward on the recliner, preparing to stand. "Who is it?"

She slipped around Lundqvist and picked up the landline receiver next to my chair, pressing two buttons and then handing it to me, saying nothing but giving me a warm smile.

Lifting an eyebrow at her silence, I accepted it and brought it to my ear. "Hello?"

"Simone?"

Gasping, I covered my mouth, tears springing to my eyes, a wave of relief and worry and love and gratitude crashing over me, sending my head spinning.

All the emotions. ALL OF THEM. At once.

But mostly gratitude and love.

"Roscoe," I said through tears that made no sense. "I love you, I love you."

"I love you, too," he said, sounding weak, and my heart gave a lurch. I closed my eyes against the force of feeling.

Tangentially, I was aware of people leaving the room, of the door shutting behind them.

"I miss you, gorgeous. I hope you're taking time to rest, get better. Don't push yourself." His voice was barely above a whisper and it made me cry harder.

But I scoffed at the last part. "Don't push myself? Look who's talking. I've been out of the ICU for days, I'm doing laps around this hospital."

"I need you to be okay," he said, a grin in his strained voice. "So humor me and take a nap."

Now I was laughing and crying. "I will if you will."

"Deal," he said, sounding tired, and I knew he needed to go.

"Roscoe, I love you." I held my forehead in my hand. "And I'll be there as soon as I'm discharged. Just, get better. Please, please get better."

"Working on it," he wheezed, and I heard voices in the background, like they were debating something.

A moment later, Ashley came on the line. "Hey, lady. We've all been praying for you."

"Ashley, thank you. Thank you so much. I'm so sorry." I couldn't stop crying, and I knew I needed to. Recovering from a gunshot wound was difficult enough without introducing mucus. Maybe this wasn't a proven medical fact, but it seemed true.

"Honey, don't you apologize. You get better."

I nodded, taking as deep of a breath as I could manage, willing myself to relax. She was right. The sooner I recovered, the sooner I could see him.

"I miss him so much," I said, no longer crying.

"I know you do. Be gentle with yourself now so you can be gentle with Roscoe later."

"Tell him I love him," I said, even though I'd already told him myself.

I wanted everyone to tell him. I wanted him surrounded by it until I could surround him with my arms, and kiss him, and show him.

"I will. Now you rest, and send our love to your family. Bye, Simone." She clicked off.

I held the receiver to my face for a long time, unwilling to let go of the connection, determination gathering within me with every breath I took. I was going to rest. I was going to rest *so hard.*

And as soon as I recovered, I was driving to Nashville.

CHAPTER TWENTY-NINE

"Scars are just another kind of memory."

— M.L. STEDMAN, THE LIGHT BETWEEN
OCEANS

Roscoe

"MOST FATAL STAB wounds are located in the left chest region." Cletus's attention was on the shaving cream he applied to my neck and cheeks. "I read something that said once a victim acutely accumulates more than one hundred fifty milliliters of blood in the pericardial sac, death can occur at any time."

"Shut up, Cletus." Duane glared at our brother.

I was glad Duane was here, he was—by far—the best at glaring.

"Fine, crusty britches." Cletus mirrored Duane's sour expression, turning back to dab more shaving cream on my neck. "I'm just saying, we're all real lucky Roscoe is still here." His eyes flickered to mine, moved over my face, and grew impossibly tender. "You okay there, buddy?"

"I'm fine, Cletus," I said, though it was hard to talk with shaving cream around my mouth.

"I'm just saying, no one wants to hear that shit. We all know how lucky we are he's still here," Duane grumbled, his hand slipping over mine. He'd done this a few times, covered my hand without thinking. In a minute or so, he would probably catch himself and frown at our fingers, as though he didn't remember reaching for me.

"You have something interesting to discuss?" Cletus murmured. "By all means, let's hear it."

"I'd rather talk about your sausage than listen to more facts about fatal stab wounds." Beau placed the razor, towel, and bowl of water on the table over my hospital bed.

"Are your feet warm enough?" Ashley currently sat near my feet, her hand on the blankets over my calf, her eyes soft and concerned. She'd been giving me the same soft and concerned look for the last two weeks now, since I'd been conscious enough to notice, and I didn't mind it one bit.

Sympathy from one's sister is as close as you get to sympathy from your momma.

"They should be warm," Jethro said from his chair by the window where he was knitting me another pair of socks. Ashley had knit the first pair and he was almost finished with the second. "Wasn't that yarn a hundred percent Shetland wool?"

"I'd like a pair of those socks." Cletus sniffed, putting the brush he'd used for the shaving cream back in the holder and picking up the razor.

I shook my head, my eyes on the blade. "No. Nope."

He paused. "Well, I'm not asking for your socks. I'm just saying, if someone wanted to knit me socks for my birthday, I wouldn't file a formal complaint with the knitters' guild."

"Knitters' guild?" Ashley asked, quirking a smile.

Cletus waved his hands in the air, including the one holding the razor. "You know, the knitting peoples' governing body."

Jethro grinned, sharing a quick look with Ashley. "Cletus, what exactly do you imagine knitters need a governing body for? We're not a militia."

"Really?" He twisted at the waist and my eyes stayed on the blade he was whipping around willy-nilly. "Could have fooled me. Y'all are more organized than most militias."

Cletus returned his attention to my chin, the razor in his left hand, and I shook my head. "Cletus, I do not want you shaving me."

My brother's eyebrows raised over wide eyes. "What?"

"He said he doesn't want you shaving him," Duane said, his stare on me, anxious. "You in any pain? We can do this later."

"I'm okay," I said, though I wasn't really. My chest hurt. Everything hurt. I felt weak, unlike myself. Restless and tired at the same time. But none of that needed to be said. "I'd just prefer if Beau did it."

Cletus's lips parted in astonishment and he blinked. "But it's my turn."

"Yeah," I drawled, "but I don't want another Batman symbol goatee around my mouth."

Cletus narrowed his eyes into slits, his mouth pressing into a frustrated line, but he said, "Fine," and handed the razor to Beau.

Beau gave me a wide grin, his eyebrows wagging. "You trust me not to shave a symbol into your stubble?"

"He trusts that you don't have the artistic skill," Cletus said flatly, shoving his hands into his pockets and adding conversationally, "For the record, I think a four-leaf clover design around your mouth would be a nice change. It has the power of symbolism. Everyone likes clovers." He turned to Jethro. "Name me one person who doesn't like clovers."

Jethro lifted his hands—still holding his knitting—as though he surrendered. "I can't name one, Cletus. But I don't know many people."

"No one wants a goatee in the shape of a clover. Beards aren't topiaries," Duane grumbled, but gave me a small smile.

"That is patently false, *Duane*." Cletus took a seat next to Jethro. "Hair is the topiary of the animal kingdom, everyone knows that."

"Besides, we can't leave a clover on his face." Beau's grin waned, his eyes dropping to my cheeks. "They said we have to keep shaving the whole thing off."

Ashley made a small sound of distress, drawing my attention. A sad smile hovered around her lips.

"Don't worry, Ash," I said. "It'll grow back."

She nodded, her chin wobbly. "I know."

"I don't understand why he has to shave it," Duane grumped.

"It's not standard practice." Ashley sighed. "A beard or other facial hair can interfere with the fitting of an oxygen mask—which I reckon is why they shaved it off to begin with. But sometimes I've seen the docs ask patients to stay hair-free, especially if there's a risk for sepsis."

"She means infection," Cletus said loudly, like one of us was hard of hearing and had no idea what sepsis meant.

Beau chuckled at Cletus and shook his head, muttering, "Thanks, Cletus," as he picked up the razor and examined the shaving cream covering my jaw.

The room fell silent as Beau worked slowly, gently, carefully scraping, all his focus on my face. After a time, my eyes—feeling heavy—drifted shut. My mind wandered. Invariably, as it did when given time to wander, I thought of Simone.

A pinching ache, up and above the constant physical throb from my injury and subsequent surgeries, arrested my heart. The pain meds dulled everything, including my mind. They made my memories less accessible, a great irony now that they were all I had of her.

The first few days after the diner were a blur. When I woke up for real, I had several new scars. The biggest one wasn't from the knife Razor Dennings had thrust into my back, but from the median sternotomy incision down my front.

I'd been in the ICU after that for a lot of days, wishing someone would fill in the blanks, but being told I needed to rest.

"Later."

"When you're stronger."

"Focus on healing."

It had been a novel experience, being the one who didn't remember.

They did tell me Simone was alive. In fact, the first words I recall anyone saying to me other than my name were, "Simone is alive."

Everyone said it, nurses, doctors, my family. My sister had written the words in my chart, instructing all medical personnel to greet me as follows, "Roscoe? Simone is alive. I will now be recording your vitals and asking you some questions. Don't forget, Simone is alive."

Apparently, I'd flatlined early on after someone informed me that Simone had been shot. Folks were still following Ashley's instructions even now, even here on the regular recovery floor.

My sister, it seemed, didn't want to take any chances.

But now, what had once eased my mind was currently making me restless. Simone was alive, just not in Nashville, and my memory wasn't working right. Not for the first time in the last two weeks since regaining consciousness, I promised myself I'd take several hundred pictures with her and of her when all this was over.

We'd talked just twice over the phone, with one of my siblings holding a phone to my ear. Not much had been said other than what one might expect from two people who loved each other, were recovering from near fatal gunshot and stab wounds, and were trying to talk with an audience.

"I love you."

"I miss you."

"Thank God you're okay."

"It's great to hear your voice."

"Don't overextend yourself."

"Get better soon so we can have a real conversation."

"Get better soon so we can see each other."

"Please get better soon."

Stunted as the conversation had been, hearing her voice made a huge difference. Nothing motivated me to get better more than thinking about being with her. I couldn't hold her yet or kiss her, but

I would. I would do whatever it took to make that happen as soon as possible.

After being discharged from the ICU—or moved, or relocated, whatever hospital folks call it—my family finally told me the full story. Or what they knew of it. Billy knew more than anyone, so he did most of the talking.

After he knocked out Razor, he didn't know which of us was worse off, so he'd covered both me and Simone in ice, he'd said, trying to stop or slow the bleeding. The ambulance arrived an eternity later, but in reality it was less than five minutes. I'd had my first surgery in Knoxville, but the other two had been here, at Vanderbilt. I'd arrived in a helicopter, or so they told me.

After Billy's retelling, I still had more questions, but I waited until we were alone to ask them. This was no small task since my second brother was splitting his time between Simone in Knoxville and me in Nashville, apparently at my request, though I didn't remember making it.

One night last week, I'd finally managed to get him alone.

"What happened to Razor?" I asked. "Is he still alive?"

My brother nodded, saying nothing, looking at his hands. I knew him too well to let him get away with that.

"What did you do to him, Billy?" My question was quieter this time, and I hoped it lacked any trace of judgment. Whatever Billy had done to stop Razor from killing Simone felt justified to me.

His jaw ticked and he sighed. "I found him over Simone, about to strike, so I knocked him out. Seeing you were both in a bad way, I covered your wounds with bags of ice from the freezer and waited for the ambulance. And then I . . ."

I waited, staring at my brother. There was more to the story. There was *no way* he'd only knock out Razor Dennings and that's it. No. Way.

Billy swallowed, frowning, his gaze coming back to mine. "I cut his palms."

I started, blinking at my brother. "You cut his—"

"With his own knife, right here"—he motioned to his own hand with a finger, his voice gravelly—"severing all the flexor tendons."

"Shit." I breathed out, alarmed for my brother. Could Billy get in trouble? Be arrested? I . . . I thought maybe he could. Actually, he definitely could. Razor had been knocked out, subdued. My brother's actions weren't in self-defense.

"I wiped my prints from the handle and pressed his fingers to it again. I wiped my own hands off on his shirt, 'cause it was already covered in blood."

"What did you tell the police?"

He shook his head, staring forward. "I told them I found him over Simone so I knocked him out and covered you both with ice. They didn't ask about his hands." Billy took a deep breath. Then he took another. "He'll never hold a knife again."

"Or much else," I murmured, stunned.

And that was the last we'd spoken about it. Partially because he wouldn't say any more, and partially because I hadn't seen him much since. I assumed he was with Simone in Knoxville. I hoped he wasn't avoiding me.

Billy was struggling. Even in my diminished state, I could see my brother was going through something big. He seemed tired and was walking slow. His eyes weren't right, dull or something, and he didn't talk at all when everyone came to visit unless asked a direct question.

He was wading through weighty matters and wasn't of a mind to share them with me. I understood why, he likely assumed I had enough on my plate, but I hoped he was talking to someone.

"When do you fly back, Duane?"

I was brought back to the present by Beau's question to his twin and Duane's answer.

"Two more days." His voice sounded subdued. "Jess has both Claire and her momma with her, just in case the baby comes early. The sheriff and Jackson are supposed to arrive first of July."

"What's the due date again?" Ashley asked.

"June seven," he replied. "We still got some time."

"It's coming up fast." Jethro sounded amused. "And then nothing'll be the same."

"That's what y'all keep saying." Duane paused here a moment before adding, "I guess we should discuss plans for this summer. I talked things over with Jess. We think it would be best for y'all to come out in the fall, once the kid here is well enough to travel."

I didn't object to Duane calling me "the kid." I was too tired to object to much of anything other than Cletus carving shapes in my stubble. But I did have something to say.

So I lifted the hand Duane wasn't holding, indicating for Beau to stop, and blinked my eyes open.

"What's wrong?" Duane's hand tightened on mine.

I found Beau standing back, his eyes wide, staring at me like he was afraid to move. "Are you okay?"

"Fine." I swallowed before speaking again. "Billy needs to go. Now. Or as soon as can be arranged."

Beau and Duane glanced at each other, silently communicating something between them—as they were prone to do—while Ashley stood to come closer. Her fingers pushed into my hair and she tilted her head to the side, studying me.

"You worried about Billy?"

I nodded.

The side of her mouth curved up and she whispered, "Me too."

"Sienna, the boys, and I were still planning to fly over mid-June. We could bump it up, take Billy with us, if y'all think he needs to get out of town," Jethro offered, and this was good news. Sienna would charter a private plane to fly her family. Taking Billy along wouldn't be any extra fuss and made sense.

"Claire is with Jess? Right now?" This question came from Cletus. He was somewhere on my left but I was suddenly too tired to turn my head.

"That's right," Duane confirmed. "She's not doing any shows this summer, but arranged for a studio in Rome to work on her next album."

It made sense that Claire would be present when Duane and

Jessica's baby was born. Not only was she a good friend of Jessica's, but she was also the twins' half sister.

Five years ago, it had come out that Darrell Winston and Razor Dennings's old lady, Christine St. Claire, had messed around while Razor was in prison for a short stretch. Beau and Duane were the result. We'd all believed our momma—Bethany Winston—was their biological mother. Instead, our momma had adopted them, raised them as her own, and never whispered a word to the contrary.

When the truth had been revealed, by Christine St. Claire in a perplexing and weak attempt to extort money out of Beau, the situation had been both sour and sweet.

Sour because Christine St. Claire wasn't a person anyone would want as an acquaintance, let alone a mother.

But sweet because Beau and Duane had gained a sister. Claire McClure—Christine and Razor's only child together—was a wonderful person. I wasn't related to her by blood, but I'd come to enjoy a connection with the tough and funny redhead. She lived in Nashville most of the year, doing her thing as a country music superstar, and we'd made a point of getting together once a week—for dinner, or a hike, or to see a movie—whenever she wasn't touring or out of town for other work stuff.

We'd even been linked romantically by a gossip magazine a few years ago, which had given us both a good laugh.

"This idea has merit," Cletus said thoughtfully, and I imagined he was giving the room his somber nod. He was entirely too fond of giving folks what he called his *somber nod*.

I'd already closed my eyes again, my mind wandering as I half-listened to their conversation.

"The more I think about it, the more I like it." Jethro sounded closer. "He's been working nonstop. When's the last time he took anything resembling a vacation? I can't remember."

"Hasn't the general assembly already adjourned for the summer?" Ashley asked. "I'm sure the Paytons wouldn't mind giving Billy a leave of absence from the mill."

The Paytons.

Again, the pinching ache. God, how I missed her. I knew she was recovering, needed rest, which only frustrated me. I wanted to be there, taking care of her, but I couldn't even shave my own face.

Abruptly, I became aware of silence and the cooling shaving cream still on my face. Duane's hand slipped from mine. My siblings had ceased their chatter, which meant they thought I was asleep or trying to go to sleep. Maybe they were even tiptoeing out of the room. I wasn't ready to sleep, not even a catnap. I wanted to stay awake for as long as possible so I could rest deeply later rather than the insufficient dozing of the last few days.

So I lifted the hand Duane had been holding and cleared my throat. "Y'all, I'm not tired. Just resting my eyes."

Fingers slipped into my grip, but they weren't Duane's. They belonged to a woman—I could tell because the palm was soft and small and uncallused—but the hand wasn't Ashley's either.

Lifting my eyebrows, I forced my eyes open, blinking until the room came into focus, and with it the woman next to my bed.

Simone.

My mouth parted and I stared, but I didn't blink again, afraid she'd disappear or that I'd wake up from this dream.

Her smile was huge, bigger than I'd ever seen it, but tears spilled down her cheeks into the happy brackets around her mouth. "Hey there, handsome," she said, amber eyes shining as they moved over my face.

"Are you real?" I whispered, but then quickly added, "If you're not real, don't answer that."

She laughed, sniffed, and sighed, pressing the palm of my hand to her heart. "I'm real."

"Hi, Roscoe," someone said from the foot of my bed, and I reluctantly swiveled my attention to the new voice. Mrs. Payton stood there wearing a small smile. Next to her was Mr. Payton, his arm around his wife.

"You got something on your face, son." He motioned to my chin, grinning and stepping forward. "You want me to help you with that?"

Overwhelmed, emotion clogged my throat, and I had to clear it a few times before I could speak. By then, I'd noticed the four of us were the only ones in the room, my siblings had cleared out.

"If you don't mind, Mr. Payton." My voice was hoarse, thick with emotion. "It seems my barber has abandoned me mid-shave."

"I think it's time you called me Trevor," he said, picking up the discarded razor and inspecting my face. "I had to do this for Poe when he broke his left hand, kind of missed it when he got his cast off."

I gave Mr. Payton—uh, Trevor—a tight smile as a familiar pang burned the back of my throat, but not nearly as bad as when I'd been a kid.

Watching Trevor with Poe had been my first introduction to the acrimonious taste of envy. Billy and my brothers were great—no doubt—and I'd reminded myself often how lucky I was. I was so fucking lucky. But seeing a father and son as close as Trevor and Poe, the mutual respect and care between them, their relationship had always made me jealous.

Presently, I pushed the sensation away, irritated with myself for allowing anything to taint this moment. I swallowed the faint echo of envy and focused on what mattered. The Paytons were here. *Simone* was here. She was alive and safe and holding my hand. I'd been dreaming about this for weeks. Thoughts of her were my constant companion, having her here the most unbelievable gift.

These reminders chased away the strange ghosts of the past as Mr. Payton—*Trevor*—picked up where Beau had left off, a warm smile behind his eyes. "Just make a sound if you need me to stop, son."

"I will. Thank you, sir."

"Trevor," he reminded.

I gave him a small smile, feeling both grateful and honored. "Trevor."

Keeping my head still, I shifted my eyes back to Simone, greedy for the sight of her. She'd dried her tears and likewise stared at me, her gaze dreamy.

My injured heart gave a sudden hard beat, like a *thwump*, but it felt good. A reminder that I was still alive and my heart could feel something other than pain.

Simone's smile softened and she sighed. "It is so good to see you," she whispered, even though her daddy could definitely hear.

"You too," I said as Mr. Payton—uh, Trevor—paused to rinse the blade, forcing myself to look at Mrs. Payton so as not to be rude. "Thank y'all for coming,"

"We've been so worried about you." Mrs. Payton was moving around the room, folding a blanket, tossing a coffee cup in the trash. "I understand your sister Ashley is taking time off work when you're discharged? To be your nurse for a bit?"

I waited until Trevor was finished with his next swipe before asking, "Is she? She hadn't mentioned it to me."

"We talk," Mrs. Payton said, a knowing smile hovering behind her eyes and lips. "As a matter of fact, I suggested you stay with us. Simone will need some tending to as well. We've already hired another nurse your sister recommended—Marissa? Right Trevor?— to help out."

"I don't need a nurse." Simone's tone was equal parts stubborn and amused.

"Even if it's Ashley during the day and it means Roscoe is staying at our house?" Mrs. Payton's eyebrows were raised, and though her words asked a question, her tone made it rhetorical.

Simone sighed, her eyes narrowing on her mother, her lips pressed together as she fought a grin.

"That's what I thought." Mrs. Payton gave her daughter a sweet smile, and then surveyed the room. "You need some flowers. Or a balloon."

I shook my head. "I asked folks to donate to animal shelters instead."

Mrs. Payton blinked at me, just once, and shook her head. "My goodness, you are the *sweetest* boy. Just for that, I'm going downstairs, buying you a balloon, *and* making a donation to your shelter."

Trevor's shoulders shook with silent laughter as he picked up a towel and dabbed at my face. "There. All finished." He stood back, surveying his work.

Simone's momma came over to have a look, standing next to her daughter. "And handsome, too."

I grinned at the both of them, finding the action easier than usual. "Thank you. Thank you both for bringing your daughter and for being so kind."

"We came as soon as we could." Simone's statement brought my attention back to her. She was still holding my hand to her heart as her eyes moved between mine, searching. "How are you feeling?"

"How are *you* feeling?" I asked, my grin falling away. "Should you have made this trip? Aren't you still healing?"

Mrs. Payton bent forward and placed a kiss on my forehead, patting my cheek as she straightened. "She's stubborn like her father, needs to do things her own way."

"Excuse me?" Trevor stared at his wife. "Stubborn like *who*?"

"Oh my, look at the time." Mrs. Payton fought admirably against a grin and began backing away towards the door. "We need to get to the hotel to check in. We'll be in town for just two days, Simone has a consult with some doctors here, so we'll be back tomorrow. In the meantime, you rest up, Roscoe. And think about staying with us when you're out of here." She then waved Trevor forward. "Come on, my love. Let's give them a minute."

Giving me a look like, *Can you believe this woman?* Trevor picked up the razor, bowl, and towel, and moved to the sink. "Fine. But I get to pick out the balloon."

"See?" Simone's mom whispered. "Stubborn."

I tried not to laugh, because laughing hurt. But Simone did laugh, which gave me another heart-thwump. I sighed, grateful for the sight of her laughter. Until I was discharged, this moment would make fine company.

Simone and I shared a smile as her parents closed the door. Her gaze studying my face, she lifted her free hand to my jaw, smoothing her palm over the skin.

"It's strange, to see you without a beard."

"It's strange to be without a beard. Do you like it? You want me to keep shaving?" I found myself grateful for the light conversation, unwilling to take it for granted.

"I love your face." She bent and brushed her lips against mine, just a light touch. It wasn't enough, but I knew it would have to do for now.

"And I'll take it however I can get it," Simone added, leaning away.

I twisted my lips to the side. "That's not an answer."

"Fine." She lifted an eyebrow, giving me a mock-irritated look that was ruined by her mischievous smile. "Here I was, trying to be polite—*like we'd agreed*—and there you go, pushing me. The truth is, I love your beard and I want it back. Happy?"

"More than ever," I said, because it was true.

We'd almost lost the chance to have these teasing moments. We'd almost lost the chance to have any moments at all. I knew the desperation to make each second count would eventually fade.

For now, I embraced it, noticing details I might've missed before, because I was anxious for each and every new memory.

EPILOGUE

✳ ✳ ✳

"I've learned that people will forget what you said, people will forget what you did, but people will never forget how you made them feel."

— MAYA ANGELOU

Roscoe

A KNIFE TO the heart hadn't killed me, but six weeks of living with the Paytons might.

Don't get me wrong, I loved the Paytons, and being with them had been awesome, just like I remembered. They had dinner together every night. Everyone helped. Everyone cleaned up. Everyone talked about his or her day, their interests, what they were reading, what they were into. And everyone else listened and asked questions.

They debated, playing devil's advocate, challenging each other. I recalled this phenomenon from when I'd come over and stayed for dinner when we were kids. Back then, I'd sat quietly and listened. This time I sat back and listened, but I was also encouraged to share my thoughts. It was so great. They were all so smart—so damn smart

—and none of them treated me like a kid, like I was the youngest and needed looking after.

Well, that's not exactly true. Daniella visited one weekend and treated me like I was an idiot. She'd roll her eyes every time I spoke —even if I agreed with her—until Simone called her on it and challenged her to a thumb war (which was how the Paytons dueled).

Daniella lost and had to keep quiet for the rest of dinner. However, she did laugh at one of my dad jokes when Trevor and I got into an impromptu contest. Unsurprisingly, he won. In all fairness, he had three kids and thirty years more experience with the craft. Maybe when I was fifty-six and Simone and I had our own kids, I'd catch up to his punny genius.

Yeah, the Paytons were fantastic, kind, and unbelievably generous. But they were also Simone's parents and—as much as I respected Simone—I was having seriously dirty thoughts about her all the freaking time, especially since the plumbing broke in her bathroom and she'd been using mine.

Even something as mundane as coming upon her while she was brushing her teeth felt erotic, likely because she wore underwear and a tank top to bed with a measly, thin cotton bathrobe thrown over both. Of course, it didn't help matters when she made a point to brush against me every time either of us were passing by the other.

We'd been good, so good, *painfully* good. Stealing only kisses, or a quick make-out session in the hallway. I stayed out of her room and she stayed out of mine, though longing glances had been sent in both directions near bedtime and I'd often had difficulty falling asleep, thinking about all that smooth skin and softness on the other side of the wall.

For me, the main hurdle had been deference for her parents. They'd been kind enough to have me stay under their roof, I refused to undermine their rules.

For Simone, and by her own admission, she would have snuck into my room weeks ago, but she was worried about my physical fitness, not wanting to push me too far too fast.

As of yesterday, that concern was a nonissue. Though I still had phantom aches along the incision line, my breastbone had healed, and my cardiologist had declared me ready to increase my level of strenuous activity. I'd been working with a physical therapist on range of motion and flexibility, but now strength training would be added.

I never thought I'd say it, but I couldn't wait to lift weights again.

The timing was perfect, too. Jethro, Sienna, and family had been back in town for a few weeks and decided to throw a barbecue and bouncy house birthday party for their second son, Andy. Sienna had been trying to talk me into moving back home. As an extra enticement, she'd offered either my old room or sole use of the carriage house, whichever I preferred.

For my immediate needs, I preferred the carriage house.

For my long-term goals, however, I preferred Simone's apartment in DC—or her apartment building at the very least, if she wanted to live separate—a topic I planned to raise as soon as I could get Simone alone in the carriage house.

My suspicions were that my family had been hoping I would look for a job at the Park since I'd left my job in Nashville. I'd turned in my notice as soon as I'd been well enough to contact Dr. Tucker, no use prolonging the inevitable.

Not one to prevaricate, Sienna had made a point to mention our family's hopes several times.

"Wouldn't it be nice if you lived in the carriage house and worked with Drew?" She'd made the statement one morning when she and Cletus had come over, using yoga as their excuse to visit.

"That would be nice." I'd given her a half-smile, my eyes wandering to Cletus. His eyes were closed and he had his mouth open, presumably to breathe.

"It would be more than nice." She'd continued to push. "With Billy gone, off gallivanting who knows where, the boys have no uncles to play with."

"Excuse me." Cletus finally spoke, but his eyes remained shut. "I am sitting right here. Do I not count as an uncle? What am I? Lima beans?"

Sienna rolled her eyes. She was one of the only people who could get away with rolling their eyes at Cletus. "I mean an uncle at the house. Ashley and Drew are nearby, so are Beau and Shelly, which is fantastic. I'm just saying, it would be great if the boys had family who lived on the property. That house is so big."

"Then have more children and fill it up," Cletus suggested, like it was the obvious answer.

This led to her making sarcastic remarks about how easy childbirth was, leading Cletus to comparing it to passing a kidney stone, leading to a discussion on the pain-scale faces one encounters in hospitals and doctor's offices, leading to them both trying to mimic each face, leading to laughter, leading to Ashley coming out and warning me against overextending myself.

That had been three weeks ago, and Sienna had brought it back up every time she saw me since, which was why I'd agreed to move into the carriage house as soon as my cardiologist gave me the all clear. Ideally, the situation would be temporary, the two-bedroom house serving as a base as I searched for a job in the DC area.

Wherever Simone was, that's where I wanted to be. From all our conversations thus far, Simone missed her research and her lab. Ergo, Washington, DC was where I would be.

With these thoughts—and hopes—on my mind, I packed my room at the Paytons. I'd told everyone last night about my doctor's visit, and we'd had a little celebration. My move-out day wasn't a surprise as I'd discussed my plans with Daisy and Trevor as soon as I'd made up my mind, but it was bittersweet.

"You know, you could just stay here." Daisy stood in the doorway, watching me pack my suitcase with a crease between her eyebrows. "The houseplants will miss you. You're so good at watering, my peace lilies have never looked so good."

Shooting her a grin, I opened the second drawer of the dresser and pulled out my clothes, carrying them to the bed. "If you want, I can stop by on occasion and see to your greenery."

"I'd appreciate that," she said, sounding distracted, pensive, which had me turning to study her. The crease between her eyebrows had intensified. "I hope you know that you're welcome here anytime, Roscoe."

"I know that, Daisy." I nodded once, the sound of her name on my tongue still tripping me up. I'd called her Mrs. Payton my whole life, switching to Daisy these last few weeks had been a struggle.

"You're like a son to us," she said suddenly, her voice a little rough. "And, whatever you do, wherever you decide to go, you have a home with us."

That pulled a grateful smile out of me and I dropped the shirts I'd been holding, crossing to her, and gathering the sweet lady into a big bear hug.

"Is your chest okay?" she asked, fretful. "Is it okay to hug this tight?"

"Yes and yes." I chuckled, giving her a squeeze. "Your kindness, yours and Trevor's, means the world to me." I pulled away, smiling down at her. "Thanks for being consistently great role models and showing me—showing everyone—how good folks live their lives."

She sniffed, sounding a touch watery, and nodded wordlessly.

I laughed, taking her by the shoulders. "I'm not disappearing into the ether. I'll be two miles away. You'll see me all the time."

Her expression turned flat, like she didn't believe me. "Oh really? You're telling me you plan to stay in Green Valley, then?"

My eyes widened, because I'd been caught.

And that made her laugh.

Taking my face between her palms, she placed a kiss on my cheek and stepped away, wagging her finger at me. "I know what's on your mind, plain as day. First chance you get, you're moving to DC."

I shrugged, scratching my short beard, and admitting quietly, "She's it for me, Daisy. She's always been the one. I live and I breathe, and I love Simone Payton."

This seemed to make her exceptionally happy, and she gave me a beaming smile. "I know, baby." Simone's momma clasped her hands under her chin, a delighted glint in her eye. "And I can't wait to help plan your wedding."

Simone

I WAS GOING to a three-year-old's birthday party and I couldn't stop wondering whether there would be clowns.

If there were, so be it. Roscoe was worth it. I'd deal. I just needed some time to mentally prepare before coming face to (freaky-and-unnatural-makeup) face with one.

Can we pause here and talk about clowns for a second? Yes? Great.

Why? And who? Who first thought this was a good idea? What possessed them? What bet did they lose and how much money had they lost? It must've been epic.

Yes, I could have Googled "first clown" and researched the topic to become actually knowledgeable about the first modern clowns, but I didn't want to risk the image results. Therefore, I dwelled in sweet, sweet ignorance and assumed a lot about clowns and their gambling habits.

But back to now and my sweaty hands.

I wiped them on my jeans after placing my car in park and I glared at the front door of the Winston house. I needed to come up with a plan to extract myself from the clown. Clowns, in my experience, are like cats. They can sense when a person isn't into them and then go out of their way to interact with that person.

Once, in my case, I'd had a clown follow me around a co-worker's child's birthday party, trying to foist balloon animals on me (I thought they all looked like genitalia, but what did I know?) When that hadn't charmed my pants off, he'd made a comment about my hair, saying we must shop at the same wig store.

. . .

. . .

. . .

So, long story short, he didn't press charges, which was nice of him. Meanwhile, I'd used turpentine to take the clown makeup off my fists.

Moving on.

I reached for the small wrapped gift on the passenger seat and gathered a bracing breath, opening my door in one bold movement. I wouldn't be intimidated by clowns. I'd just recovered from a freaking gunshot wound. I was a badass. I was TNT.

Eh, TNT might be a step too far. On a scale from water to azidoazide azide, I was TATP. Harder to handle than trinitrotoluene, but with an explosive power of about 80% of TNT.

Again, moving on.

The day was bittersweet already and it wasn't even 4:00 PM. Last night, we'd celebrated Roscoe's clean bill of health from the cardiologist, which meant he'd finished packing his things this morning while I'd been in Knoxville, meeting with the SAIC for East Tennessee.

I'd received my new assignment, which placed me firmly back in the FBI research lab. I left in a week. Professionally, I was ecstatic. Personally, I was feeling a little woe-is-me. Though I'd mentioned to Roscoe more than once how much I wanted to get back to my lab work, he hadn't shared any of his hopes and dreams for his professional future in return.

I knew he'd given his notice at his old job, but he hadn't mentioned what he planned to do next. His unemployment didn't seem to give him much angst. As soon as he'd been allowed by his doctors two weeks ago, he'd started helping Drew with Park paperwork and volunteering at two animal shelters doing light vet work. As long as he was busy with animals, going to physical therapy, and having dinner with my family every night, he seemed content.

But what did he *want*? Out of life and work? What fulfilled him professionally? Where was his ambition? These were questions that needed answering and I planned to get him alone today—birthday party or not—to pump him for information.

Climbing the stairs to the big house, I lifted my hand to knock. Before I could, the big door was suddenly yanked open, revealing Shelly Sullivan.

Dressed as a clown.

Instead of my usually instinctive repulsion, the sight of the tall, willowy woman staring back at me, a smile painted on her typically unsmiling face, filled me with a spark of amazement, followed by amusement.

"I'm a happy clown," she said, sounding as flat as a piece of paper.

Pressing my lips together so I wouldn't laugh, I nodded. "Of course you are."

"I am the only one who can juggle for an indefinite period of time." She stood back, opening the door wider. "I think that is why they made me a happy clown."

"Are there more clowns?" I asked with some alarm, quickly conducting a survey of the large living room for any additional clowns that might be lying in wait.

"Jenn is a sad clown, Sienna is the clumsy clown, and I think Ashley is a rodeo clown or a magician clown."

Usually, I'd be horrified by the idea of four clowns running amok in my general vicinity, but I wasn't.

I grinned. "I hope someone has captured this amazing moment on film."

Shelly grunted, saying nothing, which only made me want to laugh. The dichotomy of her brusque and forthright personality paired with the perpetually manic and happy paint on her face was absolutely hilarious.

I was about to assure her she was doing a good thing and would be up for the aunt-of-the-year award when her nephew—the oldest of Sienna and Jethro's children—ran into the room.

"Aunt Shelly!" Benjamin sprinted over to her, grabbing her by the hand, his gorgeous brown eyes, which were lined with thick black lashes, on his aunt's face. "I have a new thing for you to juggle."

Even with the face paint, her entire demeanor seemed to soften and she squatted in front of the five-year-old. "I'm not juggling alligators."

He giggled. "No! Not alligators."

"I'm not juggling chainsaws either," she said, her own grin peeking out.

Movement out of the corner of my eye caught my attention, and I turned to see another clown—the sad one, so presumably Jennifer—walking into the room from the kitchen, twisting a balloon animal that actually looked like an elephant.

Huh.

"Hey, Simone!" Her mouth grinned, but her face continued looking sad. It was eerie, but not as distressing as I usually found clowns to be. She came over to give me a hug, but stopped short and laughed, gesturing to her face. "Sorry, this paint comes right off. Better not risk getting it on your clothes. Come out back, that's where everyone is. We got the grill going. Are you hungry?"

"Yes, starved." I hadn't eaten since breakfast.

"Come on, come on." Benjamin tugged on Shelly's hand, forcing her to stand up. "You can juggle this, I know you can."

"Is it a couch? Because I can't juggle couches either," she teased, reaching out to tickle his side.

Benjamin laughed at her, holding his stomach. "No, it's not a couch!"

"Aunt Shelly is so silly." Jenn put the elephant on Benjamin's head and I was amazed to see the balloon animal was also a hat.

Okay, that was cool. I was seriously impressed. And I kind of wanted a balloon animal hat of my own.

. . . I wonder if she can make cheetahs?

"Quick," Benjamin was saying, pulling frantically on Shelly's hand. "Come juggle it before it's too late."

"You got me, what do you want me to juggle?" She fit her fingers in his hand properly and allowed him to lead her towards the back door.

But then he said, "Uncle Cletus's sausage," and her feet stopped.

Both her real eyebrows and her painted on ones jumped and she turned to face Jennifer, who was gaping, wide-eyed.

"Did Uncle Cletus put you up to this?" Jenn asked, her voice full of both irritation and mirth.

"He made a bet with Uncle Beau that Aunt Shelly couldn't juggle his sausage," Benjamin said, as though he was offended on behalf of his Aunt Shelly's juggling skills.

Jennifer and Shelly exchanged a look, with Shelly's real face looking exasperated and Jennifer's real face fighting laughter.

"You go tell Uncle Cletus that Aunt Shelly has no desire to handle his raw meat," Jennifer instructed. "And then tell him I'll be out later to twist it into balloon animals if he doesn't start behaving himself."

Benjamin's eyes widened, but he nodded and darted out of the room, his instructions clear.

As soon as he was gone, Jennifer and I busted out laughing while Shelly shook her head. "I don't know why I was surprised," she said flatly. "I knew we were in trouble as soon as I saw the grill."

"What's this about Cletus's sausage?" I asked, glancing between the two women.

Shelly and Jenn shared another look—sad clown to happy clown—and Jenn turned a small grin on me. "Let's go outside and find Roscoe."

* * *

"HAVING A GOOD time?" Roscoe whispered in my ear, startling me a little as his arms came around me from the back.

I grinned, tipping my head back on his chest and peering up at him. "Actually, I am. More fun than I'd ever had at a kid's birthday party, that's for sure."

The Winston women opened my eyes to the value of clowns, a feat I'd considered impossible. Jenn's balloon animals were impressive, Shelly's juggling was outstanding, and Ashley's pantomiming and magician skills—especially the tricks she played on her brothers, like pulling a sausage out of Cletus's ear—were first class. But Sienna had us all in stitches with her ability to fall down.

I didn't usually enjoy slapstick humor, but there was no denying Sienna Diaz-Winston was a slapstick genius.

Roscoe grinned, giving me a soft kiss and squeezing me lightly with a cautious hug. I sighed, leaning against him, but was also careful not to give him too much of my weight. This caused him to lower a hand to my stomach and press me backwards more firmly.

"Stop being so careful with me," he said, whispering against my neck.

Smiling ruefully, I gazed at the horizon, at the sight of the summer sun against the cloudless sky, descending into the emerald forests of the Smokies. Its last beams stretched along the wildflower field as day turned to dusk, and the witching hour dawned.

Exhaling an exasperated laugh, I caressed the back of his hand on my stomach. "Okay, fine. I'll stop being careful with you if you stop being careful with me."

His arms loosened a tad—so the opposite of what I wanted—and he leaned to the side, studying me. I loved his touch, but I'd been a tad frustrated by his gentleness. I couldn't wait until we stopped being so careful with each other. But I supposed, after so many weeks, caution had become a habit.

We stared at each other for a minute, his soulful eyes examining every inch of my face, growing from warm to hot to scorching. He released me.

Sliding his hand down my arm to tangle our fingers together, he tugged. "Come with me."

I allowed myself to be pulled, a flutter of excitement and anticipation in my stomach. "Where are we going?"

"We're going to wrestle." His legs—much longer than mine— were eating up the ground as we walked around the side of the house, forcing me to jog to keep up.

"Wrestle?" I asked, biting my bottom lip at the thought, eagerness and worry battling for dominance within me.

Pausing just for a moment to open the door to the carriage house, Roscoe pulled me inside and down the hall, stopping before we'd reached the end of it and pressing me against the wall, capturing my mouth in a hungry kiss.

My body's response was immediate, heat pooling low in my

belly, making a puddle of my insides as shocks and sparks of sensual awareness teased beneath my skin.

But then, he broke the kiss, and raised his hand to stop me before I could follow. His gaze darted over me, moving from my neck to my chest, stomach, hips, thighs. The hand he held out turned, as though he wanted a handshake, and I glanced between him and it, confused.

"Uh . . ."

"Thumb war," he said, his voice rough. "Whoever wins gets to decide what we do, and how we do it."

I slid my palm against his, our fingers curling together as we assumed the position. "You know I'm a championship thumb wrestler."

The side of his mouth hitched. "Yeah. But I've memorized all your moves."

He didn't know all my moves.

Giving him my Dirty Harry squint, I pressed my lips together and gave a single nod for the battle to commence.

"One, two, three, four, I declare a thumb war—"

Two things happened at once. His thumb came up, going to the left instead of the right, about to subdue my much smaller thumb while I stepped forward and pressed my free hand against the front of his pants and rubbed.

He sucked in a startled breath, but—to my amazement—didn't lose his concentration on our war, but he did huff a frustrated sounding laugh as I continued to stroke him while battling his other hand.

"You fight dirty," he said, losing his advantage as I worked both my hands.

"You're lucky I didn't flash a boob," I said, moving in for a final strike.

"I wouldn't say that makes me lucky." Roscoe's voice like gravel, he surprised me by navigating out of my trap, faking right, coming back left and pressing my thumb down in victory.

"Shit," I said, wrinkling my nose at my loss.

But, to be honest, I wasn't disappointed. I was thrilled.

My hand dropped from the front of his pants and he caught it, putting it back in place. I lifted my eyes to his, surprised.

Roscoe's gaze had darkened and the force of his ardor made my heart skip a beat. It also made my mouth go dry and my brain go a little stupid.

"Where were we?" he whispered gruffly, his free hand coming to my tank top and pulling down the strap of both my shirt and bra. His mouth lowered to my shoulder and he bit me, soothing the sting away with his tongue.

Suddenly, he was everywhere. His hands everywhere. His mouth everywhere. He'd won the war and now it seemed he was ready to collect the spoils.

Still in the hallway, my shirt was whipped off, my pants and sandals were next, my bra and undies quickly followed as he feasted on my flesh, grabbing and caressing, greedy and insatiable.

My hand continued to give him strokes over his jeans, because I could do nothing else. Every time I tried to remove an article of his clothing, he subdued the attempt, catching my wrist and bringing it around to my back where he'd released it to grab a handful of my backside.

Eventually though, he allowed me to unbuckle his belt, unbutton and unzip his pants, and reach my hand inside his shorts. We both gasped as my palm came in contact with the silky heat of his erection. A shiver of anticipation racing down my spine, I pressed my legs together, feeling empty and needy.

Roscoe's lips dipped to my neck, his short beard tickling the sensitive skin as he whispered, "I miss you. I miss you so fucking much. You're all I think about." He tongued my earlobe, sending an aching shock wave through my entire body as his hand massaged and plucked my breast. He pinched and tugged at my nipple, roughly, expertly, and my knees grew weak as his hand slid lower, the rough calluses of his palm delicious friction on my stomach and abdomen, his fingers moving to separate me.

Using one jean clad knee, he pushed my legs open and invaded me, my head falling back to the wall as he leaned away, his eyes ravenous for my reaction. "I want to watch you come, just like this, and then I want to taste you."

I shuddered, my body all coiling heat and twisting knots. I gripped his shoulders to hang on, my hips rocking against his hand. Roscoe glanced down, watching his fingers move inside me, and he cursed, his eyes blinking but never closing.

"You're so fucking sexy."

I gasped. Watching him watching me sent a spike of pleasure directly to my center, and my fingers curled into the fabric at his shoulders.

I was so close. So close. *So close—*

But then his hand was gone. I cried out, a jumble of sounds communicating my dismay were quickly silenced as he lifted me off my feet and carried me down the remainder of the hall, past the kitchen and into a bedroom.

Placing me on the edge of the bed, he stripped off his T-shirt, revealing an angry-looking scar traveling vertically down his chest. My heart lurched at the sight, dually mourning the loss of his unblemished skin and rejoicing in his will to live. That scar meant he was here now, we were together, and this was only the beginning.

Kicking off his shoes and jeans, he climbed over me, his eyes on my mouth. A spike of trepidation knocked me out of my sexy and sentimental brain fog, because—from all appearances—it looked like Roscoe was about to attempt missionary.

My heart didn't have time to fall, however, because Roscoe's hot, lean body settled over mine. And that felt good. So good. His erection nudged at my entrance, slick and sensitive thanks to his earlier handiwork, and I gasped at the sudden shock of sensation.

Instead of pushing into me, which was what I'd expected, Roscoe reached down and adjusted himself so that his cock slid against my center, rubbing himself against me with tortuously slow strokes that felt like heaven and madness.

"What—" I panted, my body overheated, unable to catch my breath. "What are you doing?"

His lips were at my neck and trailed biting kisses along my

collarbone to my breast, holding himself above me as he rhythmically rocked with impressive skill and strength.

"Whatever I want," he answered, swirling his tongue around my nipple, and I thought I would splinter in two.

Breath, skin, friction, heat. I felt suffocated in the best way, and yet empty where I needed him most. The best torture, the most essential agony.

"Please," I begged, tilting my hips as much as I could. "Please, Roscoe."

"Tell me you love me." His voice was rough, almost stern. "Tell me."

"I love you, I love you. Please."

"You think about me, hmm?" He was right there, *right there*, poised, but not moving. "You think about this? About how much you want it?"

My skin was ripe with goose bumps, hot with need. I would have said anything, I wanted him so badly.

"Yes, yes. All the time. I think about you all the time." The words were a struggle, a puff of air as I kneaded his body, urging him to fill me, take me.

He did. Slowly. So slowly. Earning him a moan and my glare.

Tangentially, I was surprised to find him glaring at me as well, his eyes wild, almost angry in their intensity.

"You're teasing me," I accused, breathless as he gave me another controlled, languorous stroke.

"No," he said through gritted teeth. "If I go any faster, I'll come."

I laughed, and then moaned again, pressing my head back against the bed, my body arching even though I could barely move. His weight restrained me, but somehow felt essential, like his heaviness was the only thing keeping me from shattering.

Despite his claim, he began to move faster, one hand braced on the bed next to my head, the other moving to my hip, sliding up my side, over the pucker of my scar to my breast before coming to the bed as his balance wobbled.

He cursed, his body growing tense, his movements jerky, lacking in finesse. It was this lack of finesse, this predatory mindlessness that had me soaring, the twisting knots in my abdomen snapping, my heart racing to the edge as my hips pivoted and rocked, grinding against his invasion, my movements just as jerky and lacking in finesse.

Gasping for breath, I fell back as the last tremors made me shiver and shake. Roscoe had slowed, but he was still moving, still thrusting against me, as though endeavoring to pull every last spasm from my body, his eyes on mine, loving yet still wild.

Reaching for him, I pulled his full weight on top of me and sensed his arms resist. He was allowing me to hold him, but he still carried most of the burden.

I made a sound of protest. "Roscoe, come here, come lie on me."

He shifted, bringing us both to our sides as he pulled me into his arms. I released a huff of impatience, but I allowed it, because that is what one does when faced with a Roscoe Winston who wishes to cuddle on his own terms. One huffs but allows it, and then one snuggles closer, trailing one's fingertip along the ridges and lines of his glorious, sexy body.

Admittedly, this position was probably better as it allowed him to fondle me as well, his hand performing dreamy caresses on my skin, petting me as our pulses slowed and beat in unison.

I found my hand resting on his chest over his heart, unwilling to move, and I stared at it. He felt so strong, solid. A pang of emotion, residual fear and anguish seized my heart as I remembered waking up and believing for a moment that he was no longer.

"Hey." His finger fit under my chin, forcing my eyes to his, and another sucker punch of feeling pushed the air from my lungs. "What's—"

I lunged at him, wrapping my arms around him tightly and buried my face in his neck. "Don't ever die."

Roscoe released a short laugh, rolling onto his back, his warm hands rubbing circles on my back. "Only if you promise the same."

"Okay." I sniffed, blinking against sudden tears. "Deal."

My answer made him chuckle and he continued rubbing soothing circles over my bare skin, making a low, rumbly sound of contentment.

We lay together, holding each other, breathing each other for a long time. So long, the dim light of dusk turned to night, outside illumination fading to darkness, the only light a lamp by the bed which cast everything in a gentle glow. And still I held him. I think part of me was afraid to let go.

But eventually, Roscoe stirred, returning us to our sides and cupping my face. His brow was knotted, and I sensed he had something on his mind, but struggled with how to start.

"What is it?" I asked softly, leaning forward to give him a light kiss.

"I want to be with you," he said haltingly. "And I'm taking for granted here that you want to be with me."

A slow grin claimed my mouth and I nodded. "I do."

"So we need to talk about how to make that happen, what you're willing to give me."

"What I'm willing to give you?"

Roscoe sucked in a breath, his soulful gaze bouncing between mine. "I'm going to look for a job in DC."

My eyes widened and a sudden tightness seized my chest, warmth unfurling to my limbs, my smile huge and immediate. "THAT IS FANTASTIC!" I yelled, tackle-hugging him, forgetting for a moment that he might still be recovering.

He laughed, sounding relieved. "I'm glad to hear you say that."

"What else would I say?" I leaned away, placing my elbow on his breastbone but careful to keep it away from his scar.

"I don't know, but it's what I hoped you'd say."

"Are you going to move in with me?" I asked, hopeful. "I love my building, because it has a Nancy, but we could get a bigger place, maybe two bedrooms so we have an office."

All the sharpness and uncertainty in Roscoe's gaze softened and disappeared. Grabbing my face, he brought my mouth to his for a firm kiss, now rolling me onto my back and straddling me. We kissed. We kissed and kissed, slow and fast, urgent and leisurely, until my lips felt tender and swollen. And still I wanted to suck his face.

But, alas, I could see he was tired. So I curled against him, my body relaxed, replete, my heart on wings, my brain full of ideas.

I couldn't wait to show him the city, to take him to all my favorite places, to share everything with him and muddle my space with his things.

I couldn't wait to have him in my life, for now, forever, for always. My throat clogged as I thought about it, as I considered this level of happiness and how fleeting it felt. I wanted to remember this moment, I wanted to bottle it up to keep for always, I wanted to take it out and relive it.

Maybe I can.

"What are you thinking about?" he asked, his voice sleep roughened.

I lifted onto my elbow, indulging in the sight of this achingly handsome man and his beautiful soul. "Will you tell me something?"

He opened one eye, a small happy smile hovering over his gorgeous lips. "What?"

"Tell me a story."

"What kind of story?" His hand began moving again, this time it was slow circles on my bottom.

"Tell me about the first time you told me you loved me."

His hand stilled. In fact, his entire person seemed to still.

Roscoe opened his eyes, his stare steady and guileless, and yet cloudy with something I couldn't name. "That's a difficult story for me to tell," he admitted, his voice raspy with emotion this time.

Understanding him so much better now, and what it must mean to remember everything—the good and the bad—with such clarity of detail, I nodded, placing a gentle kiss on his nose.

"Maybe one day?"

He gave me a small smile, but his eyes hadn't quite recovered. "One day."

Pushing my fingers into his thick, dark hair, I scratched his scalp with my nails. "Then tell me a different story. A good one. One you like thinking about."

The mists of discontent parted as his eyes lost focus again, and a smile tugged at his lips. "Do you remember the first time we kissed?"

I thought back, and I also smiled, and then I laughed. "You hated putting worms on fishing hooks."

"I still do," he said, and I was hit with a wave of nostalgia.

"I tricked you into kissing me," I spoke as I remembered, laughing and biting my bottom lip.

"You did not," he said, drawing my eyes back to his frowning face.

"I certainly did."

"You absolutely did not." He shook his head. "I remember everything."

"Ah . . ." I gave him my most mischievous smile and trailed a finger from his ribs to his hip. Trying not to laugh, because this was going to be fun, I reminded the man who never forgot, "But you don't have *my* memories."

The End

AUTHOR'S NOTES

Simone

Simone was a rare character for me in that, when I went back and read some of her chapters, she caught me by surprise with the things she said and thought, and made me laugh out loud. She and her family were an absolute joy for me to write. So much so, I feel we have not seen the last of the Paytons or their extended family . . .

I have to thank my sensitivity readers (LaRae, Amber, Nicole, Victoria, Jess, and Emily) for their time, effort, energy, and feedback. I also want to thank author Dylan Allen for giving critical scenes a first pass and providing insight for course corrections. If you haven't read any of Dylan's books, this is where I ask you what you're waiting for.

What are you waiting for?

Roscoe

I knew early on (Duane's book) that Roscoe would have a "memory thing." Research was required and I identified several potential culprits (time-space synesthesia for example). However, after speaking with a few folks who have what's called "eidetic memory," I decided it fit him best.

Eidetic memory, based on my research and interviews, seems to be a bit of a catch-all for someone with an exemplary situational memory, and shouldn't be confused with a photographic memory, which usually relates to things read/learned rather than experienced, or with hyperthymesia, which is considered a neurological disorder (though the two have areas of overlap).

As with all gifts and afflictions, eidetic memory impacts each person differently. Roscoe's experience was based on a real person and is not meant to be reflective of every person with an eidetic memory.

If you have interest in this topic, check out articles on "super-recognizers" who work for law enforcement. I found the entire subject to be fascinating.

Thank you to my sensitivity readers for Roscoe (both of whom preferred to remain unnamed). I won't ever forget you. ;-)

Other (important) Acknowledgements

Thank you to April, Shan, and Heather for their early reads.

Thank you also to my children for their patience. While I was wrapping up this book (writing the last quarter) I experienced an unexpected loss in my family. As such, finishing this book was delayed, which meant their mother's presence in their lives was also delayed. Putting fingers to the keyboard felt bizarre, and writing hasn't been coming as easily as it had before, but it also helped . . . I think. So, thank you to my kids for being patient and supportive. Now we can go play in the pool and would you please stop teasing your sister.

Thanks for reading,
Penny Reid

ABOUT THE AUTHOR

Penny Reid lives in Seattle, Washington with her husband, three kids, and an inordinate amount of yarn. She used to spend her days writing federal grant proposals as a biomedical researcher, but now she just writes books.

Come find me
Mailing list signup: http://pennyreid.ninja/newsletter/ (get exclusive stories, sneak peeks, and pictures of cats knitting hats)
Facebook: http://www.facebook.com/PennyReidWriter
Instagram: https://www.instagram.com/reidromance/
Goodreads: http://www.goodreads.com/ReidRomance
Email: pennreid@gmail.com …hey, you! Email me ;-)
Blog: http://pennyreid.ninja
Twitter: https://twitter.com/ReidRomance
Ravelry: http://www.ravelry.com/people/ReidRomance (if you crochet or knit…!)

Read on for:
Penny Reid Book List (current and planned publications)

OTHER BOOKS BY PENNY REID

Knitting in the City Series

(Contemporary Romantic Comedy)

Neanderthal Seeks Human: A Smart Romance (#1)

Neanderthal Marries Human: A Smarter Romance (#1.5)

Friends without Benefits: An Unrequited Romance (#2)

Love Hacked: A Reluctant Romance (#3)

Beauty and the Mustache: A Philosophical Romance (#4)

Ninja at First Sight (#4.75)

Happily Ever Ninja: A Married Romance (#5)

Dating-ish: A Humanoid Romance (#6)

Marriage of Inconvenience: (#7)

Winston Brothers Series

(Contemporary Romantic Comedy, spinoff of *Beauty and the Mustache*)

Beauty and the Mustache (#1)

Truth or Beard (#2)

Grin and Beard It (#3)

Beard Science (#4)

Beard in Mind (#5)

Dr. Strange Beard (#6)

Beard with Me (#6.5, coming 2019)

Beard Necessities (#7, coming 2019)

Hypothesis Series

(New Adult Romantic Comedy)

Elements of Chemistry: ATTRACTION, HEAT, and CAPTURE (#1)

Laws of Physics: MOTION, SPACE, and TIME (#2, coming 2018)

Fundamentals of Biology: STRUCTURE, EVOLUTION, and GROWTH (#3, coming 2019)

Irish Players (Rugby) Series – by L.H. Cosway and Penny Reid

(Contemporary Sports Romance)

The Hooker and the Hermit (#1)

The Pixie and the Player (#2)

The Cad and the Co-ed (#3)

The Varlet and the Voyeur (#4)

Dear Professor Series

(New Adult Romantic Comedy)

Kissing Tolstoy (#1)

Kissing Galileo (#2, coming 2019)

CPSIA information can be obtained
at www.ICGtesting.com
Printed in the USA
BVHW03s1234070818
523538BV00010B/3/P